ABSOLUTION

LISSA KASEY

Absolution : A Dominion Novel

1st Edition

Copyright © 2019 Lissa Kasey

All rights reserved

Cover Art by Natasha Snow

Published by Lissa Kasey

http://www.lissakasey.com

Please Be Advised

This is a work of fiction. Names, characters, businesses, places, events and incidents are either the products of the author's imagination or used in a fictitious manner. Any resemblance to actual persons, living or dead, or actual events is purely coincidental.

Warning

This book is licensed to the original purchaser only. Duplication or distribution via any means is illegal and a violation of International Copyright Law, subject to criminal prosecution and upon conviction, fines, and/or imprisonment. This eBook cannot be legally loaned or given to others. No part of this book can be shared or reproduced without the express permission of the Author.

A Note from the Author

If you did not purchased this book from an authorized retailer you make it difficult for me to write the next book. Stop piracy and purchase the book. For all those who purchased the book legitimately: Thank you!

This is for my writing family who have waited a long time for this book, and for Christy who helped me grow enough to reinvent Sam the way he needed to be.

CHAPTER 1

The cold night brushed against my skin with the sharp clarity of fresh needles as I walked through the bowels of downtown. It was the coldest winter in thirty years. I should have worn a heavier jacket, but it wasn't like I could freeze to death. One of the few benefits of being already dead.

I flagged down a cab and had it take me to the edge of downtown St. Paul. My brain was running on high gear—a million things flying through my head—and I just needed some time away from people. The shit in my head wouldn't bother most people, but I had to meet Gabe, my mentor, at a club later and make nice with someone I had yet to meet in person. Should probably show up for work for a few hours too. Though since Gabe was my boss, he wasn't likely to fire me if I didn't.

I would rather have been out stalking the night. What was the point of being a vampire if I couldn't be all dark and brooding when I wanted to be? That should be number one in the vampire rule book. If there was a rule book, which there wasn't.

I'd break all the rules anyway. It was one of the things I did best.

Not many wandered around downtown St. Paul at night, especially not in late February. There were drunks who shouted things that made no sense while they stumbled out of the bars. Homeless who hid in corners, buried in heaps of dirty clothes and praying they'd live through the frigid night air one more time. Prostitutes smiled and flirted, then cursed when I ignored them. I'd grown up here. Riverside to be exact.

The multicolored high-rise towered over the Mississippi only a few miles from Gabe's fancy condo, but a millennia away in class. Living with eight siblings and my parents in a small two-bedroom apartment had been a nightmare. Then I'd met Matthew, my first boyfriend and the first extreme fuckup of my life. I thought I'd found a way out. But false promises, abuse, and heartbreak killed those dreams. The stain of what he'd done to me—made me do—covered me with a film that never washed away. It was worse than remembering the way Andrew Roman had fed on me over and over again like I was some automatic refilling soda pop machine. I was something to kick and beat or feed on. Not a person.

Then there had been Caleb who had used me to get to Seiran. Because of course everyone wanted Seiran. He was beautiful, powerful, and perfect. I sighed.

My track record was for shit. There had to be some giant bull's-eye on my back that pulsed in neon red for only creeps to see. I was done with all of that. Relationships, men, sex, the whole deal. I was dead now and no matter what the world at large thought, that just wasn't sexy. Just because I could still get off didn't mean I needed to. What appealed to me was something much darker. And I was smart enough

ABSOLUTION

not to voice my desire to anyone in my life. They were all too goody-two-shoes to let me have any fun. Instead I'd taken to stalking the recesses of my old stomping grounds. Hiding my bit of play. No one got hurt. Not really.

The streets hadn't changed much in the years that had passed since my hopeful escape. I wondered if my folks still lived in the same cramped apartment. Would they look at me and scream monster? Run away in terror? How had they ever survived in neighborhoods that ate at the weak like maggots on roadkill?

Footsteps echoed mine. I couldn't help but smile as I fed my depression into the blood lust that plagued me from the moment I'd been reborn. They didn't know the freak they were stalking could and would eat them for breakfast.

Literally. I hadn't eaten yet today.

I turned down an alley I knew had no outlet and slowed my pace, letting them follow like I was unwary prey. They would think they had me cornered, and an easy target. Two, maybe three—all bigger than me by the sound of their feet crunching the icy pavement—followed me. The crunching of snow echoed in the dark cold as I closed my eyes and leaned against the building, letting them come to me.

"Hey, Chink! You're in the wrong neighborhood."

At least they'd gotten my heritage right. Maybe it was because they were Vietnamese themselves that they could tell. Not that it mattered. I'd eat them anyway, white, black, yellow, hell even purple. Everyone was on the menu.

"You hear me, punk?" The leader demanded. The other two shouted and joked in a language I didn't understand, but didn't need to since I was sure it was taunts and insults.

I heard him all right. More than he could imagine. The pulsing of the first attacker's blood ran excitedly through his veins, quickening his heart and making me lick my lips. He was aroused by the idea of beating the shit out of me, which would make my taking of him so much sweeter. He'd be first because the gush that always came from a surprise attack was the best. The other two might run, but this one would be mine.

Gabe hunted using sex appeal. He'd taught me how to seduce others, draw them close, feed and then fill them with memories of pleasure. I preferred something a little darker. Fear tasted better than pleasure because it was real. No false hopes or dreams were smashed to put it there, even if it soured the blood sometimes.

One of them slammed a bat against the wall near my head hard enough to shake ice from the side of the building. It shuffled around us in the eerie silence of the night, sliding to the ground and crackling like shattered glass. I waited. Letting the hunger grow as they surrounded me, hearts racing, words an angry mash of sound. I didn't need to see them to know how they moved or where they were. My own fears seeped away as I let the monster out. He was hungry and I was willing to let him go even if it were only for a few minutes. *No death*, I reminded my other self firmly before letting the red haze settle over my brain.

When I opened my eyes, they gasped. I knew what they saw. The glowing red gaze of a true predator. Gabe had never shown me this side of himself—though I was sure he had it. All vampires did. Matthew had lived in this state, which had probably driven him mad. Roman had only let the beast out in the end when rage tore away his control. I'd spent months perfecting the slip of self in secret—afraid my mentor wouldn't approve and would cast me out. Only when I let go could I truly feel free.

I grabbed the first by the jacket, twisted the arm with the bat until a satisfying pop told me I'd broken his bone, and set my fangs to his neck all in one smooth move. With my arms wrapped around him, he didn't even struggle against me. He just let me suck mouthful after mouthful of his hot blood. It stayed sweet a little longer, maybe because he was slow to realize his mistake or even too stupid to get that he'd just become the prey.

One of the others came at me, like he could help his friend. I kicked him away, landing a solid hit to his ribs that had him sliding back several feet then tumbling feet over head several times. Too much strength. I hope I hadn't broken him by accident, but he shouldn't have tried to interrupt a feeding. That was vampire intel 101. He struggled to his feet then turned to run for the entrance of the alley clutching his ribs like it hurt. Maybe I'd broken a few though I hadn't heard the crack.

I licked the wound closed on the first and reached for the third who had yet to run. He stumbled backward, falling on his ass as he realized he should have run the second I took his friend. He reeked of fear.

Bloodlust was strong in the young. I could gorge myself on all of them and still not be satisfied. Their fear poured like honey, strong onto my tongue, a slightly bitter aftertaste telling me that I should move on to the next. But they had a lesson to learn and I was nowhere near full. I gave them memories of glowing eyes—the monster I was sure I was. This is what a vampire was meant to be. Not sex and beauty, but ugly and terrifying. Death wasn't meant to be pretty.

The second disappeared around the corner as I let the third go and silently instructed them to head to a clinic nearby to tend any wounds. The first would need his arm set, but he wouldn't start feeling that for a while yet. Not that it mattered to me. These three had been out looking for someone to harass. They'd made the mistake of choosing me. The third had pissed himself. At least I'd already let him go so he didn't splash me. I hoped it froze to his dick and gave him frostbite. Maybe this little scare would make them think twice about harming someone else in the future.

I headed to the end of the alley determined to clean myself up and calm my heart before reaching the club where I was supposed to meet Gabe. He'd know I already fed. But I had to take the edge off. With my belly full I could think again. The rush of breath from my lungs formed a white mist that made me smile. For a few minutes I could almost feel normal. Perhaps that was the answer—gorge myself on blood until I felt human again. Only the lingering copper bite of pennies on my tongue reminded me that I'd just fed on the blood of a couple of thugs who six months ago would have beaten me to a pulp.

A shadow stepped into my path. Had the second come back? I almost ran into him when he didn't move, but he was larger than any of the thugs had been. For a minute I thought he was Gabe who had somehow found me lurking in the nastiest areas of downtown. I'd never hear the end of it if he caught me roughing up 'civilians.'

"You could use some polish, but not bad for an amateur."

He was dark, not blond like Gabe. I looked him over, taking in the designer pants—pressed just perfectly—Burberry coat, navy in color, and chiseled face, strong chin with dark stubble. His eyes, a warm brown, were lined with thick black lashes. Dark hair, curled just slightly, fell around his ears and across his forehead. Damn but I was a sucker for tall, dark, and handsome. It was what drew me to Matthew. This guy had trouble stamped all over him.

The stranger reached out to slowly drag his thumb over the edge of my lips. In the pale light of the street lamps I saw he drew away a bit of blood. I was usually neater than that. He didn't seem bothered, and in fact, licked his thumb then sucked on it briefly. "Thugs do have a certain vintage."

My cock hardened making my pants too tight. It'd been a

long time since that happened. Shit, who was this guy? Couldn't be human. No human would willingly lick the blood of some random person off a stranger's face. "Who the fuck are you?" I demanded. Gabe had introduced me to every vampire in the cities. He informed me it was so no random vampire would kill me for being rogue because they didn't recognize me. I figured it was more so I knew who was a potential enemy. Not everyone liked the fact that Gabe was setting up a nest and calling all his old buddies home.

"You may have heard of me, Sam. I'm Maxwell Hart. Call me Max, please. We never got to formally meet while you were visiting Los Angeles. Though I know you were there with your master. I would have loved to spend some time with you. See how your transition to our world is coming along."

Right before Christmas Seiran had gone to California to learn more about his dad. Maxwell Hart had been there, introduced himself to Seiran before Gabe and I arrived. In fact, Sei said Max had been a part of the Ascendence—the ruling body of male witches—killing other witches to steal power and make more powerful male witches. Only when it came down to it, Max had handed his power over the institution to Sei asking that the earth Pillar fix the corruption of the organization. Sei still didn't know why. He said many times that Max was scary powerful. Maybe even stronger than Gabe. I didn't have Sei's witch powers. I was just an amplifier. Plug me into a witch and we could make crazy trouble. But on my own I didn't know Houdini from Cris Angel. Hell, I couldn't recognize another vampire when I met one unless he bit into someone in front of me. Or apparently licked the blood off of me.

"Does Gabe know you're in town?" The words sounded a bit more clipped, and angry, than I thought they should have since I was facing a crazy powerful vampire alone. But my survival instinct had always been for shit.

He shook his head slightly. "I have not presented myself to him formally. However," he gestured to the darkened street around us. "Walk with me?" I nodded, whatever, and fell into step beside him. "I've not breached any protocols yet. I'm on the west side. He's claimed the east. The west is yet unclaimed. Odd since it's such a big city."

I couldn't imagine anyone wanting the west side as it was mostly abandoned warehouses and homeless. Gabe didn't have enough vampires to claim the east side, but the Tri-Mega demanded he begin building a nest since he had a Focus now. "So you're planning on claiming the west side? Not much here, you know. Maybe Minneapolis would be a better option for you."

He shrugged. "You probably know the area better than I. Though I think Gabe and I do not much run in the same circles. We are both businessmen, but my businesses aren't as *nice* as his."

"Bars really aren't that nice. Lots of drunk assholes." I followed along with him wondering if he'd sought me out to try to get something out of Gabe. Sure, hurting me would piss off my mentor, but Max would be better off fearing the witch than the vampire. Sei was sort of possessive and convinced he had to be my friend no matter how many times I'd beaten the shit out of him or tried to kill him. Some people were just gluttons for punishment. "Gabe won't let you break the law here. The Tri-Mega has sort of put him as de facto leader around here. They hold him responsible for everything." Which was stupid and unfair, but he didn't really have a choice. One man couldn't control one city by himself and technically Gabe had two since Minneapolis was just as empty of vampires as the west side of St. Paul. Maybe vampires didn't like the cold. It was a lot of layers to peel off of prey, but I didn't mind.

"What makes you think what I'm doing is illegal?"

"The whole Ascendance killing witches thing."

Max nodded and sighed. "I suppose that makes sense." He checked his watch. "I'm actually headed over to look at a new business venture. Since no humans are allowed there are a different set of rules and legalities that don't much apply to the *other* among us with the norms. Would you like to come?"

I'd been to my share of nonhuman clubs. They were a lot like watching snow—fascinating for the first few minutes—and then just more of the same. A lot went on in those places: drugs, sex and blood for sale. None of which I needed, but I was curious. I did like watching other monsters if just to prove that I wasn't all alone. "Just for a few minutes."

"Understood. Feel free to leave whenever you'd like. I would hope we can become friends. Maybe I can become a backup if you need help or advice of the vampire kind. Should your mentor be unavailable, of course." He pulled a card out of his pocket and handed it to me. "Call any time."

I took it and stuffed it into my coat, wondering if he really meant it. "If you're looking for someone to help you get at Sei or Gabe, I'm not your guy." I told him honestly. "They've been good to me. Even when I'm a total shit. I won't invite you into their house, or try to get them to meet with you, and if you don't want the witch to turn you inside out and feed your innards to the nearest tree, you're better off leaving me in one piece."

Max laughed, strong and hearty, throwing back his head. He stopped a moment later and shook his head at me. "No mincing words, eh? I have no use for those sorts of games, Gabe, or his Focus. My plans are larger and involve only vampires." He shrugged, "And for the moment—shifters." He led me down an alley where a brawny man stood at a nondescript door. He nodded to Max, barely spared me a glance, and opened the door for us. "I assure you, my interest in you is purely curiosity."

"About what?"

"Your power and how it's slipped through the cracks."

I shrugged. "Not Dominion born. So I couldn't tell you where it comes from. No one in my family has anything like it."

Max nodded. I followed him down a long hallway and to another door. He opened it and the noise hit me first. Cheering, shouting, and the smack of flesh hitting flesh. Not the soft slap like porn. No this was bone hitting muscle wrapped bone. The door closed behind us, blocking me in with the echoing thud of a body hitting the ground in the distance. What the fuck?

Max proceeded forward through a far doorway. As I moved closer the smell of sweat and drying blood wafted toward me strong enough to almost be visible. If there was one thing I hated about being a vampire, it was that everything smelled so awful. And this place stank.

The room was cavernous. A warehouse converted into a fighting room. Cages spread out across the open space. Wire bolted to the ground and looping all the way to the ceiling in intricate design over a concrete slab created elaborate fencing around each ring. Everyone moved to cluster around a new fight that seemed to just be starting in the back corner.

"Just in time for the final fight of the night," Max said. He smiled at me. "If you ever feel the blood lust getting to you, come here and the smell will kill it fast enough. Shifters stink, though their blood tastes all right. Not as good as witch blood, but better than those punks in the alley."

The stench made me a little queasy. I hadn't blown blood chunks since the first night of my change and wasn't going to do it now.

"It's really awful," I agreed. I didn't think I could get past the stink to try tasting a shifter. Did they all smell that bad? Like wet, sweaty, dog piss?

No one noticed us as we stepped in close to the last cage. I moved around to the edge, away from the others in case I needed to bolt. I had to breathe slowly to filter out the smell. Not like I had to breathe it was just habit. But, God, the smell. Gross.

Inside the wire ring something that looked like an overly muscled version of a horror movie wolfman stood, flexing his semi-furry arms and throwing spittle from his elongated snout. He wore nothing. His oddly bald sex hanging large and heavy between his legs, showing arousal. Maybe the fight got him off like that guy in the alley? His hands curled in a mix of human and wolf with long sharp talons and his legs hunched, bent wrong like a dog. Nothing about him was appealing. I wondered where all the romanticism with shifters came from. In comparison, a witch who changed flawlessly like Seiran, Jamie, or Kelly was so much more beautiful. Perhaps it was magic that made the difference. Science could only make humanity uglier, but magic—that was a dark beauty that created some of the most heavenly and devilish things in the universe.

A man moved across the ring, yanking off his shirt and pulling on a pair of boxing gloves. I couldn't imagine how they'd help him against the shifter. He looked scrawny compared to the hulking, fur-covered monster across from him. He couldn't be human though, since Max said this was a non-human event. Fight clubs for supes. The gambling portion of it probably made it as illegal as hell. The man in the corner with fists full of money probably worked for Max. But local law enforcement wouldn't care. So long as none of the norms were hurt, they'd turn a blind eye.

"Who's the human-looking guy in the ring?" I asked Max. "He's not really human, right?"

"Not hardly," Max replied. "Almost vampire, but not quite."

Was that even possible? The man was handsome enough, broad in the shoulders, medium brown hair, and just the slightest of red haze to his eyes. A vampire then, even if Max said no. Did any other creature have that red haze when they let the monster out? I couldn't recall anything from all of Seiran's lessons.

The bell rang and the fight began. I didn't watch. The beautiful man would fight the beast. Would he live or die? Did it matter? We were all monsters here. I turned away overwhelmed by my depression again. I was just like them, wasn't I? I may not look so scary on the outside, but the monster inside had claws just as sharp and bigger fangs.

I made my way out, sucking in the deep cold air.

"No one dies," Max told me, having followed me out. "At least not often. Accidents do happen."

"I don't want to be just another monster," I told him.

His smile was sad and somewhat self-mocking. "But we are, aren't we? I do a lot just to feel. You're young. You still pulse with emotion. What you saw inside scared you, depressed you, and yet excited you. I long for all of that."

Was that all I had to look forward to? An eternity searching for emotion? "I don't want to be like that." It was probably rude to say so, but the truth. "Empty."

"Happens to all of us in time. We live so long the world kills us from the inside out."

"Are you looking for a way to die, Max?" I had to ask. Gabe mentioned he'd been nothing but a walking corpse before he'd met Seiran. Max probably wasn't any younger.

"Looking for a way to live, my young friend. Call if you need me. I can show you things that Gabe would not dare."

Because Gabe was one of the good guys and Max was just fire I'd already burnt myself with twice. "Thanks," was all I offered as I headed back out into the night. It was getting late, and I had to get to the club before midnight. Gabe expected me to meet with the *cibo* I'd approve before the night was over.

I stopped at a gas station to clean up. The attendant didn't say anything about the bottle of water and chewing gum I bought. Though he did give me the stink eye when I asked for the bathroom key. Did he think I was gonna camp out in the crapper for the night? I would rather have found a dumpster to sleep behind.

When I stepped inside the stink nearly had me hurling again. Did they ever clean this place? I went to the sink and washed my face, taking time to scrub away small bits of blood spatter. The hunger must have been bad to make me so messy. At least my shirt and jacket were still clean. I could only imagine what it would be like to go meet the *cibo* with some other guy's blood on me. Sort of like paying for a second whore when the come of the first still stained the skin.

The mirror made me look so ordinary. I'd fed so my eyes wouldn't turn red even if I willed them to for at least a few more hours. Though I did try. Sometimes I let the monster out and just stared at him for hours. It still shocked me when I'd fall out of a weird trance and find only myself in the mirror.

I popped a half dozen pieces of gum. The strong cinnamon of it would kill any lingering blood and it burned my tongue. The stuff was nasty, but it was the one thing that Gabe swore by that I always used.

I made my way to the club hoping that the guy I'd spoken to online a couple dozen times wasn't some clingy jerk who wanted to be my vampire groupie. Gabe wanted me to have a regular blood source. Someone to feed on that would help me build a bond with humanity. I didn't care either way. Humans weren't all that great. I'd spent most of my life being one. Vampire wasn't much of an upgrade.

The last thing I needed was someone fragile that wanted me to be his savior. I was no one's hero dammit. No matter what Gabe and Sei tried to convince me of most days. I was okay being the bad guy. At least the role fit.

CHAPTER 2

The wailing pulse of music reverberated through my spine and the lights flashed in time to it. A headache was forming behind my eyes, and in my gut a tingling need grew. Gabe often reminded me that I was young and everything made the bloodlust worse. He hadn't been wrong so far, no matter how much I wished for a reprieve.

I shifted in my seat, turning to get a better angle of the crowd. Men and women gyrated, clothes almost non-existent. Pulses raced with lust and excitement. If I had been human it might have been appealing to join the crush of bodies, heat, and sweat. But I wasn't human anymore and they all reeked.

Still I wanted to gorge on them all.

The bottle of QuickLife in my grasp should have taken away the edge. Older vampires swore by the stuff. I could barely tolerate it. It tasted like I imagined liquefied shit to taste like. And really wasn't that what blood was? At least real people tasted better. Maybe it was the warmth or even something as spiritual as the soul, but I'd rather dine on the lowliest of people than drink the shit they put in a bottle.

That was why I was here. Even nibbling on the two thugs earlier had only dulled my hunger. I really longed to drink deeply of someone but feared killing them. Norms could only take a few gulps before they got dizzy and there was a chance they'd die. Witches, shifters, and vampires lasted longer but weren't exactly ideal prey since they fought back.

Sitting on the fringes watching the crowd made me feel like the predator I was. Gabe had frowned on my choice of seats. He wanted me to interact, seduce, and relate to them. I often wondered where the romance was. Books and movies made vampires sound so great. People didn't have a romance with their cheeseburger. Why did I have to have one with my food?

Being a vampire drew the hanger-ons like flies. Gabe warned me they only wanted to use me to be turned and that wasn't allowed. I didn't want any of them anyway. Couldn't imagine being stuck with any of them through whatever semi-immortality was granted via vampirism.

My old high school bullies would have laughed themselves hoarse at the thought of me being the guy everyone wanted. Little dorky Sam Mueller with his slanted eyes and dark clothes. They'd always called me Goth, though I'd never been. I guess now I really was.

My phone buzzed with a new text from my roommate Constantine. *Games?*

Waiting for Cibo, maybe l8er, I texted back. Con was a super-hot playboy covered in tattoos who just happened to land as my roommate when his sister had gotten involved in some shit. She'd been executed a month ago for trying to kill the Pillar of Earth, Seiran Rou. Now Con and I lived together and spent most nights playing video games until he was too tired to move off the couch and I had to hide from the light of the sun. He played viciously, killing everything in his path and sometimes screaming at the TV. I played stealthily, trying to rid myself of some of the internal demons I refused to tell Gabe about. If the *cibo* didn't get here soon I'd be finding other prey for the evening so I could get back to the exorcism.

Life was good when it was narrow. Despite Gabe's protests I didn't want a constant. My luck with lovers had been 0 for 3. It was probably better for everyone if I stayed on the edges and fed only when I needed to from random strangers. I'd been texting the *cibo* for a few weeks, talking to him online. One chosen out of dozens who had contacted me. I thought if it was someone I could get along with, it would be easier. Now I questioned the wisdom of that. If I didn't know them, I could bite them and leave them. Feeding was sort of like a one-night stand. I didn't need to get their name to suck on them for a while.

The smell of blood permeating the club warned me that my hunger had just about reached its limit before it would take over and choose for me. No matter how much I drank it wasn't enough, which was why Gabe asked the Tri-Mega—the ruling body of vampires—for help. They sent me a volunteer, a *cibo*, someone I could feed from regularly to stem the need. All I knew about the donor was that he was Italian, and a half vampire named Luca. I hadn't known anyone could be a half vampire until I asked Luca how that happened. He said his dad was a vampire and his mom was human, which apparently meant that when he died he would transition to vampire without having an official sire. I hadn't really pushed for more details.

When we talked online it was about books, movies, or video games. All the others had wanted to role play me biting them, which was why I'd chosen Luca. He hadn't talked about it at all until we arranged this meeting. And no pictures exchanged. I'd rather see his expression in person than get the brush off because I was nothing special.

Luca better be worth the wait, as I'd been waiting almost an hour. I hated places like this and stuck out like a sore thumb. The internal noise was worse than the music. For some reason becoming a vampire had tuned me into the human psychic network or some shit, because I could feel their emotions, and hear a lot of their thoughts. In the beginning I'd basked in the new ability. But now it was an incessant chatter that never stopped. Often, I didn't know whether I was feeling someone else's emotions or my own. Gabe claimed it was because I lacked focus, which was because I was always hungry. I didn't agree. I could pick a single person out of the room and get inside their head, shift their emotions if I needed to. Focus wasn't the problem, though hunger was always an issue.

No, the real issue was my ability to amplify other people's powers. Proximity to me could make even a null's expanse of power triple. After an incident where a guy doing a trick with his lighter set the bar on fire, I avoided clubs like this on general principle.

"Sam?" a voice broke me out of my brooding.

I glanced up at a handsome man. He was probably only a few years older than me—human years—with dark, bed-head messy hair, and dark brown eyes. His faded blue jeans hugged his hips instead of hanging off his ass as was the style, and a snug T-shirt outlined strong shoulders and a lean waist. The stubble at his jaw was more arty than natural. He probably spent a lot of time trimming it to be just perfect which annoyed me because I couldn't grow facial hair if I wanted too. Overall, he was good looking, the kind of guy who would never have looked my way twice before I'd been turned. It instantly irritated me.

Was this my *cibo*? Had I been played and he was just some sort of junky looking for his next vampire fix? But that was sort of the point right? I sighed. Maybe I could use that to my advantage. Keep from getting attached.

"Yeah?"

He held out his hand. "I'm Luca Depacio."

I took his hand, waiting for the touch to amplify his internal dialogue or emotions so I could read him better. But there was nothing. Just a vague hum of energy more intense than with other vampires and less annoying than humans. He also smelled heavenly. I don't mean his cologne—his blood. Did that mean he had some sort of power? Seiran smelled good, so did Kelly. Hell, even Con smelled like a steak dinner with a slice of New York cheesecake at the end. Luca's scent was mouthwatering. Maybe I was just that hungry. I took a deep breath and let go of his hand to keep from attacking him where he stood.

He slid into the booth beside me. All I could see was the sun-kissed skin at his neck pulsing in time to his heartbeat. The vein stood out like a sign in the desert pointing to a spring. Were all *cibos* like this? If they were then shit, sign me up for a dozen of them.

"God," I whispered unable to focus on his face, words, or anything but that jumping little river of life. I'd waited too long and he smelled too good.

He dragged me into his lap and pressed my face to his neck. "Feed, then we'll talk."

He didn't need to tell me twice. I latched on, sinking my sharp fangs into his tender flesh, sliding into the vein with a practiced ease and let the heat of him fill my mouth. He tasted like a thick red wine flavored with a hint of strawberries and chili peppers. Each swallow I drew from him poured through my body and straight to my groin. I had to shift away from him to keep my erection from pressing into his stomach. Feeding had become a turn-on the second I woke up from the death that completed my transition. Survival instinct Gabe had told me, because really who gets off on blood other than serial killers? Only I did now. And God did I want Luca bad.

I had to yank myself away and take a deep calming breath before I drained him dry while humping his corpse. Crap, he tasted good.

"You don't have to stop. I can handle you taking more."

I shook my head. No need to get addicted, and he tasted so damn good I was sure that had already happened.

"I can take care of your other need as well," Luca's softly accented words breezed by my ear. He pressed his palm to my cock, squeezing me through my pants. "A full feeding often makes the young very horny."

I let his touch linger a moment as I debated with myself on the pros and cons of taking him to the bathroom and letting him have his way with me or better yet bending him over a sink and filling him. He smelled so good. Slightly of blood and sweat—a shower, and vaguely wet dog. Shit, he'd been the guy in the ring with the shifter. I hadn't been close enough to see his face then, but the body type was right. His reason for taking so long made sense. Oddly enough there was no smell of injury on him. Had he won?

I sighed to myself. In the end, the choice was easy. I licked his wound willing it to shut and hoping it wouldn't look like more than a hickey since my healing skills weren't all that great yet and leaned away from him. His hand fell away from my traitorous dick. "I didn't ask you here for sex."

"No, you asked for a *cibo* with experience. I have cared for several new vampires."

The guy looked all of twenty. He couldn't have cared for that many vampires. My doubt must have shown on my face because he said, "We didn't discuss trivial things like this online because you find feeding and sex uncomfortable, but I'm not inexperienced with either."

And I was? "I have no problem with feeding or sex."

"Unless they go together?" He raised a brow in question.

I didn't need some stranger analyzing me. "This was a bad idea." I slid around him to the edge of the seat.

"Have I offended you? I didn't mean to. I'm only trying to be what you need."

"A blood bag? How is that good for either of us?" I shook my head. "You should go back to Italy or whatever. I'll figure something out. This was stupid." Even if I had to keep stalking the bowels of the west side to eat. The last thing I needed was another man I didn't want to say no to.

He put his hand on my arm. "Sam, your hunger won't be fulfilled by any normal human. In the old days new vampires slaughtered entire towns just to quiet the need. How will you continue without someone like me to help? Perhaps if one of your witch friends would let you feed from them…"

"Sei or Kelly? Fuck no." And I was pretty sure Jamie would rip my head off if he could. I'd hurt his kid brother, and nothing anyone said could make him like me. I got that, but I wasn't about to play hard up vampire just to suck on him a bit. And Con would freak.

"Then let me help you."

I stared at him. His words sounded genuine. He hadn't been a groupie like the others. But sadly, I hadn't known a lot of good people in my life. Trusting a stranger sent to me by the royal pains-in-the-ass of the Tri-Mega didn't sound smart the first time I heard the idea. Gabe told me food was food. And willing food even better. But he had donors lined up out the door with just the snap of his fingers.

I pulled out my phone. "I'll text you."

"I'm glad you changed your mind. But maybe you'd let me take you home tonight? Be sure you've fed properly?"

"I haven't. Changed my mind, I mean. I want you to think for the next twenty-four hours about why you really want to be here. If you're into getting bitten, then fine. No more games. Just be real. I'm no one's charity case, and we won't be fucking."

He opened his mouth to protest but I shook my head. One of the benefits of being the biggest, baddest things in the room now was that I made the rules. I was strong enough to keep anyone from pushing me around. Well, most anyone. Luca had just beaten up a werewolf so I wasn't sure where I ranked on that scale, but I'd be willing to lay him out if he tried.

"I will call you in twenty-four hours."

He folded his arms across his chest. "And if you don't like my answer?"

"Then you go home."

"Even though you need me."

"That's the funny thing about me. I don't *need* anyone." I headed for the door, not looking back. The man was beautiful, had an accent that anyone would fall over in adoration for, and his blood tasted like heaven. He had trouble written all over him. Been there, done that, came back undead.

My phone buzzed. I tapped the screen to answer, knowing who it was without checking the ID. He had been watching. *Him* no one would notice unless he wanted them too. The crowd of pulsing blood bags didn't bother him.

"You fed," Gabe said.

"Why aren't you home making your boyfriend happy instead of bothering me?" I snapped.

"You shouldn't be this moody after a meal like that. I could smell him across the room."

I was horny and had just turned down a hot guy. After more than two months of abstinence the blood was no longer my only need. I hadn't even braved masturbating since I'd been brought over. It just felt wrong. I was dead. I shouldn't have these sort of feelings. Then there was the red haze that couldn't figure out when to show up. Sometimes when I was turned on it came, and all the time when I let the monster out. I feared that meant the monster was taking control of me. But telling my mentor I was pissy because I hadn't been laid would only have him insisting I alleviate that problem, too. And I was pretty sure I'd kill whomever I took to my bed right now. "Look. I'm fine. I just want to go home."

"You should work for a few hours. Get some of the aggression out. I don't know why feeding always makes you so angry, but it does. Think of Constantine."

Yeah, there was no need to expose Con to my bad mood. He got real jumpy around vampires. More than once I'd stared longingly at the pounding vein of Con's throat. He'd never offered and probably wouldn't since he'd been bitten by his sister and controlled by a very nasty and now very dead vampire.

I stepped out into the chilly night. People passed by, huddled in coats and breathing white puffs of air in the nearly sub-zero temps. My coat was light-weight wool meant to help me blend in rather than warm me. I huffed out a heavy breath expecting a little white cloud, but got none. I'd just fed, should have been warmer, but the ice seemed to fill the core of me. I was a dead man wanting to feel alive. How stupid was that?

A hand landed on my shoulder. Gabe. He stared down at me in concern. His coat was heavier than mine, more expensive and stylish. His blond hair was trimmed beautifully. Face all angles and chiseled like a piece of artwork. No one ever saw him and thought "vampire." Two thousand years of practice made perfect. I couldn't imagine living that long. I put the phone away.

"Let me give you a ride." Gabe led me to his car, hand on my arm in a no-nonsense sort of way. It was a short two block walk, but the car would be better than the bus, and I did need to go home eventually.

He unlocked the doors. I got in and stared out the window not wanting to talk, though I knew he would. It was one of the things Gabe did best, though he failed miserably when he had to share private stuff with his lover. Gabe was the overprotective sort, which was both endearing and annoying. More the latter for me.

"So, tell me about Luca."

"Nothing to tell."

"You got upset when he came on to you," Gabe pointed out. So obviously he'd been close enough to watch. Did that make him a pervert? Or was I just in a pissy mood? Yeah, pissy mood.

"I don't need therapy." Well, yeah. I probably did, but I didn't want to work through the disaster that had been my life the past few years while lying on my back on a couch talking to some stranger. None of that shit helped Seiran. Hell, I was pretty sure it made him worse.

"Was he polite?"

"Yes. Of course."

"Did he taste good."

Understatement of the year. I could still taste him on my tongue and would be fantasizing about him for days to come. "Yes."

"Then why didn't you stay? Spend some time getting to know him?" Gabe started the car and steered out into the street, heading for his bar, not home. Guess I was going to work tonight after all.

"I've had that trouble before. Too good to be true."

"This isn't love, Sam. It's food. He's not asking you for any kind of commitment."

"That makes him a whore and me a john."

"Only you're not paying him."

"No, you are," I told Gabe pointedly. The *cibo*'s were paid, though I didn't know how much. It was Gabe's responsibility as my mentor to foot the cost, but it bothered me. More than I realized before. "He's a blood whore."

"He's willing. Why is that a bad thing?"

"Because if I wasn't a vampire, he wouldn't even see me."

"You don't know that."

But I did.

Gabe glanced at me, his sharp, handsome features blank of emotions. I'd seen the stoic expression enough to know it was disapproval. Gabe didn't share his emotions well. With him it was just an impenetrable wall. I pitied Seiran, because sometimes Gabe was just a jerk. He came across as cold when he was really angry. Or maybe that was just to me. "I can't help you if you don't let me."

"I'm trying. I just don't know if I'm cut out to be a vampire." I glared out the window again. Another round hole this square peg didn't fit into.

"There's only one other option. And I don't want you to give up yet."

I shrugged. It was only a matter of time. I'd never asked to be rescued from that creek. That was Kelly's doing. Choices I didn't get to make. I hoped they didn't come back to bite everyone else on the ass. "But if I decide eventually that's the right thing for me?"

Gabe let out a long sigh. "Then I will grant your request."

I sat back, relieved by the fact that Gabe would kill me if I asked. I wasn't there yet, not ready to go. But the thought constantly entered my mind. Too much pain from two lives now, instead of just one. Vampires didn't walk up to their undead existence with perfect lives and no memories of the old life. No, we dragged that baggage full of shit with us. Someday soon I'd have to let it go one way or another.

CHAPTER 3

Gabe pulled the car into the lot at the bar and parked. The place had to be jumping since the lot was full enough that people were parked on the grass. I got out without being asked. Maybe some quiet time with a lot of suds could help. I was still hungry but no longer horny. That was a plus, right?

I used the entrance in back to avoid the regular crowd and took off my coat—hanging it on the door—before heading to the kitchen. The dishes were piled up on the counter beside a giant sink and two dishwashers that swirled in a noisy gurgle. I'd never eaten here before my change, but I heard the food was good. The amount of washing I did paid tribute to that. The giant closet of dishes could get emptied in just a few hours on the busiest of nights. On the weekends I often washed twenty or thirty sink loads of dishes while running both washers constantly. People came to the Bloody Bar and Grill for more than just booze. Seiran's menu drew in even big television networks food critics to talk about the amazing meals hidden away at a little vampire bar tucked away in the corner of the city.

I filled the sink with warm water and suds, pushed up my sleeves and began to dunk dishes into the flow. The heat over my hands felt good. I began to scrub the dishes and put them in the drying rack one by one. Gabe hadn't hired me because he needed me. He'd hired me because I needed the distraction. That and I was pretty sure Sei had threatened to leave him if he didn't get me out of the house every once in a while. I'd never had a real job before this—if you could call dishwashing a real job—but I made sure everything was spotless. Seiran was a shrew when it came to dirty dishes and even though he had a real job now, solving magic crime, he was here a lot.

The rhythm of the work kept me focused for a while. Apparently Kelly and Sei were working tonight as they both had come around to drop off more dishes and take some of the clean ones to the serving area. Kelly just gave me his usual nod hello, but Sei gave me a half hug and asked if I needed a Quicklife before heading back.

"No, but thanks," I told him. I was still hungry, always hungry, but that stuff was gross. "Think of those like drinking a warm purple Gatorade." The fake flavors, too much sugar, and wallop of chemicals was nothing but nasty.

Seiran shuddered, "Gross."

"Exactly."

He left me to my washing. I'd finished over a dozen loads before the counters were finally clear. It was getting pretty late. The dining room always wound down to just boozers after midnight. Anyone could still order food until closing at two, but it was rare to see something other than chips and salsa head to a table that late.

My fingers were wrinkled little prunes by the time all the silverware was rinsed and dried. The glasses sparkled with plates stacked in neat piles. I began moving everything to the dish closet having already been in there twice checking for anything that was looking dusty and in need of washing. The dining area probably had more dishes I could retrieve to do at least another batch. But the washers were empty and I hated going out to face people who smelled like nothing but food to me.

I pulled the plug to drain and clean the sink then peered out the door to the main seating area. Gabe's bartender Michael stood behind the bar mixing up drinks. Kelly, Seiran and Jamie waited tables. The place was still packed with the regular drinking crowd. One non-regular sat at the bar near Michael, Luca.

He glanced up as if I'd called him—though I suppose since I'd fed from him, technically I could call him if I wanted to—and our eyes met. I turned away letting the door close heavily. I peeled out of the kitchen, pausing only to grab my coat. Luca's blood still ran through me, easing the need, but not enough. Maybe if I'd taken more. He *had* offered, but I would have had sex with him and I was pretty sure I'd kill him by accident.

Just thinking about it pissed me off. Maybe if he chained me down or something. Christ, just the thought of that made me hard. Fuck, was I twisted or what? How long would it take for him to fall into my bed and break my heart? What was he going to use me for? Was I just another toy to him like I'd been to so many other men?

I growled at my own self-pity. Stupid vampire bullshit. I was no Goddamned Louis. Self-hating prick that he'd been. I was a monster and that was okay. I'd done some pretty bad things before I'd been changed. Being undead couldn't be all that different. Gabe told me I was depressed and if I wasn't a vampire, they'd have me on medication for it. But since I couldn't eat and my blood moved ridiculously slow, nothing could help me. I had to suck it up. HA, vampire humor, suck it up.

This whole vampire thing happened all the time. People were changed every day. Some made it. Some just threw themselves into the fire. Most lived somewhat normal lives. Gabe was a testament to that. Michael was more normal than Gabe. He didn't have the wealth or power Gabe did, but he was smart, took care of his own and lived a good life. Most vampires seemed to be like that. I'd been exposed to the worst of them with Matthew and Andrew before I even realized I believed vampires existed. They'd taught me destruction and evil, but I'd come to the light. Crossed over to the side of good and joined Seiran and his band of do-gooders.

Yeah, right. Drafted. Kidnapped, maybe. And good was a relative term. Who made the rules of good and bad? Everyone thought they did good, or at least the lesser evil.

Most people would be happy they weren't pushing up daisies. Mostly I wasn't unhappy. More confused, unfocused, lost. When Matthew had been in my life, I'd had a goal—make Seiran's life miserable because only then would Matthew be happy. But that had all been a lie. Then Andrew had stormed in, promising things he could never provide. Revenge he had no right to, like I even cared that Matthew had been torched. It had been a bit of a relief to be free of him for the few minutes before Andrew took control of me.

I glared into the distance at the dark evening in the city. I could go home. Play video games with Con. He was sure to be awake. He'd break me out of some of the funk. Remind me what it was like to be normal. At least for a few minutes. He'd maybe tell me a joke or a story about when he and Kelly were a thing and how much of a fuck-up they both were. We'd laugh because Kelly was sort of perfect now. Poster boy for the new movement of men accepted into the magic studies program. Pillar of water, best friend to Pillar of earth. A superstar. Maybe being Seiran's friend made him that way.

I didn't hold out much hope that it would work the same for me.

The bell from the basilica rang quietly, in the distance, marking the hour. I'd come from religious stock. My folks migrated from China to have more freedoms, including that to be Christian. Was all that over now that I was undead? It wasn't something I had asked Gabe about, but I approached the church with a reckless abandon, only pausing briefly before stepping on the shoveled walk to text Constantine—*if something happens, be safe...*

The phone buzzed back almost instantly. I ignored it and followed the manicured snow drifts up to the salted stairs. Lightning didn't strike when I took the first step, nor did I burst into flames when I opened the door.

Scattered lights made the church look cavernous. Statues of angels and saints lined the walls high up, and above them stained-glass windows reflected colorful panes of darkness, probably from the snow cover. I bet during the day the sun would bounce around creating rainbows to dance on the oak pews.

I touched one of the wood pews sliding my fingers along the smooth surface of the sanded seat. It was a good memory. Times when my family had piled into the back of the church to listen to mass and kneel in prayer for something better to come.

No one screamed or even glanced my way. The few people still awake at this hour knelt with heads bowed. Either no one noticed that a vampire had just walked in or no one cared. The lack of bursting into flames made me wonder if church was all bullshit, or if vampires being inherently evil was.

The confessions closet was open on the parishioner's side. I sucked in a heavy breath and headed for the little room. Maybe talking to God and asking for forgiveness would lighten my mood a little. Maybe he could tell me what to do, whether I should keep Luca or try to find some other focus for my life. Anything had to be better than the drifting I was doing right now.

I closed the door behind me and marveled at how similar the room felt to a coffin. Was that intentional? To give people a taste of death and scare them into confessing? The door between the windows slid back.

"Forgive me, Father, I have sinned," I said in familiar fashion.

"The Lord forgives those who seek His grace, son."

"I'm not human, Father. Are the rules the same?"

"We are all imperfect in His sight, child. Yet His blood cleanses us of all wrongs. Seek Him and find peace in His forgiveness."

Blood. Yeah, it was all about the blood. The way it tasted, smelled, and how badly I needed it. I should have taken more from Luca. Maybe he'd have stilled the hunger a little longer. Gabe said I could take from the average *cibo* two or three times a night. Anything had to be better than the constant bloodlust, right? Matthew had been driven crazy by it. Revenge for blood had stolen Andrew's life from him. Those were the examples I'd begun with. Then there was Gabe who was strong, stoic, and compassionate. He could also be ruthless and cunning. Andrew had told me stories that I didn't know if I could believe or not. Things that made Gabe sound like a monster who killed anyone or anything that got in his way. He hid his darker side, wouldn't even let his lover glimpse it, but I knew it was there. We all had it. No matter how much we fought it.

Yeah, it was all about the blood.

I could smell the priest's blood and hear his pulsing heart. He was tired, old, but I could almost taste him from where I sat. "Forgive me, Father. I can't do this yet," I told him and got up from the bench, fleeing the confessional. Back out in the cold I stalked toward home though it was a several mile walk. I'd work through this just like I had everything else in the past. I wasn't an animal out of control. Just a new vampire. I could rein it in. Or let it go. I wasn't really sure which I preferred.

The quiet streets passed. I ignored it all. My gut told me sunrise was a few hours away and I should hurry home. A coffee shop beckoned with bright lights and smells of roasted beans early in the morning. I crossed the street and slid inside, enjoying the fact that the place was mostly empty. The barista smiled at me and took my order for a hot mochaccino. I couldn't drink it but it would warm my hands and smell good.

I sat down at a corner booth and opened the lid so I could breathe in the sweetness. I tuned out the world and just focused on air in and air out, letting all the rest go for now. The smell had somewhat vanished and I might have dozed because I barely noticed someone drop into the seat across from me.

It wasn't until he grabbed my cup and took a sip that I finally realized I wasn't alone. I blinked away my spotty vision and stared at Luca. "You look like a vampire when you do that," he pointed out.

"Is that a problem?"

He shrugged. "I guess if you don't have people randomly targeting vampires around here for gang beatings and stakings it wouldn't."

My smile was automatically wicked—I'm sure with more than a little fang showing. "Let them try."

"You have a mean streak." He took another sip of the coffee and frowned. He got up, threw it away and headed to the counter. The jeans he wore hugged his ass nicely. I admired it until he returned to the table with two new hot drinks. Mine was another mochaccino. I took off the top again and sucked in another burst of the wonderful smell. Luca sipped from his cup looking damn edible. Why did he have to be so damned hot?

"Does it bother you that I'm not nice?" I asked him.

He shook his head. "Nah. I sort of expected it. When we talked on the net you come across a little distant and cold. Not that it's a bad thing. Life is not all bubble gum and puppies. And anyone who tells you it is, is trying to sell you something. Talking to you was actually refreshing. Lots of new vampire are just suck ups trying to keep their master happy. It's so annoying."

"I've done my time as other people's doormats. I don't let anyone walk on me anymore. So if you're just looking for someone to push around, I'm not your guy."

"Understood. Makes sense really. I've read your file. Gabe insisted. You've had shitty people around you most of your life, you can't be expected to be perfect."

I snorted at the irony. "Have you met Seiran? He had shitty people too, but he's pretty perfect."

Luca shook his head. "He's not. I'd say he's pretty troubled. And his OCD is only part of that. You shouldn't be aiming for perfect anyway. You should just be you."

"Get that off a Hallmark card?"

"It did sound kind of cheesy as I was saying it."

"Kinda?"

He laughed. "This is better though, right?" He motioned to the two of us. "Talking, no bloodletting or anger. We talked all the time online."

"I don't want to talk about you being my *cibo* right now." I wrapped my hands around the cup and let the warmth filter through my fingers.

"Okay." We sat in silence for a minute or so before he asked, "You like to fight?"

Had he seen me at the fight club earlier with Max? "Not like you do." In a cage surrounded by cheering crazies and monsters.

"It's a hell of a stress reliever. I've been doing it for half a decade at least."

"I don't do a lot of fighting. Unfair advantage with me being a vampire and all."

He shrugged. "I'm a half vampire. In the cage it doesn't matter. They pit you against someone they think is a pretty even match. Sometimes pushing yourself to the limit is really the only way to know you're real. Alive. The anger eats at me so much that I just need to break something. It's better if it's in an open fight. Medics can help if I fuck up, or maybe I really just need someone to beat the shit out of me to get my head back on straight."

This was a side of him I hadn't seen before. Not even a glimpse of it online. "But you only fight monsters."

"Because I'm stronger than humans. I'm always looking for the next monster to break in half. In the ring I don't have to hold back. It makes me feel powerful."

I sighed and got up, heading toward the door. "I really don't want to be that monster."

"Hey, that's not what I meant." Luca followed me, throwing my cup away and holding the door. We walked in silence for a while. He wasn't really dressed for this sort of cold, but maybe he was more vampire than human. Finally he said, "I didn't mean to offend you." He stuffed his hands in his pockets. "Vampires aren't monsters. They are people, more than most other paranormals. The genetics are really similar. A hybrid, I guess you could call them. I've met ordinary humans who are more monstrous than any *other*. It's all about the mindset, I guess." His expression was neutral. "I've studied a ton of the science on vampires since I'm half one. My mom dropped me off on my dad's doorstep when I was five. I wasn't human enough for her and he had no idea I existed until that moment. Apparently I'd gotten really mad and broke the kitchen table with a single hit. Scared the cleaning lady. She thought I was gonna kill her. Cops were called and everything. No one believed her, thought she was on something. I mean, I was five. But my mom knew."

"Shit."

"It's okay. I'm grateful. I could have hurt someone. My father helped me control the rage, strength, and my hunger."

"You need blood?" The thought surprised me since everything about him said he was human, from the beat of his fast pulse to the warmth of his skin. He even smelled mostly human, under the luscious goodness of his heavenly blood.

"Yeah. Not as often as any full vampire. And the Quick-Life crap doesn't work for me at all." He got really quiet. "No vampire should be drinking that anymore."

"It's awful."

"It's more than awful. But that aside—I usually drink from my dad once a month. It's a little more awkward now that I'm older."

"I can imagine how sucking on your dad would be awkward."

He punched me lightly in the shoulder. "Smartass."

"Better than the alternative. So seriously, is that why you're here? To find a new vampire to feed on?"

He held up his phone showing the time which was just after four A.M. then shoved it back in his pocket. "Not time for my answer yet. You'll just have to wait in anticipation."

I sighed. "You're pretty sure you're staying, aren't you?"

"Not sure at all, but hopeful. You're an interesting guy." We walked in silence for a few more minutes. "It's really cold here. Been in a lot of snowy places, but never someplace quite this cold."

"You should have a coat and gloves," I pointed out. "It's probably two or three above zero right now."

"I run warmer than most humans. Not as hot as shifters, but close. Part of being half vampire maybe."

So that was why he was without a heavy coat and normal winter gear. "Did you beat that werewolf?"

"Yeah. They are pretty easy. A hit to the snout and they're out cold. They fight dirty though, lots of nails and teeth. Ever fought a shifter?"

I thought of my sparring with Seiran and of late Kelly. "No. Just a couple of witches, and a few vampires. A lot of street thugs too, though they're no challenge."

"Witches, now that's a tough fight. They are wicked scary in the ring and outlawed in most fights, especially the stronger elementals like earth and water. In California there was a network of male witches and a few females who would fight. None above level three allowed though as most often times they kill their opponent and that's frowned upon in cage fighting. No witches up here allowed at all in the ring, but I think that's because the Dominion presence is pretty strong here."

"I thought their presence was strong everywhere."

Luca shook his head. "The world is changing and not all because of Seiran Rou. He's part of it. A step in the direction of equality, but no one thinks he's treated fairly either. It's all politics. Someone always disagrees, doesn't matter on what end of the spectrum your views are. In the south there's still a pretty big movement against the Dominion because all witches should burn. Religion starts a lot of wars that politics finish. The Dominion is really just another religion."

"Sadly true," I agreed.

"As for other opponents in the ring, vampires, the occasional siren or other random supe, it's mostly a fight of who's faster. Strong is not so much an issue if you can't land a punch. And magic is banned from the ring."

"How did you get into all of this? You look so…"

"Nerdy?" he supplied

"Normal," I amended. He was kind of nerdy. Nerdy-hot.

He gifted me with a wry smile. "I mentioned I had anger issues. It's sort of a vampire trait. The older ones learn how to bury the feeling or release it in other ways. For the young it's harder to control and often comes out in bloodlust. Thus, the reason I was sent to you."

"You said thus. How old are you anyway?" I rolled my eyes at him.

He smacked me again playfully. "Older than I look. Anyway, my dad hired a vampire who was an ex-boxer to train me. He thought it would help me work through the aggression."

"It didn't work?" Was it too much to hope the deep wells of rage that ate at my gut would go away?

"Not enough. The fighting helps. But I'm not dead yet. So it could be worse in me because I'm still part human. Human emotions are intensified. It's sort of their superpower. Also one of the reasons the newly undead struggle. They are used to feeling things so strongly that when it starts to fade, they panic. Around the one-year mark is when a vampire is either safe or put down because they've gone mad." He jogged ahead and walked backward smiling. "But let's not talk about that. We have less than two hours before sunrise. Wanna fight? I can show you some moves."

The promise of violence and Luca made me hard again. Dammit. I really was twisted now, wasn't I? "Who's your dad anyway? I don't want some freaky ass vampire coming to kill me after I kick your ass."

He laughed. "I'm not that breakable, I promise. Besides, you came into the fight club with him. Max Hart."

Shit!

"Don't look so alarmed. I'm like his eightieth kid or something. He's really not all that overprotective as you'd think a vampire might be. He's kind of opposed to us becoming vampires. Since I was born half I will probably turn after death anyway. It's already in my blood. Whatever it is that makes vampires, vampires."

"How do vampires have kids?"

Luca snagged my hand in a tight grip and led me toward the main road where there were sure to be cabs. "Same way anyone has babies. Insert tab A into slot B. I've heard bullshit about vamps not being as fertile, and never heard of a girl vamp having a baby, but I know more than a handful of male vamps who are daddies. And not the leather kind."

"So do you have a lot of brothers and sisters then?" He said his dad had like eighty some kids. That was a lot. I couldn't imagine and I came from a big family.

"Alive? Just one older brother who's a vampire, but we aren't close. I have photo albums of ones who've passed. Not that they mean much. They're really just pictures of strangers. I'm sure there are dozens of cousins and stuff but it's too much to keep track of."

"Seiran says your dad is pretty powerful. Maybe that's why he has a lot of kids."

Luca shrugged. "Maybe. There aren't a lot of studies on vampires and fertility. Though Seiran being Father Earth might mean he can read my dad better since he's pretty damn powerful himself."

Did Luca want Sei too? I couldn't contain my sigh, and stopped, pulling my hand out of his. "I'm not competing with Seiran Rou. If you want him, do it on your own, and look out for the large Roman general who hangs around him. Gabe's sort of possessive."

He appeared genuinely confused. "Not sure what you mean."

I stared at his face, searching for something that said he was messing with me. Men as beautiful as Luca didn't look at guys like me. Not unless they saw a way to get to someone else. "I should go home."

"Ah, I get it," he said.

"What?"

"You have someone special at home. That's why you don't want me. You know you need my blood and are attracted to me, but you want to be loyal. That's nice. I can talk to your guy and help explain if you need. We don't have to be anything more than blood partners."

"What? Where the hell would you get that idea?" Con and I were friends of the non-sexual kind. Not that he was unattractive. In fact he pushed a lot of my buttons, but he was deathly afraid of vampires, and I sort of hated humans and players. Both of which he was. We got along simply because we were both pretty fucked up. "I don't do sex with anyone."

"Ever?"

"I'm not a virgin if you're asking. But I've had enough with people fucking me over." We caught a cab back to the west side near the club. Neither of us spoke until the cab dropped us off.

"So you like to be the fucker, not the fuckee. Okay. I'll store that away for future use. I'm versatile." His words invoked an image in my head of him riding me, that tight ass clenching my cock tight. I had to adjust myself just to alleviate some of the pressure. Of course, he noticed. "My offer from earlier still stands."

"I don't do pity sex."

"Me neither." He circled around me, stalking with a big smile on his face. "I'd rather fight you. Winner fucks the other."

"You must really get off on this fighting thing. You'll probably kick my ass."

"Not necessarily. You're faster than me, stronger. Odds are pretty fair. I don't fight full vamps in the ring. Just critters."

I was tempted. Not only to get out some aggression but to maybe win against someone I couldn't really hurt. The idea of fucking him was more than appealing. I'd probably be dreaming about it today when I finally went to bed. "How breakable are you?"

His smile said he knew he won. "Hardly. I'm really flexible though. Can bend my legs over my head and everything."

"God, stop! I want to fuck you okay. That's not a secret. Just 'cause I'm not going to doesn't mean I don't want to. It's called restraint."

He leaned in close, almost near enough to kiss. "You gotta win first."

CHAPTER 4

He led me inside the building, past the room of cages and to a training area in the back. The place was empty and the room smelled like cleaner. At least it didn't stink as bad as the main room. The floors and walls were heavily padded. A shelf near the wall was organized with a bunch of gear. Luca grabbed two sets of gloves and head gear, then threw me half and some extra padding before pulling on his own.

"This stuff isn't going to help much."

"Humor me," Luca said. "It's really not sexy if I punch you in the head and your ears bleed. The padding can stop a major injury. Shit still hurts though, I promise."

I tugged everything on and kicked off my shoes like he did before stepping into the taped red box. "So what are the rules?"

"Stay in the box. A ten second pin is considered a win. In the ring a win would be a TKO, but I'd rather fuck you while you're awake."

That was not going to be happening. "Whatever. Hope your ass is ready for me pretty boy."

He tapped his gloves together and the fight began. Luca moved like a dancer, darting around me, graceful, elegant, but fast—trying to get into my blind spot. I matched him and threw a quick jab which caught him in the shoulder. He didn't flinch, though I knew I hit him pretty hard. His first punch landed square on my chin, sending me down to the mat. I even slid a few feet seeing stars. It hurt, but not in a bad way.

He leapt on me, trying to get in a pin already, but I kicked him off and rolled away, spinning into a jump mid-move and landed back on my feet. Kelly's little self-defense classes were helping. I wasn't all swinging anger anymore. In fact, Sei and I sparred often enough to be evenly matched. Which was odd because he was mostly human. He could match my speed and flexibility though, and almost seem to predict my moves. Maybe it was because he was Father Earth and I was dead. Maybe it was because he was Gabe's Focus. All that mattered was that the practice kept the fight against Luca going.

Staying on the mat was the hard part. It was a smaller space than I was used to. Luca kept pushing in close, swinging hard enough to make me stagger and tried to get me to step outside the red box. Each time I rebounded with a harder punch or kick, sometimes missing him completely, but getting him to back off, and other times just grazing him. He was fast. Faster than any human I'd met. Neither of us connected more than two or three times.

"Stop being afraid to hurt me and fight," Luca shouted at me. But I didn't want to hurt him. No matter what he wanted me to think, he was still human. I missed him probably more than I should have, matched my pace to his, even landed a punch or two more than I would to anyone else. Luca growled and his fist found the side of my head hard enough to make me see stars.

I landed on my knees, shaking my head to clear the fuzzy

edges from my sight and ringing from my ears. Fuck that hurt even with all the padding. He bounced away, waiting, when he could have taken me down completely with another hit. But he was sweating hard. I was making him work. His pulse raced, and the scent of his blood called to me like a fucking siren's song. Red inched across my vision.

"That's more like it. Let me see those red eyes of yours. Let the rage free."

Did he want to die? I wouldn't give him that, but I could scare him, show him it wasn't all fun and games. My heart sped up to match his. A burst of energy flowed through me like a shot of caffeine and I jumped to my feet, ready. I let my other self out, telling him not to kill or maim. So far he heeded me, and I hoped this time was no different. Even if Max Hart wasn't enamored of his kid, he'd probably come to settle the score if I killed Luca even by accident. If Gabe didn't kill me first.

I zipped around Luca landing the first punch to his ribs and moved out of his reach before he could even finish his gasping exhale from the hit. Luca couldn't hope to keep up as I landed another dozen punches. But he took each one and kept coming back. Blood poured down his chin smelling like heaven. I wanted to lap it up, feed at his mouth, and fuck him until the world flipped over.

He pivoted left and bounced back to avoid another hit, then swung and connected a hard right directly to my left eye. I landed hard on my back, sight swirling in a wash of red. This time he was on me, shoving me hard to the ground to pin me. I couldn't see him. My head throbbed from his blow and the back of my skull where I'd hit the mat. I could feel him, smell him and the monster wanted out so badly I shook with need. But the glowing red took over, swallowing the world in the taste of his blood.

When I woke I was lying on the mat, high as a kite and breathing like I'd just run a race. The room spun in wild circles, twisting and shaping the metal beams above as they danced. The white spray foam looked like snow. My body ached in a good way. I was still hard as a rock.

"You back?" Luca asked. He sat a few feet away, bruised, lips swollen, clothes torn and disheveled, bloody, and a couple spots on his neck still bled pretty fiercely. He seemed dazed, but not upset.

I sat up slowly, still blinking away the weaving vision and took in the tattered remains of his jeans. "Shit. What did I do?"

Luca chuckled. "I think you need to stop your quest for abstinence. It's fueling your rage."

Had I forced myself on him? I couldn't have. I was still fully clothed. Fuck but he looked like I'd tried. "Did I…?"

"Kissed me, bit me. You were kind of rough and kinky, but I liked it. Ground me into the mat." He glanced down at his pants—what was left of them—which were wet in front. "I don't think I've come in my pants since I was a kid. It's been a while since I've actually met someone who could hold me down."

"Shit, I'm sorry." He looked like someone beat the shit out of him. And maybe I did.

"I'm not. Come upstairs and clean up. You're covered in blood. Any norm sees you now and they'll think you murdered someone." He rose to his feet and offered me a hand.

I took it and pulled him close so I could close the wound at his throat. For the first time in as long as I could remember I wasn't hungry. How much had I taken from him? He leaned against me, breathing into my neck and returning my embrace for a minute or two before letting go and tugging me through the far door and up a set of stairs.

"Don't worry, my dad's not here. He's got some new fancy loft."

I didn't much care about his dad. Luca weaved up the stairs somewhat drunkenly. He unlocked a door and leaned back, "Come in, Sam."

The place was nice. Not something I expected to find in a warehouse in west St. Paul. Everything was gray and industrial, furniture large and fluffy rather than stylish. The windows loomed large over the river, but there seemed to be some sort of film over them.

"Windows are protected from daylight. You could stare at the sun through them and probably be only slightly bothered. I've got shutters on the outside that can close in case of emergency too."

"You've been here a while. Longer than just coming to be my *cibo*, haven't you?"

"Couple weeks. This was Max's space, but he's moved to a different building. Renovating the whole thing to create high priced condos. Has a big vision to transform the neighborhood."

No one in this neighborhood could afford high priced condos. Where would they go next if they were priced out of the city they'd come to call home? Progress wasn't always a good thing.

Luca turned on the light to a large bathroom and pulled out a few towels. He flipped the shower on and stripped out of the rest of his clothes without a care that I was watching every move. Or maybe that was the point. There weren't a lot of doors, and the bathroom door was some sort of large shoji-type screen which had been pushed back to show most of the bathroom.

"You can stay the day if you want. You won. So you get to

fuck me." He stepped under the spray and presented his fine ass my way. "I clean up nice."

No kidding. That ass was the stuff dreams were made out of. I sighed. "I don't think that's a good idea."

He shrugged and soaped up his fine body. "Your loss then. Offer is open if you change your mind."

The man was evil. "I should go home. Gabe will get mad." It was almost dawn. Maybe with the bloodlust finally lulled I could sleep. Really sleep. I hadn't felt rested since long before my change.

"He's keeping you on a short leash. Was that your first redout?"

redout? Is that what the red haze was? "No," I denied. But it was only a partial truth. I'd never let it completely go before, just small tastes.

"You should clean up." He pointed to a stack of towels he'd left on the counter. "You can join me in the shower. I promise to keep my hands to myself." He winked at me.

I sighed and went to the sink instead. Wetting a towel and washing some of the blood from my face. I looked like I murdered someone. The clothes were ruined, even Seiran probably wouldn't be able to get all the blood out and he was the king of clean. Christ, how had I gotten any in my mouth? "Are you sure you're okay?"

"A little lightheaded, but it will pass. I'm fine."

He turned my way and I was hard again. His cock was a beautiful well-veined sight. I could almost taste him. Fuck. I had to go. "Sorry, Luca. I just gotta go." He'd probably never seen a guy run from him so fast. But I was out the door and down the stairs before I could suck in another breath. There was no doubt in my mind that Luca was trouble and I'd be smart to run the other way. Unfortunately, I was pretty sure I was already addicted to him.

CHAPTER 5

I jumped in the first cab I could find. The driver asked if I wanted to go to the hospital or the police station. "Neither. I'm a vampire and I just came from having hot, bloody, man love with my boyfriend. Take me home, please."

He drove a little faster to the big collection of condos that made up home. Gabe's home, not mine, but I was pretty sure Con would freak if I walked in the door looking like I'd been to a slaughterhouse. And I had questions. Like what was a redout? Should I be having them? And if not, how did I prevent them in the future. Trouble was, I was pretty sure I'd have to own up about letting the monster out and hiding it from him. Shit this was going to be a bad day.

The sun was coming up too. I could feel it—an ache that started in my gut and worked its way outward, into my skin. Outside the building, lights flashed from several cop cars, casting an eerie glow on the predawn darkness. That wasn't good. Had something happened to Sei again? I paid the cabbie and got out, heading into the lobby. Gabe stood off to one side talking with a couple cops. The whole place seemed to go still when I stepped inside.

Gabe glanced my way and frowned. Both cops went for their guns. "It's okay," Gabe assured them. "He's not going to hurt anyone." He crossed the room to my side. "What the hell happened to you?"

"Sparring with my *cibo*. That's what you wanted right? Us to bond?"

"Is he alive?" Gabe whispered.

"Of course."

"Mr. Mueller you're under arrest for the murder of two St. Paul men," one of the cops told me. He took out a pair of dull brown cuffs—a vampire specialty. The words began to sink in, but I didn't bother to resist. Who had I killed? The three guys in the alley were all breathing when I left them. And after the monkeying I did with their heads they weren't likely to remember much more than my red eyes.

"Gabe?" I called out to him.

"I've already got a lawyer on the way to the station. Cooperate please. Luca was with you all night?"

"After I left the club and work, mostly. We had coffee, sparred, kissed a little." I went a little nuts… The cops led me out the door just as Seiran was stepping off the elevator. He looked alarmed as he rushed to Gabe's side saying something I couldn't hear as the door closed. My body ached with the coming sunrise. Would we get to the station before? They wouldn't let me burn to death in the back of a police car, would they?

My heart skipped a beat. What a crappy way to go. One of the cops helped me into the back of the car and off we went. Thankfully the ride only took a few minutes. Yellow and gold tinted the edges of the horizon in warning. Fuck. The rising sun was starting to mess with my sight, and as the cop pulled me out of the car, I could barely keep my feet beneath me.

They led me to a windowless room—for which I was grateful—took some pictures, fingerprinted me, and made me strip, leaving me only with some lightweight scrubs, then sat me at a table. The sun rose. I set my head down on the table while sleep yanked at me like a persistent child. Finally I closed my eyes and let it have me. What was the worst they could do? Pick me up and drag me out into the sun? After some sleep I'd care. Maybe.

The door closing woke me some time later. I'd had long enough to begin to dream, and unlike my usual onslaught of past memories I dreamt of Luca in the shower. Though I was pretty sure his cock hadn't been that big.

Someone moved a chair beside me and shook me gently. It was never easy being awake during the day. How Gabe did it at all astounded me. Maybe it was because he was so old. And perhaps working out some of the rage and bloodlust with Luca had tired me out more than usual because it took a heavy shove before I rolled my head over and tried to open my eyes. The smell of honey and clover was familiar, comforting, though I couldn't remember why.

Someone placed blood near my nose. Good blood. Not that crap from the street punks and not Luca, but something far more tantalizing. I'd never been allowed a taste…

"Seiran?" I asked as I pried my eyes open to stare at a cup.

He guided my hands to it. "Drink please. The detectives need to ask you a few questions."

"They think I killed someone." I took the first sip of the still warm liquid and sighed. Okay this was why Gabe wanted him. Good looks and super powers aside, Seiran tasted amazing. "Crap you should charge for this stuff. It's … wow!"

"Not too fast," he grumbled at me. "Too much can make you drunk and I need you lucid not loopy."

"I didn't kill anyone," I told him seriously after I took another sip. "There's always opportunity, but I hold back, just like Gabe taught me. I'm not all fucked in the head." Only partially.

"I don't think you are and Gabe doesn't think you're to blame. Another vampire maybe, which is troubling, but not you. We can't talk about that anyway. Your lawyer is outside talking with the police. Luca is here too. Says you were with him, which is good. If they really thought it was you, they wouldn't have let me in, would they?"

More likely they didn't believe some baby vampire like me could hurt the most powerful Pillar the world had seen in at least a few centuries. Some of the fog cleared from my sight as I sipped at the blood. Seiran's wrist was bandaged. "I can try to heal that if you want." It seemed only fair to offer.

"It's okay. I heal fast now. It'll be gone by midday."

"Yeah, Father Earth and all that."

He shrugged. "You needed blood and the police wouldn't let Luca be alone with you. You're both beat up pretty badly. If this is what sex equates for you, maybe you should see a therapist."

"Don't like it rough, Ronnie?" I teased him. He hated the nickname, and I was the only one who dared, but he still answered to it.

"Not that rough."

"We didn't do anything anyway. Just fought a little like when you and I spar. Only Luca's more vampire than human, so we were pretty closely matched." Until I had a redout. "You don't need to babysit me. I'm not going to hurt anyone. I just wanna nap."

"They might hurt you. I've been in your spot before. Wrongly accused." He shivered then stretched out in the chair. He finger-combed his long black hair into a ponytail and secured it with a band that he'd been wearing around his uninjured wrist. I'd shaved his head once, more out of anger at myself for not being good enough, than anything he'd done. He was beautiful. More pretty than handsome. The perfect mix of his Japanese mother and European father. The slanted eyes and high cheekbones, black hair, delicate features, pale skin and luminescent eyes. I'd hated him for a long time for being so beautiful. Only now I knew how much he hated it too. "I'll stay until your lawyer comes at least."

"I'm a big boy," I told him, though I was thankful for his support.

"No doubt. But you're not a lawyer."

"You're too nice. You know that? You could be a real dick, but you're still nice. I don't get that."

He shrugged again. "I am what I am."

Amen to that. I suppose I should really own up in case he wanted to escape before being dragged into bad press. He was only just getting the world on board with him being the first male Pillar in history.

"I was attacked in an alley last night before I went to the club to meet Gabe. There were three guys. I fought back. When I left they were still alive. I fed on them. Broke one's arm, another had a busted rib or two, but they were all alive when I left them." Laws weren't the same when it came to vampires. We were too strong and fast. Self-defense wasn't always a valid defense, not when I could have outrun them easily.

"Self-defense then. Three against one is never good odds. Even for a vampire. They could have had weapons."

But I'd let the monster out. Maybe my senses had been off. Maybe I'd taken too much from one of them. "Do you know what a redout is?"

"It's something bad. A berserker-like rage that vampires can go into, uncontrollable bloodlust, usually with no memory of what happened. It's sort of a boogeyman tale to scare young vampires into behaving and people away from them."

Shit.

"There are some reports of actual occurrences that I read about in my Metaphysics 101 class. Usually a lot of people die. Sometimes the vampire doesn't even feed on the blood, just shreds people. Gabe won't talk about it. Not with me." He paused and frowned. "Did you have a redout in the alley?" Seiran gripped my hand like he feared my answer.

"No." Not really. I'd let the monster out, but I'd still mostly been in control. "With Luca. I remember everything from the alley. But my sight went red with Luca just before I blacked out."

Sei relaxed in his chair. "Luca is alive and well, so that's good." He sighed heavily. "There's no legal defense for redouts."

The door opened and several people entered the room. One had to be my lawyer since he was dressed in an expensive suit. The other two were probably cops.

"Mr. Rou you'll have to leave now," one of the detectives told him, holding the door open for him. The cop put his hand out for my empty cup and I let him have it. He'd probably take DNA off it or something, fingerprints, whatever. I couldn't stop it. If I killed those men, I deserved whatever they did to me. The fine line I was walking between hurting them and killing them was far too narrow. Gabe was going to rip me a new one if I made it out of this.

Seiran squeezed my hand before he left.

"Later, Ronnie," I teased him. Everyone sat down. The suit took his place beside me and said, "Please note that I will advise him not to answer any questions that may incriminate him. He has also cooperated without resistance, so let's make this fast so I can take my client home to bed where he belongs."

"Understood, Mr. Janovich," the cop said then turned to

me. "I'm Detective Rice and this is Detective Moore. We just want to ask you a few questions about last night."

"Okay," I told him.

"Let's start with how you got so banged up, Sam."

"I was sparring with my friend Luca."

"He beat you up? He looks pretty roughed up too. Maybe you both went for a little walk to find someone else to beat on? Maybe you get your kicks that way," the other detective said.

The lawyer interrupted before I could reply, "If you don't have any actual questions, Detective, this interview is over."

"Is there anyone who can vouch for you other than Luca Depacio?"

Were they questioning his credibility too? "Not when we were sparring. It was just the two us, but before that we were at a coffee shop for a while."

"Name and location of the shop?"

I rattled it off. I wondered if I should tell them about the fight in the alley. Would they automatically assume I'd killed the guys even though they'd been alive when I left? I leaned toward the lawyer who tilted his head to listen. "Three guys attacked me in an alley early last night. They had bats. I fought back, but they were all alive when I left. That was before coffee and before I met Gabe at the club."

"What time?" He prompted.

"Eight thirty. Then I went to the club where I met up with Gabe and Luca. I worked last night too. But I'm sure Gabe told you that."

"And where did this incident occur?"

I gave him the exact location. West 7th wasn't a great place to be in broad daylight. After dark it was brutal. Just being there was bound to start something, but I kept my mouth shut about the fact that I'd been looking for a fight.

Mr. Janovich relayed the events to the detectives. "I think

that settles this. Since Mr. Mueller was otherwise engaged. He has a solid alibi from after eleven p.m. Probable death for your victims was after two a.m." I was at the bar working until just before two a.m. "He was on the other side of town working until two a.m. and then with a lover, who is out in the lobby, until early this morning. Since you have no reason to hold him, it's time for him to go home." He got up from his chair and I followed. I really hadn't killed anyone?

"It's daylight. He can't leave anyway. And we can hold him for up to twenty-four hours without charging him."

"You have no reason to hold him other than the fact that he's a vampire. That would be racial profiling, Detective. Does your department want that lawsuit?"

The detectives glanced at each other. "So be it," Rice said. "I suggest you don't leave town, Mr. Mueller. Forensics will be combing your clothing for DNA evidence."

"You should probably swab Luca, since it's his blood all over my clothes," I told them as I followed my lawyer out the door. Were they really letting me go?

Seiran and Luca waited in the entryway outside the main desk. Luca looked like he'd been hit by a bus. Face swollen and turning colors, one eye almost black. "Shit! I'm so sorry," I told him. He hadn't looked that bad when I left him in the shower.

He snickered. "You haven't looked in the mirror, have you? We could be twins. I gave as good as I got. And I'm a quick healer, so no worries. I'll be mostly normal by the time the sun sets."

Seiran grabbed my hand and squeezed it. "Can you go home?" He glanced at the lawyer, "Can we take him home?" The man nodded. "You need sleep, Sam. You should be better healed already than what you are, especially with my blood in you." He pulled me toward the door.

"It's light out," I reminded him. Matthew had done it

pretty regularly—walked around in the sun. I wasn't that crazy. It hurt. Even if I covered up in a layer of clothing and hid every inch of skin it still hurt like a really bad sunburn. Heated skin, tightness, sensitivity, the whole shebang. Prolonged exposure only made it worse. I could only tolerate a few minutes before I'd probably start screaming like a baby.

Luca grabbed a bag off a nearby chair and then dug out a large black piece of cloth. "Put this over your head and we'll pull it down over you. Think of it as a blackout condom. It has UV protectors in the fabric protecting you from all the sun's evil rays."

I went from tired to horny in half a second at the mention of condom. Damn. I was probably going to have to fuck Luca just to get him out of my system.

He gave me a knowing smile and kissed me on the cheek, then he tugged the fabric over my head. I let it cover me as they adjusted it and pulled it all the way down to my feet feeling a bit like a sausage. I hope they didn't expect me to walk in this thing. A second later someone grabbed me and threw me over their shoulder. It had to be Luca. Seiran wasn't tall enough to pick me up and not be dragging me.

We left the building and I could still feel the sun looming overhead, hot and dangerous. The thick fabric barrier helped, but I knew it wouldn't last as my skin began to itch. I prayed the drive back to Gabe's place was fast. I couldn't go home. Not without knowing if I would have another redout. Con would freak if he found out. He'd probably never heard of a redout before, just as I hadn't, but he embraced nothing vampire, even with me as his roommate.

The car stopped. Luca helped me out of the car, but someone else picked me up and almost threw me in the air before settling me on his shoulder. His gait was heavy, and the only one I could think of that would be that big and strong would be Jamie. Hopefully he didn't just dump me in a snowbank somewhere to roast. At least it meant that we were at Gabe's since Jamie was almost always around to guard his little brother.

The automatic doors swished open and the elevator dinged. Only when everyone finally stepped out of the elevator, was I set down and the bag yanked off. The light of the room flooded my eyes and I had to blink away tears. Crap I was tired.

"Are you okay?" Con was suddenly standing in front of me looking like he'd just jumped out of bed—edible. He was in nothing but socks, sweat pants, and a tank top, but with all his ink showing and his dark hair messy around his face he was stunning. "You look like someone beat the shit out of you."

"That was me, sorry," Luca spoke up. He held out his hand to Con. "I'm Luca, Sam's *cibo*. You must be his roommate Constantine."

Con took his hand hesitantly. "Did you guys have to mess each other up to see who was the bigger, badder one, before letting him eat?"

Luca laughed, and I looked away since that was sorta right. "Just helping him work out some of that vampire aggression."

Con dropped his hand and looked at me. "What the fuck was with that text? I thought you were going to go lay in a snowbank until the sun came up or something."

Text? Oh, shit. I felt my face heat with embarrassment. "I went into a church. I thought maybe I'd burst into flames." Since I was a monster and all that.

A chuckle from across the room made the fire in my cheeks worse. Dammit. Gabe sat on the chaise with Sei in his lap, stroking the witch's back. He smiled at me and shook his head. "Just another monster movie mistake. Other than our allergy to the sun and the invite thing they got it all wrong."

"So I could stare at crosses all day and not burst into flames or melt into a puddle of vampire goo?"

"Correct. There's a few night services I can hook you up with if you're looking for them," Gabe said. I knew he was strongly Christian but figured he didn't practice it much because he was a vampire. Though it made more sense that since his lover was a different religion, he had to make allowances. "Okay, anyone not staying the day needs to go."

"I'm headed back to bed," Jamie said and pressed the button for the elevator. "I'm on the late shift at the hospital tonight."

"I'd like to stay," Luca said. "Since Sam is staying. I should probably be here when he gets up so he can eat right away."

I would be staying until dark. The library had a daybed in it that was mine. Seiran had put it in there after we'd gotten back from California. He even added a dresser and a hanging rack for clothes since I was here so often. Our fight must have resolved more for him than it had for me. I didn't hate him anyway. Never really had. Just spent a lot of time wanting to be him or at least have what he had.

Con shook his head and backed away. He and Gabe didn't work well together, though not for lack of Gabe trying. Con was just really jumpy around him. More so than he'd ever been around me. Sei held out a key. "You can use the couch at my place. Just keep it down, Kelly is probably still asleep since he worked the bar last night and doesn't have class till noon today."

Con took the key and nodded gratefully. He squeezed my shoulder. "Try not to let anyone else beat you up. And no more freaky texts, okay?"

"Sorry," I nodded. "No more freaky texts." Con headed to the elevator and I went to my "room," sleep heavy on the brain. My body was so weighty now that I didn't think I could get it up if I tried. The bed was made up, fresh sheets, everything put away and staged. Like a showroom. That was Sei's doing. Even if he hadn't picked up the room, Jamie or Gabe would have. I could never live with Sei's OCD like they did. He had to clean things a certain way and shower so often and check to make sure appliances were off like twenty times before feeling the world wasn't going to implode. It was just too much for me.

Luca sat on the end of the bed while I kicked off my shoes. "Small bed," he remarked.

I shrugged since it wasn't really mine. Nothing was. The money I got from working at the bar went into a savings account I rarely touched. Gabe paid my rent and for anything else I could possibly need. When I protested, he insisted it was his responsibility as my mentor. "I don't know how to do this, you know."

"Do what?" he asked, kicking off his own shoes and stripping off his shirt.

I waved a hand between us. "This. You and me. Whatever we're supposed to be. You're sort of pushy, and I'm not ready."

"You've been accused of murder and you're worried about what I'm still doing here?"

"You have a kink for murderers?" I asked as I crawled into the bed and yanked the blankets up to my chin.

He sighed and reached out to turn off the light. "You make yourself hard to like because you don't want anyone getting close. I get it. Spent my whole life thinking that any sign of weakness would get me killed. That's how this world treats people, but that's not reality. Being vulnerable isn't a weakness. It's part of being human."

"I'm not human," I reminded him.

"You are. Just an upgrade. It's not until you lose all those crazy thoughts circling in your head that you cease to be human. Even my dad is still human, though he complains all the time that it's a battle to not just let it all go. I've seen a lot of true monsters. Some of them physically human. None of them mentally human."

"So why are you still here?" I asked. He slid into the tiny bed beside me. Close enough to feel his warmth but not actually touch him. It was a little awkward how good it felt to have him close. He took the position between me and the door, leaving my back to the wall, which made me feel oddly safe. I hated that I was beginning to like the idea of having him around. What about when he left or used me like every guy in my history had?

"Because you need me, and I like being needed. Now get some sleep. We'll analyze the great donkey asshole of the world *after* we've gotten a few zz's. And shit, can I just say your friend Con is hot? You haven't tapped that yet?"

"He doesn't like vampires."

"Hmm. Looks at you like he likes you just fine."

"Not happening." I'd never hurt Con that way. He'd done too much for me.

"We'll see. Get some rest. You need to heal."

I would have argued, but I was too tired and the sun would no longer be denied.

CHAPTER 6

Usually I tossed and turned until the sun finally set. But I slept like a rock until the stench of food woke me up with the urge to vomit. God, I hated the smell of food. Every spice or added flavoring made it worse. Gabe said the sensitivity would pass by the end of my first year and I couldn't wait. Seiran loved to cook and his nose was as sensitive as mine. I think he wasn't bothered only because he actually got to eat the stuff he made.

I grabbed my robe, a little sad to find Luca gone, and darted to the three-quarters bath to shower away the bad morning. The bruises had vanished and I looked normal enough. One of the few perks of being a vampire. The slight ache in my limbs reminded me of the fight. It was the feeling many got after a hard workout. I liked it, had earned it, and hoped it lasted more than a few hours.

After the shower, I dressed in a pair of jeans and a tee and headed to see what the stink was about. It was just after five, so almost dinner time for humans. The sun wouldn't be down for another hour or so, and I would be stuck until it set.

Seiran and Kelly sat at the counter. Kelly had a book propped open and his bleached blond head bent over it while he scribbled notes on paper beside him. Seiran had a handful of photos spread across the countertop and he kept shifting them like it was a puzzle he was trying to solve. They were both sort of brainiacs—always thinking.

"What are you cooking, Ronnie? It smells gross."

"Smells like heaven," Kelly said into his book.

"Mexican-style stuffed bell peppers. Lots of spice. Sorry. Was craving it and forgot you were still here. You're usually not so quiet when you sleep."

"Must have been the hot boy toy he went to bed with," Kelly teased without looking up.

"If only," I grumbled. My dreams had been filled with fantasies of that hot boy toy and his flexibility.

Gabe stepped out of his bedroom looking GQ ready as always. He'd probably been up for hours. I guess old vampires didn't need to sleep as much as newbies like me. But I was pretty sure no amount of time was going to make me like him. He'd been older when he'd been changed, more mature. I'd never get there. Had he always been so suave and polished? Or was that just his few millennia as a vampire? No one knew much about his past. Just generalities. He had been a Roman general way back in the day. No one was sure exactly how long ago. He'd had a lover who died. Which had him seeking out immortality and strength for revenge. Yet here he was, with someone else, and neutral. A good guy for the most part. I wondered what had changed to end his quests for vengeance.

"Glad you're up, Sam. I want you to work on your concentration today."

My concentration was fine. And why wasn't he yelling at me about the redout?

"I want you to try to get one of the boys to do something. You had Seiran's blood yesterday. That should help."

Oh, that kind of concentration. "But I haven't bitten Kelly."

"No biting," Kelly said, not even looking in my direction. "Only Jamie gets to bite me."

"Gross," Seiran said. "That's my brother you're talking about."

"And he's way hot," Kelly said. "You know he is."

"Argh," Seiran said, going back to his studying. "Don't make me think about you and sex with my brother. I'd need brain bleach."

"I'm hot, too," Kelly pointed out. And he was, for a white boy. Blond hair, hazel eyes, pretty, and fit. He was a runner with a total runner body, full of sleek muscles and definition that Abercrombie and Fitch loved. Totally not my type.

"Not my type," Seiran said.

"Right," I interrupted and pointed at Gabe. "'Cause the hot blond isn't your type?"

Seiran blushed. "That's different."

Yeah because Gabe was another dimension of attractive. I patted Kelly on the back. "It's 'cause Ronnie has a daddy fetish."

Now Seiran turned red. "I do not!"

"It's okay, Kelly does too. That's why the giant muscleman turns him on. He wants someone to spank him when he's a bad boy."

Kelly sputtered, his face turning red. I snickered at them both.

Gabe just shook his head. "Focus. If your potential target is strong you may have to keep biting them to control them. But you can do small things without ever having a sip of their blood—like steering them in the right direction or making someone run away."

"In case you haven't noticed, there are two of the five Pillars sitting at your kitchen counter. I would categorize that as too strong for anyone."

Gabe smiled and winked at me, then flicked his eyes in Kelly's direction. Kelly suddenly slapped his hand to the back of his neck. He looked up, eyes wide and glanced behind him. "Did someone just breathe on me?" He shivered. "Wow, that was so not cool."

"What was that?" Sei asked, now paying attention to his lover as well.

"Kelly has a sensitive neck," Gabe said.

"You did that from way over there?" Kelly asked.

"He can do a lot of stuff from across the room," Sei said and wriggled his eyebrows.

"Wait..." It couldn't be the same right? All that stuff about feeding people feelings. How could I make someone feel that from a distance? I know feeding on people was a way to keep them compliant. But I never really understood how to get someone who would normally have no interest in me to let me bite them. Gabe and I spent weeks on sex appeal, and I'd come to decide that I just wasn't cut out to be the sexy night stalker he was. I could read people's body language, learned their subtle cues, but none of it had worked for me so far. Now he was telling me there was a magic to it? "You've been holding out on me."

"You weren't ready. All baby vamps start off full-of-themselves and on a power high. And don't think we aren't going to talk about your redout issue, but I want to focus on the guys in the alley. You could have scared them away without even touching them. And feeding on them? Don't you think Luca is a better meal than a couple of punks from Riverside?"

"I'm from Riverside," I protested.

"Still a punk," Seiran said.

"Shush, Ronnie."

"Sure sure, Sammy."

I growled at him.

"Enough you two. Sit, Sam. Let's work on this."

I slid into the chair opposite Sei and Kelly. "You guys okay being my guinea pigs?"

"Not sure you can make me do anything, Sammy."

"Just don't make me dance around like a monkey and I'm good," Kelly threw me a smile then went back to his book. "And no forget stuff. I have a metaphysics test tomorrow."

"I'll do my best." Hopefully Gabe could undo anything I accidentally did, if I could do anything at all.

"We'll start small," Gabe said.

I shrugged not thinking for a minute it was going to be that easy. "Is this something that actually happens or are you just making them think it happens?"

"Good observation. It's an illusion. You may gain some telekinetic powers as you age, but probably not for another fifty or so years. The bigger powers take time to develop for most vampires. Some never gain any at all. This is more of a planted mental suggestion, much like you do when you make someone you bite feel pleasure. Only this is from a distance." He pulled out his phone and a few seconds later mine buzzed.

Pull Seiran's hair.

"Just concentrate. Focus on your goal. Want him to feel it," Gabe coached.

I let out a deep breath I didn't need and stared at Seiran's hair willing it to move or feel like it moved. Whatever. Nothing happened. Seiran glanced up and frowned. "Do you need blood? Your eyes are red. I thought they were supposed to be black when you guys haven't fed." He glanced at Gabe.

Shit. I shut my eyes and turned away from them. Usually my eyes only went red when I let the monster out, but I didn't feel any different. No anger or irritation, just normal, everyday Sam.

Gabe tapped my shoulder and handed me a pair of sunglasses. "You'll get better at controlling your eyes in time. Black when you haven't fed. Red when you're using your vampire power, or if you've gained enough control the color will glow more along with your natural eye color."

"I thought they turned red when I'm mad." I put on the glasses.

"Anger is a lack of control. Which means you're letting your powers take control of you instead of controlling them. Try again. With Kelly this time."

This time I focused on Kelly, letting the brown haze of the glasses fuzz through my vision as I thought of the way his blond hair barely touched the nape of his neck. It was straight and sloppy, like he spent a lot of time on a wind-blown beach, but I knew the truth. Kelly spent a lot of time on that hair, dyeing it, bleaching it, cutting it, styling it. He was about as metro as a guy could get.

Gabe patted my shoulder. "You're not focusing. I can almost see your thoughts wandering."

"Sorry," I grumbled and he was right. I returned to try to get Kelly's hair to move. "There is no spoon," I said to myself gaining a snicker from Kelly. "Shush," I told him. I must have stared at his hair for a good half hour with no result. He seemed more bothered by my gaze than any suggestion I tried to put in his head. The elevator dinged, knocking me out of focus. "Maybe we should go to a playground and practice on some little kids. You know, like non-Dominion kids. Start on the super easy."

Gabe shook his head. "Keep trying. You'll get it and when you do, you'll be surprised how easy it is."

Luca sat down beside me just as Sei got up to pull food

out of the oven. "I was hoping to be back before you woke up," he told me. "Hungry?"

Starving, but I shook my head. Oddly enough the smell of the food wasn't bothering me as much anymore, but maybe that was because Luca smelled pretty damn good. He must have gone home because he was wearing different clothes. And like mine—his bruises were gone.

"That smells amazing," he said to Seiran. He turned my way and smiled at me, though I was pretty sure he couldn't see my eyes through the sunglasses.

Jamie trudged into the apartment from the door that led to the underground parking lot with grocery bags in hand. Kelly and Sei went to work helping him put things away as the food cooled on a rack on the counter. Jamie's long hair was pulled back into a ponytail, and he looked like the sort of guy who did personal security rather than the nurse he was. But he did work as Seiran's private bodyguard whenever Gabe wasn't around. The two of them looked nothing alike, Sei and Jamie, though they were biological half-brothers, sharing the same father. Jamie was brown all the way around, skin more tan than white, pale brown hair, brown eyes, and so muscular that he always looked like he could burst out of his clothes any minute and become the Hulk. He was attractive in a male physique sort of way, but way too much man for me.

Beside me Luca, dressed in fitted jeans, a snug T-shirt, and a draping zip-up sweater, open and hanging off his shoulders, made my mouth water. I knew what was under those clothes. The tight ass, the flat, muscled stomach, the smooth chest and long legs. Fuck, I longed to have him wrapped around me.

Luca must have felt the intensity of my gaze because he looked my way and gave me a sexy smile. He flicked his eyes toward the bedroom I used, and I shook my head. I was not getting off with him while everyone else could hear.

Gabe took a small dark cooler from Jamie and popped it in the freezer. I returned to my silent brooding over not being able to make Kelly think I was moving his hair by thinking about it. They all began to dish up and Sei offered food to Luca who accepted quickly.

The microwave whirred and I suspected Gabe was warming a QuickLife. I hoped he didn't want me to drink it. A second later he set a mug steaming with dark liquid down in front of me. It smelled like blood, old blood. Gross, dirty blood. At least QuickLife smelled clean, fresh. It had always been a bit like water, bland, with a horrific aftertaste. This was…I swallowed back a gag. Gabe laughed. "It's real. Human. Not as fresh as from the vein, but not as bad as QuickLife."

Real? I put the cup hesitantly to my lips. The first sip had me sputtering and coughing. The guys in the alley had tasted better than this. I took another sip. Okay that was really awful. "Why is it so bad?"

"Donation blood is not the same as someone you'd be naturally drawn to feed from. We may think we choose someone based on availability or even appearance, but it's the smell that draws us. You do it now, gravitating to those more powerful like Seiran, Luca and even Con." Gabe pointed out.

I gulped. Was he going to say I couldn't live with Con anymore? That I was a danger to him? I really didn't want to be part of their romance novel by living with Sei and Gabe full-time.

"We're not always lucky enough to find willing donors that we'd prefer. This is what all vampires used before QuickLife."

"And after they become civilized," Luca whispered. He sat

down beside me with a plate full of food. "Bet that stuff doesn't taste as good as me."

Understatement of the year.

"Wear something nice for tonight," Luca said.

"What's tonight?" Was I working? I glanced at Gabe who was typing on his laptop at the counter beside Seiran.

"I thought we'd do a little dancing. At least until your deadline is up and we can actually talk about vampire things."

"Deadline?" Seiran asked. "What deadline?"

"It's no big deal," I told him, not wanting them involved.

"If I don't answer his one question the way he wants by eleven tonight I turn into a pumpkin and get the country boot in my ass."

Suddenly everyone's eyes were on me. "What?" I demanded. Wasn't I allowed to make my own damn decisions? Feeding was a lot like sex, intimate, and dangerous, opening yourself up to the other person like that. It was only fair I got to pick who that was. I sighed and pushed away from the table not able to handle being in the room a moment longer.

I texted Con who was still upstairs at Sei's place. He had it closed up tight so all I had to do was make it from the elevator to the door before I burst into flames. "I'm going to hang with Con for a bit. Make sure he's not weird about this morning." I knew he wouldn't be. He'd never had a chance to see the bloody clothes. But it made for a good excuse. I left the mug of nastiness and everyone's prying eyes behind as I jumped in the elevator and headed up ready to run for the door.

The metal double doors slid open. Light blasted me with blistering heat from the entry. I practically flew past the few random people that always seemed to linger in the building's mailbox area to where Con waited with the door to Sei's apartment wide open. He let me run past him into the shielded living room where he'd hooked up an Xbox to Sei's rarely used TV.

I should have brought up the mug of old blood. The added sunburn just made me hungrier. Con sat next to me and handed me a controller. We played in comfortable silence. He never expected me to talk about my day or what was bugging me.

The smell of fresh blood and ink tickled my nose. "You get a new tat?"

He nodded. "Beau is working on a picture of Cat for me. It's gonna take a few months since there's so much detail and color. But I had to have her close, you know? I sort of feel like I failed her and maybe I can keep her alive like this. Even if it's just in my head."

I should have said something inspiring like she wouldn't have wanted him to mourn, but I didn't know the girl at all. So I just said, "Sorry."

"No worries. We've all got something right?" We went back to playing and not talking.

The smell of Con's blood made me salivate even though it was laced with chemicals from his new art. If what Gabe said was right about me gravitating toward the strong, then Con was a more powerful witch than he let on. God, I was such a monster. He'd just lost his sister and I wanted to jump him. Not just his blood, but his body. He was that lanky sort of guy that made most people wary. Covered in tattoos. His face lots of angles, sharp, high cheekbones, eyes set just a little too wide for his face. The mess of dark hair falling around his face softened the edges a bit. And he had a great mouth, lips pale rose and defined. I'd dreamt more than once about having them wrapped around my cock. Fuck. Maybe if I just fucked Luca already, some of the sexual tension would ease.

The silence that stretched between us for the next few

minutes was almost painful. Finally Con broke the silence. "So how did it go with your *cibo*? He's pretty hot. I'd do him. Seems nice."

"He's kind of pushy."

"And you don't like pushy?" He asked because he knew I did.

"He wants to have sex with me."

"*I* want to have sex with you. That's not a stretch you know. You're an attractive guy."

"Vampire," I corrected him.

He sighed and took the controller from me; pausing the game by pressing the start button. "I know. I don't blame you for what happened to my sister. I don't blame you for being a vampire. No matter what you think, you are not a monster. Not so long as you still feel something for other people, even if you hurt them. Cat had lost that. She hadn't even been undead that long…"

"I am a monster. Didn't you hear? I attacked a couple guys in an alley last night."

"Not unprovoked, and yes, Kelly told me. It's like a game of telephone around here. No secrets. They came at you, you rewarded them with the fight they wanted."

"Wasn't much fight in them."

"Not the point. But yeah I heard."

I wished I was home so I could retreat to my room to analyze all the whirling thoughts in my head. Con's presence was usually soothing. But learning he wanted to have sex with me just added stress to our relationship that we didn't need.

"Con. You and me. I can't do that." I'd break him. My best friend. Hell, my only real friend. No matter how much I wanted him…

"Hey, I hear you there. Maybe you can bite Luca and do me? I don't mind being held down." And now I had more fantasies of him I didn't need. I opened my mouth to protest, but he put his hands up in mock surrender. "I know vamps have this whole thing with sex and blood going together. I just want you to realize you're not a bad looking guy and most of the time—when you're not being a dick—we all like you. So it makes sense that this Luca guy would be interested."

"Even though he's super-hot? Guys like him never looked at me before I became a vampire."

"Because most guys are idiots. That should not be a surprise to you. Dead or alive, men are wired by their dicks. You don't come across as prey, and that's what most guys want. Someone easy. Not dangerous."

"I'm dangerous?"

Con shrugged. "Bad boy vibe is alive and well with you. Work it."

That was news to me. I'd never considered myself a bad boy. Just a not nice guy. "You're the one covered in ink."

"Doesn't mean I'm a bad boy. I'm more by the book." He looked me over again, gaze traveling down my body like he wished I was naked in front of him. "For most things. You strike me as the kind of guy who's read the rule book and said fuck it, then set it on fire." Argh, so much sexual tension.

I shook my head at him and took back the controller to un-pause the game. "Kill some zombies damn you. You're supposed to have my back."

"I do, my friend." And we played.

CHAPTER 7

Seiran arrived an hour or so later and kicked Con out. He shooed me into his room with the command that he would be helping me prepare for my date. A date with Luca. How did that happen? He hadn't even asked, just assumed. Not like it was a bad thing. He was good looking, smelled good and tasted like chocolate and spice. I should be excited. Instead I was nervous.

"You're pretty grumpy. If I give you some blood will you stop being so miserable for five minutes?"

"I don't need your charity, Ronnie," I groused at him needing to be contrary just because teasing him actually felt good. "Go back to your Roman lover and leave me to my brooding."

Seiran grabbed my hair and yanked me around hard enough to hurt. I had to meet his eyes or have the hair ripped from my scalp. His grip wasn't human, and even as a vampire I couldn't free myself. Shit this was the Father Earth power. Apparently, I'd pissed off the earth witch.

My filter must have been malfunctioning because I said, "I thought you didn't like it rough, Ronnie."

"You're a really ungrateful little bastard, Sam. Gabe is bending over backwards to keep the Tri-Mega and Dominion from just putting you out of all our misery. And you spit in his face."

"I never asked for—"

"Not done," Sei interrupted. "None of us want you dead. You don't even want you dead cause if you really did, you'd have found a way by now. So why don't you pull up your big boy britches and suck it up. Do this thing right." He shoved me onto his bed and climbed on top of me, holding me down, like I had a chance to move anyway. He could crush me if he wanted to. "You're making Gabe unhappy. Unhappy Gabe means unhappy Seiran. You know what happens to people who make Seiran unhappy?"

I sighed. It was about time the witch showed his true colors. I'd pushed him hard before but apparently not hard enough. "You fuck me up. I get it."

"I don't think you do." He closed his eyes and suddenly the room went black, or maybe that was just my sight. I fell out of myself and landed hard in a heap—surrounded by dirt and wood. A grave. The feeling of life poured into me like Luca's blood magnified by ten thousand. I gasped as it kept coming until I was sure I'd burst. Then it was torn away and I died again, slowly, painfully, lungs gasping for air and cold bitter water filling them. He slammed the life back into me again just as I was ready to give up to death only to pull it away again. The cycle continued several times until I was sure it was going to be my fate to live it forever, then as suddenly as it'd begun it ended. I sat in the dark, all sense of feeling gone. I couldn't move, or even scream, it was just a void. Was this the true death?

"It's your choice this time, Sam. No more blaming others. Do you want to live or die? The earth is willing to take you back. I can give you to it." Seiran's voice whispered in the dark.

Christ, anything had to be better than this miserable emptiness. Was this what Con was talking about? How a vampire truly lost his humanity? The void of everything? No pain or joy. Fuck. I wasn't ready for this great box of all-consuming nothingness. I wanted to live. Even if that was as a blood sucking vampire freak. Christ Almighty I wanted to live.

The room came back into focus and I sucked in a deep breath. Seiran sat beside me, no longer holding me down, but his arms around me. I trembled. He stroked my head like I was some frightened child. I suppose in a way I was. Dead at nineteen. Stuck undead forever just shy of drinking age. Tears seeped down my cheeks. It was an odd feeling, but it'd been so long since I'd let myself feel something other than anger.

"It's okay. You'll make it. You're strong enough. I know sometimes it feels like you're not, but you are," Sei whispered to me. He smelled good but the bloodlust had faded. Not that I could have attacked him even if I wanted to. He got me like no one else did. Had been through a lot of the same horrors. Matthew had twisted us both. It had just taken me longer to realize it.

"Those memories don't control you. The bad things he did to you don't define you. Being a vampire probably sucks, but it's better than the alternative. Kelly didn't want you to die. Gabe and I don't either. I know it's hard but can't you stop living in the past and try to find something to make yourself happy?"

"With Luca?" I asked him. "You get that he's Max Hart's kid, right?"

He sighed. "I wondered about that, but whatever. With Luca or someone. I sorta hoped you and Con would bond."

"We have bonded—as friends. Romantically, that's not happening. He's breakable."

"He's not. If he was, Andrew Roman would have broken him." Seiran sighed. "You realize he's probably powerful enough to be the Pillar of Air, right? And that you're an amplifier? Meaning you'd make him stronger? As much as we claim we are human, witches aren't. There's something more in our DNA. It makes us less breakable the more powerful we are."

That was a sad truth. I'd seen plenty a dead witch in my time, but regular humans were little more than ants on the spectrum. I really had to stop thinking of Con that way. "He's terrified of vampires. Of being bitten. That's become part of sex to me." And fuck didn't I hate that.

"So bite Luca and fuck Con. Hell, fuck them both. They're attractive, right?" He stared at me. "You strike me as more of a top than a bottom. How did Matthew convince you otherwise? That monster never bottomed."

And wasn't that the truth. "I'm verse." I couldn't believe I was having this conversation with Seiran. If there was any person on the planet I was less sexually into, I had yet to meet them.

"And have two hot guys who'd give it to you anyway you want. I sort of thought your sparring with Luca had come to that…but he said no."

"He offered."

"And?"

"Why did I say no?"

Seiran nodded.

"It's still weird for me. Being dead…"

Seiran waved a hand at me. "But you're not really. I've seen plenty of dead. Vampires are something else. Magic? I can feel it through the earth whatever it is that animates you guys. I think you have to get out of that mindset. You're reborn as something different. But dead is dead. Dead is unmoving, rotting, reclaimed by the earth."

"Which just proves the dead thing. Since you feel me through the earth."

"I feel it from regular people too. Different, but not all that different. A vampire's connection to the earth is stronger."

"Are you saying I still have a soul?" I'd wondered about that. The whole church thing had been part of that morbid curiosity. Growing up with the extremes of Christianity had really warped my head in a lot of ways. It was a constant battle, the right and wrong of things like sex, blood, and death. All things that had become part of who I was now.

"Maybe? I think it's more complicated than that. We consider it your spirit, but even that is a mild term compared to what I feel in the links bound to the earth. When someone passes, sometimes the spirit stays. Not like a ghost, but energy. Strong energy. Our theology is that the earth reabsorbs the spirit to continue its growth. So, if you still have spirit bound to your flesh then you're alive, aren't you?"

I thought about that for a minute. Maybe the whole blood thing was an attraction to that energy. Maybe vampires scented it instead of felt it like Seiran did. "This is so confusing."

"Life?"

Well yeah, if that's what I was truly doing. Unlife sounded stupid. "I guess."

"Love is complicated too," Seiran sighed. "Doesn't conquer all, and all that shit." Were he and Gabe having problems? "But you'll be open to someone, right? Live beyond what Matthew did to you." His voice hitched a little when he said Matthew's name. "Do you think I feel any different about the way he abused me? That I don't know the number he did on your head? He left you wounded and you are refusing to heal."

It wasn't about Matthew. He was ancient history. Wasn't he? I was undead now, but still Sam. And who would want me. Fuck it *was* still about Matthew. Damn him. I hoped he was suffering in the foulest pits of hell. "I'm so messed up."

"Aren't we all," Sei joked. "Now you have a hot guy who's waiting downstairs to go out with you in a normal sort of way. Maybe he's not the one. But you'll never know if you don't try." He pushed himself up off the bed. "He even promised to not push for sex, which is probably unheard of for a guy like Luca. That guy is sex on two legs. Whatever reason he volunteered to be your *cibo* isn't from some sort of obligation or trick."

"You can't know that. For all we know Max put him up to this to get closer to you."

"Right. 'Cause I have so many secrets? And I share them with you?" He had a point, but Luca had been sitting at the counter in Gabe's apartment. "You're attractive. Get over it. Maybe he's got an Asian guy kink." Sei wriggled his eyebrows at me.

"You're a dork, Ronnie."

"I'm okay with that."

I sighed. Fine whatever. It was just a date. "I've never really been on a date before. Matthew just took me somewhere to fuck. Roman just fed on me and locked me in a tower like some damn princess." Crap this was all fucked up. "I need to move on."

"I agree. And there's no better time to start than right now." He yanked me up from the bed and shoved me toward his closet. "Let's give him a bit of a show. Let him wine and dine you like a proper gentleman should."

"Seems unfair if I'm not going to have sex with him?"

"Ever?"

I shrugged. Maybe someday. "Not tonight."

"Anticipation is good. Gabe does that to me all the time. Sends me naughty texts or voicemails while I'm working. Had to wait months to get into his pants the first time. I thought I would die before it finally happened."

"Oh the hardship," I teased.

Seiran's smile was radiant. "Yeah, he'd be perfect if only he talked more. And I think this unrest with you is making him grumpy 'cause he's been in a terrible mood the past few weeks."

"Sorry."

"Whatever. It's my problem not yours." Sei clapped his hands. "Now I need to find you something to wear that isn't black and screaming Goth."

"I'm not Goth. I'm a vampire."

"So is Gabe and he never wears black."

He was also pale, blond, and looked washed out in black. He had two thousand years to figure out what looked good on him and what didn't. I was still nineteen and perpetually awkward. "I don't own anything else. Just T-shirts and jeans." Most in black.

"Good thing I do and we are about the same size." He began pulling things from his closet and pressed them against me murmuring to himself. He made me change twice before nodding and smiling. The pants were snug, and bright purple. The shirt he'd chosen was full-sleeved and high collared, but thin and pale lavender. Every nook and cranny of my chest was visible through the shirt—nipples and the tiny bit of belly that made me frown. "You have great arms. Good muscle tone," Sei remarked.

The shirt had something interlaced in it that made it sparkle when I moved, a trick of the light, I think. It was almost like my skin glowed. "You know vampires aren't supposed to sparkle, right?"

"Tonight you're not a vampire. You're just Sam who has a date with Luca." He tugged me into the bathroom. The things he set on the counter were products and tools I had no idea what to do with. But he set to work, first brushing out my hair and adding some goop to spike it. He styled a small patch in front to sweep over my left brow.

He rubbed something cool and soothing all over my face and neck. My skin seemed to suck it up because he cursed and applied it twice more. When he came at me with something that looked like a black marker, I grabbed his hand. "What's that?"

"Just eyeliner."

"Girls use that."

"I use it all the time."

"Not endearing it to me, Ronnie."

"Trust me. It will make your eyes pop. I'm glad you don't wear those contacts anymore. You have great dark and smoky eyes, long lashes and no caterpillar eyebrows. The liner will help your eyes stand out. I promise I won't use much. Just look up toward the ceiling. You won't even notice it after a minute."

I sighed and looked up. He applied it quickly enough. And I did only feel it for a minute or so.

"Don't rub your eyes. It won't come off without a wipe but you don't want it to smudge either." He stuffed an individually packaged wipe into my pocket. "You look great." He picked up mascara and I bit my tongue to keep from protesting.

After a minute he stepped back and motioned toward the mirror. "Take a look."

I turned and glared at my expression. "Holy shit!" Was that really me? The paleness of my skin only made the stark black of my hair and lined eyes stand out even more. A hint of glitter in the liner matched the shirt that flashed sparkling color at me. I could have been a model for some glam rock band. Thankfully I didn't look at all like Seiran Rou. This wasn't androgynous pretty. The guy that stared at me in the mirror was hot in an 'I'm trouble' sort of way. I touched my face since the skin didn't feel tight for the first time in ages.

"I put three rounds of moisturizer on you. You really need to take better care of your skin. Being undead doesn't mean you want it to flake and peel, right?" He handed me a bottle. "Keep it. Gabe buys it in bulk since he goes through a ton of it himself. Works great for solo activities too." Sei winked at me.

"You're a pervert," I told him.

He laughed. "Guilty. You should also carry grave dirt around with you. I'll make a little necklace for you like the one I made Gabe last month. You'll have to refill it a couple times a week, but it will help keep the circles from under your eyes and your skin from looking waxy." He fluffed my hair a little. "You're hot. Like man hot. Trouble. The guy that walks into the club and everyone goes, wow, who's he? I figured you'd want man hot since you're going out with Luca."

"That's a lot of man to compete with," I admitted before I even realized I was going to say it out loud.

"Why compete? Just enjoy the hotness and forget the scorecard. Do you think I'm anywhere close to Gabe's league? Hell, when we met I was just a kid. High on power and so fucked in the head I didn't care if I got him killed by coming on to him. So how about you just go and enjoy it for what it is? If you like him, great. If not, well I'm sure there will be plenty other attractive men to step up if you looked their way."

For once I agreed with him. It made sense. Even if I fucked up this date, I could find someone eventually. It had taken Gabe two thousand years to find his match. I really had to stop bitching about looking for mine. There were bound to be bad relationships in the bunch, but not trying was just accepting defeat, right?

"Oh, you need a coat." He rushed out of the bathroom and to the closet by the main door throwing it open to sort through the many hangers. "This one is perfect." He handed me a pale purple leather jacket. The cut was good though it pulled through the shoulders a little. Zipped and buttoned covered up the sparkling shirt a little.

"I look really gay," I commented. What normal guy wore purple?

Sei got really close and whispered all secretive-like, "Hate to break it to you, princess. But you *are* gay."

"Yeah, yeah, Ronnie. You're just jealous 'cause you didn't get to have my ass before you committed to the big guy." It was easier to tease him when I was in a fairly good mood. If the night went sour, I'd call and bitch him out even if I woke him at two a.m. He wanted to be friends then so be it.

"I'm more of a bottom myself," Sei said. "But yeah, there would have been a point in my life that I would have let you screw me. Good thing my tastes have improved, eh?"

"Har har," I groused, but couldn't help but smile.

"There's a smile. You have great teeth, even the fangs, which are barely noticeable."

Immediately I felt self-conscious about my teeth. Would Luca freak if I flashed fang? Gabe almost never did and I was getting better about not doing it in public, but it was hard sometimes when I was so used to them being there.

"I bet Luca will dig them. Since he's the kid of a vampire and all that."

"Yeah. I just wish he'd be straight with me."

Sei raised a brow. "Straight?"

"You know what I mean. I don't really have anything to offer him, so why's he hanging around?"

"Why would you need to offer him anything other than a good time? He's Max Hart's kid so maybe he's looking for a break from the super vamp lifestyle. It's got to be like being the heir to some Fortune 500 company. Hart has more money than pretty much every vampire in the midwest combined. Luca was handling some Ascendance paperwork stuff so he's probably being groomed to be a CEO." He scrunched up his face in distaste likely because he'd experienced the same thing with his mother pushing him to be the first male witch to lead the Dominion—which I was sure was going to happen sooner rather than later. "I'd hate that."

"Some things in life just bite."

"Like you wanna bite him."

I shrugged. "He did say he has to drink blood from another vampire every once in a while."

"Sounds kinky. You going to try that?"

"Letting him suck on me?" Burst out of my mouth before I forgot who I was talking to.

Sei laughed. "In more ways than one."

"You have a one-track mind."

"I like sex. Don't you?"

Did I? I guess. "Maybe another night."

Sei nodded. "Your say. Come on. Your prince awaits!"

CHAPTER 8

Luca looked edible. He'd changed again at some point into pale green pants that hugged his ass and rode low on his hips. His shirt was a button up, white and tight enough to outline his strong shoulders and flat stomach. He'd shaved, but not enough to get rid of the stubble, more just to tame it, and his hair was product free falling around his face in waves. He looked like he'd just stepped off the cover of one of Seiran's many romance novels.

"You look damn good," Luca said approaching me with a look in his eyes that said sex. He opened his mouth to say something else but Seiran must have done something behind me because he stopped and held out his hand to me. I took it and enjoyed his warm grip.

"Thanks. You look great too." Smelled even better, but I was hungry. Maybe I should have taken the witch up on his offer for a nibble.

"Where are you guys headed?" Gabe asked. He'd been pulling things up on the computer and didn't look happy about whatever he was reading.

"Loco Mojo," Luca said. "Mostly shifters, but I've heard the dancing is good there."

I'd never been, though I'd heard of it a time or two. I hoped the place didn't smell like wet dog.

"I want you guys to be careful of any vampires you meet tonight and don't recognize."

"Has there been another incident?" Luca asked.

Like the two dead guys I was blamed for? I tried to get a look at Gabe's computer screen but he had it turned away. "Nothing important," he told us. "Jamie is going to drop you guys off downtown. Call if you need a ride."

Something was up. Jamie appeared as the elevator doors slid open. Kelly stood beside him looking ready for a night out himself. I couldn't recall a time I'd seen the water witch so dressed up, but he was in a pale blue suit tailored to fit him perfectly. Jamie wasn't any more casual in neatly pressed slacks and a button up that could barely contain his wide shoulders. Was there a party we were interrupting?

"What's the occasion?" I asked Kelly as we got into the elevator with them.

"Date night at the 'rents. My mom and his mom." Kelly put his arm around Jamie's waist. "He has the overnight shift at the hospital tonight so we won't be out late." Jamie tensed but Kelly leaned over and kissed his cheek which brought a flush of color to them.

Dinner with the 'rents. That was commitment. And probably what was making Jamie nervous. I wondered what it would be like to have someone that I cared about enough to introduce them to my parents. Though again my parents would likely throw holy water on me and curse me for the evil thing I was. Gay and undead—which was worse? I sighed and stared at the wall instead of probing for conversation.

Luca talked with Kelly about some Ascendance thing I

tuned out. Everyone liked Kelly. He was just that sort of guy. Friendly, outgoing, good-looking, and powerful. My date wasn't cruising him, and I knew Kelly was pretty into Jamie, so I wasn't worried. I wondered more if they thought it was odd that I didn't try to strike up a conversation, but since Jamie didn't either, I figured I was in the clear.

Once we were all loaded in the car and heading across town, I let myself study Luca as the street lights passed overhead. I realized that last night he'd been dressed for the club and using all his come-hither sex vibes. Tonight he seemed to be laid out bare. Sure he was still dressed nice and cleaned up okay, but this felt more natural. Maybe this could work. I squeezed his hand and he gripped mine. If anything, I'd have my first date. Might as well make it memorable.

A line wrapped around the block to Loco Mojo. Jamie pulled up to the door to let us out. "Remember what Gabe said, Sam. Stay away from vampires who aren't his and don't wander tonight. If you need a ride, call."

"What's with the vampire thing?" I asked him, wondering if he'd tell me more than Gabe would.

"No one knows for sure. Just be on your guard."

"Okay." Cryptic much? I got out and glared at the beautiful people waiting in the cold, huddling together, flirting and generally just standing around. I didn't really want to spend the next hour waiting to get inside so I could dance a little with Luca. Maybe there was some place else we could go?

Luca tugged my hand and led us straight to the door and the bouncer who stood in front of the rope. "Johnny," Luca held out his free hand and shook the other man's. The bouncer made Jamie look small which I'd have thought impossible until just then.

"Depacio, you little shit. Heard you were in town. Was

going to hit the club, but haven't had time. You up for sparring?"

"Sure, anytime. Just ring me."

"Why Minnesota, man? I thought you were a permanent Cali-boy. Weather sure is better there."

"And the people fake."

"I get ya, man, I get ya." He nodded his tiny head like a bobblehead doll. "Come on in." He waved us through the door. "This one's a little different than your usual playmates, eh?"

Luca put his arm around me. "Yeah, this one bites back. Hot, right?"

"If you like 'em dead, I guess. No trouble. No provoking the locals. You know the drill."

"I'll be good. Or at least as good as usual." Luca tugged me inside.

The music was loud, but not uncomfortably so like it was at most human clubs. People danced. There were tables scattered around the edge of the room where people ate food and talked. There was a second-floor balcony that appeared to have mostly diners on it, but a few danced near the railing, which also had a very fine netting over it. The place smelled like people: blood, sweat, and food, not dog, for which I was grateful.

"You need to eat first?" I asked Luca wondering if he wanted to get a table. The dance floor was filled with straight couples, gay couples, and everything in-between. All moving erotically. Some obviously didn't know how to dance and no one seemed to care. I was pretty sure I couldn't do much more than sway myself.

"How about you eat first, then we'll dance a little." Luca pulled me over to the side and helped me out of my borrowed coat, swinging it over the back of a chair at an open table. "No coat check here, but no one is likely to take our stuff either. Pretty hard to steal in here when the door guys can smell the stuff on you."

So the bouncer outside had been a shifter? I had no idea. He hadn't smelled like anything, but the cold often messed with my senses. Luca hung his coat too and stepped into my personal space, wrapping his arms around me and pulling me close. I tried to move back, but he pressed my head to his neck. "No sex, just food for now. I promise. Eat."

He smelled so good I couldn't resist. I licked along the pulsing vein in his neck, savoring the salty taste of his skin and the jumping beat of his heart. He shivered, but everything about his body language said he was relaxed, prepared even, for the bite. I carefully broke the skin and let the taste of him fill my mouth, gulping heaps of him down in a slow sensual draw. Not that I should have been gorging myself on my date, but he didn't pull away or even seem to mind. My cock hardened and pressed into his thigh. Yeah feeding and sex went hand in hand.

Finally when I couldn't hold anymore I licked his wound closed. The hickey made me proud. People would see it, see us together and know I'd done that. Marked him. That he was mine even if it was just for tonight.

Luca made no move to step away. He rested his lips against my throat, arms wrapped tight around my torso. We swayed a little though we were nowhere near the dance floor. His breath warmed my skin and I tilted my head up and away to allow him better access. Small kisses danced along the cords of my neck. I wondered if he hungered the way I did. How long had it been since he last had vampire blood? Most of my memories of being bitten were harsh and brutal. Not all that different from rape—and I'd experienced that before as well. But Luca's touch wasn't about pain or power or having control over me. His kisses were soft and body pliable. I could have shoved him across the room with a small nudge if I wanted to. He would just as easily step away if I did anything to tell him that his attention was unwelcome.

"It's okay," I told him. "Do it." Better to learn now rather than later once we'd really started something.

"You sure?" he whispered, glancing up to meet my eyes.

"Yeah. Eat so we can dance."

He didn't ask again. The sharp prick of fangs pierced my skin, a quick but passing pain. This was nothing like the gnawing hunger that Matthew had shown me, or even the angry ripping of Andrew Roman.

Luca's lips sealed around the wound and drew my warmth into his mouth. He should have been sucking on my cock for how erotic it felt. Did he have some sort of power to make it feel that good or was I wired that way?

When he finally let go, we were both trembling. He licked his lips, and I thought about the fangs he must have but I'd never seen. Maybe we weren't all that different. Both exiles in a world were sameness was rewarded.

I leaned into him and brushed his lips with mine. Nothing demanding, just the barest of touches. He could have backed off the kiss easily if he wasn't interested. Instead he opened for me, letting the taste of my blood and his on our tongues, mingle. He didn't shove his way in, just gently explored like he was curious. He showed great care around my fangs and I did the same for him. They were small, but just as sharp. I accidently pricked my tongue on one of them. A rookie mistake, but he sucked at the wound until it stopped.

He tugged me away from the wall and toward the dance floor, lips still locked to mine, arms strong around me. He could lead and I was okay with that as I closed my eyes to all the other moving bodies that annoyed me and focused on him. We swayed to the beat. The music meant more for actual touching rather than the frantic gyrating I'd seen so many times at other clubs. Our bodies touched and fit together, melding, mouths feeding at each other, and minds solely on the man who danced with us.

I couldn't feel Luca's emotions. Not in the sense that I could tell what the people around us were experiencing. But his body was expressive. Sure he was hard, but he didn't dig his erection into me or grab my ass like it belonged to him. He barely touched me below the waist. Just a hand in my back pocket resting like mine did on his lower back. His arms were a warm weight against me, strong, solid.

When we finally broke the kiss all I could see was him. He looked at me like I was something. It was odd, and weirdly exhilarating. All he seemed to see was me. This gorgeous guy in my arms wanted me. It didn't matter that we were on the dance floor at a crowded club. The music played and we moved, eyes locked on each other, his breath mingled with mine. I couldn't recall a time ever feeling so close to anyone that I didn't even need words.

Time passed, though I couldn't remember anything specific other than being in his arms. For a while I rested my head on his shoulder and just swayed with him. The music slowed and we barely moved. Cheek to cheek. People circled around, but I didn't notice unless they got close enough to nudge us. Luca looked up twice to snarl at someone who must have gotten too far into our space. Someone nudged him a little harder and he shoved back, letting go only for a second, before his arms returned to their rightful place around me.

Someone whispered in my ear, asking me to dance. Like somehow I was going to let go of the guy in my arms for some stranger. I shook my head. Everyone stayed away for the most part. I'm sure we could have stayed like that for hours and I'd have been just fine. For the first time in as long as I could remember, I felt normal. Like maybe I could do this. Be a real guy, someone that was wanted by someone else.

Luca put a hand in each of my back pockets, cupping my ass, but only lightly. I ran my hands in circles over his arms, shoulders, and back. He was strong, defined in a way I'd always wanted to be but now could never achieve. I sighed into his shoulder happy that my first ever date was quickly becoming the perfect evening.

Until someone slammed into me from the side and sent me careening across the dance floor on my ass. I blinked up at the room for a minute trying to refocus my brain and understand what had just happened. The low lights and thick crush of bodies separated Luca and me. Was he okay?

Someone helped me up, which was good because I still felt disjointed, almost lost. The crowd moved finally, showing him to me. He stood ten feet away arguing with a guy, posture tense. The other man was larger, mocha-skinned, and very angry. I didn't have to be close to feel that he nearly seethed with rage. Little veins popped and jumped at his forehead and neck, and his tone was harsh.

I shoved my way across the room to Luca's side and touched his back in a show of support. If this bruiser thought he had a chance of hurting Luca while I was there, he was mistaken. No one would look at me and think I could have taken a guy that size, but they'd have been wrong.

"You okay?" I half shouted as I leaned into Luca. His body was taut with tension. "Let's just go. We can go to your place or something." I'd have even promised to have sex with him if he left before whatever was starting could escalate. I gripped Luca's arm and tried to nudge him toward our table. The other man was having none of that.

"Fucking fag, bringing your queer ass self here. This ain't a club for blood suckers. Take your nasty little corpse friend out of here." He lifted Luca up by the front of his shirt, tearing the fabric and holding him off the ground a half a foot. Oh hell no. The SOB smacked a meaty paw in my direction, which I caught and twisted, making him drop Luca as I forced the meathead to his knees.

"You just wish I was fucking you, Kenrick. Let him go, Sam. He wants to fuck with me then fine, I'll play." They were both shouting now. The bouncers were on their way over so I let go of the angry giant. Luca took that moment to lunge, a quick fist to the man's nose—which burst like a melon—and another to his stomach which doubled him up. Blood spattered over me in a hot wash that reminded me of Matthew when I'd shot him point blank. Only this blood stank like dog.

Luca didn't let the lycan up, instead he pounded him to the floor in a flurry of fists. I stepped back as others waded in to join the fight. Shit. What the hell was I doing here? This was so reminiscent of the time I spent with Matthew that I just had to leave. I returned to the table we'd saved, used a napkin to wipe the blood from my face and grabbed my coat —I was pretty sure Sei would want it back.

The air outside was no less cold than when I went in, but the eerie empty streets made my heart sink. I'd had such great hopes for the night. Was it something I did? Or was it just that I attracted men who were on the verge of a mental breakdown?

"Sam," Luca called as he was shoved out the door, his coat thrown at him by the very same bouncer who let him in.

I waved at him instead of stopping.

"What the fuck? You see something you don't like and you bail? What are you, a fucking kid?"

I paused but didn't look back. Whatever angry face he

was making I didn't need in my memory. "Gabe said you would have researched my past. I guess you skipped the part where I dated a psychopath who loved me with his fists. Thanks for the dance, Luca. Have a nice life. Don't call me." I walked off, heading for only God knew where. Maybe back to the church, maybe back to Sei's. It didn't matter.

CHAPTER 9

The heat of tears burned my eyes. Fuck, twice in one night was a record for me. I'd never been a crier. The dark empty streets taunted me. If I'd been able to find a cab I would have gone home. So Luca wasn't the one. Didn't Sei tell me that was okay? To just enjoy him for a while? And I had until he'd gone all Rocky on me. At least I wasn't hungry. I was so gonna call the witch to bitch him out later. Apparently we were both really bad judges of character.

I sent him a text instead: *U suck*.

The buzz back was immediate.

What happened?

He started a fight—well insisted on finishing it at least. Reminded me of Matthew.

That sucks. Did you see anyone else worth dancing with?

No, but I hadn't been looking. I sighed and glared at a 24-hour Walgreens—the only thing open in sight. How long had we been in the club? Must have been a few hours since the city had gone deadsville.

Maybe I'm not ready. I sent him.

Are any of us? How will you know if you don't try?

Why did he have to be so damn smart? I glared at the phone.

"I'm surprised to see you wandering around again. Didn't your mentor put out a curfew for his nest? There has been some vampire trouble of late and you shouldn't be out alone." Max stepped out of the Walgreens, bag in hand.

Not many could mess with a vampire. "You mean with no alibi?"

He nodded and smiled at me. "I expected Luca to be wooing you. He has a way with people and seems to like you."

"I don't think he's my type." Problem was he was exactly my type.

Max shrugged. "Luca is very young. I'm afraid I haven't been very good about letting him stretch his wings."

"He's got anger issues."

"Indeed. That's a vampire trait. Yet you seem to be handling it well."

"I've sort of always been angry. Being undead didn't really change that."

"I'm headed to the fight club would you like to come?"

"Will it smell like last time?"

He laughed. "Unfortunately it pretty much always stinks." He dug in his bag to pull out a small bottle of vapor rub. "A dab under each nostril will help."

"Seriously?" I took the jar and followed him down the street, surprised how close we were to the fight club. Was there supposed to be a first rule "there is no fight club" type of thing?

"Seriously. Careful though, the first kick of this stuff will make your eyes water."

I dabbed a tiny bit under my nose and oh yeah that burned! "Crap!"

Max took the jar back. "Potent, but it works. If you ever go someplace you think the smell will bother you, either by making you hungry or just because it stinks, use this stuff."

"Tricks of the trade, eh? Thanks." I walked with him a while and wondered where I was going. Did I really want to watch people pound on each other when I'd just left behind a guy for doing the same? Only there was a difference wasn't there? Control verses loss of control. Luca had lost control. "He started a fight with a lycan. Maybe I overreacted, but he just reminded me of bad things. Does he do that often? Get into fights?"

"Not as much as he used to. Mostly he keeps it in the ring. Have you shared blood yet? Both of you?"

"Yeah. Right before we started dancing." Which had been a few hours ago according to the rotating digital clock on a bank sign.

"He was territorial then. Someone got too close to you, yes? Perhaps interrupted or broke you apart? The dhampirs have always been that way. Vampires are territorial, but not as much so as their human counterparts. Luca has never liked feeding from just anyone. Even I, who am his father, can't flaunt my lovers around him, though I do nothing more for him than give him a cup of blood once a month."

That was an interesting revelation. "It was no big deal. Some guy was kind of pushy. The bouncers were coming to remove him."

Max nodded. "Gabe hasn't spoken to you much of territory and vampires?"

Gabe didn't speak to me about much of anything. Just the basics on how to bite and attract people so I wasn't blood-raping them, but I wasn't about to tell this stranger that. "I'm sure he's got that planned for down the road somewhere." Along with the discussion on redouts we had yet to have.

We arrived at the club and the same guy was there as last night. He opened the door for us. "Let me give you the bare bones of it then," Max said. "When a vampire feeds on someone, they become his. Sometimes it's about controlling their emotions so they will come back to us later—our influence on them. Other times we simply enjoy their company."

"I've fed on a lot of people and never felt any of them were mine."

"I think you do. I think that's why you're so angry. You've not claimed any of them. Though you were obviously close to claiming Luca if you let him feed from you."

"I don't understand. You mean like make someone my Focus?"

"Not at all. It's more a scent. A pheromone perhaps. We vampires don't discuss much with science or let them study us. Secrets protect us in times of trouble." He paused, stopping in the middle of the hallway. "Does your friend Seiran smell like Gabe?"

"I guess. I never really paid attention, but yeah, it's there, usually faint, but there."

"That is what it means to claim someone. Seiran would have had that scent before Gabe made him his Focus. Though it is a step in the process to making someone a Focus. Often *cibo's* smell of the vampires they serve too."

"You think if I claim someone I'll be less angry?"

"I do. We are very territorial around those that are ours. Luca saw you as his. He's fed on you and maybe not yet scent marked you, but the thought was still there. I'm not sure he could scent mark you if he wanted to as that is a purely vampire trait, and he's not yet one."

"How does one scent mark someone?"

"Sex is the easiest way. But exchange blood enough and they will start to smell of you anyway."

"And it's some sort of invisible sign to tell other vampires to keep away?"

"Other supes in general, I suppose. Anyone who could smell it, which would extend to higher level witches as well as lycans and vampires." Max headed toward the fight room where a small man met him with a tablet in hand. "Perhaps you should call Luca back and discuss his outburst? He should have enough time to calm down and realize his error was territorial anger. He's old enough to recognize it even if he can't always control it."

I sighed, not ready for that yet. Sure, I'd probably overreacted. If Gabe had been more forthcoming maybe that wouldn't have happened at all. But there was no point in playing the what-if game. "I'd rather fight. Burn off some aggression." The place was packed tonight. First fight already a mash of grunts and hard flesh hitting flesh. There were cheers and jeers from all around. How long would I last in one of these? Would it clear my head at all like beating up those thugs in the alley last night had?

Max studied me for a moment before he finally nodded. "I can arrange that."

"I don't want to fight Luca." I didn't know how I felt about him right now and didn't want to spend too much time analyzing it.

"All vampires are in level five. Luca is not a vampire yet so he is only a level four fighter." He flipped through a few things on the tablet. "Riley, is this right? We have Hanson, James, Pickerson, Ryerson, and Flay on for tonight?"

"Yep. All shifters. No vamps in tonight. At least not so far."

Max nodded. "Put Sam in against Ryerson." He patted my back and gave me a little nudge toward Riley who was the small man who had handed him the tablet. "Ryerson is high level, street smart. He's strong and fast. Should be a good match for you. Follow Riley. He'll get you gear. Most of our lycans fight naked with no padding, but almost none of our vampires do."

Riley nodded his head at me and turned toward the locker room area. He smelled human but I was beginning to think there was no such thing here. "Can't I fight another vampire?" I didn't want to take the chance of hurting anyone, but really wanted to let go of the rage for a while. Lycans were only slightly more durable than humans, right?

"Not yet. Win this one and we'll see about pitting you against another vampire. Most of the vampires who come here are older and have more skill. You'll likely have to undergo some training if you wish to continue in the circuit." He waved toward the locker room area where Riley had gone. "Go get ready. You're up next. Tell Riley I'm your sponsor and will fund your start-up."

"I can pay for whatever. I don't need help."

"You do if you want to fight here. Bringing in a new fighter costs ten grand. But you can win twice that in your first fight."

Holy crap. No one just paid ten grand for someone they barely knew. "What do you expect me to do to pay it back?"

Max's smile was sardonic, "Win."

No shit! I headed toward the locker room and caught up with Riley who handed me a bag full of clothes and some basics like a brand-new jock. At least my junk would be protected if this Ryerson guy mopped the floor with me. I dressed in a bit of a daze pulling on a tank and shorts that were that odd sports material. Sturdy, but not protective. It was more like a basketball uniform than something I expected for boxing, but it fit so I wasn't the only small guy here.

Riley waited until I was done to guide me to the cage I'd be fighting in. He handed me a mouth guard that must have been custom made for vampires because it had room for my fangs. "Busted fangs are a bitch to fix," he told me. "If you continue to fight you'll have to get one made just for you."

"What are the rules?" I asked before putting the guard in my mouth.

"No rules. You can even feed on your opponent if you win. The spectators like dirty fights. Lycans use a lot of fangs and claws, usually not high on skill. Ryerson is big—almost twice your size—but you're stronger and faster. Since you're a challenger you're expected to win or else this will be not only your first fight, but your last. Max doesn't like to be disappointed, so don't. When the bell rings, you fight. Knock him out for a win. Killing someone in the ring will get you killed by the mob of fans, which is never pretty, but it's been known to happen a time or two."

"How breakable is he?"

Riley frowned, appearing to think about it, then said, "Not very unless you rip out his throat. Good luck getting past the fangs and claws to get there."

"Noted." That probably went for tearing out his stomach too. I could avoid soft squishy areas with my fangs easily enough. Riley taped up my hands, but didn't bother with boxing gloves. The cage we stood beside was empty, but a group was beginning to form around the edges as the other fight seemed to have ended. Maybe they were curious because I was new. I stepped up to the cage and Riley let me in, where I leaned against the wire mesh and waited. Silver?

Huh. Did that sort of thing bother shifters? It didn't do anything for me but almost make me sneeze.

The door across the way opened and a large man stepped inside. He was the ugly sort of man who looked like he'd spent his life getting his face punched. His nose was crooked in several places, hair buzzed down to almost nothing, and he was covered with more body hair than I think I'd ever seen on anyone. He stretched his shoulders, swung his arms and in less time than it took to blink an eye—shifted into a human/wolf combination. On two feet he towered over me with claws as big as my head.

Shit! What the fuck had I been thinking?

The bell chimed signaling the beginning of the fight. He took a swipe at me balancing on odd backward-bent legs. I darted around him, using my small size and speed to deliver several quick hints to his back and abdomen, only it was like hitting concrete. Crap this guy had really been eating his Wheaties, and probably Mikey too.

I danced around him, avoiding his claws like I'd seen Luca do, then bounced low, sprung up and hit him hard with an uppercut to the jaw. The guy didn't even stagger. The crowds jeering grew louder. Fucking ass-wipes. They wanted me to lose. And I wanted more than ever to win if just to prove them all a bunch of spineless wannabes.

Ryerson slashed and caught me across the back before I could move away, opening me from shoulder to hip. The pain seared through me and blood poured down my back. All that tasty blood I'd gotten from Luca, wasted. Fuck but I was pitiful 'cause I was pretty sure I could smell him. The volume of the crowd grew to a deafening white nose and I vaguely remembered Luca telling me to aim for the snout.

I had to keep moving to keep out of reach of those damn claws, but my sight was starting to go red. Not so much with rage, but with pain. Fuck did I hurt. How bad was the wound? Probably worse than a paper cut, but since I wasn't tripping on anything internal, I figured he hadn't cut all the way to my guts. And the slice was more off to the side than along my spine. I was losing blood fast and sliding in the mess. This fight had to end soon. Could blood loss kill me? Probably not. Render me unconscious likely, which meant losing the fight.

He sliced me twice more before I took a small opening to hammer his nasty face in. The swing tore something in my back and while I connected with his face and he actually staggered back a few feet, the weight of the pain slammed into me. The red haze completely obliterated my sight and I sank to my knees letting my other self go. He could win even without any bats in the belfry. If he didn't, I'd be dead and that would end it all anyway, right? Not that it mattered as consciousness swirled me down into the red-tinted darkness.

CHAPTER 10

I awoke to screaming. A deafening cheering that made me aware of my surroundings as well as the unpleasant stickiness of blood that covered me like bad sex. The lycan lay at my feet, out cold and bleeding heavily from the neck. A nasty aftertaste flavored the back of my tongue. Had I fed on him?

The cage door creaked open but the medics hesitated to enter. Max brushed by them and wrapped a thick towel around me, leading me out and down the stairs. The world shifted, and I wobbled on my feet, but he kept me upright.

My feet made bloody footprints all the way to the locker room. Max had another medic follow him and I barely remember the man prodding me in several places that hurt bad enough to make me snarl at him. It wasn't a sound I was used to making, and it startled me enough that I shook my head and cleared the last of the fog out of it.

"He'll need stitches, but he'll have to hold still."

Max nodded. "Lay down on the bench, Sam. The good Doc here is going to stitch you up."

It was that bad? Just moving hurt. Hell, just breathing

hurt. So I stopped. Not like I needed to anyway. I lay down and Max handed me a fresh towel that smelled laundered and slightly damp. It felt good against the heat of my skin. Heat. Wait. How was that possible? Crap was I on fire or what? My body just about burned.

"Why am I so hot?"

"Lycan blood," Max answered as if that was all I really needed to know. "You should know pain meds don't work on us, but you need about three dozen stitches down your back," Max told me.

"Fuck."

"Agreed. He's fast though." He nodded to the medic who began stitching me up. After the eighth or ninth prick and tug I tuned it out and focused instead on calming my head. The anger wasn't there anymore, which was a good thing, but I felt kind of weird and spacey. "You drank a lot of lycan blood. It has a bit of a kick. More than human. Probably more than Luca. Though they don't taste as good as most witches or most *cibos*."

Was that what the nasty taste in my mouth was?

Riley appeared with a stack of cash in hand. Max took it, counted out a huge wad of Benjamins and put them in a plastic bag and handed them to me.

"Did I win?"

"You did. But you had to use a redout to do it. We'll have to work on that if you're going to continue fighting." Hell yeah, I was going to continue. I hurt like a son of a bitch but it was an amazing high. I'd beat that scary ass MF. "Have you been having a lot of redouts?"

"Not sure what you mean exactly by that. A lot how?" Luca had just told me what they were yesterday. Was I supposed to be timing them or something?

"Blackouts. Though your vision goes red first. It's the blood filling your eyes, and then the blood lust takes over.

You almost killed him. I'm surprised you stopped. It's very hard to stop a redout short of a kill, or even a dozen kills."

"I had one yesterday with Luca and he's just fine. I didn't kill anyone then either. But I've sort of had the weird vision for ages now. Some red, but not loss of consciousness like this time or yesterday. That's new."

"Have you told Gabe?" The fact that Max didn't seem to care that I could have killed his kid really irritated me. Maybe I still needed to get Luca's answer. Or even to talk to him about why I'd been so upset at his outburst. I was just so unprepared for all this. Was anyone prepared to be undead? And yet it made me angry at Gabe too. He was supposed to be helping me, but instead complete strangers were telling me things I probably should have known months ago. The doctor finished and mumbled something about the stitches disintegrating on their own within forty-eight hours.

"Why does it matter if Gabe knows? It's a vampire thing, right? I just have to deal with it like all the other shit."

"If the redout was once a year maybe, or even once a month. But two in twenty-four hours means you need to go to ground. Death sleep in real dirt. Even having a *cibo* won't stop the blood lust for you this time. Eventually you'll just come undone and murder everyone within reach."

The thought chilled me to the bone. They were going to bury me? But I wasn't dead. Not technically. Seiran had just told me I wasn't dead. And Gabe would insist, wouldn't he? He wouldn't want me to endanger Sei, Kelly, Con and Jamie. Oh God. They were going to bury me alive.

I got up on autopilot, retrieved my clothes and began stripping off the gear they'd given me.

"You should shower. You're covered in blood," Max pointed out. "Anyone on the street will assume you just came from slaughtering a couple of families. The stitches won't come out. It's a blood laced thread that will fall apart after your body absorbs all the blood in it."

Whose blood, I wondered. And gross. I looked down to find my arms red, stains running over every inch of me and blood dripped forming puddles around me. The heaviness of my shorts and tank meant blood, not sweat. I sucked in a deep breath and made my way to the shower, dropping the soiled clothing as I went.

My heart beat furiously, maybe because I'd had so much blood from the lycan, but I stayed under the spray longer that I probably needed to. When I returned to the bench in just a towel it was to find it had been wiped clean of all traces of blood and Riley waited there with my phone in hand. "Your master wants to speak to you."

I raised the phone to my ear expecting a lecture. "Hello?"

"Are you okay?" Gabe sounded worried, but I had no idea what he'd been told.

"I'm fine." Shaky, tired, and aching slightly with a gash down my back, but mostly unhurt.

"I'm on my way to get you."

"I can find my way home on my own. I don't need a babysitter."

"Sam," the quiet tone that said he was unhappy undid me, and suddenly I was sobbing again as I pulled on my clothes. What the hell was wrong with me? Did I have a time of the month now or something? Crap.

"I'm sorry," I told him.

"You've had two redouts with full loss of consciousness. Any others you haven't told me about? Hart's assistant called with an update."

"I don't want to go to ground. Max told me and I don't want to be buried."

"Sam, you have to be afraid of the redout. You can really hurt people. You might think you can handle it, but waking up with the scattered remains of people you love around because you killed them in a fit of blood rage, will really fuck you up. Some never even come fully back from them. Nowadays vampires are often killed before the redout is finished to stop the bloodshed."

"You want to bury me. Alive. I'm alive, Gabe. Not a corpse. You can't put me in the ground."

"It's not as scary as you think. Wait for me. I'll be there in five minutes. We'll talk about this. It's just a really good nap."

"Buried," I repeated. "Like a fucking corpse."

"I promise that it's nothing to be afraid of."

Only there was. Hadn't Seiran given me the experience earlier this evening? An empty void filled with nothing but darkness. I couldn't do it again, that chaos of nothingness. I gathered up my stuff, including the cash, and headed for the door not planning on waiting for him. I could run for a time on the cash. But what if Gabe was right and I went killer crazy?

"Would it be easier to talk to one of the guys instead of me?" Gabe finally asked when the silence stretched too long.

"Maybe."

"Okay. Hang up. I'm still coming to get you, but keep your phone out. I'll have Sei call." He clicked off. I was already out the door. No one tried to stop me. Thank God.

Sei called a few seconds later. "You okay?"

"I guess." My heart thudded in my chest like I'd run a marathon, helping me decide that lycan blood was not good the whole way around. Vampires shouldn't have anxiety and if eating a shifter meant feeling like I'd just downed a thousand espressos, I didn't need that sort of trouble. "I don't want to go to ground."

"Sam, you're hyperventilating. Slow down. Breathe with me. I know you're scared. We can work through this."

"They're going to put me in the ground. Alive. I'm alive.

You just told me I'm not dead." I had no idea where I was headed as I wandered back to the streets of downtown. The cold had obviously driven everyone off because the streets were empty. I didn't remember waking up from my first death, though Gabe said he'd put me in the ground so I would be reborn from it. If my lungs had been full of dirt and the world around me a black cage of darkness then I wouldn't want the memory.

"But if you need it to get better…"

"How come I've never heard of Gabe having a redout?"

"He said he hasn't had one in decades. The older the vampire you are the longer in between them, I guess. Besides a vampire like Gabe having a redout would probably mean a major world war at this point just to stop him from killing half the population."

"All this 'wait until you're older shit' is getting old. I'm a grown-up dammit." I wove through alleys and avoided major roads that Gabe might take to get to me. It was one of those rare moments I was happy that vampires didn't have the ability to shapeshift or fly. Gabe's sense of smell was better than most, and he could levitate, but he couldn't track me or get to me faster that way.

"Where are you going?" Sei asked after a quiet minute. At least I'd gotten my breathing back under control.

"Somewhere Gabe can't find me."

"What if you have another redout and kill someone?"

"So I'll go somewhere there are no people."

"Where in the world is that, Sam? What will you do when the sun comes up?"

"Would you let them bury you?"

"I think you're asleep when it happens."

"Pretty to think so. They're never gonna put you in the ground while you're still kicking."

He sighed heavily. "I can find you, you know. Gabe may

not have that ability since you're not actually his vamp, but I do. You're a part of the earth just like every other being walking around out there. I can't let you hurt anyone."

I stopped dead in my tracks a pulse of fear trailing down my spine. Of course he could find me. He was fucking Father Earth—tuned into the big network in the ground—and I was just a particle on the rock. "Please," I begged him.

"I will be with you. Until you sleep. I won't let you do this alone."

"But you can't go in the dirt with me."

He snorted, a weird sound for him, but it almost made me laugh. "Technically I could. Father Earth, remember? Gaea likes me. I could probably set up shop in the dirt for a few days and nap. I could use a nap."

"This is not some game," I growled at him.

"No, it's not. You don't get points for the number of civilians you hurt, and you're not trying to find the castle before someone bigger and badder offs your ass," Sei said. "I know sarcasm is your defense mechanism, but you aren't safe right now, Sam."

"Fuck!"

"There's a special cemetery for vampires just east of downtown. Tiny little place with really high walls. Can you meet me there?"

I didn't want to, but he was right. Hell, I just wanted to sit down and cry like a baby. Why couldn't life be more like a video game? At least then it was obvious who the good guys and the bad guys were. "Give me the address. I'll map it on my phone," I finally said. "You better fucking be there, Ronnie." My gut churned, and I couldn't get the taste of the lycan out of my mouth. Never again.

"Meet you there in twenty. Don't make me come looking for you, Sammie."

"I'll be there." I hung up the phone and programmed the

address in. It wasn't that far. I followed the directions having to stop twice to throw up—a new experience since I'd never done it as a vampire before—blood and chunks. Apparently I'd more than just sucked on that furry bastard. God, my stomach hurt. Was that part of the redout issue or the aftereffects of lycan blood?

Someone patted me on the back. "You okay man? You don't look so good."

I shook my head hoping the guy wasn't going to try for my wallet, phone or the stack of cash in my jacket pocket. He didn't smell like a homeless person but that didn't mean he wasn't trouble. "Too much to drink," I gave him a lame excuse.

"Yeah, shifters will do that to you."

WTF? I looked up. The guy was blond, willowy, longish hair pulled back in a ponytail and cheekbones sharp enough to cut glass on. He had to be a vampire since he didn't smell human or even lycan. Or maybe I was just getting better at sorting that out. "You're not one of Gabe's."

He shrugged. "Technically neither are you since your true sire is dead."

Right, except Gabe and Jamie had said to stay away from vampires I didn't know. "You're not doing all that vampire shit around town are you?"

He raised a brow. "Not sure what you mean."

"Okay then. Nice meeting you." I turned to head back to the cemetery. If the guy followed me, at least Gabe could get him and turn him in to the cops. I couldn't imagine any of Gabe's vampires doing crap to get us all in trouble. He was really good at holding a tight leash as I'd experienced for myself.

"Careful out there," the vampire said and patted my arm. A flash of power surged through me like I'd been hit by lightning. Brightness flooded my sight and I was sure I was going to burst into flames any second. Then just as quickly as it had begun, it ended and I was standing alone.

"What the fuck!" I screamed out at the empty street. No one answered, for which I was grateful. Now I ran. Eager to get away and find safety. Seiran was safe. He was probably the most powerful being on earth. And fuck if I didn't need that right now.

The cemetery came into view with towering white walls and bright lights. It looked a lot like a prison. The walls were twenty feet high, made of concrete, and topped with barbed wire. Spotlights glared and circled with cameras watching their every move. Armed guards in heavy Kevlar stood outside the main gate and on the wall. I shivered.

"Creepy, right? I was expecting some ritzy hotel setup or something. Not this." Seiran said as he suddenly appeared right next to me.

"Jesus!" I screamed at him. "Are you trying to give me a heart attack?"

"Nope. Just Father Earth. Sorry. Calculating distances is sort of hard." His hair was green again with flowers growing in it as he spoke. I'd heard of this version of him, but never seen it up close. He was a living, breathing embodiment of the earth. No wonder everyone was scared to death of him. "The whole astral travel thing is pretty easy if I follow the lay lines of the earth. It's just a little jarring when I stop." He shook his head like he was trying to clear it but smiled at me. "So tell me about the date."

"It started okay, but ended in disaster."

"How so?"

"He got pissed off when some bruiser was pushing us around the floor and went postal on him. Then yelled at me when I walked." I sighed and looked away. "He reminded me of Matthew. Max said he got territorial because I shared blood with him. But all I saw were his fists beating on that guy…"

"You shared blood with him?"

"Yeah."

"That was good?"

It had been better than good. Almost hypnotizing. "Yeah."

"I see." Seiran was silent for a moment. "It happens sometimes. Even Gabe will on occasion remind me of Matthew. The memories have faded, but they never really go away. Don't blame that on him, it's mostly in your head. Did he hit you?"

"No. Just called me a kid, but he was really pissed."

"You are a kid."

"Fuck you, Ronnie." He was only a few years older than me. What right did he have to call me a kid?

"You went to fight. I heard that much from Gabe. Did it help?" Sei and I walked together close to the wall with me glaring at it the whole time. Was I really gonna do this?

"Some. Max has this supernatural fight club on the west side. Mostly lycans, though Luca goes there. I thought if I could get the aggression out everything would be okay and I'd be able to think clearly about what I should do."

"Do?"

"About Luca."

"Ah. So you like him."

Fuck me, but I did. "It was great for a while. We both fed and we danced and kissed and it was good, and then it was chaos."

Sei reached out and gripped my hand. "Love is chaos. Why anyone does it is beyond me." The pulse of life poured from him to me, soothing and breath-stealing all at once. I clung to him, opening myself to the power. He was warm, and I wanted to feel human again.

"But you love Gabe," I pointed out.

"And he still drives me bonkers."

"Says the same about you."

Sei nodded. "See, chaos. He shrugged. "Gabe isn't happy Max is here. But Luca is fielding all his calls. Won't even let Max and Gabe talk on the phone, and refuses to set up a face-to-face meeting. Any idea why? Does Max seem to have something bad in mind for Gabe?"

"He seemed pretty business focused to me. Didn't ask me any specific questions about you or Gabe. Not really." We approached the entrance. There were enough armed guards stationed there to prevent a minor zombie apocalypse, or perhaps just a bloodlust-driven vampire from escaping. I pulled back before we reached the gate. "I can't, Ronnie. Please."

"We have to talk to Gabe. He's already inside waiting for us. Wouldn't you feel stupid if you put up this huge fuss over something that is not a big deal? Like you walk in and fall asleep and wake up all refreshed like nothing ever happened?"

"You don't know it will be like that. It looks like a fucking prison."

"To keep people out. Vampires are at their most vulnerable here. Some zealot could come in and slaughter the lot of them without all the precautions. You'll be safe here."

I gulped. "Fuck…"

He tugged me through the open gate. The guards let us pass without question. I couldn't imagine any of them wanting to tangle with Father Earth.

"I don't know why you bother trying to help me all the time."

"You're right. You're kind of an ass. But I like you anyway."

"You're messed up."

He nodded. "That's not news." Gabe leaned against his

car, looking tired, lips in a thin line—an expression of irritation I was quickly becoming used to from him.

"I'm sorry," I said, clinging to Sei like they were going to drag me off to be buried at any second.

"You don't even know what it means." He sighed. "Answer this for me, Sam. Are you tired?"

"Yeah." I was always tired and when I slept it was because of the sun. Though I never woke up really feeling rested.

"How many times have you blacked out in the past week?"

"Just the two times I told you about." I looked away and frowned at the icy ground. "You should probably know. I've sort of let the red come out. Like in my sight and stuff. Let him do his thing as long as he doesn't kill, but I'm there. I remember all that."

"For how long?"

"A couple months."

Gabe groaned and dry washed his face.

Sei looked back and forth between us. "But he's gonna be okay, right? We can fix whatever this is?"

"He has to go to ground. He's young and the vampire side of him is taking control. If it completely takes over there will be no more Sam. He'll be a revenant. A mindless killing machine and I'll be responsible for putting him down."

My whole body went cold, and I took a step back. "I haven't hurt anyone."

"Yet," Gabe pointed out. "Why are you fighting this? I promise it doesn't hurt. You will fall asleep and even dream. Then you wake up. Usually some time has passed—a few days maybe. You'll be monitored so we can give you blood as soon as you wake. Then you'll return to your normal life. But you'll feel better, rested, and in control. It's the earth that gives us that." He reached out and took Sei's free hand. Some of the exhaustion eased away from his face. I wondered how long it had been for him since he'd actually rested. A couple decades sounded like a really long time. He tugged us forward. "It's not scary I promise. You're making yourself sick over nothing. You just lie down and close your eyes."

We followed him through a maze of buildings, all had individual guards. Inside the walls it seemed like winter hadn't happened here. Everything was lush and green with life, trees, flowers, planters filled with ivy, all blooming as though it hadn't been the coldest winter in thirty years. Was it the vampires that did this? Even the air felt warmer. Were there giant heaters somewhere that I couldn't see?

We stopped at a large mausoleum-like building. The side of the building was etched in what looked like Latin but it could have been Greek for all I knew about ancient languages. The guard opened the door for us and nodded his head to Gabe. Inside the room was just a huge open space with a dirt floor. The walls were thick, several feet of rock on each side. But the interior was warm, the dirt smelled fresh, and pulsed with a welcome feeling of earth magic. I'd feared there would be a grave dug and ready for me to be thrown into, but it was all just semi-soft ground. Maybe I was expected to dig it myself. Only no one had a shovel and there were none leaning on the concrete ledge where we stood.

"So what do I do?" I asked staring at the dirt feeling weirdly drawn to it. It looked really soft and inviting like I could imagine a sandy beach to be. If I sprawled out in all that warmth, would I actually be warm for more than a minute or two? "What if I don't wake up?"

"You won't be out long. A week, maybe? If it seems like too long, we'll soak the ground with blood. Oftentimes that will stir a vampire who's been in the ground too long. Doesn't always work, but I don't think you'll need that." Gabe waved at the dirt. "I suggest you strip. Maximum contact with the earth will help recharge you. You just lie down and close your eyes."

"But what about like bugs and stuff?" I didn't want anything gnawing at me while I slept—if that's what I would really be doing.

"Bugs don't much like vampires. We're toxic to most of them, and since you're not in a self-dug grave out in the middle of nowhere, I think you'll be fine."

The guard closed the door, probably to give us some privacy. But I wasn't planning on stripping in front of either of them. I took off the coat since it was leather and Sei's. "Can't Sei just recharge me?"

"He can fill you with life, but you're not really alive, Sam. The grave is death, and while the Dominion doesn't recognize it as an element separate from earth, death is a different magic. Sei can't bring people back from the dead, and he can't bring the undead into new life. He can give us back to the earth, but I don't think that's the solution you're looking for."

"Yeah, no." We'd already resolved the whole I didn't want to die thing. "Will it be like the last time?" All I remembered was the pain of icy water filling my lungs and the final darkness setting in no matter how I struggled. My limbs had stopped responding before my brain knew it was a hopeless cause. I didn't wish drowning on anyone.

"Not as long as you don't fight it."

"But I feel alive." Fuck did that dirt look good. Why was I so afraid? They had made me this way, hadn't they? Dependent on them. Used to having others around. What if I was just stuck in the dirt alone for days?

Gabe took my hand. "Your skin is cold and hard. Can you feel the warmth of my skin? No? But Sei's, you can feel his?"

Sure. Sei always felt warm. Odd that he only seemed

slightly warmer than me when he normally ran hot as a furnace. "He's warm."

"He's standing here as Father Earth and running hot enough to burn footprints in the concrete, but he's only warm?" Gabe asked.

I glanced down at where Sei's feet met the pavement and sure enough the ground around him smoldered. Green things usually bloomed at his feet. Was something wrong with him? Oh shit, it was me wasn't it? I was always fucking with his power. I let go of his hand. The warmth and calm he'd given me vanished. Plants began to curl around the edges of the concrete and pour up from the soil.

"I'm so sorry," I told him. "I wasn't trying to mess with you. I promise."

Sei just shrugged. "It was kind of cool. Usually you're just static. Today you're a lightning storm. Like flashes hitting the ground and it sort of tickles. I liked it."

"Take a step back into the dirt, Sam," Gabe said. He moved toward me which forced me to take a step back. I almost lost my balance but grabbed Sei's hand. A hot blast of air hit me hard and strong enough in the small space to blow the door open. Gabe fell back against the wall, hands protecting his face, burns darkening his fingers and cheeks. Shit.

"I don't know what happened. I'm so sorry." I told them both. Sei dropped my hand to go to Gabe. A half dozen guards lingered around the edge of the tomb with automatic weapons locked and loaded.

Oh God. I was in a tomb. All the carvings and sleek designs inscribed into the wall suddenly made sense. I sucked in deep breaths, but lightheadedness made me flounder. I stumbled off the edge of the platform and landed on my back in the dirt.

The ground began to pour over me like a living thing,

sucking me downward. I fought and screamed fearing that the weight of it would fill my lungs like when I'd drowned. Sei reached for me but Gabe held him back, arms locked around him. I held my breath as the dirt covered my head, sinking me deeper until I was certain it would crush me. I didn't need to breathe, but my lungs burned as if they remembered that it was better when they had oxygen in them. I couldn't keep from opening my mouth and instantly the dirt filled my lungs as the world began to blacken around me. It was terrifying and painful right until the moment I died.

CHAPTER 11

The day I met Matthew had been my seventeenth birthday. My family had too many kids to really celebrate anything, and since I was the oldest it meant I was on my own for pretty much everything. I don't think any of them even remembered that it was my birthday.

I found my way to the movie theater with the cash I'd stolen out of the apartment's laundry room. The quarter slots were easy enough to jimmy and always filled with a good chunk of change. I'd escaped the confines of the apartment as soon as the sky grew dark with the plans to enjoy time away from the siblings my parents expected me to raise for them.

I bought a pizza with my quarters—a good one—and spent the day playing Resident Evil on the machine in the back of the rundown theater. There were movies playing that I'd like to have seen, but the cost was too much. Food and fun lasted longer without the expensive screen time. And I'd been pretty involved in the game when Matthew showed up.

He kind of loomed over me at first, like a shadow of someone who was maybe a little irritated that I was playing his game, but when I looked up he smiled. Something bright lit up in his dark eyes. He looked like a soldier just back from war, dressed in fatigues, hair trimmed super short, nice body, strong shoulders, good posture. I'd never been with a guy before but had fantasized about it. A red-blooded all-American boy like him could never have been interested in me, could he?

I think I figured in that moment—because it was my birthday—what the hell? Why not? What was the worst he could do? Kick my ass? Been there done that a few dozen times. I could give as good as I got if we went that route.

"Like something you see?" I asked, daring him to continue staring. He'd looked me over more than once and I'd never met a straight guy who did that to another guy. Seen them roll their gaze over plenty of leggy chicks, but never a short chink from the bad side of town.

"Yeah, actually I do." He leaned against the side of the game. "You done playing?"

"Depends on what you're offering? If you want the machine then fuck off, I was here first."

He laughed and with it showed fang. Vampire. I should have been afraid. Had heard enough evils about them in church and from my family, though the news reported daily that advancements were being made toward equality, but I was seventeen. He was attractive, interested in me, maybe. "I bite," he teased.

"What's in that for me?"

He grinned and held out his hand. "Name's Matthew."

"Sam," I told him as I shook his hand.

"Well, Sam. This is what's in it for you." He yanked me forward into a kiss. It was brutal, amazing, and invigorating all at once. He fed at my mouth, teeth scoring my tongue. The taste of my own blood should have clued me in that the guy was bad news. But we were all young and stupid once. I followed him home to an apartment that wasn't much better than the one I lived in.

Whatever dream god worked for vampires, thankfully, didn't make me relive that first night for which I was thankful. It had been awful. Painful, humiliating, and yet I'd come a half dozen times. Matthew would bleed me until I passed out, and then bleed me some more. When he thought I was halfway awake he'd fuck me or bring in some "buddy" to fuck me. Looking back, it was a nightmare.

Why did I go back to him? I knew I'd gone home at some point because I would go to school all day feeling like a zombie only to have him pick me up as soon as the sun set. On the rare occasion I tried to avoid him he always found me. I guess that would have been the blood. He fed from me so much he could probably have told me to pretend to be a monkey and dance on my head and I'd have done it.

Two months after that first day we met and he took me with him one night. Told me that I would be leaving it all behind. I hated them anyway. Hated my life, so it was okay. I changed my name and became his. Sadly, all I was was a possession to him.

If going to ground was just a replay of the highlights and lowlights of my life it was going to be a short trip. But there was no hashing through Roman's time or the horrible hours spent in that fucking tower. I did remember the first time I realized Matthew didn't see me because he really wanted Seiran.

We were watching the news. Well, he was watching. I was on my knees with his dick down my throat while some guy I never even heard his name plowed my ass. Matthew got off on sharing me. It did little for me as proven by my limp dick. He didn't care so long as I kept sucking.

"Breaking news. Dominion's Regional Director Tanaka Rou's son Seiran has been accused of murder. A co-worker has been found dead on his doorstep, and a professor killed with his wards. Police

are investigating possible magic for both homicides. The Dominion has claimed that this is an attempt to frame the Rou family and remove them from power. The Director has yet to make a statement."

Seiran's picture flashed up on the screen. It wasn't a mug shot, something from school maybe. He was smiling, long hair, almond-shaped, bright blue eyes, pretty enough to be called androgynous. And apparently some rich bitch's son.

"Damn that kid grew up fine," Matthew said. He gripped my hair and forced me to take him in further, gagging me with each thrust. At least I hadn't eaten that day. The consequences of throwing up on him were never good. "I had him for years. Was his first. Taught that pretty little boy to sing. I bet he misses me." He came, shooting down my throat at the same moment I stared at Seiran Rou's picture thinking that I kind of looked like him. It suddenly made sense why Matthew always had me wear colored contacts. At the time I thought it was because he just hated the boring dark brown of my Chinese heritage, but staring at Seiran, and his pretty blue eyes, it all clicked into place. I was a replacement. I'd hated Seiran for that, which was stupid because it wasn't like it was his fault.

I dozed for a bit, memories leaving me to rest a while before returning. I guess it wasn't really dreaming since I was dead. The experience was certainly more relaxed than I recall death the first time around. That had been a cold searing pain until my heart stopped, then nothing until I awoke undead thinking I was still drowning. The fact that I was sort of dreaming meant I was still alive right? It wasn't a full stop. More like a semi-consciousness. I couldn't feel the weight of the dirt anymore, or even my body. Instead I just seemed to be in a warm cocoon of random memories. I dreamed of dancing with Luca again, letting that one linger a while and pushing away the intruding thoughts of his anger at the shifter. Yeah, he'd gotten in our space, but I'd handled him. Could have thrown him out myself. Maybe I would apologize and we could start over. Talk it out, set guidelines. If it was a territorial thing I could learn to live with it as long as he learned to minimize it.

I dreamed of kissing Con, though it had never happened. I'd fantasized about it often. Sometimes when he slept at night, he had nightmares. More than once I'd curled around him in his bed, offering him soft words and touch as comfort. Nothing sexual, but it often made me hard lying next to him. He rarely awoke to find me there, but my presence always seemed to calm his nightmares. Too bad the same didn't work for me.

I sank into a deeper sleep for a time. Dreamed of new things that I knew had to be all in my head because they'd never happened to me. I'd never even been on any airplane and yet I dreamed of flying over the city. When I'd been locked in the tower at Roman's mercy to fuel his spell against Seiran and Gabe I'd often wished I could fly away from it all.

Seiran, Jamie, and Kelly could all change—escape the human form that bound them by strict rules—I longed for that. Seiran would often forget he was human at all when he changed into a lynx. Kelly never talked about it, but I'd spent enough new moons with him at his parent's Olympic-size pool to know that it wouldn't take much for him to lose himself in the wild. He'd turned down an invite by the former water Pillar to spend the winter training with her in Cancun using the excuse that he was in school and didn't want to fall behind. I was pretty sure he feared that he'd swim out into the ocean and never come back. Humanity really sucked sometimes. I could totally understand wanting to leave it all behind.

No one spoke of it, but I knew. Jamie watched him sometimes like he was worried. I got that. I sort of liked

Kelly too and didn't want him to swim off into the sunset never to be seen again. But that didn't stop me from wondering what it was like. I was some sort of witch, right? I had weird powers that amplified everyone else's. I borrowed abilities from others sometimes, and with Sei's help in the past few weeks had learned how to cast a few very basic defensive spells. The Dominion was against my training, which made sort of sad sense. I mean if I could fuck with the power of a Pillar, did they really want me to be fully trained out there somewhere strong enough to take over the world? I laughed to myself. Dictator Sam—how stupid. I'd have made a horrible ruler since I hated people. *Kill them all!* Sei and Kelly were better at that. But the ability to change, even just a few nights a month, I'd like that.

I let the dreams of flying take me for a while. I soared over open fields covered in snow and forests of trees, riding on thermals, relaxing into the flow. I lost another chunk of awareness. My body felt light as a feather. I thought I heard Luca's voice, Con's calm tones floated through quite often, urging me to come back. Come back from where? Flying?

I thought maybe I heard Sei's voice too. But it was too far away. I focused instead on the flight—found myself as a raven with thick black wings. The feathers were soft and warm.

I dozed in and out, finding myself back in the dirt, but waking up as a bird. The last time, I sat on the ledge next to an air vent inside the top cathedral-like ceiling of the tomb. Another dream I was sure, since I looked down to find Luca sitting on the concrete lip by the door. He was just in jeans and a T-shirt, jacket behind his back to cushion him from the wall. He had a deck of cards set out in a game of solitaire. He was talking, but I couldn't understand the words. That was often the way of dreams. He looked good at least, not angry. I wondered if we could work it out. Or if I was just asking for more trouble like I had every time I'd gone back to Matthew.

The thought made me turn away and tuck my head under my wing for a while. It was a tiny nap. The next time I roused it was Con sitting on the lip, bare feet buried in the dirt. He wasn't playing solitaire. Instead he seemed to have laid a gash in his arm and was sprinkling the blood around the dirt.

The droplets felt like ice. Stinging needles that awoke my senses. Jarring in the cold absence of physical sensation. It no longer felt like a dream, but something more real, yet still blurry at the edges.

I swayed slightly and let the fresh air from the vent soothe me. Cold wind breezed through, taunting from the outside. The slats were small and edged to keep out the light while letting air inside. A few strands of dried brown grass near the edge meant there'd been a nest there at one time, or an attempt to make one that had been removed. I squeezed though the tiny opening wondering where this new dream would take me.

Outside I stood on the edge looking down at the giant rocks all around me and in the distance even larger rocks. I'd have preferred to have flown over a forest or even an icy lake, but I would take to the sky anyway. The cold wind blew through the stone village. I could see thermals circling upward. If I could catch one of those maybe I could cruise all the way to some nice trees.

I spread my wings, flapping them like I'd done it all my life, but didn't get any height. Was I doing it wrong? In the rest of the dreams I'd already been in the air. Maybe I just had to catch the wind. I stilled my wings and studied the ledge. A small thermal swirled near the edge. I wandered down and felt the warmth blow at me and began to move my wings again. I stepped off the ledge and was flying, well hovering, but hot damn, close enough!

The thermal kept me up until I found the steady beat of wings that would move me around. I figured I could ride it up to the next one and do a lot of gliding which I seemed to be good at. Not that it mattered if I fell since I was dreaming and all.

I left the stone village and rose up above several much larger stones—mountains perhaps—riding the heat waves like I was a master surfer. I watched a few other birds navigate, and fly together in synchronization. I wondered if I could find that—my own flock. I got so caught up in watching them that I ran into the long branch of a tree, clipped my wing and sent myself into a spiral. A moment of utter panic consumed me as I twirled—free falling, feet over head in a maddening swirl. My stomach lurched and screamed, and my head and wing throbbed in time. I had to stop the descent. The ground was approaching fast.

I flapped my wings, trying to slow myself down. Pain seared the left one, but they finally caught the wind so I could straighten myself out and slow my fall. I landed a little bruised on the icy pavement, glaring at the tree in the distance. Stupid tree. Stupid birds for distracting me.

I hadn't been hurt in the dream before. Maybe it was a sign of waking up. Gabe hadn't mentioned anything about waking being painful, but he'd been lacking in the training department lately.

Someone called me. I paused cocking my head to listen. It was a bit like a melody I could barely remember, a haunting tune that made me spread my wings—despite the pain—and reach skyward. My ascent was awkward as the wing was injured, but I followed the sound like it was some sort of siren song. The thermals helped ease some of the pain in my wing as they were warm and would let me glide long distances until I reached the window where the sound came from. The music played sweetly from here—loud, clear and soothing.

A strong breeze swept past me, seeming to wrap me up in its embrace and heal my wing in an instant. I stretched the wounded appendage and marveled at the lack of pain. Maybe I could nap here, rest a bit then take to the sky again. The song was peaceful and the flight had made me tired. There was a whole world to explore after all and dreams were endless, right?

The pinpricks of stars spanning into the distance spoke sweetly of adventure. I'd be sure to explore them all once I'd let my wings rest a bit. The heat from inside the window drew me in closer. I walked through the open frame onto a flat sort of tree and enjoyed the warmth of the room. I hadn't realized it was a mistake until the window closed behind me. I turned to peck at the clear wall, irritated that I'd not be able to return to explore the stars.

"Welcome, Sam. I've been waiting for you."

I turned my feathered head, shifting it around a few times until the words came into focus. Though the vision made little sense. Someone knew me? Well of course someone knew me, this was my dream wasn't it? Only I couldn't imagine why Max Hart would be in my dreams. He was hot and all, but I didn't have daddy fantasies. He had some odd aura, like two people splayed across one another. How was that possible?

"Won't you change for me so we can talk?"

Change? Oh right, because I was a bird. I laughed to myself thinking it so silly. I was a bird because I wanted to fly and in dreams we could be anything, right? So all I had to do was want to be human again. That was easy enough. The change poured over me, knocking me off the dresser—that was the word for the flat tree—and onto the floor. Pain ripped through my back and arm. It was a bone-breaking shift that left me gasping for breath and panting to keep consciousness. I didn't understand how this could hurt so much in a dream.

The weight of my limbs returned, throbbing with needles like they'd been asleep for days. A long gash on my left arm dripped blood, and I could feel the hotness of liquid on my back.

"With a little blood you'll be able to finish healing both of those fairly quickly. Going to ground often suspends our healing skills since we're in a comatose state. Not sure of all the science behind it, as I don't subscribe to that religion, but I'm sure there's some proper justification," the fake Max said.

"This isn't a dream?" I asked realizing that everything was just a little too real to possibly be a dream. Did that mean I'd really changed? I'd been a bird? Holy fuck the Dominion was really going to want me dead now.

"Your long nap began to awaken the rest of your power. You've only begun to tap your potential, Sam. Your raven was lovely. Do you realize you're the first vampire in all of history to ever be powerful enough to change on a non-new moon night? I'm very impressed."

I sighed and grabbed a blanket from the bed to wrap it around myself. Whoever this guy was didn't need more of a show than he'd already had. I was pretty shaky on my feet and wondered how I'd get home and explain all this to Gabe and Sei. "Take the mask off. The illusion or whatever the fuck it is you're wearing. You're giving me a headache. I know you're not Max."

"See. So much more powerful." The illusion faded and the man who stood before me was the blond man I'd met in the alley right before I'd gone to ground. "You're a treasure, Sam. Can I call you Sam or do you prefer the name your parents gave you?"

"My name is Sam," I growled at him. Any other name belonged to a life I no longer had. The facts began to fall into place. The man was a vampire with illusion skills. Some pretty powerful illusion skills if he'd been in town a while and no one knew he was here. There was only one vampire that I knew existed with those powers. "Galloway, right? Nathaniel Galloway. The Tri-Mega is looking for you."

He smiled and sat in a chair beside the door, crossed his legs and leaned back. Was he going to stop me from leaving? "There's no such thing as the Tri-Mega anymore. I was part of it, Himdale is dead, and Tresler knows where to find me. He's just not ready to play that game yet. He may not survive it, and then his little coup will fail."

"Whatever. Am I free to go? I'd like to go home."

Galloway got out of the chair and went to a table where a chess game was set up. The pieces were laid out as though he stopped in the middle of a game. He moved a single piece. "Don't you wish to know of the danger to your friends? Perhaps you don't care about them as they do about you. They've been visiting you often as you slept."

"I'd like to go home and tell them I'm awake."

"And if you've returned to chaos?"

"I have powerful friends. I'm sure they can handle whatever is coming their way."

"What if it's Santini that breaks? Did you know he's one of the oldest vampires alive? He and Maxwell Hart. Both older than Tresler and I combined. Santini is very quiet about his power. He reins it in and hides it from the world as he has no wish to be king. What better mate could there be for Father Earth? Hmm?" He moved the black knight. "He plays the role, stays under the radar. Not because he's not powerful enough. No vampire could be more powerful. But Santini has always been a simple man. Always focused on love."

And that was a bad thing? Didn't everyone want someone to love them? To care about?

"It will be love that breaks him. It always is. And not even the first time it will break him." Galloway pointed to the black king on the board. "That is Tresler controlling the powerful through fear. He pretends to offer order and protection while building chaos and panic." He picked up the black queen. "This is your friend Seiran. As much as Tresler hates humans he wants the Pillar so he can have control. He fears Gabe but has been moving in the background to take Gabe out of the picture."

"But you just said that Gabe is stronger than any of you, and Sei would slaughter anyone who hurt Gabe."

"Not death, child. A Focus flounders without his master. The oldest of us forget that. Which means Tresler thinks he's strong enough to keep your friend from falling to madness once Gabe is gone." Galloway glanced at me. "Out of the picture. Much as you have been for almost two months."

I blinked at him. Two months? I'd been in the ground for two months? It felt like a few hours at most. "I thought they were supposed to wake me if I was out more than a week. Fuck. I gotta go."

Galloway shrugged. "Your *cibo* has just arrived. I will send him up as you'll need to eat. I look forward to spending more time with you in the future, Sam." He swept out of the room closing the door behind him. Luca? He knew Luca? Well fuck, didn't I just have to be right about everyone?

I opened the drawers to find them all empty. That was just great. When the door opened again it really was Luca standing in the doorway. Was he working with Galloway? He stripped off his shirt and threw it in the chair. Chest and defined arms looking as mouthwatering as ever. Fuck him.

"It's good to see you. Eat." He reached for me and bared his neck. I let him pull me into his arms and took his invitation to bite into the sweet pulsing vein in his neck. The taste of him was even better than before, likely because I hadn't fed in two months. I took long gulps of him, waiting for him to pull away or tell me to stop. But he did neither. I wanted to drink him dry for betraying us. To hurt him as I felt in my gut he planned to hurt me. But I couldn't. Even if I wanted to. I finally stopped when I could hold no more, licked his wound, which healed perfectly, instantly. Fuck!

Apparently going to ground had fine-tuned my power. What else would work better?

Luca tugged his shirt back on and handed me a bag of clothes. "Let's get you home."

"Are you working with him?" I pointed toward the door. "Galloway? You know his Focus tried to kill Sei and Gabe."

"And he had nothing to do with it. He'd gone to ground himself. Spent almost five centuries asleep which is likely why Jonahs went mad. He'd like to prevent the same thing from happening to Seiran and ending the world. Now get dressed. I have to sneak you home before someone sees we're out after curfew. Con will be ecstatic to see you."

Curfews? I'd never had a curfew in my life. My bleeding stopped at some point and Luca retrieved a damp towel from the bathroom to wash my skin clean. There was no sign of any former wound. Not from hitting the tree or the claw wound on my back. Did Luca know I had changed? Would I be able to do it again on command or was it just a fluke? I so needed to talk to Seiran.

I dug through the clothes, glad to see they were mine, but when I put them on they were all a little loose. The socks were warm and fuzzy and my shoes felt right. I zipped up the coat and started for the door.

"Don't you have more questions?" Luca asked.

"Oh, you're planning to be forthcoming now? Did you

know the last time some guy introduced me to a strange and powerful vampire I was used to fuel a death spell?"

"That's not fair. I'm not Matthew and Galloway is not Andrew Roman."

"Then explain it to me. Tell me you didn't volunteer to be my *cibo* so you could get close to me for this guy."

Luca looked away, which was answer enough.

"Wow. I really do pick the winners, don't I? Later." I walked out the door and found myself in the hallway of some weird loft very similar to Luca's. At least it meant I could find the main door and get the hell out. Galloway had vanished completely.

"Sam! Dammit. You can't just walk out onto the streets. There's a vampire curfew in place. No one is allowed on the streets. Anyone they suspect of being a vampire will be shot on sight." Luca followed me out of the apartment and down the stairs. "Let me drive you home. You can be angry with me all you want. I'm okay with that. But shit, let me get you home safe."

"My home. Not yours or Gabe's. Assuming I still have a fucking home." Two months!

"Gabe is your registered sire. I have to take you to him. Anything else will get us both killed. The guards at the grave should have notified him of your departure. I don't know how you got all the way out here for Galloway to find you first."

I sighed and followed him to a car that was parked in a lot below the building. At least we didn't have to wait for it to get warm. Though I felt okay now, not cold, or really all that tired. More irritated and curious than anything, but I needed answers from someone I could trust first. And there were only two people on that very short list.

CHAPTER 12

The drive through the city was like traveling through a movie set. Storefronts were boarded up, graffiti scrawled over newer buildings, and the flashing lights of police cars lit up every corner. No one tried to stop us, but even heading to the suburbs didn't improve the scenery. The snow had melted to wet slush and mud, but there were endless homes standing like burnt out shells. Cars flipped over and charred. Lawns were brown and looking like fresh graves.

The highway digital boards said the city was on lockdown. Any and all vampires needed to be registered with the government and monitored. The curfew was military enforced and police had been authorized to use "lethal prejudice" when finding a vampire out after curfew. "What the fuck happened?" I said out loud while Luca drove. The world had turned into some dystopian nightmare. Was this contained just to the Twin Cities? Or was everywhere like this now?

"The vampires have lost it. Tresler's war. Half of congress

is telling the president to bomb the Twin Cities to kill all the vampires," Luca said.

"There aren't even that many vampires here." I could think of a little more than a dozen that lived in the area and were in Gabe's nest.

"They've been coming in droves. Nate thinks there are probably hundreds of them now. Maybe even over a thousand."

"Yeah, Galloway seems a stand-up guy. No reason to disbelieve him."

Luca sighed, but didn't reply.

"If they are coming to fuck with Gabe they're messing with the wrong guy. Seiran will fuck them up." The car pulled up to the door of Gabe's condo. I was surprised to find armed guards around the place. There had always been security but never like this. I wondered if they'd shoot me.

"Gabe isn't…right. Max is fine, but Gabe is not. Something's off. The government thinks Gabe is part of the problem." Luca frowned at me. "He might be, even if it's not his fault."

"What is that supposed to mean?"

Luca shook his head. "I can take you down to the parking garage, but it's no different there. I can't go in. Seiran won't listen to me. He won't even take my calls anymore. I think Sei blames me for making you go to ground. Though I'm pretty sure you were on that path before we met," Luca said.

"I'll be fine." I assured him, not feeling sure at all that they wouldn't just open fire on me the second I stepped out of the car. Thankfully no one moved, so I cautiously approached the door. "Let me pass, oh sweet Jesus, please don't shoot me," I whispered as I walked through their ranks. Would I survive a hail of bullets? Probably. And wasn't that just the shit. It wasn't likely to tickle. And I wasn't a pain slut by any definition.

The door opened, and I stepped inside pausing to suck in a deep breath before heading to the elevator. I punched in the code that would let me into Gabe's place and the elevator descended.

I could hear raised voices before the door even opened.

"I don't know why this is an issue for you, Seiran. I need to go out. I promise I will be back later." Gabe had his back to the elevator as the door swung open. Seiran was pacing the living room with a baby cradled in his arms.

"Because I need you here. The twins are fussy and I have to work early tomorrow. You've been out every night this week and it's not safe. The news keeps saying—"

"The news is over sensationalizing this just like it does everything else. I'm a vampire for fuck's sake. Other than a bunch of overzealous militia wannabes shooting at me a few times there's not much that can happen to me," Gabe interrupted. I couldn't recall ever hearing him so irritated. And it was rare to hear him swear, even rarer that he seemed in a state of agitation that he couldn't see that Sei was beside himself with worry. "They can't hurt me. I walk right by them all the time and they don't even notice me."

"Sam!" Seiran cried spotting me as I stepped out of the elevator. "You're awake! Oh, finally! Thank Gaea."

Gabe turned my way his face a mask of exhaustion and irritation. Gone was the stoic man I'd come to know as my mentor. Usually he was the picture of perfection, but he was wearing faded baggy jeans—like he'd lost weight—an oversized T-shirt and a pair of dirty canvas shoes. He looked like he was headed to a kegger. "No one called to say you had risen. How did you get out of the tomb?"

"Wow. I guess I was hoping for a good to see you, Sam. Not what the fuck are you doing here, Sam." I told him and walked past him to Sei. "What's going on out there? The guns and the signs. What happened?"

A baby began to cry. Not the one in Sei's arms, but from the library. Gabe's face completely shut down, his shoulders tensed and he turned toward the elevator. Sei went into daddy mode, heading to the other room to coo the second baby while whispering, "Shh, you'll wake your sister. Hush now. Daddy's here. Would be great if daddy had more arms."

Gabe didn't try to help out. He didn't respond at all. What was wrong with him? "I'm going out," he finally said, motion coming back into his limbs like he was a doll whose strings were finally pulled. He pushed the button for the elevator. "Sam, you should stay here. There's blood in the freezer. I'll take you hunting tomorrow night." He stepped into the elevator and the doors closed before I could think through the insanity of what I'd just witnessed. The world had really gone insane.

Both babies were crying now, and so was Seiran.

I headed into the library, which was now a nursery with a giant crib and a changing table. My bed had been pushed to the opposite side of the room but was unmade. Not like I'd needed it lately. I scooped up the crying baby from the crib. Male—I could tell by the smell of him, which was odd since I'd never have noticed that before. But he needed a diaper change. I'd only done that a million or so times in my life. I took the boy to the changing table, cleaning him up and even dressing him in a new onesie that said "Son of a witch." By the time I had him bouncing and making happy baby noises, Seiran had gotten the other baby to calm down as well.

"I'm sorry," Sei whispered. "Thank you for helping me. It's so much stress. I never expected to be doing this on my own. My mom offered to help and all I can remember is the horror of my own childhood, but now..." He looked between the two kids. "I'm getting desperate."

"No biggie, Ronnie." I carried baby two to the living room where there was a playpen set up with bright hanging toys overhead for him to reach for. I set him down on his back and he began reaching for the dangling fun. "I've done the baby thing before. I was the oldest of five, you know. Changed lots of diapers and entertained plenty of babies." It'd been two years—almost three since I'd left home. Longer than that since any of my siblings had been in diapers, but it wasn't a skill that was easily forgotten.

"What's his name?" I asked, thinking that the boy's pretty blue eyes matched Sei's so well. He had little wisps of red curls decorating the crown of his head, which were all Jamie's side of the family. I didn't know Hanna—Sei's baby momma—that well, but I knew she had red-gold hair.

"Mizuki. It means beautiful moon."

"And her?" I asked as I gently took the little girl from him. Her eyes were the same blue but her hair jet black like her daddy. "You are going to be beating the suitors off with a stick, baby girl. Both you and your brother are going to have them lining up."

"Sakura," Sei whispered. He looked so young and tired with his tear streaked face that it reminded me of how young he really was. Only a few years older than me, and an only child who'd never been allowed to play with others. The children had been forced on him. An agreement struck with Seiran's mother to bear an heir for his freedom. Tanaka Rou was a real piece of work. I avoided her like the plague. If there was someone less prepared to have a baby it was probably Seiran Rou.

"Cherry blossoms, right? I think I learned that from watching Naruto," I told him and set Sakura down beside her brother. They both wiggled and reached tiny hands toward the dangling mobile. "Let them play a bit, then we'll swaddle them up and put them back to bed. When they're little like this their brains get engaged so quickly. They might not have the same focus we do, but they'll wear each other out in just a few minutes, but it's good to keep their minds engaged. It'll help them sleep longer." I watched them wiggle and coo at each other. They were probably just over a month old. Tiny enough to not have a lot of motion yet, but just enough so they weren't just crying, sleeping and pooping. "They were early?"

Sei nodded. "Just a little, but it was pretty hard on Hanna. She's still on bed rest. They spent the first few weeks in the hospital. But I've had them home a little over two weeks now."

I went to the nursery and found blankets for the two of them since they were winding down already and started by swaddling up Sakura. "You've probably had people show you a million times. But practice makes perfect. The more they swing their arms and legs, the more they escape the blankets, but it's cold yet and babies are used to being just this side of roasting." Once she was covered, I handed her to him and she blinked sleepy eyes at him.

It was oddly calming taking care of the babies. Like being back home only without my parents or siblings fighting in the background. I got Mizuki squared away and took him to the nursery to set him down. They had an extra wide crib with baby bumpers on the side. We laid them side by side like two little sausages.

"I had them in separate cribs for a while but they just cried and cried. Jamie found the big crib and the hospital says it's okay to have them together." Sei looked about ready to keel over himself. New babies meant not much sleep. Why wasn't Gabe here? He would have been awake at night anyway and could have allowed Sei some rest.

"I need to get cleaned up," I told Sei more than a little surprised that he didn't react to me being covered in dirt from the grave still. I could feel it like a fine layer on my skin, but his hair was a messy ponytail, and his clothes looked a little disheveled. Even his socks were mismatched, which just wasn't normal for him.

He nodded and sat in a chair beside the crib. The room was really cramped. But then I guess Gabe had never planned for kids. Maybe if he'd been buddies with Max, he would have added it into the cards somewhere since that guy had a million kids. Would a gay vampire ever think he might have kids? Was Gabe gay? Or bi? I'd never really thought about it. Older vampires always struck me as sort of the opportunistic sort. Food was food. Sex was always on the menu. Gender didn't matter that much for food, but when sex was combined with food?

My brain hurt with the philosophy.

I headed into the bathroom, stripped out of everything, and turned to examine my back which didn't look like I'd ever been scratched. This vampire thing was kind of crazy. Okay more than a little crazy. At least my stomach wasn't gnawing away at me with hunger. Maybe drinking that much from Luca had helped. I stepped under the warm spray and washed away two months of grime.

When I got out of the shower, I found clean clothes waiting for me beside the sink and a new toothbrush. I changed, brushed both my hair and my teeth—I'd need a haircut as I'd gone really shaggy—and went searching for Sei. I found him curled up in his king-sized bed in the master bedroom. Baby monitor clutched in his fist.

I took it from him and set it on the nightstand then crawled in beside him. "When's the last time you ate?" I asked.

"I had a sandwich a while ago."

I wondered how long a while ago was, but wasn't going to push. He needed sleep.

"Sorry about Gabe," he whispered. "He should have stayed to help you now that you're back. Did you eat?"

"Yes, Luca brought me home."

Seiran stiffened. "I'm not sure I like him."

"Why?" I asked. Wondering his take. "You were gung-ho for me dating him before I went to ground."

"He's working for Max."

"That's also not news." Did Sei know about Galloway? Did Max know about Galloway? Crap, I hated being involved in the middle of all of this.

Seiran looked away. "He says Gabe is in trouble."

"He might be right."

Seiran said nothing.

I sighed. "We will figure this out." Though I wasn't sure how exactly that was going to happen.

"Luca says Gabe's not right. That something is off in his head." Sei's tone indicated he wasn't all that uncertain Luca wasn't right anymore. "I thought it was just the babies. Extra stress, you know. But he's been distant a while. He should have stayed to welcome you back at least."

"He should be here," I agreed. "Not because of me, but because you need him. Luca is not the one who made me go to ground." He might be part of this whole mess, but I'd been losing it before I'd ever met him. "Gabe should have seen the warning signs before I got as bad as I did." I could have hurt people. Only now, with my mind clear, no hint of the monster creeping up, did I realize how far I'd gone into the madness. Almost a revenant. Was that what Gabe had called it? Only I'd still felt emotion. Just an insatiable need to destroy, feed, and rage.

"I thought he'd help bring you back."

"Who? Gabe?"

"Luca," Seiran corrected.

"And he didn't?" Had I just dreamed of him being at my grave playing cards?

"He said he did. I know he was there. The visitor log

scans everyone in and out. Both he and Con were there a lot. But nothing seemed to help." He frowned and looked away. "I wanted to give you my blood. Would have soaked the ground with it, or even tried to pull you out, but Gabe refused. Said it wasn't my place, that you'd wake when you were ready."

"He's been at this longer than either of us. The whole undead thing," I pointed out. The idea of Seiran ripping me from the grave gave me nightmares. It was probably a kindness on Gabe's part to not let Seiran do that.

"He's been off for a while. Even before the twins were born. I thought it was stress from my new job and work, and the Tri-Mega…" He sighed as I wrapped my arms around him and buried us both under the covers. It wasn't something I would normally have done, but he looked for a minute like he was just going to fall apart.

He began to sob, a heart wrenching sound that actually had me tearing up. I fought it and just held him. "He's not been himself for a long time. I've been denying it." He sniffled and wiped at his eyes. "Not since Matthew put a knife in his chest and we dug him up. Was I wrong to bring him back?" Seiran asked. "Did I break him? Or was it my love that broke him? Our commitment?" He buried his face in my chest. "For years I put him off, refused to settle down in fear of just this. All I ever do is fuck everything up."

Funny how his words echoed what Galloway had said. Broken by love. I wasn't sure that was quite it. Maybe Gabe needed to go to ground and not have Sei pull him out of it. Maybe that had been part of it, but not all of it. Gabe was old enough to know better. "It's a lot of chaos for someone who's used to organization," I told Sei. "I think you both need time to adapt to the changes. And it sounds like the world has gone a little nuts while I was out."

His subdued attitude toward my presence was odd. Sure, I was clean now, but the apartment around us was still in disarray. A consequence of having children. But even this was a lot for both of them. Clothes heaped in a basket, some dirty, some clean, the bed unmade. The kitchen counters packed with bottles and baby supplies. Sei smelled vaguely of chemicals. "Did they put you on medication?"

"And upped my dose," he whispered. "I get shots every day now. I didn't want to. Jamie insisted. I've been having some bad panic attacks. Hasn't been this bad in years. A couple times a day. Haven't been to work, but they granted me paternity leave anyway. Am supposed to start back tomorrow."

Gabe should have been helping with that. Their connection had stabilized Seiran. Unless it wasn't Seiran who was unstable and it was Gabe's chaos leaking through. Then we were all in trouble. "Sounds like the world is sort of driving us that way. To fear everything."

Sei snorted. "Nothing scares you."

"A lot of things scare me. You having kids scares me. How crazy fucking powerful are those kids gonna be?"

"They are just babies," Sei defended.

Yep. Just babies to the Pillar of Earth and a woman almost his equal. "They do anything weird yet?"

Seiran hesitated.

"Ronnie?"

"I heard them when they were still in the womb."

That didn't surprise me. It had seemed like he'd been talking to them for a while. "Okay. And now?"

"It's hard to understand them now. They are louder, yet not as clear? I thought it would be easier once they were born. Gabe says it's all in my head. But I wake up when they do. I know if they want to eat or need to be cleaned or held. But it's just me. Two babies at once is hard. I know Hanna wants to be here. She needs to heal first. I thought Gabe would be more involved…"

"What about Jamie and Kelly? Can they help?"

"Jamie tries, but he's working and Kelly has school. I can't make them take care of babies that aren't theirs. They've been having some issues anyway. Fighting a lot. I'm worried it's because of me so I'm trying to leave them alone to sort it out."

"Okay, but you didn't sign up for this daddy gig alone. Ally should be able to help even if Hanna can't, right?"

"She doesn't like the babies," Sei said.

"How can she not like your babies? They're adorable little spit and poop makers. And half Hanna's, whom she's married to."

"'Cause they aren't hers." Sei buried his face in the pillow. "She makes excuses to not help or see them. Even when Hanna tries to push. And she's cold to me when she does come over. I don't want to war with her because they aren't her blood. She's even pushing Hanna to give me full custody. We agreed to half, but that was before Hanna got so sick from having the babies. I think I've gotten more help from Bryar than anyone else."

"The fairy?" I didn't see him much but knew he lived more upstairs in the plants that bloomed in Sei and Kelly's apartment than down here. "Where's he off to tonight?"

"Some meeting with other fairies. He's not all that good with babies. Follows instructions well, but apparently they have kids and after a few weeks they are grown enough to live on their own."

"Scary," I told him.

"Yeah. I think he was a little disappointed when I told him human babies don't grow that fast."

"Ah, but they do!" I teased him and got up, pushing the blankets around him. "Before you know it they'll be dating and off having babies of their own. Get some sleep. I'll keep an eye on the babies while I watch some TV and read some news on the computer. I need to get caught up on what I missed in two months."

"Seventy-six days. We tried to wake you," Seiran said. "Soaked the ground in blood. And everyone visited to talk to you. Even Jamie, though he grumbled about it. Tresler too, but I didn't stick around to find out what he had to say to you. He's creepy with a capital C. I don't know why you slept so long."

"It's okay. It's not like I was gone years. And I actually feel pretty good."

"Yeah?" He looked at me funny.

"Why wouldn't I?"

"You're much calmer than you were before. I'm not sure if this is real or if I've fallen asleep in the nursery again."

I smacked his ass, hard enough to sting my hand. "Feel that, Ronnie?"

"Ow, damn you."

"See, you're not sleeping, but you should be. Now get some rest. I've got baby duty."

"K. Thanks. Your phone is in the desk drawer. You left it in the coat. Gabe put the money you had in your pocket in your bank account. Oh!" He rolled over and dug in the drawer beside the bed, then pulled out a bracelet. "I made this for you."

"I'm not really a friendship bracelet kind of guy," I told him, but held out my hand. It was a thick leather cord with purple, blue, and green beads on it. They felt like glass, and when I slid my fingers over them, a sleepy sense of calm warmth eased through me.

"I made them from your grave dirt," Seiran said. "They should help keep your energy up when you're out and about." He laid back down and closed his eyes. "They don't work at all for Gabe anymore. He won't even wear them anyway."

This was all a big clusterfuck. I clipped the bracelet onto

my right wrist. "Thanks, Ronnie." The warmth of the bracelet rolled up my arm, and spread through my body slowly, uncomfortable at first in its intensity, but then it lapped away like waves on a beach, leaving behind a tingling of life I hadn't realized I'd been lacking. "Wow. Maybe glass bead bracelets will become my new kink."

Seiran cracked the barest of smiles for me.

"Sleep now," I commanded. I tugged the blanket over him and turned off the light before grabbing the baby monitor and heading to the living room. If the babies stirred I'd probably hear them without the help of an electronic device since I could hear their little hearts beating in the next room. I could even tell when Sei finally drifted off to sleep by the sound of his breathing.

Weird. I'd not been able to do that before. Gabe should have been here to explain it to me, which just pissed me off. What was wrong with him?

Seiran was twenty-three. He was the Pillar of earth, researcher for the Magical Investigations department of the Dominion, the father of newborn twins, and Focus to one of the most powerful vampires alive. How the hell did Gabe think he could just walk away? I thought about Max Hart and how he hadn't taken responsibility for Luca until Luca's mother had dropped him on Max's doorstep. Maybe it was a vampire thing. If so, it really sucked and I totally planned on giving the big guy a piece of my mind.

I plugged in my phone so it would charge then pulled up the grocery ordering website that Sei always used. The cupboards were almost bare and the fridge had no food in it but was stocked with QuickLife. What the hell? The freezer was packed with frozen blood packs, all untouched but dated. I grabbed one and nuked it. Then opened the cupboard below the sink to find the recycle bin. Sure enough the blue bin was full of QuickLife bottles. How much of this stuff was Gabe drinking? He said we'd need two to three bottles a day. This was more like ten to fifteen. Crap. I needed to talk to him about that.

At least Seiran had his password saved as well as his normal grocery list. I checked through it and added a few things for the babies before ordering a quick delivery. I began to pick up the apartment. Habit ingrained even after only living with them a few months. The babies slept pretty soundly, though I did hear them stir once or twice, which had Seiran tossing and turning. Mizuki opened his eyes to stare at me once when I'd entered the room to look at them. His blue eyes glowing in the dark.

Yeah, that wasn't normal. I put my finger to my lips and mimicked closing my eyes. Mizuki blinked twice, slower each time and fell back to sleep. Yeah, so not normal babies.

CHAPTER 13

My phone buzzed now that it had enough juice, telling me I had several text messages. A lot from Luca. A lot from Con, lots of short texts separated over a series of days and even weeks. They had both apparently been texting me the entire time I was in the ground. I sent Con a quick text letting him know I was back and at Gabe's place. He responded immediately that he was upstairs and would be right down.

Quietly. I wrote back. *I'm babysitting the next generation of Pillars.*

All I got back was a thumbs up. The elevator dinged a few moments later. I was grateful the ding didn't wake anyone. Con rushed into the condo looking like he'd just dragged himself out of bed. He smelled of warmth, sweat, and cotton. The tank top, pajama pants, and slippers attested to the fact that he'd been sleeping somewhere.

He raced across the room and had his arms around me before I could think to react. His grip almost crushing. I didn't realize he'd wrapped himself around me and buried my face in his neck before I smelled his blood, close to the skin. I wasn't hungry, at least not unbearably so.

"Hey, it's okay," I said to him, returning his embrace and patting his back, while breathing in the scent of him. He didn't smell like the nectar that Luca did, but it was almost as good, this sense of peace and home. "I'm back, sort of don't remember being gone long, but I'm back. The world has gone to shit while I was gone. Thought you were supposed to hold it together for me." I half joked.

Con pulled away enough to grip my face in his hands, staring intently into my eyes. "Don't leave like that again."

"Wasn't planning on doing it the first time," I defended.

Con growled a fiercely angry sound that tightened my balls and made me hard as a rock. Fuck.

Then he kissed me.

Not some brush of the lips or peck on the cheek, but a full devouring, suck on my tongue kiss. At first I was at a loss, trying to understand what was happening. My body reacting to him like we were attached to an electric circuit. I opened my mouth, taking his tongue, tasting his lips, swallowing his gasps as our hips moved together. Friction amazing after wanting it forever.

His hold on my face just shy of pain, and so fucking good. I trembled, reaching a hand up to cup the back of his head and change the angle, pressing us both backward until he tripped onto the couch, dragging me on top of him. He let out a little oomph, but Con slid his hand down my back, to the top of my jeans and beneath the fabric to squeeze my ass. I didn't like to bottom anymore, but if that's what he needed I could make it work.

I growled at him, nipping his jaw, while my hips ground against his. He stiffened, his passion fading away, and I thought for a minute, he'd come, but the scent of fear hit my nose. I froze.

"Con?" I whispered, pulling away to look at him. His eyes were squeezed shut. "Con?"

"Just need a minute," he whispered.

I scrambled off of him, realizing we both looked disheveled and I was supposed to be babysitting newborns. I listened for the twins, but heard only their steady breathing and heartbeats. Seiran too, still fast asleep. At least we hadn't been too loud.

Con didn't move. At least not consciously. A fine tremor ran through him. Barely visible, but I was a vampire and little changes didn't escape me. Had I done something?

"Con?" I reached for him. He put a hand up to ward me off.

"I thought I was ready," he muttered, still not looking at me.

"I would never push you..." It hadn't even been me who'd started it. Con had always been on my do not touch list. Fuck. Back a few hours and already fucking things up. "I'm sorry."

"It wasn't you," Con said. He sat up, folding himself in half to bow over his knees. "Not really. I mean, I felt teeth on my jaw."

I hadn't broken the skin. It wasn't even a real bite. "Did I hurt you?"

"No. No, just...I thought I was ready. It connected in my brain. You being a vampire, the teeth, the fear." He shook his head. "I need to work on it more with my therapist."

I hadn't known he'd been seeing one. "Okay." My stomach ached with the idea that this could be the end for us. A beginning and an ending all at once. Fuck. "Con, I don't want..."

"We're fine," Con promised.

But it didn't feel like we were fine. It felt like we were breaking. "You're my best friend, Con."

He nodded. "Yeah. Ditto, right?" He looked toward the elevator and I knew he wanted to escape.

"It's okay. You can go," I told him. "Maybe we can talk when you're more awake, eh? Not at o-dark-thirty or some shit."

Con nodded. He got up slowly, still not looking at me. "I'm sorry, Sam."

So was I. "We're good," I told him, putting more confidence in the words than I felt. "Once I'm done watching the rug rats we can play some games, yeah?"

He smiled. "Yeah. Games would be good." I let him leave and sat down on the couch staring at the small remains of the mess I had yet to clean up. Alone in the silence of night was always hard. I didn't want to be alone. How weird was that? I had spent most of my life wishing people would just leave me the fuck alone, now it was the last thing I needed.

I could crawl into bed with Seiran and he probably wouldn't care, but I wasn't tired, and didn't want to chance waking him when he obviously needed the sleep. I picked up my phone and scrolled down to view the messages I hadn't read, which was most of it.

Luca's first text right after I'd gone to ground made me pause. The answer began a long list of daily texts.

Answer to your question: A vampire asked me to be your cibo. You seemed nice when we talked, a good match, and I agreed to meet you.

You weren't my first newbie vamp.

I thought it would be okay, just like any other assignment.

Then I saw you sitting there at the club and you just looked so lonely.

I thought "that's me." Alone in the crowd. Invisible. Unlovable. Again, I thought we'd be a good match.

You rejected me. I was hurt. Angry. Stupid. Followed you.

Found you at the coffee shop, again alone and lost.

You remind me of myself. The part of myself that I bury to stay safe.

Not that it's a bad thing...

We fought and you were so hot even covered in my blood I wanted you to fuck me.

You've got a mean right hook.

But you ran from me.

What did I do wrong?

Seiran says I'm too pushy.

But you're a strong guy, you can handle pushy. I think you like pushy in some ways. I can be that if you need.

I liked dancing with you. Kissing you.

Sorry I went territorial on you. I should have known better. I'm working on it.

ABSOLUTION

My dad says Gabe isn't training you very well.

You shouldn't have had to go to ground so soon.

You should have been more prepared.

Gabe is pissed that my dad won't take his calls.

Seiran is mad at me. He acts like he's the ruler of your life. It drives me nuts because I know he's just trying to protect you.

That's not his place though. I want it to be mine.

Sigh.

You've been asleep a long time.

Things are bad topside. Folks are talking war.

We're pretty sure it's the QuickLife.

Something in the formula.

Don't drink the synthetic crap.

When you're back, pick me.

I talk to you sometimes when I'm visiting, but I don't know if you hear me.

I miss our online chats and your sarcastic emails.

The weather is warming up, you should wake up now.

I lost a cage fight yesterday. My face hurts from the beating I took. My pride hurts more.

Will you fight me again?

The lost fight was less than a week ago, though he'd looked okay when he'd brought me home. Crap, he was sappy. Was it funny that even his random texts made something in my stomach clench? Damn Luca Depacio for getting in my head.

I sent him a text.

You still awake?

It was almost one in the morning.

Yes. An immediate reply.

You're kind of a text freak. Texting me the whole time I was to ground. Why not just keep a love diary or something?

Jerk.

Asshole.

Your asshole if you want it.

I laughed out loud and had to cover my mouth so I didn't wake the babies or Seiran. Crap where had that come from? When was the last time I'd laughed? Grade school maybe? Fuck.

Come over.

Would Con get mad? Was I cheating on Con by seeing Luca if Con had never told me he wanted me before? Wait, he had, I just thought he was being nice. Fuck. I so didn't need this insanity in my head. Going to ground should have fixed all my life troubles, right? I laughed again. Life. I was a vampire. I didn't have a life.

Seiran's? My phone buzzed. Technically Seiran's place was upstairs, where I was pretty sure Con was staying.

Gabe's. He's not here. Seiran is asleep.

Give me ten.

Be careful. I sent him.

I opened Seiran's computer and began to surf through weeks of news stories about vampires gone wild. Not mild stuff like flashing tits or anything. No this was smashing windows and randomly feeding off people who passed them in the streets. Apparently everything began here. What an odd place for a vampire war. Why not California or New York?

But then it did make sense. Gabe was here. So was Max. Apparently Galloway and now Tresler who had done several interviews for the press citing that he would tighten the reins on his people until they behaved. The four most powerful vampires in the world were all in one place, not a coincidence.

Was Galloway right? Was Tresler trying to get Gabe out of the picture? And what about the QuickLife. Luca said not to drink it and Gabe was drinking it by the ton.

I sipped at the reheated old blood. It didn't taste any better than I remembered. And since my belly wasn't whining that it was starving, I was okay with just sipping it. Why couldn't the bloodlust have been this manageable before?

I researched the internet about the rise in vampire attacks. The two that I'd been accused of were actually done by a Wisconsin man who'd crossed the border to try to hide his kills. He'd been caught by Mike—Gabe's right-hand man—and publicly executed. I didn't watch the fire knowing it would be something I'd never be able to erase from my head.

There were hundreds of reports. Christ. What the hell was happening out there? More were popping up across the country, but most centered here. I dialed Mike just as the grocery order arrived. I directed them quietly to the kitchen and just to leave the bags and boxes there so I could go through them. The group of three humans were efficient, silent, and done before Mike picked up his phone.

"Are you awake or did someone steal your phone?" he asked.

"I'm awake. I think. The world has kind of gone crazy while I've been to ground."

"That happens a lot actually. I went to ground in the fifties. Woke up in the seventies. Longest nap I'd ever had, felt like the blink of an eye but the world had gone nuts. War and drugs and madness. The free sex part was the best part of it. Oh and weed. Weed is great."

I liked Mike. Probably should have talked to him before going to ground. "You slept over a decade then? And I thought two and a half months was bad."

"Nah. The older you get the longer you get between, but when it hits, it hits for a long time. Could be decades or even centuries before we wake up."

Hadn't Galloway slept for several centuries? "So it will get longer?"

"Not if you do it regularly enough. Most of us older

vampires try to go to ground once a decade or so. Keeps us from getting overtired. Then it's a week to a month on average. Back before the humans knew about us, we'd go to ground each night for protection, never had these long naps then. But that's only been the last century. No idea why yours was so long since you're still so new. You feeling better though? More in control?"

"Yeah. Though everyone else seems to have lost control. And Gabe…"

Mike was silent for a minute. The call box buzzed from upstairs. It was Luca. I unlocked the elevator to let him down. I had to ask before Luca was close enough to hear. "Does he need to go to ground?"

Mike's sigh was heavy. "He won't. You know he won't."

"Any idea how long it's been for him?"

"Too long. Centuries, I think. Before he met Seiran he was little more than a zombie, existing within the set rules. Lots of murmurs back then of him looking for an easy way to die. Then he met Seiran and he changed. I'd been watching him deteriorate for a while, and poof, like magic, he was the guy I remember from the days we first met, happy and willing to live. When Sei buried him after that Roman thing, he should have left him until he was ready to dig himself out."

Fuck. That's what worried me. "How are you holding up?"

"I'm okay."

"Nothing like any of the other vamps are experiencing?"

"No. No more crazy than usual."

A thought occurred to me. "Do you drink QuickLife?"

"Nope. Wouldn't touch that shit. I've a couple regulars that I circulate through not unlike a *cibo*, only not officially designated as them. It's cheaper for me that way. *Cibo*s aren't cheap."

"Lovers rather than blood whores."

"Mundane, yes, but effective. You're better off with the real thing if you can get it. I've been hearing rumors about the QuickLife being part of the problem. So steer clear."

Meanwhile Gabe was drinking it like water.

"Luca tell you that?"

"Heard it from some of his people I'm sure. Could have been him. He's in the bar enough. Hot for a blood whore. I'd do him, couldn't afford him, but I'd do him. That boy looks like he comes from expensive tastes."

"He's Max Hart's son and my blood whore, though Gabe is paying him." I was a little possessive and hadn't known Mike was into men. But again, maybe he was just into whatever was attractive food, like a good-looking burger might lure people in. "Thanks, Mike." I told him as Luca stepped out of the elevator, and hung up the phone.

"Bed is off limits," I told Luca. "There are babies in my room."

Luca nodded and joined me in the kitchen as I put away the groceries. Hopefully Sei hadn't moved anything around since the last time I'd been here so I wouldn't freak him out if I put something away wrong.

"Heard about the babies. It was huge news on TV. Even with all the vampire crap going on. They are like baby celebrities or something. Only Sei pretty much went into hiding the second they came home," Luca said. "No one has seen even a glimpse of them. That's why security is so heavy outside of the building. Lots of paparazzi hanging around. If this is how bad it is for his kids, I can only imagine what your friend Seiran grew up with."

Prince of the Dominion, I had once teased Seiran. And while the witch hated it, it was more than a little true. Tanaka Rou had created an empire of power despite her parents cutting her off for bearing a male child. She had made it clear several times that her power would go to

Seiran. I wasn't sure if she meant the inheritance ceremony or just her wealth and title. Seiran did not need any more power. I wasn't sure he was in control of what he currently had.

"Gabe left. Sei needed him and he just left. Like he couldn't handle the babies crying," I told Luca.

"Some people can't. That's why they don't have kids. Gabe's pretty old. I'd be surprised if he never had any, but not wanting them now makes sense. He's sort of set in his ways. My dad is the same. I was raised mostly by nannies. The Hallmark shit with dads reading to you and kissing you good night, that's not my life."

"Mine either and my dad wasn't a vampire."

"So am I forgiven?" Luca asked suddenly.

"Not completely. And I don't want to talk about Galloway or whatever you do for him." I paused and looked at the hot guy who said he wanted to be mine. "Are you fucking him?"

"Pretty sure Galloway's asexual. He has groupies galore throwing themselves at him and he's not interested in any of them. Uses them as blood whores, that's all, but he has a menagerie of them."

"So he's not drinking from you either?"

"Nope. I'm your blood whore."

I felt my face heat. "Heard that part?"

Luca shrugged. "It's pretty close to the truth. Most *cibos* are blood whores. They don't have regular jobs. They use the excuse of recovering from the blood loss not to work all day. For humans, that's pretty much spot on, they don't regenerate blood cells as fast. A vampire would need a dozen human *cibos* to survive. I'm not human, and I have a job."

"You work for your dad," I said.

"Yep. Mostly just as a liaison. I schedule meetings, gather research, work up documents and get them approved by lawyers or finance people or whatever. It's a boring job I could do in my sleep, but I make good money. Max says it teaches me leadership skills. Mostly I think it just keeps me out of his way."

I opened the fridge to put stuff away and just stared at the QuickLife. What if it was like booze? Could it addict you and then make you nuts? Maybe that was why Gabe had come unglued. I began pulling bottles out, opening them and dumping them down the sink.

"Do you know what's in it?" I asked Luca after he joined me at the sink to run the water and empty the bottles. I'd smelled it and tasted it before, but couldn't say there was anything that made me think it was addictive. The stuff was awful. Like watered down Gatorade, the sugar-free kind that tried really hard to be real despite the fluorescent-colored additives.

"I'm not a scientist and Galloway doesn't believe in them, so I have no idea. Did someone alter the formula or has it always been funny? Maybe the real issue is that it's not like blood at all. So vampires drink it, thinking it helps with the thirst, but only makes it worse? How would we tell?"

"Have you talked to Max?"

"Max has always thought the synthetic blood was a sham. And he's wrapped in a big sports sale thing, so I've barely heard from him. Max always puts Max first. Power and money are his focus. I think that's why he's never had a real Focus."

"It's weird that you call your dad Max."

"He's never really been dad. Haven't seen him in a while anyway. He was more interested in seeing you when he got here than me." His words weren't bitter, just matter of fact.

I looked Luca over for the first time since I'd woken up. Really looked him over. He looked tired, and a little thinner. He also said he'd recently lost when before he'd made it sound like he always won. "When was the last time you ate?" I asked.

"I had pasta at Bucca's. Surprised you can't still smell the garlic on me." He patted his stomach.

"I mean blood."

His face shut down and he turned away to grab another stack of bottles.

"So your dad's been absent, Galloway is a bastard, and I've been mostly dead for a few months. Am I the last one you got to snack on? You have to feed on a vampire, right?" I took the bottle he was holding and stared at him until he looked at me.

He nodded. "That went sort of bad. So maybe we shouldn't repeat it."

"Because you went nuts."

He sighed and leaned against the counter. "I was totally stupid. Kenrick always gets in my shit. I dunno why I let him. But it was so good and then it was like he was suddenly stepping all over what was *mine.* I can't recall a time when I've been that possessive. Not since I was a kid at least."

I stepped in close and wrapped my arms around him, hugging him. "I'm broken, Luca. I don't know if I should trust you, but damn I like you anyway. How fucked up is that? Drink from me you hot bastard so we can finish being domestic and putting stuff away before the babies wake up with another dirty diaper."

Luca chuckled. "You're just the little daddy's helper, aren't you?"

"Play nice, or no bite," I told him as he nuzzled my neck. It was only fair. I'd taken a truck load from him earlier. His bite was mild and sweet. Mouth sucking away at me and I just leaned into him. It wasn't as erotic as last time, likely because it was more necessary. He drank deeper only to finally come up gasping, and staggering.

"Wow. You weren't that potent before," he grumbled and licked my wound to heal it. I helped him to the couch. "Oh shiny," Luca stared at me his eyes dilated like he was high. Had my blood changed somehow?

"Eat something solid, maybe that will help." That's what they told drunk people to do to absorb and dilute some of the alcohol right? I pulled out a banana and handed it to him. Even had to unpeel the end for him.

"I'd rather eat your banana," he said, but took it anyway.

"Oh my God, you're one of those drunks, eh?"

"Did you just say eh? What's next? Ya-sure-you-betcha?" Luca laughed at his own joke. "Minnesota humor."

And the man was a total loon. "I'm not sure you should be drinking from me regularly if it makes you this loopy."

"Oh, I'm sure," Luca said waving his hand. "This is fantastic. Never knew what it felt like to be drunk before. This is great!"

"Yeah? Maybe you're a chatty drunk?" I asked him. "Finally loosen those tight lips of yours and answer some questions?"

"You can loosen all my tight places if you want," Luca said.

I groaned. "Bad pickup lines, great."

"They work fine on Con," Luca grumbled.

I frowned at him. "What?" Had he and Con…?

Luca shrugged. "He's hot, what can I say? The tattoos and the brooding. Pretends to be a bad boy, but so isn't. Meanwhile you're all clean-cut and adorable and a total bad boy in disguise."

"I'm not adorable."

"Yeah, you are. Even all glammed up like you were on our date. Then you get all red-eyed and brooding, which makes me hard enough to spill in my jeans."

"But you and Con?" That confused me. "He's terrified of vampires."

"I'm not a vampire yet."

That was splitting hairs pretty finely. "You and Con have been having sex?" The idea should have pissed me off, but instead it filled my head with images of the two of them together. Fuck that was hot. Con's tattoo covered body with Luca's Abercrombie physique? Wow, who knew that was a kink I had?

"Sure."

"But you can't bite him."

"Wouldn't do me any good to bite him. He's not a vampire. Until I'm actually a vampire, all other blood just tastes like blood. Which is kind of gross."

I thought about that for a minute. Gabe said death was magic just like earth or water, an element of its own. Maybe he was right. If Luca needed the *magic* of death found only in vampire blood because he wasn't yet undead, that made sense. "Have you shown Con your teeth?" Luca had fangs too.

"He knows they're there. I don't pretend to bite him. We're good. I give really good head. He's got a nice cock. Likes it a little rougher than you'd think for a guy who tries to pretend he's a badass."

I tried to imagine that. Okay, that made me hard. I shoved away the last of the groceries, and stopped in the spare room to check on the babies again. Still asleep. Seiran was also out cold. I could sense the deepness of his sleep like a thrumming lull of the earth's energy.

"Are you mad at me?" Luca asked.

"I'm not sure," I answered honestly, needing time to think. "Am I just blood to you? Have I been wasting my time thinking we should have more than just a blood whore relationship?"

"No," Luca said firmly. "I like you. More than just your blood. I knew that before we even met from all our conversations online."

"And Con?"

"I like him also. I thought you did too?"

"Are you suggesting…?" Was he? Or was he too drunk to realize what he was saying. "That we all fuck?"

Luca grinned. "Oh, that would be the bomb. You fuck me while I fuck Con? Wow, your blood makes me super horny too. Or we could both take him. I bet he'd be up for that. It's been a long time since I double-teamed anyone."

Okay, that thought almost had me spurting in my pants. I frowned at Luca, trying to be stern and thoughtful instead of horny. Porn fantasies were rarely reality. "What if he's not into that?"

"What, us? I know that's not right 'cause he's already doing me and has wanted you for ages."

"Bottoming," I clarified. Had Luca topped Con?

"Aw. I think he's verse. We haven't gone that far yet, but I don't think he's as much of a top as he pretends to be. He likes to be told what to do. Likes when I grip his hair and fuck his mouth. He makes lots of noise when I finger his ass." Luca's gaze trailed over me. "You can top me anytime."

I sighed. "You're drunk."

"A little, but it's still true." He laid back on the couch with a dramatic sigh. "Take me, my sweet prince."

I scowled at him. "I'm not a sweet prince."

He began to laugh, but slapped his hands over his mouth to stifle the sound. "Forgot…Babies. Okay, how about we make out then, you badass son of a bitch?" He held out his arms.

"No sex," I told him. Not with Sei and the babies able to wake up any minute.

Luca pouted. "You keep saying that to me. Am I not sexy

enough for you? Should I cover myself in tattoos like Constantine?"

Sprawled as he was across the couch, his body relaxed, tight pants tented with an erection I knew to be impressive, he was sex. His whole being screamed sex. And yeah I wanted him. I just didn't want more nightmares. "You're hot. Someday I'll do you. Just not while babies, with more power than either of us can ever imagine, sleep in the next room."

He grinned. "That's awesome. And we can do Con too."

"I don't want to fuck up what Con and I have."

"Why would you?"

"Because sex has a way of messing up everything."

"Or being really good," Luca said.

I sighed. Nothing was ever that easy anymore. "The world is in chaos. I don't think sex is on the top ten most important concerns right now."

"For vampires, maybe. But you either spend your life worrying or you live it. Your friend Seiran spends his life worrying. What joy does he get out of it? Do you want to be like that?"

Sei was more than a little neurotic. "He can't help it."

"Maybe. Or maybe it's just so normal for him that he hasn't realized he doesn't have to live that way? You once told me when we were talking online that you spent your mortal life wishing you could die. Now you spend your immortal life afraid to live. Is that what you want?" Luca waved his open arms. "Come here. No sex required. Even badass sons of bitches like to snuggle sometimes."

I gave him a skeptical glare, but really he was right. I'd been asleep a long time. Spent months barely existing on the edge of insanity. A lifetime without really being touched by anyone who wasn't ultimately out to hurt me.

Fuck. I was just like Seiran. Afraid to really live. I was a fucking vampire. Almost unbreakable. Alive, or not really? Did that even matter?

And there was Luca, offering nothing more than physical contact. Would I be just like Seiran and push everyone away? Or embrace something that could either be heaven or hell? What the hell, it's not like I wasn't used to a little pain.

I crawled onto the couch with him. Letting him wrap his arms around me, and rested my head on the decorative pillow beside his. It didn't matter in that moment that we were both hard, or that the world was caving down around us. For the first time in what felt like my entire life, I just let go of the worry, the expectations, and the instinct to run, and settled into his embrace. I closed my eyes and breathed in his delicious scent, promising myself a little bit of rest, even if it was only for today.

CHAPTER 14

The babies woke around four for a diaper change. I got to them before they even began to cry. Luca was surprisingly efficient with baby clean up. And I was thrilled that we got them fed and back to sleep without waking Seiran, the man probably hadn't slept well in a while, and there was no sign of Gabe.

I texted Jamie, wondering just what was going on there. His phone buzzed back some auto text about him working a shift at the hospital and would be available when the shift was over. I was a little surprised when he showed up just after five a.m. looking tired but a lot relieved.

"You're awake," he said as he stepped off the elevator.

"Yep. What was your first clue?" I groused at him.

"Forever a smart ass." He fought a smile and shook his head, then frowned at Luca.

Luca sighed. "Yeah, yeah. Persona non grata. I get it. I'll go upstairs and crawl into bed with Con. He won't mind the company." Luca pulled me into a hug and kissed me lightly on the lips before letting go to smack my ass and head to the elevator. "Text me when you're up later."

I nodded. The sun would be up in a little more than an hour. There would have to be a changing of the guards. Luca left and I stared at Jamie wondering if he'd answer questions, and where to start.

"What the fuck is going on?" I began because bullshit wasn't something I liked to wade through.

"You didn't look at the news?"

"Not that." I waved my hand dismissing the whole vampire chaos. That was more my problem than his. "With you, Seiran, Kelly, and Gabe?"

Jamie sighed and seemed to deflate. He sat down on one of the barstools at the kitchen counter. "It's complicated."

"Right, 'cause that's new? I'm pretty sure you all have complicated for middle names. What the hell, Jamie? I thought you'd be here to help Seiran with the babies?"

His face flushed pink. "I want to. Gabe and I have had some screaming matches about that. He doesn't want me to interfere. Kelly wants me to take Seiran away from him. But…"

"But what? Gabe is unstable. I watched him walk out as Seiran and the twins were crying. That's not him. I barely know the man and know that's not him. He's lost weight and was dressed like he was headed to a kegger. What the flying fuck?"

Jamie flinched. "I thought they were perfect for each other. Gabe took such good care of Seiran. Now he's just —cold."

"I don't think Gabe is really Gabe anymore," I offered.

"That's what your friend Luca says."

"I don't think Luca is as young as he looks. His dad also happens to be one of the most powerful vampires in the world, so maybe he knows what he's talking about?"

Jamie scoffed. "Yeah, I looked him up. He's seventy-five.

And his dad…Maxwell Hart, how do we know he didn't do something to Gabe? Start all this mess?"

Luca was seventy-five? Holy shit. Talk about good genes. "Now you sound like Seiran, paranoid and afraid of everything."

"Isn't that how we should be? Aren't you the king of that yourself?" Jamie threw back.

Well yeah, experience was a bitch. "I have seen nothing so far that leads me to believe that Max is fucking with Gabe. Seiran said Max refuses to talk to him, even on the phone. Max has kept out of Gabe's side of the city and seems more focused on business than vampire bullshit."

"Which is weird."

I shrugged. Who was I to tell old vampires how to socialize? "What about you and Kelly? Seiran said you've been fighting."

"About all of this." He let out a long deep breath like he was trying to keep calm. "And he has another training offer from the former water Pillar. She wants to help him dive. The Dominion thinks spending time in his element will increase his control of his power."

And Kelly was afraid to swim in the ocean for fear of never returning to humanity, but I had often wondered how much it limited him. "He has you to come back to."

"And if I'm not enough?"

"Fuck you, Browan. That boy adores you. He's as moon-eyed over you as Seiran was over Gabe." Was. Fuck. Were Seiran and Gabe over? And since they were metaphysically bound, how could that be possible.

Jamie bowed his head. "I don't know what to do. I can't leave unless I know Seiran is taken care of, and Kelly really wants to go. *Needs* to go, I think. Kelly thinks they need time apart. He believes Luca when he says something is wrong with Gabe, with most vampires. But what's the solution to that? Kill them all like the government suggests? Even if we went to that extreme, killing Gabe might kill Seiran, which in turn would cause a catastrophic world event which could kill millions if not the entire planet."

"Whoa, big guy. Hold up those black-eyed horses of doom for a minute. No one is suggesting we kill Gabe."

"The government has. They've even contacted me to see if any of us are willing to do it in private. Only my warnings about what it might do to Seiran, and the rest of the world, has kept them at bay," Jamie said.

"Well isn't that just the good old American way? If it can't control it, kill it? Fuckers." I didn't think Gabe was the root of the problem. He hadn't been this bad when I'd gone to ground, though he had been floundering for a while. "Gabe needs to go to ground. Not in the permanent sort of way. More in a very necessary nap sort of way."

"I've suggested it to him. He snaps at me."

"Because his head is off." I recalled my own being terrified of the very thing. "He's not rational because he's fighting to keep awake when he's so far beyond exhausted, he's barely on his feet." Because that's how I had felt. Now I felt tired, sure, but more like that normal, hey I had a long day tired, than the dragging agony of exhaustion with life.

"It's not like we can just kidnap him and shove him into a plot of dirt."

I wasn't sure that was impossible. The earth had grabbed me, pulled me back like a living thing. Had that been Seiran's influence? Somehow I didn't think so. Perhaps that death magic I'd been suspecting was a whole other thing, rather than anything scientific, and had been the key. Could we get Gabe to the tomb and shove him in? That was a hard no. We'd have to trick him somehow, and Gabe always saw through that shit.

"Maybe we're overthinking this. We just have to do something to make him want to go to ground," I pointed out.

"Like what?"

"Everyone's been telling me that before he met Seiran, Gabe was just looking for a way to die."

"Okay?"

"So if we separate them, and give him an ultimatum, go to ground or you can't have him back?"

Jamie thought about that for a minute. "But Seiran is Father Earth, which means he'd have to be on board."

"Yeah, there would be no way to remove the witch without his consent, but that's okay because he has other priorities right now." I pointed toward my room where the twins slept.

"Fuck," Jamie swore, like he rarely did.

The solution was simple enough, while being complicated at the same time. "We need to get Seiran out of this situation until we can fix Gabe. You and Kelly can go do your tropical honeymoon, and Seiran can catch a break."

"Where will he be safe? He and the twins?"

"Again, Father Earth. You all worry like some old woman. He'll be fine."

"With a bunch of crazies always out to kill him or control him?" Jamie pointed out.

That was true, though I didn't think any of them could really hurt him at this point. His kids on the other hand… "He owns a giant magic house in California."

Jamie blinked at me as though the cogs were working in his head. "But who will help him with the babies?"

That was an easy enough solution too. "Tanaka."

Jamie jolted back. "No. Fuck no! Do you know what she did to Seiran?"

"Sure. Mothers fail spectacularly all the time. She's a tiger mom, which I guess you wouldn't understand since it's a cultural thing. I think she's also learned a few things. She's the one changing laws in the Dominion to make them more accessible for men. Sure, it's probably because Seiran is her son, and she should have done something sooner. But she's also sort of protected by the mob. You know, the mob of witches called the Dominion?" Tanaka had spent a lot of time visiting Seiran, bringing him gifts, both for him and the babies, and providing him with books on Dominion governance to help with his job. Was she fucked up? Sure, but weren't we all. "It's not like he's a pushover anymore. He's Father fucking Earth. You all treat him with kid gloves and I think sometimes he forgets that he could blow up this rock we are on without breaking a sweat."

"What if she treats Mizuki like she treated Seiran?" Jamie said.

"He'd kill her. Hell, I would kill her." I grinned at the muscle man who shouldn't have been so afraid of a tiny Asian woman. "I'd enjoy that. I'm not a fan of bullies. I really love to teach them their place."

Jamie deflated. "I'll think about it. If I could go with them I'd feel better about it, but the house is nowhere near the coast and Kelly needs the water. Fuck," he swore again.

I shrugged. "Anyway you have about half an hour before someone else has to be on baby duty. Seiran needs the rest."

"I'll stay until he's up. I can sleep on the couch."

"And what about Kelly?"

"He's going to be up and off to school in another hour. We've been on opposite shifts for a couple of weeks. But his classes are almost done for the semester. He was going to take the summer off for the trip…"

"So you both need to get away and fuck like bunnies."

"Sam…" Jamie warned.

"What? You're cranky. Seiran's cranky. Gabe is nuts. Kelly's probably cranky. I'm the only one who isn't."

"This isn't cranky?"

"Nope," I said. "This is about as good as I get." I glared at the clock. Gabe should be back by now. He was going to be cutting it very close to sunrise. I could feel the heat of it rising even though I was underground. "Gabe needs to stop drinking QuickLife. I dumped it all out. Don't order him more."

Jamie frowned, seeming to think about that for a few minutes. "Is it that simple?"

"No," I said honestly.

"He'll unravel even faster without blood. That will kill Seiran."

"It's already killing Seiran. He thinks his love broke Gabe."

Jamie was silent for a long time. I checked on the twins and Seiran again. Everyone slept soundly. Good. I hoped they all caught up on rest a little. When I returned to the living room Jamie was on the computer.

"I blocked all the links for ordering QuickLife," Jamie said. "I'll call the store too, make sure they don't send any over."

It was a start. "There's plenty of the real blood in the freezer."

"Yeah, I've been ordering it, and keeping it stocked. Making sure it was ready for your return. I didn't think Gabe was drinking any of it."

He probably hadn't been. "Any idea where he would have gone?"

Jamie shook his head. "No, but he's out almost every night. Rarely works at the bar anymore. Mike's been running it."

Chaos. Of course, I'd wake up to fucking chaos. The sun did another insistent tug, almost six a.m. and I was going to bed. Fires could be put out later. "I'm headed to bed." I handed him the baby monitor. "Seiran said something about going back to work today? I think that's probably not a good idea."

"Agreed," Jamie said. He let out a long sigh. "I'll call Tanaka."

"Better you than me," I told him and headed to the baby's room and my bed. It smelled like Seiran. He'd obviously spent more than one night in that bed trying to rest and keep an eye on his kids. I didn't really mind. It reminded me that I was no longer in the grave, though I still had a million questions. Had I really turned into a bird? Should I tell anyone or was that just a bad idea? Not that it mattered much in that moment. The sun rose as I heard the door from the parking garage open, and Gabe's footfalls enter the apartment. I closed my eyes hoping he would finally see the light and give us all a break.

My phone beeped, and I was suddenly annoyed that I'd forgotten to silence it. At least it hadn't bothered the babies. I changed the setting and glanced at the text. It was actually a picture from Luca, in bed with Con, both looking warm and sleepy. It read:

You could be here.

Fuck.

Bastard. I texted back. *Sun's up.*

But oddly, unlike before I'd gone to ground, while it tugged at me to sleep, it wasn't a fierce smack down into unconsciousness. More of a "hey, you're pretty sleepy."

Apartment is sun-free. Blackout drapes everywhere, came the reply.

Which made sense since Seiran and Kelly both worked late hours sometimes, and Seiran was dating a vampire. I thought about it for a minute.

Jamie was here to watch after the twins and Seiran, and it wasn't like Gabe was helping me with any vampire stuff. I looked over the picture again, the two of them wrapped up in the blankets, bodies close, sleepy eyes, and bed hair. Did I want to be part of that sandwich? Stupid question. Yes. Even if I was too tired to do more than the vaguest lift in attention.

I crawled out of bed, checked on the babies again, who slept soundly, and peeked out the doorway. Jamie was alone at the counter. He glanced up as if he could feel my eyes on him. He raised a brow in question.

"Is it okay if I go upstairs to Sei's place?" Normally I wouldn't ask permission, but I didn't want to leave Sei or the twins alone with Gabe. "You're staying right? To watch over everyone?"

"I'm staying," Jamie agreed. "If you're going upstairs, I'll even be taking your bed for a bit. It's more comfortable than the couch and then I don't have to use the baby monitor which their powers keeps messing with."

I swallowed a laugh. Of course they did. Normal babies, my ass. "That's fine with me." I found my slippers and put them on before carefully leaving the room, and tiptoeing around the apartment. I took two blood packs out of the freezer to bring upstairs. No reason to freak Con out by biting Luca when I woke up hungry. I glanced at Sei's room. Would he be okay?

"He's fine," Jamie said.

That was wishful thinking. Seiran was not fine.

"He will be fine," Jamie amended. "I'm working on a few things. I'll catch you up later. Go get some sleep. If I had two attractive men waiting for me, I'd be moving my ass a lot faster."

I gaped at him. How had he known?

"They haven't been subtle, and I'm not blind," Jamie said.

"Do you think it's stupid? Am I making the wrong choice? My relationship history is for shit."

He shrugged. "No one can really know until you try, right? Love is always a crapshoot. Either you win or you lose. But you never know until you play the game. I know they are both interested in you for you, not because you have some weird amplifying power. I'd say that's a good start."

"Even with all the vampire chaos going on?"

"Only time you have guaranteed is the present."

Fuck. When did the muscleman get so damn smart? Dammit. "You've got Sei."

He nodded. "I do."

I shouldn't have cared so much. Seiran had been my arch enemy for a while. Only that had been in my own head. He never felt that way about me. More annoyed that I bothered him. Now I guess I considered him a friend. Fuck but life, or unlife if that's what I had, was complicated.

"Go," Jamie insisted quietly. "They're fine."

I rubbed the bracelet Seiran gave me and tiptoed to the elevator. "The dinger on this thing is really loud," I remarked when I pushed the button and the box appeared a few seconds later.

I sent Luca a text, *Coming.*

"Only to vampires," Jamie said. "The tone is set for your hearing range. I don't even notice it. I think Seiran hears it, but not the same way the rest of us do."

Well fuck. Something else to make me weird. I stepped into the elevator, waved goodbye and hit the button to jump up a floor. Sei and Kelly's apartment was on the inner courtyard just across the lobby. I hoped Seiran hadn't change his wards too much because there was about fifteen feet of direct sunlight separating the elevator and their front door.

The last thing I wanted was to be stuck in the lobby outside the door feeling like my skin was on fire. How long would it take before my skin actually began to burn? I hadn't braved being outside in the sunlight long enough to know.

Luca stood beside the elevator door when it opened. He had a blanket, which he wrapped around me and guided me into the apartment. As soon as the door closed we were encased in darkness and he took the blanket back. He turned the light on over the sink in the kitchen. I headed to the freezer to store the packets of blood.

"I can doctor that stuff up for you later, but it still won't taste as good as me," Luca said.

I was pretty sure that was true. "I don't want to freak out Con."

Luca nodded. Once I'd put the blood packs away he tugged me toward the bedroom. Technically it was Seiran's room. There was nothing of him in it since he lived mostly downstairs. I think the only thing that really reflected him in the room was the last remaining bookshelf filled with a handful of romance novels. My vision adjusted to the darkness enough to see Con's outline in the bed. He could have been sleeping, and I might have thought that's what his stillness was, if it hadn't been for his heartrate, which I knew was higher than his regular sleeping rate.

"You okay with this?" I asked Con, kicking off my slippers. "I can sleep on the couch."

"Come to bed," he said.

Luca climbed into the bed, setting himself in the middle. I was okay with that. If Con needed a buffer from remembering I was a vampire, that was fine. I couldn't change what I was, and he'd had just as shitty of an experience with vampires as I had.

I made my way to Luca's side of the bed and crawled in beside him. The queen-size bed should have been enough for all of us to have our spots, but Luca wrapped his arms around me and tugged me closer, throwing the blanket over us and snuggling until his face was buried in my neck. "Sleep," he said.

I could hear Con's breathing. He shifted around until he spooned Luca and could touch me. His breathing hitched a little, but he didn't bolt. I closed my eyes, bowing to the sleepiness and the heat of the bed. Their problems weren't mine, I reminded myself as I let sleep take me. I couldn't save anyone and wasn't obligated to. All I could be was me.

CHAPTER 15

I awoke in a sandwich of limbs. Luca mostly, though Con perched over us playing some sort of game on his phone. The sun was still up, which felt odd, like a tingling in my veins. A reminder perhaps. The one perk of being a vampire —or maybe it wasn't a perk—was that I never woke up hard. My dick did a little tiny jolt of "hey, that's nice" when I realized Luca's hand rested on my hip right next to it, but that was all. I'd need blood before any games were had.

Had Luca gone to bed in just a pair of tiny undies or had he stripped down to them as I slept?

The fact that Con was still in bed, awake, but unfazed, gave me hope that maybe he wasn't as terrified of me as a vampire as he let on. Did vampires die when they slept? Did I stop breathing? My heartbeat still? Did my flesh go cold? I felt warm. But that could have been Luca's heat absorbing into me. Or the zinging warmth of the bracelet still wrapped around my wrist.

Luca smelled like a steak breakfast with a side of bacon and a huge glass of orange juice. Fuck. His neck was only inches away, pulsing with sweet life that my stomach decided it really wanted with a loud grumble. Con froze and glanced our way. I jolted up out of the bed, unseating Luca, and rushed into the kitchen. The blood in the bag wouldn't be nearly as satisfying, but I wasn't going to send Con into fits today either.

Luca appeared a moment later, rubbing his eyes as he headed to the coffeepot, put in a pod and hit the button. He watched me empty a packet into a mug. I nuked the blood for almost a minute to take the chill off. Not much was going to help the flavor. It smelled like old blood I realized. I carefully lifted the warm mug out of the microwave, trying not to cringe at the smell.

Luca took a knife out of the cutting block and sliced his arm, drawing a thin line of blood. He squeezed the wound, letting the droplets pool for a few seconds. My mouth watered at the thought of licking that wound. Fuck, was I twisted or what? But he let the drops fall into my mug, squeezing a few more out before offering me his arm to lick the wound closed.

I ran my tongue along the length of it, wishing it were his cock and I was already full of blood for the day. I kept my eyes locked on his. He shivered.

"Fuck," he grumbled. "Did you mean to send me that thought?" His wound closed, and I took a sip of the blood in the mug. Not terrible. It was like adding a bit of cream to coffee. An edge of bitterness, not enough to make it good, but just enough to make it palatable.

"What thought?" I asked, watching Luca rinse the knife then put it in the dishwasher. He picked up the mug of coffee and took a large gulp, black.

"Of you sucking my cock."

I had thought it, but hadn't realized I'd been sending it. Was that what Gabe had meant about giving someone we fed on pleasure? "Wasn't intentional."

"Not unwelcome," Luca said. He sipped at his coffee for a few minutes longer, still rubbing his eyes like it was five in the morning instead of two in the afternoon. "You can suck my cock anytime." He raised an arm and sniffed. "But I need a shower. Sleep stink isn't attractive on anyone but a vampire. You guys don't sweat like the rest of us plebes do."

I gulped down the blood, trying not to think of Luca naked in the shower, covered in soap. He'd showered in front of me before, so I knew how tight his ass was, and the width of his thick cock, which I had yet to taste. My body was starting to wake up. Blood beginning to move again.

"In case you need an official invitation," Luca continued as he set his cup down and headed toward the shower. "The door will be unlocked, and I'd love to have a naked vampire for breakfast." He disappeared around the corner, fine ass fading into the shadows of the apartment. I stood there, contemplating a thousand things, but only really one. Sex with Luca.

Fuck.

I finished the mug in several huge gulps, rinsed it, and added it to the top rack of the washer before finding my way to the bathroom. I hoped Kelly wasn't home because there was only one bathroom in their apartment. It was huge and had been remodeled recently with a large walk-in shower, and a separate clawfoot tub, but there was still only one toilet. He might not like walking in on Luca and I fucking in his shower.

I passed Con, who still sat on the bed playing a game on his phone, and paused. "You okay?" I asked him.

"Yeah," he said a little tightly.

"I didn't bite him."

"It's okay if you do."

"We don't have to do it in front of you."

He shrugged. "Luca said you guys have a twenty-minute head start."

It took me a few seconds to process that. Did that mean Luca expected Con to join us in the shower? Was I okay with that? I thought of all Con's ink and water running over his skin while Luca and I tasted him…

Yeah, I was okay with it. Consenting adults, learning to live, and all that shit. I walked into the bathroom. Luca had the shower on and had stripped out of his little undies. He was a fine man, honed muscle tone, olive skin and pretty eyes. I didn't really care for the facial scruff. A beard would have been okay, but the artful mess that was popular right now did nothing for me.

"Any chance you'd shave?" I asked him. What was the worst he could say? No? Fuck you, get out of the bathroom? Whatever.

He glanced my way, then at the sink, before padding over to the counter and pulling out an electric razor. "All of it?" He wanted to know.

"Yes." I'd never had scruff, and since I was full blood Chinese, I might never have any. On Luca, I just wanted those lips pure and clean. The idea made me hard as I watched him stand at the sink, shaving off the shadow, naked ass swaying to some song I couldn't hear. He was so attractive. The kind of guy all the girls wanted and all the boys dreamed about. I'd never be that. In the reflection in the mirror—yes, vampires have reflections—I felt very pale next to him. Pretty, I guess. Not as pretty as Seiran, but not the masculine beauty that was Con either.

"What's with the expression?" Luca wanted to know.

"Don't know what you're talking about," I lied.

"You're brooding."

I was, wasn't I? "Just thinking how different we are."

"You could undress," he said. "Make us less different."

I could, and had been too busy thinking about all the things I wanted to do to him, and how inadequate I felt. I stripped off my shirt, throwing it to the floor and stared at our reflections another minute. Somehow I'd gotten leaner too. Part of being a vampire, Gabe had once said. Hard to maintain body fat when your body is essentially on an extreme no carb diet. I realized in that moment how much I'd hated myself. Everything about myself. My Chinese heritage, my pudgy stomach, my less than stellar brain, and my entire life. But that wasn't me anymore, was it?

The mirror reflected back something I'd never seen before. A dangerous man full of sex appeal and desire. My expression one of attitude and contempt. For myself? More for my views of myself. I was a vampire. Not dead. No longer someone's plaything. I was an amplifier, a witch unlike anything ever documented with the Dominion before. And I had not one, but two attractive men wanting me.

What was left to hate? Wasn't I Sam now? A vampire, creature of the night and all that bullshit? Reborn from the Earth, wasn't it time to make myself who I always wanted to be instead of wallowing in who I'd been?

I stripped out of the rest of my clothes and stalked to the counter as Luca was finishing up. He rinsed his face, not bothering with aftershave likely since we'd be going into the shower in a minute. I stepped up behind him, grabbed his hips and pressed against him.

He sucked in a deep breath, his eyes closing like he was in heaven. I leaned my head over his shoulder so I could rub my cheek against his and used one hand to cup his cock which was already engorged and leaking come.

"Fuck," he groaned when I touched him. He thrust his hips into my grip. "Been waiting for this."

I squeezed him a little harder, enjoying his tiny grunts of pleasure as I worked him. In the mirror I could watch his passion, loved the way his head tilted back to rest on my shoulder and mouth lay slack in pleasure. I rocked my hips into his, using the counter for extra leverage, pressing my cock into his crack and sliding along his skin. He was so warm.

I nuzzled his neck, hungry, but not for more than just a little taste. Would it be sweeter if I drank from him as he came? I kissed his throat, laving it with my tongue, following that little line of pulsing warmth beneath his skin.

"Fuck," he said. "Do it."

"Hmm?" I asked him, easing my grip down to squeeze the base of his cock and stave off the orgasm he had coming. "Who's in charge? I thought you sad I was a badass son of a bitch?"

"You are. Dammit." He pressed his butt back into me. "Don't stop. Please."

I slid my hand back up again, tickling along his shaft in more of a whisper of a touch than the tight friction I knew he craved. Come wept from his tip as his cock strained toward his stomach. "Shaved your balls, but not your face, eh?" I asked.

"Shave everything for you, if you want. Just fuck me."

"Yeah?" I asked. "Bend you over the counter and slide in dry?"

"There's lotion," Luca nodded his head to a large bottle of lavender scented beeswax lotion. "I won't need much prep. I like it hard." He groaned as I found a rhythm on his cock again. "Fuck, do I like it hard."

I reached around with my other hand and picked up the lotion bottle, skirted some over my moving fist, tightening my hand around him, and watched him come unglued. Luca's eyes rolled back in his head, and he leaned into me, letting me take his weight while presenting me his neck. I took that offered sip by just edging the tip of my teeth into his vein as he spurted his come over my fist. I continued to pump him, listening to his heavy breathing, and enjoying his weight against me while my cock still sat nestled between his crack, tiny movements adding pleasure.

He tasted as amazing as always. Sweet with a hint of spice which warmed me from the gut on outward.

"Okay, that was worth the wait," Luca said after a minute. "And shaving."

He pulled out of my arms to turn around and wrap me in his. He found my cock and started pumping me. He leaned in for a kiss, which I accepted.

"Mm," I said, freeing his mouth for a minute. "Shower. Then more play. Stinky human and all," I teased him, pulling away. His neck was already healed, but I was sure our time was almost up. Would Con be coming in soon? Would he chicken out? Looking at Luca and I in the mirror, how good we looked together, naked limbs and flushed faces, it didn't matter. I wasn't going to make time for all the worry anymore.

"Are you saying I stink?" Luca asked.

"Always smell good to me," I said honestly.

A sweet smile touched his lips and he made his way into the shower. The spray ran over him, drenching him in a warm wash of water that since I was in Kelly's apartment, and he was the Pillar of water, I could feel running over Luca's flesh. I stopped and let the sensation roll over me for a minute while Luca stared at me, eyes still filled with lust.

I'd do a lot for that look. I stalked toward him, stepping into the spray and reaching for him as he turned into my embrace. We kissed, a fierce battle of tongues, arms crushing as the heat of the water flowed over us. His erection was growing again, and I wondered what it would be like to see him on his knees, lips wrapped around my cock. His clean-shaven face made him look younger, more innocent than the hedonist I knew him to be. I swallowed one last kiss and shoved him to his knees.

Luca didn't even hesitate. He took my cock in hand and began sucking on the tip. Fuck that was good. How many times had I done this for someone else only to never have it reciprocated? I shook my head, forcing the memories away. That was in the past. Another life ago. Now I could just enjoy the way Luca's warm lips wrapped around me, and the play of his tongue on the underside of my cock. He pumped at the base of me, grip firm, but not painful, and took me down the back of his throat.

"Fuck!" I cried. He swallowed around me, and squeezed my hip to get me to move. I fell into a rhythm, thrusting my hips, fucking his face, while he made wet sounds barely drowned out by the falling spray.

I was on the edge when the door to the bathroom opened. Facing it, I knew Con had a view of the entire event. His decision, I reminded myself. I wanted him. My standing erection was proof of that. Luca glanced back briefly, but not long enough to lose his rhythm. He was a pro, pulling back to nip the tip of me in a stinging bite that kept me from coming.

Luca stroked himself while he worked me, half turning to look in Con's direction. An invitation if there ever was one. I bit my lip as Luca took me down again. Con watched a minute longer before nodding, then stepping in our direction and shedding his clothes. We watched him, not stopping our play, but both careful, I could sense it. What a picture Luca made, kneeling on the floor, my dick in his mouth, his big cock in his hand, ass splayed like he was ready for more. He nipped me again.

"Jerk," I scolded him.

He winked at me and placed a soothing kiss to the tip.

Con stepped into the shower. His body was all tattoo and sinew. Beneath the tattoos were a network of scars that we never talked about. His pain put to skin. Years of family trauma broken down to cutting that even endless days of video game demon slaying could not exorcise.

I reached for him, hand sliding up his shoulder to cup his face. He worried at his bottom lip and I pulled him forward into a kiss. A few seconds passed, and I feared he'd pull away since he didn't respond, but then he was kissing me back, a heated battle of lips, tongue and need. Luca's rhythm changed, and Con gasped. I looked down to find Luca stroking us both, tasting one and then the other, bobbing back and forth.

I fell back into Con's kiss, careful of my teeth, though he didn't seem to notice. My hand on his face moved to a grip on the back of his head, turning him just so we could meet for a better taste. He groaned into my mouth. I reached down and found Luca's hair with my other hand, gripping it, letting him feel the slight edge of pain, and hearing his pleasured gasp as he worked Con and I together.

And wasn't that an amazing feeling. The hot brand of a dick against mine, slick with spit, water, and pre-come. We both moved our hips, Con and I in flux. Luca used a hand for each, licking the seam between us. It didn't matter in that moment all the backgrounds we'd come from, our history, baggage, or memories. We were one, a lightning rod of pleasure, awakening in a fury of sensation. Con let out a strangled cry, the first of us to come as he let loose in Luca's fist.

Luca's hold on us loosened as he came, his face buried against my thigh, where there was the tiniest little sting. I said nothing, though his mouth sucked at me, making me feel like I could come over and over again. His face so close to my balls, teeth in such a sensitive area of my body, that I trembled with the force of my orgasm. My body erupting in a final bit of heat I couldn't recall ever being so sweet.

Con took my cries and fed at my mouth. If he saw Luca's

bite, he didn't react to it. Luca finished with a firm lick to heal my thigh, and let out a long sigh. We all sank to the floor encased in a mass of arms and legs, the water streaming over us, washing away spunk, sweat, and sleepiness.

Luca lay his head on my shoulder, while Con sprawled against my side. "I could do that again in another twenty minutes or so," Luca remarked.

Con snorted. "He's like the energizer bunny on heroin."

I smiled. "I could be up for another round in a bit. But maybe you plebes should clean up a bit?" None of us were really under the spray anymore.

Luca pointed to a smear of come on my hip. "Whose was that?"

I didn't know. Mine? Maybe Con's? Or had Luca scored a shot that high. "I guess we should all get squeaky clean." I reached for the shower sponge and soap.

"That gel makes for great lube," Luca remarked.

"Energizer bunny," Con restated.

I laughed.

CHAPTER 16

Two more rounds of blow jobs and hand jobs in the shower and I was not only well fed, but well fucked to start the day. Who knew having two lovers would be such a good thing? At least I'd chosen these men. I sighed as the old memory of Matthew's many *friends* crept up, irritated with myself that I hadn't been able to just leave it all in the dirt where I'd been buried.

We dressed and Con was digging through the fridge trying to find normal food when the door to the apartment opened. We all froze, that sort of deer in headlights look on our faces, like we were caught doing something inappropriate, only we were all dressed and being domestic. But it was Seiran with the twins in a stroller. He glanced in first, saw us and then entered the apartment before closing and locking the door behind him.

He looked better rested, but no less stressed.

"Everything okay?" I asked him.

He gave me a tight smile. "I was hoping you were done with your little party, and when things quieted down, I headed up." He glanced at Con and Luca. "You guys want some food? I need to cook to de-stress and have no one to cook for but me."

Little party? Had he somehow sensed we were having sex?

"Food is always good," Con said. "Just nothing too spicy."

"And no mint for you, right? 'Cause you're allergic. How about you, Luca? Any allergies?" Seiran parked the twins and locked the wheels of the stroller beside the counter and began unpacking their things.

"No allergies," Luca said. "Other than intense sunlight."

"Yeah?" Seiran said. "Are all dhampirs sensitive?"

"I've heard it's common," Luca agreed.

Seiran nodded like he was filing it away for later knowledge. He opened the hall closet and pulled out a big cylindrical bag. It wasn't until he pulled out something full of rods that I realized it was a portable playpen. He set it up like he'd already done it a hundred times and then got the babies settled. They couldn't move much yet, but the pen kept them from wiggling into something.

"The pantry should be full, right?" Seiran asked as he parked the stroller by the door and kicked off his shoes.

"Kelly unpacked a bunch of stuff yesterday. Said it was for meal prep," Con answered.

"Good," Seiran said as he headed into the kitchen and began pulling out ingredients.

Con escaped to the living room, and I heard the Xbox boot up.

"You work at the bar tonight," Seiran called to Con.

"I know," came an annoyed reply.

"Con's working at the bar now too?" I asked.

"We all are," Seiran said. "Even Luca has taken a few shifts. Mike and Jamie are back to managing it."

"While Gabe is off doing who knows what," I said. Seiran

flinched. He glanced at Luca who put his hands up, and backed into the living room.

"I'll just join Con for a rousing game of kill something not real," he said.

I looked at Seiran. He refused to look at me. "Ronnie?"

"I can't," he said.

"Can't what? Talk about it? See the forest for the trees? Leave the vampire? Break it down for me, witch."

He paused in his quest for pantry items, staring blankly at the countertop for a minute. "I'm all he has."

"Which is sort of the point. I'm assuming Jamie has already talked to you."

"And Kelly." He sounded miserable.

"Sucks when the people who care about you make sense, right?"

He returned to his search for items. At least this was something I recognized. A form of a panic attack for Seiran was order to chaos. A way to control it. As long as he wasn't reaching for the cleaning supplies, we were okay. So far he was just organizing vegetables and bakery items. "Sweet or savory, Rou, make up your mind," I teased him.

He sighed. "I wish I could hate you."

"Yeah? Right back atcha, Ronnie."

Again he was silent. Moving with purpose but emotionally blank, though I could feel the stir in the earth from his unease. If he didn't reign that in soon there'd be some minor quakes on the news tonight.

"You shot him," he finally said.

"Who?"

"Matthew. I always wondered. You wanted him, but you shot him. Cut off his head. Like it was so easy for you. I thought you loved him."

"I wanted freedom. Matthew was just another chain. He liked to track young vampires and kill them. It was how I knew his head had to come off. By the time he'd been reminded of you, I was already his slave." I sighed, hating the memories. Another life ago wasn't long enough. "For a while I thought he could make me powerful. That was always a lie. And then I died. Death really is a bitch."

"So is life," Seiran added.

"Not always," I pointed toward the living room. "Party? Could you hear us all the way through the floors?"

"No. Just the earth doing a weird little thing when a powerful air witch, a dhampir, and a vampire with amplifying magic all get busy. At least I didn't get visuals. I'd need brain bleach."

"Like I haven't seen enough of your naked ass?"

"Sexing with Gabe?" He wanted to know.

"Thankfully, no." I frowned. "And um, gross."

"Gabe's hot. I'm hot."

"You're pretty. Like bend over and give him that boy pussy of yours pretty. Gabe is like…stuffy. It takes away all his attractiveness."

"Boy pussy?" Seiran seemed to think about that for a bit.

"When your hole looks a lot like a lady hole?"

"How would you know what my hole looks like?"

"I don't and would like it to stay that way."

He blinked at me. "How do our conversations always spiral like this?"

I shrugged. "It's a gift. Anyway, so you want to know what to do? Advice from the king of screwups? Give him an ultimatum. Leave the big man if he doesn't go to ground."

"And if he doesn't pick me?" He sounded so broken asking that question that I took the container of ground oats from him and put it on the counter so I could wrap my arms around him. I'd never been a hugger before this group. Still wasn't really, but I knew sometimes it was necessary just to keep us from falling apart.

"You are the Pillar of fucking earth, Ronnie. First male in known history. You're Father Earth. Connected to the big rock unlike anyone could ever dream."

"Which isn't always a good thing," Seiran grumbled.

"Agree with you there. But stop thinking of yourself as less. You're not weak, you're a Pillar. You're not unlovable, you have a whole slew of us idiots following you around. You're not useless, 'cause the earth would explode without you right now. So why do you let someone make you feel that way?"

"Never pegged you for a pep talk."

"Yet you came to me and shoed my guys from the room so we could talk. You could be with Kelly or Jamie right now." I let him go, and he returned to his kitchen chaos.

"They're upstairs at Jamie's place." His face flushed. "Sort of doing what you did."

"Party?"

He nodded.

"Wow, that's some power." I wondered if I could tune into it and then why I would want to. "You maybe need some more training to focus that power?"

"I have to take care of the twins. They are my priority."

"Not blowing up the earth should be at the top of that list too. The whole world-go-boom thing would make for no babies."

"Haven't blown it up so far," Seiran said.

"Luck. Pure luck. I'm sure of it."

"Bastard."

"Jerk."

"Help me cook while I think."

"I suck at cooking, but I can clean and hand you ingredients." Best to keep the witch focused on chemistry rather than biology. "It can't be just Jamie's suggestion that has you up here ready to cook for an army."

"He's mad," Seiran said.

"Gabe is mad? Why?" I said, knowing instantly he was talking about Gabe and not Jamie.

"Because he can't get any QuickLife. Jamie disabled his wi-fi and phone. He'd have to leave the building to get it, and he can't do that till dark. I offered him blood. He refused. I pointed out there's blood in the freezer. He said he hates the stuff. I understand it's not great. But why refuse me?"

That was an interesting revelation. "How long has it been since he fed on you?"

Seiran shook his head. "I don't know. Months at least. Since long before you went to ground."

Was it Gabe's last way of protecting Seiran? Maybe he was so hungry that if he started he wouldn't stop? Or maybe he feared the witch would bring him clarity he didn't want? I really was at a loss for what might be going on in his head. "If it makes you feel better, you're still the best blood I've ever tasted. Even better than Luca who is like a fucking Dom Perignon." Not that I'd ever tried the wine, but it was the principle of the thing.

Seiran didn't say anything, instead focusing on the food. It seemed to be some sort of stuffed potatoes, with bacon, broccoli, ranch dressing and dill pickles, which sounded weird. He set me up on cleaning an entire four pounds of strawberries of which he planned to dunk in chocolate. "Are you making a romantic dinner?" I asked him.

"Seems to fit," he said. He added some fresh steaks to a bag of marinade. "Since you had sex already. Sort of like a date at home, right?"

I didn't think I needed to wine and dine Con or Luca, but I didn't point it out to Seiran that he was being romantic when he'd always thought of himself as practical.

"Luca could probably use the iron anyway," Seiran said.

"He's had plenty of iron," I assured Seiran recalling the bite to my thigh. Who knew that could be so erotic?

"Don't rain on my parade, Sammie."

I put my hands up in surrender. "Okay, okay."

"Do you need more food? You're so thin. Not unhealthy, but very lean."

"I ate well today," I promised him. Wasn't hungry at all. But I'd had the first blood pack, nibbled from Luca twice, and finished off the second doctored blood pack right before Seiran had arrived. "I thought the vampire thing was why I'd gotten so lean."

He stared at me for a while before finally saying, "I don't know much about vampires."

"And yet you're practically married to one."

Again he flinched. I think it was the reminder that they were bound. "He hasn't slept. Even today when he came in late. Jamie said he paced the apartment."

The agitation sounded a lot like Matthew's. He'd gotten worse without sleep and no amount of blood could have fixed him in the end. Would he have been saner if he'd gone to ground? Somehow I didn't think even the earth could fix that sort of crazy.

"I told him I was taking the babies out for a walk."

"You lied to the big guy."

His shoulders slumped. "I did walk them around the lobby."

I snorted, that did not fix the lie. "Seiran…"

"I know. I just…"

"You have babies to focus on." The twins were awake and mostly just making tiny noises at each other. I kept an eye on them as I dipped the strawberries and put them on a parchment-lined pan to harden.

"They're talking to each other. I can't understand it, but I feel the change in their emotions. They're worried. Brand new babies and they are worried. Pretty sure it's because of me. They shouldn't have to worry about anything."

I agreed, but Seiran hadn't signed up to do this himself. Hell, he hadn't wanted to be a dad at all. His anxiety planted too many scenarios in his head of what could go wrong. And wasn't that exactly what was happening?

"I talked to my mom," he said after he put the potatoes in the oven for the second time. We'd already been in the kitchen for over an hour. I could hear Con and Luca chatting in-between the small noises of the conversations in the game. They were playing Witcher 3, as far as I could tell. I loved that game. Would have enjoyed it more if the MC, who was a hot daddy, could buy more than just female whores at each town. But the game had plenty of gore and violence to suit most internal demon slaying needs.

"And?"

"She is giving me a house. Not the one I grew up in, but one she had built for me here. She wants me to take a look with her, see if there's anything else to change before I move in with the twins. It has a lot of the same things my dad's house had, or so she tells me. She wanted to make it an ideal place for two earth witches to grow up."

"So you don't have to go to California?"

"No. I wouldn't anyway. The California house has already been converted into a safe house for young male witches. Last I heard it was full, and thriving. They don't need my trouble."

"How is your mom with Mizuki?"

Seiran finished putting everything away except the steaks, his eyes focused on the counter mostly as he seemed lost in thought. "She's very animated with him. With both of them. Brings them gifts, holds them, feeds them, changes them and doesn't seem bothered if they throw up on her."

"Baby throw up is unavoidable." I knew from experience.

"When I was little…" he began, "I sort of remember her always being there. Then she changed. What if she does that again?"

"Then you fuck her up," I told him. "Pillar, remember?"

He let out a long sigh. "I don't know if I'm strong enough for that."

"How about you worry about that when it happens? If it happens?"

The timer beeped and Seiran took the potatoes out and set them on the counter to cool, then added the steaks to a pan. "How do they like their steaks?"

I had no idea. "Luca? Con? How do you like your meat?" I called to them.

Seiran flushed bright pink, and I couldn't help but chuckle when Luca called back. "Long and uncut."

"Good thing I'm both," I told Seiran who mock growled at me. "I mean your steak, dumbass."

"Rare, soaking in its own juice," Luca threw back.

"Is everything he says related to sex?" Seiran wanted to know.

"I'm pretty sure everything he does is sex," I assured him. "'Cause really, who wouldn't want to tap that?"

"He's sort of boy band cute without the facial hair," Seiran allowed.

"I heard that!" Luca sounded indignant. "And Con wants his steak medium well. Boy band…the fucking nerve of some people! I'm at least Adam Levine hot."

"Not without tattoos," Con said. "I'm Adam Levine hot." And he kind of was. I agreed. Seiran nodded and cooked their steaks while they continued to argue.

"Epiphanies?" I asked Seiran once he'd removed both steaks from the stove to rest before adding his own. At least he was planning to eat.

"Still thinking."

"You think too much."

"We both do," he said. Wasn't that the truth. "Are you happier now? You've only been back a little while and you seem happier. More calm at least."

"I have two hot guys in the living room waiting for me, why wouldn't I be happy?" I was happier. Not so much because Luca and Con, though that was great, but because I was no longer looking at the world and waiting for it all to end. "I'm alive, Ronnie. You know that's a good thing, right?"

"Is it?"

I remembered Luca's comment about how Seiran spent more time worrying about life than living it, and how I didn't want to be the same. "I want to live the life I have. Sometimes that's going to suck. Sometimes bad things happen. But sometimes good things happen too." I pointed to the living room and then to the babies. We both had good things, even if sometimes they confused and stressed us out. "You gotta choose how to live your life, Ronnie. Either spend every day wishing you could die, or live it until you do. I'm choosing to live."

He went silent again, staring at his steak like it held the answers to all his questions. "Gabe said he'll be up right after dark to take you hunting tonight."

I frowned. "Why would I need to go hunting if I have Luca?" Wasn't that the point of having a *cibo*?

"I asked him the same thing. He said that your *cibo* wouldn't always be available so you had to master hunting. He didn't make it sound like you were just going to a club to convince some cute boy to let you close for a nibble."

Was Gabe hunting hunting? Like stalking people and taking them by force? Was that why he was gone every night?

"Will you go with him?" Seiran asked. He took his steak off the fire and turned off the burner.

"And if I see something we both don't want to know about him?"

"I don't think he's hurting anyone," Seiran said softly.

"Just because there hasn't been bodies, doesn't mean he's not hurting anyone." Vampires didn't need to kill to eat, but a vampire as old as Gabe probably knew how to hide bodies if he'd lost that much control.

"Gabe isn't like that," Seiran continued.

I wasn't so sure.

"It will make the decision easier." He fell silent again for another minute and began plating up the food like he worked in some high-end restaurant. It surprised me in that moment to realize, while I smelled the food, it didn't irritate me like it had before. It looked tasty and smelled pleasant, not overwhelming to the point of making me gag like everything had before I'd gone to ground. That was a bonus.

"Do you have any spells you remember that might help?" Seiran finally asked as he was putting together the last plate. "From the books Roman gave you?"

We didn't talk about those. In fact, I let no one know that I still had those books. Most of them. Some had been damaged by water, but borrowing Kelly's power I'd been able to dry them out easily enough. They were currently buried and spelled to protect them from insects and elements. I had hoped to find enough clarity eventually to begin searching them for what I really was. Make some sense of my power.

"Help how, Ronnie? He just needs to go to ground."

"Maybe so he's not so against it?"

"Control him? I'm pretty sure that's your job as a Focus. I don't know of any magic to control a vampire other than the sire-baby vamp dynamic. And last I heard his sire is dead." Andrew Roman's wife had been the one who made Gabe as far as I knew. And he'd turned around and killed her for killing his lover Titus. We all knew just tiny bits of the story.

I had a feeling there was a lot more left unsaid than anyone realized. "You have the power to put him in the ground if he won't go willingly," I pointed out.

"I don't want him to hate me."

"Seiran, I'm pretty sure Gabe hates himself right now. This self-destruction? And you realize that's what it is right? Because he knows that he could fix this with going to ground. This is something inside him that is broken. Not because of you, or the babies, or even life. It's something in him that has gone wrong." I knew that Gabe knew that. It was common sense and the man had never lacked common sense. Maybe it was more complicated. Maybe Tresler was keeping him above ground with threats. Gabe wasn't sharing with us, so it was hard to know all the details. "He needs to rest. I just did it and I'm now a fan."

"Vampires used to go to ground every night," Luca said, coming into the kitchen. "They didn't have cushy lives to live, so they could do that. Now they try to maintain the status quo and it wears at them. My dad still goes to ground every night—well every morning. I think that's why he's so powerful. He's also never lost centuries like Galloway did."

"Hard to have a lover that way," I pointed out. "I kind of liked sleeping with you guys today."

"I don't think it's absolutely necessary to go to ground nightly," Luca said. "But maybe on a set schedule? Once a month? Like on the new moon or something?"

That reminded me. "So I have something to confess and I want both of your takes on this," I said.

Con appeared in the kitchen. Seiran pushed their plates towards them and pulled up his own. "Should we not start eating before this confession? Is it going to be gross?" Seiran asked. "Like boy pussy gross?"

"I like boy pussy," Luca said.

"I'm pretty sure you like boy everything," Con pointed

out.

"I'm trying to be serious," I told them. "And um, no. Just what do you think I'd be confessing?"

"Maybe you like to be double-teamed and haven't shared that with us yet," Luca said.

I blinked at Luca.

Seiran pointed his fork at him. "I don't want to know that."

"I don't mind being double-teamed as long as I've been appropriately stretched," Luca said. "Can be really good with the right pair."

Con and I exchanged a look. My pants tightened. Seiran growled. It was funny because it sounded more like his lynx than him. "Okay, Ronnie. Nothing I can do about the porn star sitting over there. But my confession has nothing to do with sex. It has to do with how I got out of the tomb."

"I was wondering about that," Luca said. "Those things have a ton of safety features to keep people out and vampires in."

"How did you get out?" Seiran asked.

"And all the way across town for Galloway to find you?" Luca wanted to know.

Did Seiran know about Galloway? He waved away the question he must have seen on my face. "I've already questioned Luca at length. He might not be undead yet, but all humans are a product of the earth."

"He can be very persuasive, and terrifying," Luca said, for the first time not adding any innuendos to his comment. The witch scared him, which I thought was a good thing. Anyone with half a brain should be scared of Seiran Rou.

"I flew," I told them. "That's how I got out."

"Vampires don't fly," Seiran said.

"You wouldn't have gotten through the door that way," Luca stated.

"I changed into a raven and walked through the slats in the grate at the top, then flew. I thought it was a dream at first, until I ran into a tree, and then Galloway siren-called me to his window." I blurted out all the details, waiting for the shock and disbelief.

Luca looked thoughtful. Seiran seemed confused. Con was frowning.

"What?" I demanded.

"Seems odd that you manifested as an air animal," Seiran said. "Your power never seemed set to one specific element. Maybe it was because Roman was your sire?" Andrew Roman had been an air witch, and because he'd fed from me until the point of death, Gabe had been able to bring me back as a vampire. So technically Roman was my sire, though Gabe had been the one to give me his blood to raise me. Did that mean I still maintained some of Roman's abilities?

"Vampires don't change," Luca said.

"Vampires aren't normally witches," Seiran pointed out.

"I think it's sort of my fault," Con said. We all looked at him. "He'd been under so long, and I knew they'd tried blood, but I went to the grave and thought if I added a little of my own, maybe it would help?"

We all blinked at him, processing his words. It was Seiran who said it first. "Can you change on the new moon?"

He nodded. "I don't have to. Not every month. But I can."

"And it's a raven?" I asked.

He shrugged. "Never seen my bird. Just that I fly. I've always been alone. Cat didn't know. I don't think she could change. It started for me after Kelly and I broke up and I lost the baby…" Around the same time Con had turned to cutting as his past time.

"So I can borrow a shapeshift now?" Was that possible? I looked at Seiran who didn't seem to have any answers either.

"We can try on the next new moon. See if you can borrow

from me or Jamie. It's in a couple weeks."

I'd be sad not to fly again. If I borrowed it once, would I have to keep borrowing it to use it again? I still felt Seiran's power and Kelly's. Hell, I was pretty sure I could still pull up a null field of Matthew's power if I really tried. It all sat like seeds of energy inside of me. What if I was just collecting everyone's power and it never faded? How much would be too much?

"I'll talk to Max. He might have heard of it happening before," Luca offered.

"Galloway had obviously seen it before," I said.

"Galloway doesn't answer questions. I'm not sure he's all there or still half asleep. I think the death of his Focus really screwed him up," Luca said.

"I don't trust Galloway," Seiran said. "Or Max."

"And we can't trust Gabe," I pointed out. "So who's left? The Dominion doesn't know. Are there any vampires left who might know and we can trust?"

"Mike?" Seiran asked.

I shook my head. Mike was old but only a few centuries old. "I'm pretty sure Luca knows more than Mike."

"I'll vouch for that," Luca said. "Super nice guy, but not quite two centuries old and since Gabe is his sire, Gabe could keep him from sharing stuff with us."

I hadn't thought of that, and neither had Seiran from the expression on his face. He sighed. "Fine. You can ask Max." He cut furiously into his steak, breaking it into small pieces. The babies started to fuss. I patted Seiran's wrist and got up to take care of them so he could eat in peace.

We needed some answers. I wondered if there was anything in those books I had hidden. Maybe I'd take a short trip to retrieve them. Although if Gabe was coming for me after dark, I had a feeling the evening would not be headed in a positive direction.

CHAPTER 17

The sun set and I felt Gabe at the door almost like he'd magically manifested there. He looked tired, thin, face stern. He didn't even look in Seiran's direction. I could feel the anger wafting off him. "Let's go," he said and turned to leave, not bothering to see if I was ready or not.

Seiran gave me a shooing motion, begging me to go. He wanted to know what Gabe was doing, only I knew that was masochistic. Neither of us wanted to see Gabe fall apart. Seiran because he loved Gabe, and me because Gabe was my mentor and I looked up to him.

I waved to Con and Luca and followed Gabe out. He said nothing as we got into his car. "I know how to hunt," I told him as he pointed us toward downtown.

He said nothing.

"Why won't you drink from Seiran?" I asked.

"Because Seiran feels pain when I bite him."

"Well, yeah, doesn't everyone? That's why we do the whole sex thing or suggestion sex thing, right?" It took me a few seconds to catch up. Was he saying he and Seiran hadn't had sex in months? No wonder Seiran was falling apart. "You need to go to ground," I told him no longer willing to mince words.

He gripped the steering wheel. "I won't leave Seiran alone."

"You're already leaving him alone. In case you've forgotten he has two brand new babies that you promised to help with."

"That's temporary."

"Uh, not sure how babies were done when you were young, but babies are sort of a permanent fixture. They grow up yeah, but they are your kids for life."

Gabe pulled into a downtown parking garage with covered parking and took us to the first spot he found. "I'd be gone centuries."

"You don't know that."

"It's been almost a millennium since I went under. Other than when Seiran put me in the ground." Only to pull him out way too soon. "What would that do to Seiran? And why do you care? I thought you hated him."

If I'd been born to a different family, I could have been him. And wasn't that just the kicker. There was a time I'd have looked at Sei and Gabe and thought they were the perfect couple, madly in love and unbreakable. Love didn't conquer all, but sometimes it gave us the strength to do the right thing. "What are you doing to him now?" I threw back. "To all of us?"

"Holding it together," he said through clenched teeth. "Now shut up and get out of the car."

I swallowed back a hundred things I wanted to say and got out of the car letting the anger build. I wasn't hungry. Had no desire to hunt. And was so mad at Gabe I wanted to hit him.

We exited the parking garage and crossed the street in silence, taking a backdoor into a building that I didn't recognize. The smell hit me first. Blood, sex, and death. Lots of disinfectant, but nothing could cover the smell of old blood and spend. I followed Gabe down several curving hallways until we passed an area like I'd only ever seen in porn videos. There were naked people everywhere, women and men, most of them lying on tables with their legs spread, some on their knees sucking men off, or bent over a table taking someone, or even two at a time.

The entire place had one common theme, vampires. Everyone getting off was also eating; necks, wrists, thighs, wherever. Nothing about this appealed to me at all. It didn't arouse me, it didn't make me hungry, it just made me angrier.

Why was Gabe bringing me here? Why was he here? Hadn't he told me all about what it meant to be a gentleman when I fed? To make them feel good and treat them with respect? This was the complete opposite.

I reached out without even thinking about it, tapping that tiny seed inside me that was Seiran's energy. I could feel him sitting in his apartment watching Con play a video game while Luca read. Kelly had joined them too, but was on the floor playing with the twins who were giggling at faces he made.

Seiran looked up like he could see me inside his head. The link tying us together through the earth strong enough that he could follow it. Did he really want to see? I wondered. Did he want to know what Gabe had been up too? How far he was gone?

Seiran's answer was a painful, *"Yes."*

I closed my eyes and let the feeling of him settle over me. The weight of warmth and calm that only the earth could provide, with an undercurrent of chaos just waiting for release. He saw what I did, and was mostly nonplussed.

I was never really into porn, he told me.

Me neither. At least not like this. There was no illusion of shared pleasure here. It was all about the vampires, feeding, getting off, while humans were little more than blood bags with holes. *Maybe I'm still too human to see the difference.*

Vampires are essentially humans, Seiran reminded me. *All creatures of the earth, taken as easily as given.* And he was right. There wasn't a creature who walked the earth that couldn't be taken back into it. That alone was the reason Seiran should have scared everyone. Earth was both the most fundamentally powerful element and the most vulnerable. Little shifts in human existence could tear it apart, or tiny ripples from the earth could destroy humanity. Seiran should have been the one to feel all-powerful and omniscient, since he practically was, only I never got that feeling from him. Even with his senses laid over mine in that moment.

I'm just me, he told me. *Beautifully fucked up, me, as Gabe always used to call me.* I could feel his sadness at the reminder.

We'll get him back, I told him. He wasn't at all sure about that. And really, neither was I. I hated standing there in that room, watching the vampires pretend to be more important and treat the humans like nothing more than blow-up dolls filled with blood. It reminded me of my time with Matthew, and how much I'd come to hate him in the end.

I'd always hated the superiority complex some people had. That their skin tone or race meant they were better than I. This was no different. Being a vampire didn't make them greater. In fact, I was pretty sure it made them weaker. Vulnerable to being seduced by blood, power, and destroyed by sunlight.

Seiran silently agreed.

Gabe didn't stop. He passed through the room and into one beyond where the lights were low and music played softly. People were dancing. I realized then that the music must have been set at a vampire's hearing level because it didn't hurt my ears at all. And once again the crowd was filled with vampires dancing with humans, feeding.

"What is this place?" I demanded of Gabe.

"Feeding Ground," Gabe said like it was a title rather than a thing. "Should have brought you here right after you changed."

To feed on emaciated humans looking for a way to die? Couldn't he smell the sickness in them? How many vampires could they feed before they succumbed? "Are these people here because they want to be turned?"

Gabe shrugged. "Some. Though most are fed on by too many different vampires to ever survive a transition. Not enough of a bond built up. Some vampires even refuse to heal their wounds as it creates a tie that might eventually be used to change them."

I frowned. "Healing the bite?" Did that mean when I'd been feeding off bullies I'd been creating bonds with them?

"Our saliva is part of the change, more so than any mental bond. It's why Roman was your sire. Every time he healed you, kept you from dying, he was creating a lasting link that could have ultimately forced your transition when you died, even without my help."

It was the first I was hearing of all of this. I'd sort of thought making vampires was like the movies portrayed, an exchange of blood or something. Only Roman had never given me blood. Gabe had, though I'd been mostly dead for that. "That just means all these people are going to die," I said looking out into the crowd of sluggish humans clinging to vampires as though they were in some renaissance film.

"Everyone dies. Even vampires. Humans are short lived. Stupid humans even more so. They made their choice." Gabe waved to someone across the room. A moment later a small Korean kid appeared. The guy didn't look legal, and like most Korean men I'd met, he was more pretty than handsome.

"Who's your friend?" The kid asked Gabe.

"This is Sam," Gabe said taking his offered hand and squeezing it. He tugged the young man forward and gave him a little nudge toward me. "Sam's here to practice."

The kid smiled. He let go of Gabe's hand and stepped into my space. "I love helping with practice." He put his hands around me and tilted his head so his neck was bared. The skin there was scarred, and he smelled of anemia.

"I'm not sure I need practice," I told him, trying to unlatch him from my side.

"Practice sending him images," Gabe instructed. "He tastes all right."

I felt Seiran try to swallow back his hurt.

"You'd drink this over Seiran?" I had to ask. This kid wasn't even on the same planet as Seiran's blood was.

"Who's Seiran?" The kid asked. "I'd let him have a taste too. Gabe makes it really good."

Gabe was already up and moving away, disappearing into the crowd. My anger at him grew. Seiran retreated, though I couldn't help but feel his heartbreak through the shared bond. Rage grew in my gut over all of this. I felt a bit of the red haze settle over my vision as the kid nuzzled my neck like he could bite me.

I pushed him away. "Not really in the mood," I told him. Never really had found a good mood for nameless strangers who wanted me just for the kink of getting bitten.

The kid shrugged, muttering, "Your loss," and wandered off. I wondered how many times Gabe had fed on him. Even as pretty as the kid had been, he couldn't compare to Seiran. Why the replacement? Because Gabe wasn't feeding on Seiran or having sex with him. And that was another question. Why?

I pushed my way through the crowds, watching in disgust at the blood orgies. Two died while vampires fed. No one seemed concerned. The vampires just stopped and went on to their next living victim. Dead blood was just dead blood, I guess.

I felt sick. This was not the civility Gabe had taught me to expect. He'd told me that vampires were just humans with special powers. And it was our responsibility to be aware of how those abilities affected the world around us. Biting people could kill them. Messing with their minds could drive them crazy. I couldn't imagine him letting this sort of debacle even exist in his city.

Was all of this new? From the change in vampires due to the QuickLife? Had this been going on all along? If so, then the humans had every right to be afraid of us. This was more monstrous than me hunting bullies in Riverside. At least there no one had died. I'd never lied to them about giving them new lives only to destroy them.

The bodies were hauled away quietly, like none of it mattered. I found Gabe surrounded by groupies, all taking turns feeding him. They were aroused. I could smell that from ten feet away. He was not. They were just food to him, and so much so the one he drank from right then was almost done.

I stepped forward to pull him off. "Stop." I yanked the girl away and shoved her toward her group. "She'll die," I told Gabe.

"They're all dying," he said, a red haze tinting his normal green eyes. "Everyone is dying. The whole fucking world is dying. You spent months wishing you were dead and blaming me for bringing you back to life. Why deny them the same?"

"Because you're not a murderer."

He stood, towering over me and gave me a hard shove.

"Says who? Do you know how long I've lived? I've killed thousands." He gestured to the crowd. "They are just food."

"Is that all Seiran is to you? Food?"

"He's my Focus. He belongs to me. He is no longer human. He is no longer food." The red in his eyes intensified. No comment about love. No emotion from him at all except the anger. I realized then that this wasn't even Gabe I was talking to anymore. It was his *other*.

I could feel Seiran recoil. Had he ever seen a vampire so lost in the revenant? He likely never expected to see it from Gabe.

"And if Seiran knew you were here? What would he do?" I demanded trying to bring Gabe back into some common sense. "This is perilously close to cheating on him."

It was cheating on him. Seiran looked at the crowd and saw lots of replacement faces, some even witches, though none could compete. Gabe may not be sexually aroused, but that could have been because the revenant was out. I'd been the same before going to ground. Finding little to lift my attention other than just blood. "Seiran should leave you."

I didn't see Gabe move. The next second, I was up in the air, slammed against a wall, pain shooting from my chest where he crushed me into brick. His fangs bared and eyes flashing, he snarled at me. "You know nothing of what we are."

"And whose fault is that?" I demanded unwilling to let him bully me. I tried to move his hand but it was like an anvil, solid and damn near unmovable. "You told me we aren't monsters. So what is the point of all this? To prove we are? None of this will keep him with you."

"He can't leave me. He's *mine*. We are bound."

"And he is earth itself. Do you think he can't tell it to take you back?"

"He would never hurt me."

That was true. "Not like you're killing him. Is that the point of all this? Are you looking for death?"

"You wanted to be a monster. This isn't good enough for you?" He growled and gripped my shirt, dragging me out the door. "Fine. We'll do it your way."

My way would have been to go home and play games with Luca and Con. But Gabe dragged me out of the club and into the darkness of downtown. We were far enough downtown that I could hear the noise from other clubs, sirens from passing cop cars, and chatter from bars. There were also armed soldiers standing at every corner.

I struggled to free myself from his grasp. "I'd like to not get shot, thanks."

"They won't even see us," Gabe said, dragging me toward the noise of the bars. People came and went along 1st Avenue. A game or maybe a concert had attracted a crowd of people lined up to get in. And just like he said, no one seemed to see us. Was this another power he had yet to tell me about? Some sort of suggestion? Or real magic?

Gabe steered us toward the crowd. "You want to be the monster, fine." He shoved me toward a group of teen girls standing off to the side. "Be a monster."

"I don't need any little kids." And I didn't hunt people who didn't hurt others.

"Those girls snuck out." Gabe tapped his forehead. "Can't you hear their chatter? They are all excited about how bad they've been and how much trouble they could be in for if discovered."

"They don't deserve to die," I said.

Gabe shrugged. "So don't kill them." He approached the girls, looking every bit the tall and sophisticated man we'd all thought he was, smile in place, but eyes tinted with a hint of red. "Ladies, how are you fine women tonight? Looking forward to the show?"

And it was that simple for him. They all fell under his spell, if that's what it was. I'd never seen it before, not like that. One moment the girls were animated and talking to each other, the next their expressions were blank and they stared at him waiting, like he was some goddamned puppet master. I hadn't even known group influence was a thing. Yet he'd just done it as easily as breathing. He reached for the first girl, and I slammed into him, using my entire body weight to knock him away.

He growled, his connection to the girls lost, they screeched and scattered, rushing off into the bigger group and lighted areas.

"Are you fucking insane?" I demanded. Not only were they underage and couldn't consent, we were in the middle of a fucking crowd. "We're done here. It's time to go home."

Gabe rose slowly, eyes looking like pools of fresh blood instead of his normal green. He grabbed me by the throat, and slammed me against the wall, teeth bared. That was okay. I was pissed too. He could kill me if he wanted, and legally that was his prerogative since he was officially listed as my sire. He could just tell the authorities that I'd gotten out of control. Even if he was the one out of control. But I wasn't alone in my own head.

He began to squeeze my neck like he was going to take off my head. I closed my eyes to wait for the end. At least Seiran would know. He could put an end to this fight since he was still with me.

And Seiran was pissed. His rage fueled my own, his as hot as lava building in my core. "You guys always forget about the witch," I said and put my hand on his arm and Seiran poured power through us. I just let it flow, had practiced it quite a bit with Kelly's power, letting the energy slide through me, amplifying with my own power before being directed elsewhere. Gabe's arm sprouted branches, leaves, and flowers, the earth eating away at it. His grip crumbled with his strength as the muscles dissolved into fine particles of earth.

He growled and pulled away, dropping me, cradling his injured and disintegrating arm. I sucked in a deep breath and sighed at the feeling of my ribs being broken once again. It was sad when you recognized that sensation because it happened so often. "We're done," Gabe said.

"Yeah, we are," I agreed. I was so done, with him and every other abusive bastard who decided I was prey.

"The Tri-Mega will kill you. The Dominion will kill you," he said.

I shrugged. "They'll have to get in line." I pulled myself up, using Seiran's offered strength to heal my ribs. It hurt and I bit back the cry of pain, but it eased fast enough. It's something he should have been able to do for Gabe too. Except Gabe was completely closed to him.

"I revoke my mentorship of you, leave you adrift, and unrestrained," Gabe said. I didn't really think much about those words in that moment, instead I left. Turning my back on him as my mentor and my friend. I couldn't save him, I reminded myself and Seiran who was sobbing. I could feel Kelly's arms around him even though they were across the city. At least he wasn't alone. Gabe was now, or what was left of Gabe. Was there any other way to fix a revenant? Could going to ground bring him back or was he too far gone?

It was the first trickle of red easing over my vision that clued me in on the change. Subtle for a few seconds, the rage and hunger began to fill my stomach. I swallowed back the urge to scream.

CHAPTER 18

One of the groups of soldiers approached as Gabe backed away, vanishing into the crowd. "That guy is a vampire," I told them. "He was after those girls." I pointed in the direction Gabe had gone. They scattered around the group, searching it with weapons pointed. It was unlikely they'd catch up with him, but they'd be keeping a better eye on the crowd.

The clarity in my head began to fuzz, and soon I wasn't seeing straight anymore. I stumbled, trying to find my footing through the red haze. What had he done to me? Revoked his mentorship? No longer my sire? Is that what he meant? I hadn't realized it was much more than a title as he'd been telling me since I'd been brought over that Roman was technically my sire.

Hunger poured into my gut. A mindless bloodlust filling every ounce of my being like a cup of water overflowing. Rage snapping through my veins with weight I couldn't ever recall feeling. It made me sluggish and heavy, slow and disoriented. The world pulsed around me, no longer living beings, but food and outlets for rage, the rational part of my brain drowning under the onslaught.

I found my way back out to the main street where I caught a cab, one thing on my mind. The anger and bloodlust needed to be redirected. I could have gone back and beaten the shit out of Gabe. He probably would have killed me, so that wasn't the wisest course of action for release. Going home to Con and Luca was out of the question. They didn't need the red eyes or vampire rage that Gabe had brought back to the surface, or the well of energy still pooling in my veins from Seiran's power.

Maybe I could work it off. My hands itched with the need to rip something apart while my mind seemed to be coming apart at the seams. Which way was up? And why did everything look so goddamned red? Life everywhere, pulsing, screaming for me to release it with the ripping of a vein.

Fuck!

Would there still be fights? Luca said Max had been busy with business stuff. Luca had been fighting before I came back. It was my only hope now. Maybe they had a vampire I could fight. Someone to remind me of Gabe while I worked out all the aggression taking control.

And how angry did that make me to learn things tonight that I should have known right away? Saliva created a bond that could change a person into a vampire. Vampires used to go to ground every night. Vampires could mind rape a group of people with little effort. Vampires had blood sex clubs where people died and no one cared. The sire bond was some sort of magic. Vampires were monsters.

I'd known the last. Thought I'd embraced it. How dumb I'd been.

Don't go, Seiran said through our bond. *I'll come get you.*

I was too lost in the rage to see anyone fragile right that moment. I needed violence like I never had before in my existence. Something had to die. Maybe that would be me, and in that moment, that was okay too. Better me than Seiran.

I'm Father Earth, or so you keep reminding me, I'm not fragile.

But he was. Still breakable, and I really wanted to break something. *It's just a fight*, I told him, as I arrived at the club and was let in by the same bouncer. Inside I found Riley, the guy who scheduled the fights and said, "I need to fight, anyone strong enough to match me?"

He looked at me, then at his list. "Hart said he'll fund all your fights. We have a few other vampires in tonight, but none I've seen fight before. I can put you with one of the shifters."

"No. A vampire." I could pretend it was Gabe and smash them to bits.

"We have rolling rounds tonight. Beat the champion and we keep sending you another fighter until you get beat and they become the champion or we run out of challengers."

That sounded like heaven. "No one fragile?"

"All level five and up fighters. They know what they are signing up for when they step in the ring. But you have to beat the champion first."

"Done, point me in his direction," I demanded. My skin begged for the fight, muscles aching, energy still rolling through me as I remembered Gabe's arm almost disintegrating under Seiran's power. I absently pushed the energy back at him. *Put a lock on it, Ronnie. I don't need your help to fight.*

I staggered for a minute from the loss of Seiran's energy laced over my own. The last grounding force, I realized as I blinked through the red haze. Someone was going to die. "If I kill someone?"

"It happens with vampires. A lot lately."

"If someone kills me?" I wondered. Would someone tell Luca, Con, and Seiran at least?

"Your friends will be notified." Riley pointed toward the dressing room. "Get changed. I'll put you in rotation. They'll call your name when you're up."

I found a pair of shorts and didn't bother with anything else. Blood would ruin it all anyway. It didn't take long before my name was called, though long enough that my vision was completely gone. Someone said something I didn't quite understand but they led me to the cage. I could smell blood everywhere and once the door clanged shut behind me, the rank odor of another vampire filled my senses. It didn't matter that I couldn't see him, or that his stillness meant he was old. I envisioned Gabe and how he had failed Seiran. Him tossing me away like worthless trash wasn't so bad. It wasn't like I was worth much. He'd only saved me because Kelly had asked. Matthew and Roman had taught me the truth of vampires, they were selfish, heartless, and utterly ruthless when it came to power. I was probably the shittiest vampire on the planet because none of that appealed to me. But Seiran, who had embraced me as a friend despite everything I'd done to him, deserved better.

The bell rang. Pain came first. A blow to my head that sent me careening into the cage. People cheered. Another hit exploded my nose and sent black tendrils of oozing unconsciousness into my brain. That was okay too. The rage, hunger, and need for self-destruction would go silent if I was knocked out, or at least I hoped it would.

Only it didn't feel like unconsciousness, instead it was something else that took over. The *other*. He opened his eyes to briefly glimpse the crowd and the monster looming overhead, but in that instant, as he leapt to his feet, he shut me down. The rational, moral, and human side of Sam Mueller going dark as the revenant took hold. It was a strange thing, being locked inside my own body, unable to see, hear, or really feel anything. It was a lot like that dark place Seiran had given me a glimpse of, death without being truly dead. I fought it, trying to tear free of the abyss, but nothing seemed to help.

I crested three times, coming briefly back to myself in a glut of blood and screams. Nothing hurt. In fact all I could feel was hunger, anger, and a need to destroy. I fed, over and over, though it did nothing to satiate my bloodlust. Too much blood as I spewed each time, spitting out gallons of the noxious stuff, only to be rewarded with more hunger. What was taking them so long in sending me the next challenge?

The scent of others tickled my senses. The blood around me was old, stale, and dead. Vampire blood, I realized. It couldn't satisfy me, no matter how much I might want it to. But there was living blood in spades nearby. I could smell the stench of shifters, a few others I couldn't identify, and witches…

I licked my lips at the thought of tasting a witch right then. Drinking down the power of someone like Seiran Rou might satisfy the monster. I took a step in their direction, but met resistance. A wall of some kind, though I still couldn't see straight. It looked like some sort of mesh, dripping with gore. It didn't taste like anything living so I shredded it with my claws. The wail of metal tearing hurt my ears, but at least now I could continue my quest for that delicious scent.

What was that again? The familiar delicacy of smells that lit my senses and tried to pull back the weak side…the human side of my brain. I refused, too far gone in need to pursue the link. They weren't moving, and I could hear their voices, though not make out their words.

Someone stepped in front of me, forcing a pause in my movement. That someone died a second later. I felt their blood run over me in a cold rush. Another vampire. Useless.

I needed real food, not this dirty mess of rot.

Yet another stepped in front of me. I reached for them, only they smashed me into the floor with so little effort it took a few extra seconds for the monster to realize we'd been temporarily immobilized by magic. But the real blood was so close.

The one who held me was a vampire too. Strong, yet weak. Made powerful by magic that wasn't his own, instead it was layered over him, like unmatching condiments on a slice of toast. There were gaps in his magic, holes as though something had been ripped out of the grid. I could feel the pulse of his energy, recognized it vaguely as someone I'd met before, but couldn't place. The monster didn't care. It struggled against him. Reaching out now with something more than just physical energy. Little fingers of magic wove through him, finding a light inside, a different sort of energy than blood, digging into those little tears. It was a sort of unrestrained magic, old and unfamiliar, a shadow of change that brought the flash of my one flight as a bird, then a roll of people through my spotted vision. Some familiar, others just a crowd of faces.

He wanted me to come to him. Accept him. Like I knew at all what that meant. He tried to force more of that vile dead blood into my mouth, but I refused it, needing something more vivid, living, and terrified, beneath my jaws.

He tried to drink down my power, pulling at it like he could peel it off of me and wear it as another skin. Only the more he tugged, the more his own power stuck to mine, ripping away from him in chunks when he tried to break free.

The glow engulfed us both. He fought me, trying to hold me down as I fed on the power that he'd stored away for years, only daring to use with an occasional illusion. So much power, almost like Seiran…

Seiran, who I thought I heard somewhere nearby. Seiran, who I remembered I had hated, but now...wanted to eat? This was a different sort of lust, not for blood or sex, but energy and power. *Not my power*, the one who held me, said. His, and I was using it to destroy him. Borrowed and amplified, I drank him down, swallowing the light, illusion, and electricity like it was water. It burned through me, flashing a word of pain and dizziness, but I couldn't stop.

The noise around me of cries, screams, and pleas, all meshed into a hum of white noise. I fed at the source of him, eating away that supernatural liquidity of magic until there was nothing left. He struggled against me, trying to push me away until he became too weak.

I caught a glimpse of blond hair and thought briefly of triumph that I'd destroyed Gabe. That he could never hurt anyone again. He couldn't abandon Seiran or strip away my control. He couldn't leave everyone floundering for a way to save him from himself by putting him back in the grave. Only the taste of him was unfamiliar. Gabe had a power, stored away and barely touched, a part of my subconscious brain recalled. This wasn't his power. And that was okay. I took it in anyway, rending apart the last of the energy and devouring it.

The power of the other faded as the vampire did. His form becoming dirt in my arms, the earth taking him back, leaving me floundering in a blinding light, every pore of my being singing with lightning-deep pain. Like being shocked by a billion volts of electricity, I convulsed and shuddered. Still the hunger rode me; bloodlust back again, I crawled toward the smell of witches and power, despite the pain.

It didn't matter if they all died. Not as long as I could finally rest that endless need in my gut. A small voice inside my head said it would stop when I died too, but wasn't sure if anyone could achieve that in that moment. I felt invincible, and lost all at the same time.

Another vampire appeared in front of me, and I reached for his leg, only he stomped down on my hand, breaking every bone in my fingers, causing the lightning network of energy to crackle through me. I howled. He turned then, lifting his other foot to smash down between my shoulder blades, crushing me into the floor.

Bones broke, a lung punctured, skin broke as bones protruded through it, and I only barely felt it. Now I'd need more blood. The pulsing energy throbbed inside me, burrowing itself deep in my core like a pit of lava waiting to be released. My blood smeared the pavement, a nasty mess of useless rot just like the rest of the vampires.

I reached for the new vampire with the power, trying to find his magic, only he came up blank. Powerful, yes. His strength echoed through the hunger as danger—this was not prey—yet not from magic. No, his power was something more human, physical. His energy seemed to be from pure will rather than something tangible. Death magic coursed through him, something that my body recognized immediately, but could do nothing with. It was just something that animated us both, connected us, yet couldn't bridge the gap.

He held me effortlessly, turned me like I was a ragdoll and forced his blood, not into my mouth, but into the punctured mess of my chest. When had that happened? I vaguely recalled the pain.

His blood was like a brand coursing through my veins. The pulse of magic faded, quieting, though it still sat hot and livid in my gut ready to be called in an instant. The bloodlust began to ease and I blinked through the red haze to stare into the bright lights of the fighting area outside the cage. The cage looked like it'd been ripped open by the Kool-Aid Man, a huge gaping hole in the center of five layers of stainless steel mesh. Inside the cage a mess of blood and gore dripped off all the sides making wet plinks and splats.

My world tilted with nausea and I gasped for breath. Luca, Con, and Seiran stood huddled together a few feet away, kept back by a handful of shifters in fighting clothes. Everything else was carnage. Blood, gore, and the dirt of dead vampire.

My stomach rolled in disgust as my brain struggled to catch up. The revenant faded as something—someone else— took control. His strength and calm settled over me like a finely woven net.

I closed my eyes and could see a wash of memories, more than a single person should ever hold, but there were innumerable faces, lovers, friends, business partners, and even children. I caught a glimpse of a little boy my brain tagged as Luca, afraid and lonely, standing on a doorstep. I saw a man with dark hair and sapphire eyes dressed in clothes from the fifties who smiled tenderly my way, then glimpsed a raging fire as he died. I saw a thousand others cascading further into the past until it came to a pause in a time I didn't know enough history to understand. This was an intimate embrace with another man, blond hair curling around his forehead in honey-wheat waves, eyes a bright shade of green. Handsome, and young, probably early twenties at the latest. My mind recognized him, though in a different way than the person whose memories I walked through.

Gavriil. The man was called, though I knew him as Gabe, younger in the memory than I knew he'd been when he'd changed. The image shifted, like I'd directed it somehow, to the Gabe I knew, dressed in the different clothes of a generation long dead, reaching for me, covered in blood.

The memory was shut down hard. The whole walk through places and people closed, like a door in my face. The vampire let me go, though his presence still lingered in my head, binding me like a lock on a door leading to the monster I'd become.

I gasped for breath, trying to control the influx of processing thoughts, memories, and confusion. Too much for my brain, my head throbbed, and my stomach churned. I rolled over and vomited, heaving up blood and gore like a cork had been pulled.

The person who had held me down stepped several feet away so as not to get splashed. "This is why I don't create or blood bond vampires anymore," Maxwell Hart said. "Disgusting."

CHAPTER 19

Once I'd stopped heaving, Luca and Con dragged me into the shower to hose me off. I didn't have the energy to do much more than stand there. Max leaned against the wall outside the shower talking to Seiran. I could feel Max in my head, needed him close for the moment, which I suspected was why he was still there. It was a little unnerving, yet he didn't seem to be trying to intrude on my thoughts.

"You're back, right?" Luca asked for the twentieth time.

"I think so," I replied again, not sure where I had been, other than lost in the haze.

"That was a redout?" Con wanted to know.

"That was a revenant," Luca said. "Way past the redout stage."

"But he just went to ground." Con dried me off and they found clean clothes for me, dressing me with the little help I could provide. I was exhausted, and healing very rapidly from a dozen or more broken bones. The hand was the worst. It throbbed like an open wound, but I felt each bone as it knit itself back together. Even after it healed, it ached in warning that it was too weak for any sort of battle.

"Gabe abandoned him," Seiran said appearing beside us in the locker room. "He's too new to survive without a sire."

"How does that even work?" Con asked. "Some sort of magic bond? Was it the blood? He didn't stop until Max covered him in his own blood."

"Blood bonding can override the sire bond," Luca said. "It's the only other option if the sire is dead. I assume that's what Gabe originally did."

If what I had with Max was a blood bonding, then something had been really wrong with my bond with Gabe. I'd never felt him in my head like this, never felt his control quite so firmly, or saw anything from his past like I'd gotten from Max.

I had a million questions, just as soon as I could hold my head up without crying like a baby. Max had blood bonded me, so he was my sire now? What was with the walk down memory lane? And he knew Gabe? What the fuck?

"He'll need to feed," Max said. He was near the sink wiping blood spatter off his wingtips. "The healing needs blood."

"Will he throw it up again?" Seiran asked.

"Not as long as he doesn't feed from a vampire. We can't take blood from our own for anything other than bonding," Max informed him.

Seiran growled. "Is there a book on all this? I need a book on this vampire shit."

A smile cracked the edges of Max's lips. "Several actually."

"Can I read them? I think I need to read them."

"Me first," I grumbled at them. If anyone needed a clue on how to be a vampire it was me.

"Can I give him blood or does he need someone else?" Luca asked. I was practically sprawled across him, my head resting on his shoulder, propped up with an arm around Con's neck. "I've never seen a revenant come back." He actually looked scared. Of me? I didn't want Luca to be afraid of me. "He killed Galloway. Even a revenant shouldn't have been able to kill Galloway. He was one of the Tri-Mega."

Galloway was dead? Holy fuck. *I* had killed Galloway? How did that happen?

"Galloway was weak. The loss of his Focus broke him. I warned him that he would not be strong enough to quell the siphon. Stolen power never undermines natural power," Max said. "Feed him. He'll need rest."

"Need to know what the fuck happened," I grumbled.

Luca pressed his wrist to my lips. "Drink."

I didn't want to. Didn't have the energy to make it not hurt him. He must have seen it on my face because he pulled his wrist back, sliced it with his own sharp teeth and then pressed it to my lips. Con flinched and looked away, but didn't try to leave. I closed my eyes as the taste of Luca's blood filled my mouth, sweet as rain in a desert. It didn't take much to fill my stomach, though it did another gurgle that made me worry I'd lose that blood too. I lapped at Luca's wound, willing it to close, knowing now it was more my saliva than any magic power. Bonded, I thought. Could I create that between Luca and I? Would it ensure he changed when he died? I swallowed back that thought, not wanting Luca to change. He didn't need to know what it was like to be a monster and he wasn't one yet, not really.

"Thanks," I told Luca. "I didn't want to hurt you."

"You're sweet for a badass motherfucker," Luca leaned forward to give me a kiss. When he pulled away, he kissed Con too. "Don't freak, okay?"

"I'm not freaking," Con promised. "I'll just insist Sam brush his teeth before I kiss him."

"We okay?" I asked Con. He'd seen a lot of bad vampire

shit. I hadn't wanted to be part of that bad vampire shit, but couldn't change that now. "I'm sorry. For all of this."

"Wasn't your fault," Con said. "We called for you. Tried to get you to stop. You didn't hear any of us. Or anything, really. You decimated the first two challengers in the cage and they were trying to keep people out and you in. You broke through the cage, ripped it open like it was nothing more than paper. Galloway tried to step in."

"Which was stupid," Luca said. "Fuck. You killed one of the Tri-Mega and didn't even break a sweat." He looked at Max. "And you reigned him in. Is the Tri-Mega all bullshit then? Just more political crap to keep vampires in line? I thought they were supposed to be the be-all and end-all power."

"I think we all have a lot of unanswered questions," Seiran said.

And wasn't that the truth?

"Let's go upstairs and we can talk privately, yes?" Max said waving a hand toward the elevator.

"I don't trust you," Seiran said honestly.

"I'd expect nothing less from Father Earth," Max said. "Your grandfather was much the same. But I can answer a few questions and direct you toward some legitimate reading if you'd like."

Even with Luca's blood in me it was hard to stand up, like my limbs didn't quite have enough electric pulses to actually animate them. Con and Luca helped me balance. "Let's go, Ronnie. I'm needing some details myself. Someone needs to answer some shit already."

Seiran walked to the elevator and pushed the only button and a moment later the door opened.

"Where are your tiny Pillars?" I asked him as I hobbled into the elevator.

"With Jamie and Kelly in the loft. Bryar's keeping an eye too."

"Gabe no longer has an invite I'm assuming?"

Seiran got into the elevator beside us. Max stepped in last and hit the button for the top floor that I knew to be Luca's new place, Max's old place.

"Correct." His voice was tight and careful, tired I realized. Emotionally rather than physically. Had love broken him?

"That will only work for homes that are not yours," Max told him. "Since you're his Focus, your home is his and he will always have an invite."

Seiran frowned. "Can he cross my wards just because we are tied together?"

Max shrugged. "I'm not sure I know of any vampires who are bound to witches. You'll have to let me know."

"Fuck," Seiran muttered.

I agreed. We needed to put Gabe in the ground fast and pray it fixed whatever in him that was broken.

Luca's loft was as I remembered it, open and very modern, lots of space with almost no room separation. Max went to the minibar in the kitchen and poured himself a few fingers of scotch before making his way to a slatted wall that slid back to reveal a bookcase. "You'll find all the reading you want, right here. First shelf on the bottom are vampire memoirs, ridiculous in my opinion, but insightful about some of the variations of vampires. Second shelf is law, human, lycan, vampire, and witch, in that order. Third shelf is reference, with a handful of guides written by former masters about vampirism. Fourth is witchcraft. Spell books and the like. Though you'll find them mostly useless as spells are individual rather than universal, or so I've discovered over the years. Top shelf is current reads, useless works for entertainment." He sipped the scotch and didn't to seem to be much interested in us. Was it an act?

The entire wall was filled with books. I didn't even know where to begin, but Seiran went right to the reference shelf, gliding his fingers across the spines as he searched the tomes.

Gabe had given me one once. It read more like a memoir and had been boring as hell. Lots of talk of seduction and keeping to the shadows. I hadn't done more than skim it. Would any of those talk about some of the powers Gabe had used? Group influence? Mind control? What other powers did vampires have that I needed to know about? And what was a siphon?

Luca and Con practically had to carry me to the bed, and I dropped onto it like a limp noodle. Why the fuck was I so tired? "Is this from turning into a revenant?" I asked Max. "This exhaustion? I feel like my limbs aren't quite working right." It was more than a little unnerving.

"I suspect it's a number of things. The revenant eats away energy, but so did Galloway's power and blood bonds also take energy. You'll be fine in a few hours. Everything realigns on its own in due time."

"Tell us about Galloway. He was a siphon?" Luca asked. "How did Sam beat him so easily."

"Sam is a siphon. Galloway was just a wannabe. He'd spent a millennia learning magic to steal power from whomever he could. I suspect Tresler is much the same." Max shrugged. "Power is a thing of perception. Those with true power are often smart enough to keep to the shadows instead of making for easy targets. Those who dream of being all-powerful step into the spotlight only to have it eventually burn them."

"Gabe was powerful," Seiran said. "Almost as powerful as you."

"Likely more so, if he was sane. I suspect he's been walking the edge for years," Max said. "Unwilling to go to ground because he had nothing to come back to, and now because he fears leaving you long enough for you to abandon him."

Seiran looked at him, pain clear on his face. "Do I know him at all? Has all of this been a lie? Our entire time together?"

"I can't answer that because I simply don't know. Speaking to some of the vampires he's created might give you more insight."

"But he can command them to say certain things, hide stuff from me, right?"

Max looked thoughtful but nodded. "Yes, and no. It would be a very specific command to keep all his vampires from telling you about him. If they couldn't speak of him at all, that would be suspect, likely a command, but for them to just not say small thoughts or opinions of him? Too individual to really control. And the older the sire-bond, the less strength it has. After a decade or two, most vampires don't need the bond at all, though it remains until the sire passes or a new blood bond is sealed."

"So you could talk to Mike," I said.

Seiran rubbed his face and turned back to the shelf. "I hate all of this. Not knowing. It's like driving down the highway at eighty miles an hour in the dark with no headlights."

"Ditto," I agreed because fuck wasn't this all a big mess. Luca wrapped around me was nice though. He rubbed my back while I used Con as a pillow. If my body didn't still feel like it'd been put through a meat grinder, I might have been a bit happier to be sandwiched between them.

Seiran took a book off the shelf and looked around a bit like a cornered animal. He needed to just breathe for a few minutes. I could feel it, the tie between us stretched, but awake and liquid. He met my eyes like he knew I could feel him, was partially in his head. "Is this part of the siphon thing?" He wanted to know.

I shrugged, just as clueless as him.

"Yes," Max said. "Once a siphon tastes your power it's a permanent bond. Not in the same way of a vampire to a Focus, but more a link. The siphon will always have the ability to borrow and enhance your power. It's one of the reasons the church, and later the Dominion, hunted them to oblivion back in the day." He walked to the shelf, took the book from Seiran's hand and chose another before placing it in his grasp. Apparently he was getting what was in my head due to our bond. It was a dizzying web that I was too tired to contemplate. "Start with this one. It has a good overview."

Seiran took the book, flipped through it for a moment before nodding.

"There's a sun porch up the stairs and to the right," Luca said pointing to a spiral staircase off to the side. "Has comfy chairs, a nice view of the stars, and a door."

That sounded like a good idea. "You can close us out for a little while. Take a breather, and still be safe, knowing your kids are safe," I pointed out. Luca's place or even if it still belonged to Max, would be a no enter zone for Gabe. I couldn't do anything to heal the hurt Seiran was feeling, other than letting him rest and regroup without all the responsibilities of being a new dad and the earth Pillar. Jamie had the twins and I knew they were safe with him. So Seiran just needed some time to decompress, I could give him that.

Seiran looked at me. I gave him a raised brow. I'd be fine just as soon as my limbs stopped feeling like lead weights. He gripped the book and headed up the stairs. I was pretty sure the book he had was a guidebook on vampires. I hoped it helped settle some of his worries about Gabe. He needed a break from all the madness. Too bad his kids weren't older so he could take them to Disneyland or something instead of basking in the paranormal bullshit that was our lives.

"So you wanna tell me how you know Gabe?" I asked Max once Seiran was gone, and I heard the door close upstairs.

"I don't," he said.

"I saw him in your memories. He's in there. Just like Seiran's grandfather was in there." The man with dark hair and sapphire eyes. I recognized him from pictures in history books. John Ruffman. He'd been executed, supposedly for crimes against the Dominion, which of course I wondered now if it was propaganda. Apparently Max and John had been lovers of some kind. He hadn't been the only one in Maxwell Hart's memory that I recognized. I glanced at Luca. "And Luca."

"The vampire you know as Gabe and I have never met."

"You knew him before he was changed?" Luca asked.

Max shrugged. "Several lifetimes ago. Neither of us are the same as we were then."

But Gabe was super old. That meant Max was just as old? No wonder he was so powerful. "I didn't feel Gabe like this," I said. "In my head."

"Then he was already gone when he brought you over. That he managed to bring you over at all is a surprise. Perhaps that was Roman's power rather than his." Max said. "You should know I don't take apprentices anymore."

"I didn't exactly ask you to."

"No, your friend Seiran did. I got the call from Riley that you weren't right, but they thought they could distract you in the ring until I got there. They expected me to put you down. I've done it more than a handful of times in the past few months. Vampires have been losing themselves to the revenant far too frequently lately. Then Seiran called to tell me Santini had revoked his mentorship, leaving you floundering. I knew you'd be a revenant by the time I got here. I explained to Seiran you might be unreachable. He asked me to try anyway."

So I owed Seiran *again*, for saving my life *again*, without asking me *again*. I sighed. "Are you going to cut me loose too?"

Max didn't look at me at that moment. He looked at Luca who was staring down at me, eyes half-lidded. He was tired too, but happy to be wrapped around me with Con's hand in his hair. Max hadn't done it for Seiran or even for me. The son of a bitch actually did it for his kid. It made me think better of him.

"Consider yourself bonded. I expect rules to be followed to the tee. You'll be learning business, helping Luca with management, taking some of his workload, so I expect you to work hard. I also expect you to read every book on those shelves." Max pointed to the wall of books.

"I'm not a big reader," I admitted.

"You will be soon. I don't give second chances, and I will put you down if I have to, even if you're not a revenant."

I gulped back that bit of news. "Is there a book of rules I should be following?"

"Luca will walk you through it. You have twenty-four hours before I come for you to begin your training. Expect to be busy, exhausted by the work." He glanced at the elevator. "You'll also be fighting regularly. Riley will put you on the schedule. Luca can help train you."

"Hmm," Luca hummed. He combed his fingers through my hair. "I like sparring with Sam. Gets me all riled up."

Max's expression changed a little, just the barest glimpse of a smile on his lips. He met my gaze and I saw the challenge there, knew his unspoken deal. Luca was something I wasn't supposed to fuck up 'cause then the big man would kill me. I nodded my agreement. All I could do was my best. At least I wasn't taking care of the masochist porn star all by myself.

Con wrapped one of his long legs around Luca and I, and snuggled close. I was tired, but being curled in their embrace made me struggle to keep my eyes open.

"I wanna know about other stuff too," I told Max. "Like the mind control Gabe did."

He pointed to the bookshelf, "Best get reading then." He looked thoughtful. "You speak and read Chinese, correct?"

"Uh, yeah." Had spent the first seven or so years of my life only speaking Chinese. But had picked up English pretty quickly in school. Some things you never forgot.

"Fantastic. I have several business ventures I'm working on with China. I will see you tomorrow evening." With that, he left. And that was okay because I seriously needed a nap.

CHAPTER 20

I dreamed of being Max. Or maybe I was just in his head as I slept. He sat on the couch in a very posh looking apartment, which didn't appear all that different from Luca's, petting a man's head with absentminded affection.

The sleeping man was one I vaguely recognized from somewhere. He had to be some sort of *other*. His muscular frame and short cropped hair made me think he'd been some kind of soldier. Maybe a shifter?

Max waved off my thoughts as it didn't matter to him, all the titles and judgments of humans. I was still very human in his opinion. The man in his lap was simply food, and he assured me that someday I'd have my fair share of those. Humans of all kinds couldn't sustain a vampire forever, even the hybrid types.

Good to know, but I was happy with Luca at the moment.

Max nodded, pleased at my affection for his son. There was also an underlying threat there, a *keep him happy and safe or else* type of feeling. Yeah, yeah, I'd try.

Max's phone rang. I knew it was his because he recognized the ring tone and was instantly annoyed. He picked up the phone and glared at the screen which read: *Tresler*.

Fuck. Was Max part of this mess too?

Max answered the phone and put it to speaker. "What do you want now?" The irritation in his tone left no question that he was not happy to hear from the final remaining member of the Tri-Mega.

"Galloway is dead."

"I did report as much earlier this evening. It was his own damn fault."

"Did he know the boy was a siphon?" Tresler demanded.

"Since he tried to take control of his power, I would assume so. I knew from the moment I met him. It's unlikely that Galloway would not have known."

"And yet you didn't tell me."

"Tell you what? What you should already have known? Wouldn't it have been Gabe's job to report his charge's power to you?" Max nodded as if he knew the answer to his own question. "Gabe didn't know what he was. Perhaps he's never met a siphon before. I remember the days of the witch trials which eliminated entire family lines of them. Apparently our reach did not extend to Asia. Gabe actually spent a good portion of his life living in the East, didn't he? Hiding from memories and constant wars, among people who thought he was some sort of kitsune."

"It's better off if you let the boy bond to me," Tresler said.

"He accepted my bond. He destroyed Galloway with little effort. Would you really like to try?"

Tresler was silent for a minute. "You should accept my bond as well. How long until your mind frays like the rest?"

"My mind is fine," Max assured him. And it was. He was clear, unclouded by doubt or scattered bits of emotion like Gabe had always been. I had thought that was what made

Gabe more human, but perhaps that just meant Gabe had been broken a long time.

"There are so few left it is better for us all to unite. You could be part of the new Tri-Mega. You and Santini. You could have him back."

"Did Santini let you blood bond him?" Max asked. My heart flipped over as the cold realization slipped through me.

"Of course. He wants to protect his lover and was willing to accept my help and strength."

How many of the crazy vampires were blood bonded to Tresler? Had that happened before or after I'd gone to ground? Fuck. No wonder Gabe was completely batshit crazy now.

"You rejected my business proposal, how is that of sound mind?"

"For a stake in QuickLife? How many are blood bonded to you through the QuickLife?" Max inquired. "Without knowing it."

"You know that was necessary. The young are so wild." Tresler sighed whimsically. "Do you remember the old days? When we were worshipped and feared? When we didn't walk among the cattle wining and dining them to our side?"

Max had thought those times very uncivilized and had found building his empire difficult. Too much unrest in the world at large. He thought the new ideas of diplomacy so much better for power consolidation and wealth building. "So you wish to return to the days in which the humans fear us and we were driven to hide from them? How is that a sound business decision?"

"I never hid from them."

"Yet somehow you survived? Their numbers are so much greater than ours. It would take little effort for them to destroy us now. Even now they contemplate if that is a better course of action than diplomacy." Max knew this for fact as he had several meetings with high-up members of the government speaking to him about that very issue. Asking questions. Demanding answers. If he hadn't been tied to the government with a couple hundred contracts for goods and services through his vast array of businesses, he might have already found himself dead. Stupid, Max thought. This whole thing. A waste of energy over baseless greed.

I agreed.

"I am all-powerful, they would not dare."

Right. The USA was a ballsy government who did it's best to railroad anyone into their control, even decimating entire nations when it was convenient to them. A couple thousand vampires was nothing. Max nodded at my opinion. He'd seen it himself over and over again.

"I will think about your request," Max offered, though had no intention of doing so.

"It's not a request. You will accept my bond, as will the boy."

I wasn't a boy, and it irritated me that he thought of me that way. Hadn't I just destroyed one of his equals? Bastard.

"The boy is bonded to me. It's unlikely you can take his bond from me without my death. Perhaps you're looking for a challenge?" Max suggested it as though it were no more consequential than the weather, but I felt the threat in him. He did not want to be pigeonholed. "Perhaps you forget that I have an organization of over one million witches at my beck and all? Or that Seiran Rou, the Pillar of earth, is currently the leader of that organization and the son of one of the most powerful Dominion witches in the world? The boy, as you call him, is theirs, I only bonded with him to control the revenant at Rou's request. Take him from me and you take him from them." There was silence over the line so

Max added. "The last time you fought the witches the humans were on your side, eliminating them because it was convenient for them. Now the witches and humans are united. There are millions of them. Don't think that because I am not the magical power that Galloway was, that I am weak. My allies are many."

"You ask for war."

"No," Max said. "That is what you're asking for. It's what you've been planning for years. I will have no part in it." Max clicked the end button and glared at the screen. This was all coming to a head, and he was not thrilled by the direction in which it was leading. He let me feel his frustration and worry for a few minutes as he thought of options.

Funny how a vampire who claimed to feel nothing, felt so much. Perhaps he just didn't understand what he felt was still human?

"You think so?" Max said out loud, asking me. "Are they not muted?"

I couldn't tell that by being in his head. Only that he was angry with Tresler, worried about protecting Luca and the vampires he'd created, and frustrated with how his hands were tied with human diplomacy. All strong emotions in my opinion.

"Hmm," he said. "I will have to think on that." And with those words he pushed me back into myself, a sensation that felt a little like falling. I jerked awake. My limbs snapping back to full function hurt more than I thought anything should. The fire through my nervous system burned until my eyes twitched.

The energy began to fade, leaving my fingers tingling and me blinking at the ceiling, the room dark. I could feel eyes on me. Not Con or Luca who were asleep. Seiran sat in a chair and stared out the window instead of at me, though I could feel his attention.

"Creepy, Ronnie," I whispered. "I dreamed of Max."

"Like sexing him up?"

"Um, ew, and no. Why does your brain go there?"

"'Cause I'm talking to you and that seems to be where your brain goes."

"Jerk."

"Bastard."

"I might know some stuff."

"Okay," Seiran said.

"Do you know if Gabe accepted a blood bond from Tresler?"

"I don't know. He doesn't talk about vampire stuff with me. It's almost like he was embarrassed to be one."

"'Cause sucking on people to survive is embarrassing?"

"See!" Seiran said pointing at me. "Your brain."

I waved off his comment. "Seriously. I think Tresler put his blood in the QuickLife and that's how he's controlling all the vampires." No wonder that shit tasted like ass. "Or maybe it's not control so much as lack of control? Breaking their bonds with their sires?" Was that a possibility? Fuck, I needed to know more about vampires.

Seiran seemed to think on that for a minute. "Gabe's sire is long gone as far as I know."

"But a blood bond to another vampire works the same way." Could it let the demon loose, as much as it could reign it in? That felt right, even if I wasn't sure. Gabe's bond to me had done something for me, and its loss had nearly been my undoing. Even if he'd already been broken when he'd done it, he'd kept me from going revenant.

We sat in silence for a few minutes, both of us processing the implications behind all of this. Finally Seiran said, "Why?"

"Why does any crazy ass bastard do anything?"

Seiran sighed. "Power corrupts, but does it really make us all mad? Is that what I have to look forward to?"

"We'll keep you sane, Ronnie," I promised him.

He nodded, but I could feel his worry. This link between us wasn't fading. "Mike is coming to pick me up. I need to talk to him." More like interrogate him. "Find out how much of Gabe I really know."

"Okay. You gonna be okay?" Where those really answers he wanted?

"No," Seiran said honestly.

"I'm sorry." And I was. I hadn't created the problem, though I was pretty sure I was part of it. There was also no way I could fix it either.

"Let me worry about Gabe."

"That's the plan."

"I need you to find out about Tresler," Seiran said.

"Find out what? If he's nuts? Pretty sure most vampires are nuts. Me included. Even if what I dreamed was just a dream, it's a pretty solid theory. Though it felt pretty real to be a dream. Can a blood bond let him in my head? Max, I mean."

"It's different for each vampire," Seiran said. "At least according to what I've read so far. Though there is some level of metaphysical bonding that goes on with a blood bond. Some vampires report being about to hear each other's thoughts, some merely feel their sire's presence. You didn't feel anything with Gabe?"

I thought about that for a few minutes. "Faintly. Sort of like I could tell if he was in the room and what direction? Sometimes I'd get an edge of his emotions, but nothing else."

"Hmm. If Tresler put his blood in the QuickLife and Gabe's been drinking it by the ton...how long has it been there? He's been drinking that stuff as long as I've known him." Seiran got up and began to pace. "Would going to ground even help him at this point? Or is it Tresler's bond that is driving him mad?"

"Only one way to tell," I said. At least if Gabe was out of the way we could maybe deal with Tresler head on. "Gabe's a pretty powerful vampire to have under his control, especially since he's bonded to you."

"But he's been closed off to me for months. I only get tiny glimpses through our bonds every once in a while."

"Maybe Gabe's still in there," I pointed out. "Maybe he's trying to protect you."

Seiran stopped pacing and looked at me, his eyes looking watery in the dark. He clutched a book to his chest, holding on to it like it was a life raft. "If Tresler's the reason the vampires are going nuts, is it a loss of control of vampires that is making them all crazy, or is he doing it on purpose?"

"I thought that was a given."

"Maybe he's not strong enough to control them all?" Seiran shook his head. "It could be the unraveling of the ties. Tresler takes a strong vampire but he's not strong enough to control all the vampires that vampire sired? The government thinks it's Gabe. But he hasn't made enough vampires to be causing this mess. When I asked, Gabe said he'd only created two dozen vampires in his life."

"He could have been lying."

"Maybe. But why about that? He also has never seemed the type to just go and create vampires for the hell of it." Seiran sighed. "I mean, back when we first met, he always came across as responsible. Not an act, not just words, his actions."

"Stuffy," I agreed. If there had ever been a word to describe Gabe, it was stuffy.

"Responsible," Seiran amended. Which was why his

collapse hurt so much now. Everyone relied on him, maybe too much so.

"Okay, so what if it's all Tresler. Whether it's his control or lack of control or whatever? What then?" I wanted to know.

"You killed Galloway."

"By accident." And by going revenant which I didn't want to ever experience again. "Do you want me to go nuts again just to kill that monster? I might not come back." And that was what terrified me the most.

"Are your bonds with them strong enough to keep you here?" He asked and waved at Luca and Con who were wrapped around me.

"They weren't enough to call me back just a few hours ago. I think the whole revenant thing is a little more than just losing your shit. That bond unraveled something in me. I wasn't me anymore. I was just hunger, rage, and destruction. Love doesn't conquer all, Ronnie. No matter what the romance novels tell you."

He sniffled. Fuck.

"Death magic is pretty strong," I said. "I think that's what the revenant is."

"The Dominion has never recognized it as its own element."

"And yet it takes us all, doesn't it?"

He resumed his pacing. "So say we take down Tresler then. Would his death end this madness or just add fuel to the fire? Let's say that death is an element like earth or water..."

"What happens when an earth witch dies?" I asked.

"The earth takes them back."

"And a water or air witch?"

Seiran frowned at me. "The earth takes them all back."

"And if a vampire experiences true death like Andrew Roman and Matthew did?"

"The earth takes them back."

I nodded. Exactly. "He's just a vampire. The earth likes vampires. Full of nutrients for the soil."

"Talking about murder, Sammie. I'm not sure I can just kill him that way."

"Extreme circumstances call for extreme actions." I understood. Seiran was the good guy. The world relied on him to stay that way. After all, what would happen if the Pillar of earth happened to be a bad guy? Seiran had killed before, but it had been self-defense. Was I splitting hairs? Was there a difference? Premeditated murder felt like a different level of extreme. Was it premeditated if we knew Tresler was ordering his flunkies to kill people, or self-defense? I'd never cared much for philosophy for exactly that reason. I also wasn't bothered by the idea of premeditated murder for someone who deserved it. So maybe it didn't have to be Seiran. After all, I could borrow his power. "Let me worry about vampire problems."

"I'm a vampire's Focus," Seiran pointed out.

"And a new father, and Pillar of earth."

"That doesn't make me more important than the rest of the world."

"No," I agreed. "But it does put you pretty high up there. It's not all on you, Ronnie. Saving the world and all that shit. Your white knight syndrome is annoying."

He mock growled at me.

"Get pissy all you want, it's true. The whole fucking lot of you have it. Your muscle head brother, the blond swimming freak, even Gabe before he went completely bonkers."

Seiran fell silent, likely thinking about their time together. I knew it was tearing him up because he was completely closed off to me.

"Not your fault, Ronnie."

"But I'm not enough to save him either."

"Sometimes we have to save ourselves, otherwise it doesn't mean much and we don't learn anything." It was why I was so frustrated that they kept saving me. The other option was dead, of course, and I wasn't sure I wanted that, but I hated being a fucking damsel in distress always being saved. Wasn't I strong enough to save myself?

He let out a long sigh. His phone beeped and I saw him glance at it. "Mike is here to pick me up. Don't go home." He paused, "Well not to Gabe's or my place, and I know Con let the lease on your place expire. He's been living with Kelly since you went to ground. You can stay here with Luca or I've texted you the address for the new house. After sunup I'll be moving my stuff and the twins into it. You'll have an invite and your own space. Hell, there's enough room for you to have a whole wing if that's what you need. My mom was a little over the top with her McMansion building. Said there would be plenty of room for more kids. 'Cause I need more?"

"I'm thinking the big guy and his little merman boyfriend might want some kiddos eventually."

"Yeah," Seiran agreed. "Jamie wants them bad. He looks at the twins and I see it in his face. I just hope he gives Kelly some time to finish school and stuff. Though it'd be nice to have some friends for the twins. Hanna had a bunch of her eggs frozen when we were mixing up the twins."

"If Jamie used those and mixed with Kelly, your kids would technically have siblings/cousins."

"Yeah, but family is okay, right? The family you choose." He stared at me and I realized then that was what I was. Part of the family he'd chosen. And not only that, he was part of mine. Fuck.

"Feelings," I growled at him.

"Yeah, but you're a vampire and still feel them. Hold on to that, yeah?"

"Jerk," I said.

"Bastard," he threw back as he got up. "Text me before dawn so I know you're safe, no matter where you'll be. I don't need details," he waved at the piles of limbs and warmth that was on the bed.

"Will do, Ronnie," I promised. He nodded and left quietly.

CHAPTER 21

I untangled myself to pace and think. Seiran had taken a book with him, and I stared at the shelf in the dark, thinking maybe I should find a place to begin, but I really hated reading. It made me tired.

I heard Con take a deep breath and glanced his way. He was staring at me through sleepy eyes. After a moment he got up and went to the kitchen and poured himself a glass of ice water. There was almost no food in the fridge, just a few condiments in the door.

I leaned against the kitchen counter and stared at him. Con was the sort of beautiful a man with a lot of ink should be, all lean lines and bright colors. His ears were pierced and gauged, dark hair trimmed short on the sides and left long enough on top to tangle in his eyelashes. The ink covering him was more about hiding scars than elaborate storylines, and that was okay. I knew some of the stories, small things he'd been willing to share over our months together, and would listen each time he needed to open up about another one. Sometimes the internal demons just needed to bleed, he often told me. I agreed, but was glad he was using tattoos instead of cutting to get that feeling.

He actually had a new wash of color that decorated his back with wings. Not one giant set like an angel, but dozens of birds. Birds of various colors, flying outward forming a tree-of-life type shape. There was no rainbow, more variation from the birds of prey, eagles, falcons, ravens, and hawks. I reached out to touch it, running my fingers across a raven or two, detailed despite the black outline.

"Was this inspired by your change?"

"Yes. Seiran actually drew it for me a while back. I asked him for lots of birds, but told him it needed to be more badass than just a bunch of black winged shapes." He shivered under my fingers. "We're all connected through the earth, so that's why it's the tree. Birds land in the tree, rest, and nest in a tree. Earth and water make the tree grow. Fire burns it down to make way for new growth. It's a balance. Took five sessions to complete. Burned for a long time, but you were in the ground and the pain made me think of you. It kept me from cutting again."

"Sorry," I said and withdrew my hand. I never wanted to hurt him.

"Don't be." He turned and stepped close. "I like you touching me."

"Even though I'm a vampire?"

"I think that's more your hang-up than mine. I don't want to be bitten, but I don't mind that you're a vampire. You're still just you."

"With fangs," I pointed out thinking about the whole revenant thing. There was an edge of that inside still, wasn't there? I could feel it waiting, just like all the energy from Seiran, Kelly, and now Galloway. Was that part of being the siphon? I glanced at the bookshelf again. Stupid books. "I hate reading," I said, "but I have so many questions."

Con laughed. "Unless it's a video game." He wrapped his arms around me and pulled me into a hug.

"I do like video games. Too bad there's not a video game that teaches me all this vampire shit for real," I agreed, sighing as his body pressed against mine. This was nice. I'd fallen asleep on the couch with him before and tried really hard not to focus on how nice it had been to be there. "Is this real? You and me?"

"Yes."

"And you're okay with Luca?"

Con snorted. "He's hot. I wanted to hate him, you know? 'Cause you'd talk about him when you guys were chatting online. You liked him. He made you smile sometimes with silly things that he said. And I tried to be happy for you. Thought that it was good that you could like the guy you'd have to feed from. And maybe you'd find out you loved him. But man did that piss me off."

"Sorry," I said.

"Don't be. That was me, not you. I was jealous. Wanted you to want me."

"I did…do want you." Fuck, had since the moment we'd been thrown together as haphazard victims of Kelly's white-knight syndrome. "I just don't want to lose our friendship." Con was part of what kept me feeling human, real. He grounded me in a way I feared I'd lose without him.

"I'm not going anywhere."

"Even if Luca sticks around?" I had to admit the guy was really growing on me.

He sighed and pressed a light kiss to my lips, which I accepted and returned. "I'm not the badass you are." He rested his forehead against mine, leaning down, and stared into my eyes.

"Okay?"

"I'm a little needy."

"Okay?"

"You were gone a few weeks, and he was around a lot. Making passes and playing games with me. We talked about you at first. He's nice. Smart. I wanted to hate him, but I really like him. He gets me in a lot of ways. And yet is so different that I find him fascinating. Then it just sort of happened. He kissed me and we made out...which led to other things. You were still gone. Sometimes we'd sit together at your grave and play card games to pass the time. Thought you could maybe hear our voices. I kissed him there once. Hoped you'd wake up because you were so mad. Are you mad?"

"No." And I wasn't. I had no right to demand anything of either of them. If they found comfort in each other, who was I to judge? Well, and quite frankly, the thought of the two of them together was really hot. "Do you want me to find someone else to feed on?" Did he want Luca instead of me?

"No. I want all of us to work this out. Fuck the Western view of monogamy. I've never been good at having just one lover. I thought maybe with the two of you...we could find something that works. If you're open to it."

"Uh, since we all had sex several times already today, or yesterday now I guess, I think that means I'm on board."

"But I don't want to always be all of us," Con said as he wrapped his hands around my face and pulled me close for an intense kiss. This was no glancing touch of the lips, but a full onslaught on my mouth, lips, teeth, tongue. I closed my eyes and enjoyed the taste of him. He pressed his hips to mine and I felt his erection. When he finally let the kiss end, we were both breathing hard. "Sometimes I want it to just be me and you. Is that okay?"

"Sure," I promised him, turning us to press him into the counter and grind my hips against his. "I'm all for that. Same goes if you just want Luca sometimes too."

"You too," Con said. "He gives amazing head." Con closed his eyes like the memory was enough to get him off. "Never thought a blow job could be that good until I met Luca."

"Wow, I have some standards to live up to then, eh?" I teased.

Con smiled. "Maybe. Your blow job in the shower was good. Might have to try it again to compare…"

"Jerk," I said. "You're supposed to say I'm better. I was a little nervous about the fangs. Luca probably has more practice too."

"No favorites," Con said. "No competition. I want it to just be Zen with us. We all get what we need."

That sounded too good to be true, but wasn't I the one who wanted to live again? Experience life for real this time, even if I was undead? "Okay. I'm willing to try."

Con kissed me lightly again. "Yeah, that's a good start."

I wallowed in his kiss for a moment, enjoying the slow, sensual break of it. Nothing rushed or rough like most of my life had been. It was sad how I'd been conditioned by those things. Rough turned me on, and that was okay, but I was happy that it wasn't just the hardcore that turned me on. I reached down and rubbed Con through his jeans. "Can I jerk you off?" 'Cause how hot was that?

He laughed lightly. "You don't need permission for that."

"Good," I kissed him again and unbuttoned his jeans to reach my hand in. His cock was thick and not overly long, but I liked the weight of him in my grip. He sighed into my lips, eyes closing in ecstasy. I found a rhythm that had him hitching his breath and my hips humping his legs in time to it. We ate at each other's mouth. Not the fierce devouring I always found myself lost in with Luca, but a delicious exploration of sensations.

We swallowed each other's little sounds, both gasping and moaning, leaning into each other. My grip on him quickened. I rolled my fist over him, then thumbed the head to tickle his slit. He was so sensitive.

"Fuck," he cried as he let go and painted my fist with his come. I groaned and let myself go. The pleasure pinged through me with the energy of a lightning bolt, stinging, and empowering all at once. Since we stood next to the sink I reached over, rinsed my hand, dried it on a towel and then tucked his spent cock back into his pants. Con wrapped his arms around me, and we stood there together for a few minutes. Not talking. I wasn't even really thinking, which was a nice break. Though I needed clean underwear. Maybe Luca had something I could borrow.

"Fuck," I groaned to Con.

Con nodded his agreement. "I, however, need food. Apparently that's a foreign concept in this house."

"I never eat here," Luca grumbled from the bed. "Always ate out or with you."

"Yeah, well it sounds like we have a new haunt," I told them. "I'm sure the witch will cook for you both."

"We're going to stay with Seiran?" Con asked.

"You don't want to?"

"I don't know. Seems like someone is always out to fuck with him."

Which was why I planned on sticking with him. He didn't make himself a target. He'd been born one. Just like me. He was a powerful earth witch in a world that didn't believe a man should have that power. I was some sort of power siphon and amplifier. Not something either of us had asked for. And how was that fucking fair? "Someone is always out to fuck with me too," I pointed out.

Luca crawled out of bed and to our sides where he wrapped the both of us in a warm hug. "Probably won't stop either since you killed Galloway. Vamps will come after you just to prove they are better or more dangerous than you."

"That's stupid," Con said.

"Yes," I agreed, but knew it was true. "The siphon thing made me a target before I even knew what I could do." Matthew had known. Somehow through his insanity he'd sensed it and used it. Roman had done everything he could to exploit my power for his own gain. I had no delusions about people leaving me alone now. Galloway's attempt to control me had been another grab for my power. Only my power had turned on him, ate him down, and destroyed him. It made me worry about Max. He wouldn't be so easily beaten. But I also had yet to see him actually try to use magic for his own gain.

And what if I went revenant again? Who would protect the world from me? I had no doubt that Seiran could have ordered the earth to take me back, a true death. Instead he'd asked for help to save me. If I got lost again and he had no choice? He could be ruthless, right? He'd killed before to save himself and the people he loved. I hoped he could save Luca and Con if I ever turned again. Yeah, staying close to the most powerful witch in the world was a good idea.

"How do you feel about it, Luca?" I asked him.

He shrugged. "I'm not really attached to places. Moved a lot my whole life following my dad's business stuff. I don't care where I sleep as long as it's with you guys. 'Sides, the witch is probably as safe a bet as any. If I've learned anything about being the kid of a vampire over the years, it's that powerful allies are important. And he cooks." Luca patted his stomach. "Man, I love that guy's food. Hope he has good Wi-Fi. I work from home a lot when my dad is traveling. Lots of phone work."

I groaned.

"Yeah, we'll have to work on your bullshitting," Luca patted my cheek. "You gotta say pretty things to people even when you hate their guts. That's how business works."

"I hate this already," I told him.

"Nah," Luca said. "I think you'll be great. You're a bit of a shark like Max. Put up with no one's bullshit. He's sort of the master of calling people on it while still sounding like he's the most intelligent and nicest person in the room. I aspire to such greatness someday."

"I'm glad I work at the bar. Hope I don't lose that job when Gabe isn't around anymore," Con said.

"Sounds like Mike has been running it anyway," I reminded him. "But we'll worry about that bridge when we cross it."

"Max could buy the bar. If Gabe goes to ground all his assets will be Seiran's since Seiran is his Focus. It's part of the official filing of a Focus with the Tri-Mega," Luca said.

I shook my head. "Seiran loves that bar."

"Sure, but he's got bigger problems than that."

And that was true. I sighed. More problems I didn't want to think about. "Okay, let's get your stuff packed up then." I shifted my hips. "Maybe I can borrow a pair of clean undies?"

Luca laughed lightly. "That was hot."

"Coming in my pants is not hot."

"It was from my place on the bed."

"Jerk," I said. He grinned. Con laughed. Luca finally pulled away to dig in another hidden wall cupboard for clothing.

He held out a pair of undies for me. "Here you go, princess," he teased. "Or, I mean, you badass bitch."

I snarled at him, let Con go and crossed the room to swipe them from his grasp.

"We should bring the books," Con said from his place by the counter. "I'm sure there's room. Sam doesn't like to read, but I do, and I know Seiran does. Maybe we can get the whole lot of us up to speed."

"I've read most of them," Luca said. He squinted at the bookcase. "Once or twice. I don't have great recall or anything, though. So I'd have to look stuff up. I think the book Seiran took with him had info about siphons."

Con tapped his forehead. "My recall is excellent. My sister's was too. It was one of the reason's Roman wanted control of her. She could see a spell once and memorize it."

No wonder he'd brought me a handful of spells written on scratch pieces of paper. I hadn't yet searched through the books I had stashed for them, but if Max was right and spells were individual, then I wasn't sure it mattered much.

I headed to the bathroom to wash up and change. We needed a plan. Something to stop the vampire's insanity, put Gabe to sleep, and maybe take out Tresler. However, I was not the brains of the operation. New adventures and enterprising ideas had a way of backfiring when I did them. But I wasn't alone anymore. Con and Luca chatted as they packed up his clothes into a suitcase he'd dug out from somewhere. I had a dhampir, an air witch, two very powerful earth witches, a water witch, and a master vampire on my side. It sounded like the start to a great RPG video game. But time would tell.

CHAPTER 22

I sent Seiran a text asking him if it was okay to bring the guys to the house. He said it was fine. There was only another two or so hours before dawn. He wanted me at the house as soon as possible because he had a long list of wards he wanted to create and thought that my ability could strength them. I agreed, and let him know we were on the way. Instead of taking a cab, Luca said he would drive and led us down to an underground garage and a giant black Hummer.

"Holy fuck," Con said.

"It's my dad's," Luca said. "Built like a tank. I wanted something more practical, he insisted on this." He put his suitcase in the back, and I added the box of books we'd decided were essential.

"For all your smack talk about your dad, he really cares about you," I commented.

He side-eyed me. "Just because he gives me stuff, doesn't mean he cares."

Did he really have no idea? Maybe being linked to Max gave me a different point of view. The empire he built, had trained

Luca to command, the loft, the car, and now me, a powerful vampire to watch over him, was all just to take care of Luca. "Was it just Galloway who wanted you and me involved?"

"No," Luca said. "Max brought you up first. Since I've helped other vampires, I thought it was just that he didn't think anyone else could tame you at the time."

"Tame?" I squinted at him.

"Your bloodlust. My blood is a bit supercharged and not all *cibos* are. Most are just human, and the few who are hybrids like me aren't nearly as powerful as I am. Probably because my dad is so powerful. I'm also older than most other *cibos*, so I have more experience in redirecting hunger."

That all made sense. "So your dad said, 'Hey, feed this almost feral vampire?'"

Luca blushed. "I sort of have a thing for Asian guys…"

Con snorted. "You have a thing for all guys."

"True," Luca agreed. "But lots of fantasies…So my dad pointed you out, knowing my kink. Asian, rough, tough, and a little snarky."

"A little?" Con asked.

"Asshole," I threw back at him.

"Exactly that," Con replied.

"Anyway, after we talked online the first time, I knew we would click in person. My dad made the arrangements for me to move here and still have a large part of his business."

I smiled at Luca.

"Don't be creepy," Luca told me. "Did he tell you something?"

"Just to take care of you," I assured him.

"And he gives you a cushy loft and a fancy super car? Makes sure you have a good job?" Con teased. "All housed in a building with heavy security?" He pointed toward the guard station which was manned with big guys with guns.

Luca frowned as he got in the driver's seat. I got in the passenger seat and Con jumped into the back. "He's never said anything. Always says his emotions don't work right."

His emotions worked just fine. I think he'd just had far too long learning to ignore them. "Maybe you should talk to him about it sometime. Though not right now. He sort of has someone over…" In that moment I realized who it had been in his lap. Kenrick, the guy from the club.

Fuck.

Didn't Luca say he got jealous of his dad being with people? That was a blood thing, right? Territorial or something? He froze, staring at his hands. And I wondered if I'd made a mistake. Would he freak?

After a minute he shook himself and started the car.

"You okay," I asked.

"Yeah. Thought the jealousy would rise up like it always does. But it didn't." He looked at me, and for a second his eyes seemed to glow, a bit of the vampire in him coming out. "It's you I need now."

"But you're not jealous of Con," I said, pointing toward the backseat.

"No. He doesn't get to feed you. Only I do."

"For now," I allowed. Max had suggested that even Luca wouldn't be enough on his own forever. Would I have to hide others from him? I hoped not. I really just wanted it to be the three of us for a while.

"I'll work on it," Luca said. "Some of it is instinctive." He used the GPS on his phone to navigate us to the new address Seiran had sent me. It was actually outside of the cities a good way.

"How well did you know that guy at the club?" I asked Luca. "Kenrick, I think his name was."

"Not well."

"How long has your dad been sleeping with him?" I clarified.

He glanced at me and growled.

"Thought you said I was what you need now?"

"He says he doesn't sleep with Kenrick. Just feeds on him. And um, gross, thinking of my dad with anyone."

"Your dad is hot," Con said.

"Truth," I pointed out. "If you like the tall, dark, and dangerous businessman sort. Total daddy kink."

Luca narrowed his eyes at us. "Really? What the fuck is wrong with you two?"

"You look like your dad," Con amended.

"Just not as big and dangerous," I agreed.

"I hate you both," Luca said without heat.

Con and I laughed.

"He doesn't talk about anyone. Never has. Not in a relationship sort of way. He's all business," Luca said. Max did have a very black and white view of food so maybe that was true.

"Is that why you went off your rocker? 'Cause you thought Kenrick had taken your dad's attention and was trying for mine?" I asked.

"You make it sound like I was screwing my dad. It's just instinct to protect those I'm feeding on. Don't you have an instinct to protect me?"

I laughed. "My instinct to protect you has nothing to do with the fact that I occasionally munch on you."

"Is it 'cause I'm hot?" Luca asked.

"You are hot," Con agreed.

"Stop fishing," I told him. "I'll be all over you like Donkey Kong later. I protect you because I like you," I admitted.

"That's a rousing endorsement," Luca gripped.

"He *like likes* you," Con said laughing.

"This is not high school," I said. "I'm not in love with you yet, but it's more than just plain like. Is that good enough for now?" No more bullshit. It wasn't likely they were walking away now. Not with all the super vamps trying to rule the world and the Pillar of earth falling apart. I loved Con. Had for a while now, and Luca wasn't there yet, but he also wasn't far out of that zone.

"Yeah?"

"Yeah," I said. "You're more than a blood bag with a hole to me," I said with a straight face.

"Another rousing endorsement."

"I like all his holes," Con pointed out. "Can't wait to explore more of them."

"That sounded kind of creepy," I said, but the idea still made me hard. "Like you could be cleaning wax out of his ears or something."

"Or fucking his boy pussy," Con said.

"You can fuck my boy pussy anytime," Luca promised. "Either of you."

Okay, totally hard. Fuckers. "You both realize I have to do magic shit with the witch, right? So we can't show up at his house and fuck like bunnies?"

Luca shrugged. "He said we could have a whole wing. Once he's got his little magic shindig done, we can go play. I brought lube."

"Is that all that's on your mind?" I wanted to know.

"No, but it sure makes life worth living sometimes. You still need to sleep some today and then get started at my dad's business tonight. He wasn't kidding about you being busy. You'll be begging me for a blow job in the bathroom just to get your mind off contracts for five minutes."

"Okay, now I want a job with you guys. As long as I get blow jobs during the work day," Con said. We all laughed.

The drive was long. I began to wonder if the GPS had sent us to the wrong place or if we were moving to

Wisconsin or something, but finally we pulled onto a street lined with a massive brick fence and in the distance a giant house.

"Boonies…" Con grumbled.

"Better have Wi-Fi," Luca agreed.

I laughed. What better place for a bunch of crazy powerful witches and a vampire who just happened to amplify their power than the middle of fucking nowhere? "It looks more modern than I was expecting," I admitted when we pulled through an open metal gate and onto a long circular drive.

"McMansion is right," Con said.

The towering building was easily four stories high, though it didn't seem to have enough windows to accommodate that many floors. It was painted a pale shade of green, almost so pale it looked white in the dark, but when we stepped out of the Hummer and up to the entry, I could tell it wasn't white. There was a huge double door entry, columns on each side and an awning overhead. I expected something with gargoyles on the top, or turrets, but it looked like a normal house from the front. Just huge. There was a wrap-around porch, but no furniture or adornments outside.

The wall encased the house and what appeared to be a couple acres. There were already gardens planted in the front and trees around each side. I had to admit, that despite the giant, starkly new feeling of the house, the grounds pulsed with warmth and life. I'd have to walk the grounds to know for sure, but I could almost feel the pulsing of ley lines. Seiran's father's estate had intersecting ley lines that blew power out of the universe. It didn't feel quite that level here, but still strong. Perhaps not intersecting. Or maybe the intersection just wasn't through the middle of the house, which I thought could only be a good thing. No one needed to live in that constant buzz of energy.

Before we even got to the doorbell the door opened and Seiran stepped out. He was in full Father Earth form, green hair, flowers and ivy woven around his clothes and hair, and glowing eyes that swirled with shades of the planet. It was both creepy and awe-inspiring because my mind instantly thought God with a capital G, and he sort of was one, and yet not. The earth had chosen him as her husband, and her voice. She was also a fickle thing that could take all that away in seconds.

He smiled at us. "Glad you're here. I'm finished with the upper floors, just have to link it all to the lower floor and hopefully add a bit of your strength in to tie it all together. I'll work on the grounds tomorrow."

"How many acres?" I wanted to know.

"The yard or beyond the gate?" Seiran asked.

"Yard."

"Two. Not as big as my father's estate."

But still huge. "You inviting your fairy friends to take care of the yard? I'm calling 'not it' on lawn duty."

"Bryar is working on it. Until then my mother has a crew of gardeners on the schedule."

"Okay, Ronnie. Tell me what you need." I didn't know much about spells that weren't words of power. Seiran was power, so he didn't use words much, though I knew he had a handful of spells he'd written. He could make other people's spells work because he just had that much power. It was also why spells often worked when other people used them around me, since Andrew Roman had used spells that weren't his, and Maxwell Hart stated that magic was individual.

Seiran held out a hand. "It requires you to plug in to my power and walk the floor with me."

"You mean tune into the psychic network? Lightning-is-us? Jerk." I said to him knowing the buzzing of his energy was going to hurt, especially since my senses were still so raw from the revenant thing.

"Bastard," he replied in a teasing tone. "I wouldn't ask if it wasn't necessary, but the twins are upstairs." And he had to protect his kids. He glanced at Luca and Con. "You guys both have an official invite already, but if you could wait in the entry until Sam and I are done linking the wards? Too much movement in the house makes it hard to layer them properly." And he was trying to keep a vampire linked to him, out, and away from his family.

"Sure," Luca agreed.

"Okay," Con said.

"Movers will arrive a little later to get everything from the old apartment moved over. But your game console and games are here. I had Jamie grab that stuff and a bunch of you guys' clothes. My mom will be here to oversee the movers. The windows all have that UV safe glass, but you'll probably want to add curtains or blinds or something. Right now I've got a handful of sheets we can hang for a few hours of sleep. Once this ward is done." Seiran reached out a hand for me.

I took it and felt the blast of his power, let it roll through me like a wave of fire and electricity. It didn't hurt this time. Not really. More the sensation of having too much energy at once. It was almost the buzz of anxiety rising up from a well deep in my gut, a vibration of power. Feeding on Galloway had been similar, only I had no temptation to take from Seiran. My inner power, or whatever the fuck it was, must have realized that we could drink him down forever and never stop. Self-destruction. And we weren't on board with that anymore.

Luca and Con rushed up the stairs and into the house. Flowers bloomed around Seiran's feet, while cacti cropped up around mine. He looked at them thoughtfully then dragged me into the house.

It might have looked a little like the gothic monster mansion his father had designed on the outside, but the inside was very modern and clean. No tree in the foyer and instead there was a giant split staircase that curved against both walls, with a walkway in the middle beneath it that appeared to lead to the kitchen. There was also a door on each wall leading to different areas.

Seiran closed the door, then pressed his hand to it. I closed my eyes as the power rolled through us both with all the subtlety of an E5 tornado. Vaguely down the link of our bond I could feel Max who seemed to sense us and perk up, focusing in our direction. He did something, though I wasn't sure what, and the blast of power suddenly became a gentle rain, the layers of the wards almost visible in the droplets as they fell and spread, covering the door, the windows, the walls. Max had done this before. Perhaps not set wards himself, but helped someone else direct their power.

"Wow," Seiran whispered. The drops expanded like dough set out to rise, growing along the walls, covering the windows and linking the entire house in one finely woven thread of power. "I didn't expect it to be that easy. Not after I just spent the last two hours warding the rest of the house."

We both could feel down the line to Max who withdrew back to virtual non-existence, and shared a look. Could Gabe have done that if he'd been sane? What the hell was Max? Seiran frowned at something he caught in my head.

"Max knew Gabe?"

"Not Gabe," I said. "Before they were vampires." Vampires didn't always take on new names. I think that was more common when so much time passed and they had to change identities to hide. Or maybe they just hated their birth names and changed it like I had.

Seiran took a deep breath and pulled the power back. Father Earth receded into the pretty Asian man with black hair and blue eyes. He let go of my hand and I had to shake mine just to get the feeling back in it. Seiran looked tired. He'd lived on a vampire schedule for a long time. Sleeping during the day and awake at night. Now he had a real job and kids. He'd have to live when the rest of the world was living, which really just translated to him not sleeping much at all.

"Are we safe now, Ronnie?" I teased.

"As safe as we can be, I suppose. Do you need a tour? Or can you guys find a space for yourselves? There are supplies in the kitchen. Food, cleaning stuff, personal products. The twins and I are in rooms over the arboretum. Kelly and Jamie are close to the pool."

"You have an arboretum?" Con asked.

"And an indoor pool?" Luca said.

"Mom went a little overboard, eh?" I teased him.

He smiled, though it looked forced. "It will be work to make this a home. Feels like a hotel instead of a house. But the kitchen is nice and the kids will love the playset in the backyard."

"Go get some rest," I told him. "Well find our own way. Plus Con needs food."

"Me too," Luca agreed.

"There's a French toast bake in the fridge that was leftovers. Just heat in the microwave for a few seconds and it should be good to go." Seiran headed for the stairs, going up the right side. "If you do your weird boy pussy things try to find a room away from the twins, yeah?"

"Fuck you, Ronnie."

"You wish, Sammie," he threw back and disappeared into the doorway and to the right at the top of the stairs.

"Food," Con said, heading for the kitchen.

"That French toast thing sounds good. Where's that?" Luca followed.

"Typical men," I grumbled after them. "Thinking with your stomachs first."

"Sure," Luca agreed. "I plan to feed my tummy then feed one of you my cock. Pretty sure we all can find an appetite for that."

Con laughed. "You are such a horndog."

CHAPTER 23

Our brief exploration of the house proved it to not be as large as we originally thought. The pool and arboretum, both on the first floor took up the entire back of the house. There was a den, a small library, a large family room, a small receiving room, and a huge kitchen with an attached dining room on the first floor. The second floor was a network of bedrooms. From what I could tell there were only eight, which was a lot, but not the dozens I'd been picturing from the outside.

Jamie and Kelly's room was at the end of the hall near the back stairs that led down to the pool. Since we could feel the humidity in the stairwell, we found a place on Seiran's side instead, choosing a large room in the same wing as he and the twins, added some sheets to the window, and made up the California-king bed within. The room itself was huge, with its own bathroom and a walk-in closet that would make any clothes whore salivate. It was a little overwhelming for me who'd never really had a space of my own bigger than just a twin-size bed. But Luca was all over the room, talking about paint colors, the view from the window, and what furniture he might add to make it more comfortable for the three of us. He whistled at the size of the closet. "This is totally enough room for the three of us as long as you guys don't have a lot of clothes."

It was the size of an entire other room. "Um…" I said.

"He is a boy whore," Con pointed out. "Clothes whore is just another step on that spectrum."

"Assholes," Luca griped without heat. "Sam will need some new stuff for work. Suits and the like." His gaze fell to me, eyes narrowing like he was picturing me naked, or maybe in a suit, though those bedroom eyes said more sex than business. "I bet you're hot as shit in a suit."

"I hate this job already," I said.

They both thought that was funny.

I placed the bottle of grave dirt Seiran had left for me on the bedside table. The sticky note attached to it explained the dirt would help me rest better, and once we picked a room he would have a box made beneath the bed to fill with grave dirt, like Gabe had for years. It sounded weird, but if the witch wasn't freaked by having dirt in the house, neither was I.

Luca and Con had scarfed down the entire rest of the French toast thing Seiran had made, and then we'd run out of time. The sun didn't demand I sleep, but I'd had a really long night, so when I laid down, they curled around me and I passed out. Since they didn't move enough to disturb me, I suspected they did as well. I expected at least a few hours of sleep. And seemed to fall into a deep dream-filled sleep very quickly.

It was hostility that woke me. A rolling energy like a tiger pacing nearby waiting for the moment to pounce. It took a moment to identify the feeling as it wasn't something I was used to. Anxiety. Fear. Worry. Panic.

The sun was still high overhead. The feeling of anger alive

and whipping like an agitated cat's tail through the house though it wasn't actually in the house. I don't think I'd been asleep long, and I could sense Seiran was awake and anxious. The fear was his. The rage wasn't. It was downstairs...close but not inside. I was surprised that I could still feel Seiran so clearly, like he had his power layered over me still, but perhaps that was my own abilities again. It wasn't a drain of power between us, more a link like taffy that could stretch and expand or tighten and contract.

I asked him without words what was happening, but his thoughts were a chaotic mix of anxiety. Panic. A panic attack and the Pillar of earth were not a good thing. I got up, and made my way to the door. Something vibrated in my gut. Almost like someone was pulling on something inside of me, calling for me. Not all that unlike the siren call I'd felt when Galloway had dragged my raven form to his window. This was faint, weak, but still a pulse of energy. Was it Max?

As I made my way into the hall, I tried to trace down that invisible connection between Max and I. He was there in my head, but not physically close. He was also not sleeping. For a second I was layered over him again, seeing his world as if I were him. He was reviewing documents and frowned at the angry presence I felt. He seemed to ask, without saying anything, what was wrong? Since I didn't yet know, I didn't answer.

Seiran's door was open, dark and he wasn't inside. The babies' door was closed, and I crossed the hall to check on them. Inside, I glanced at the crib to find both babies awake, eyes glowing. Both quiet, and both focused on the door. Seriously, not normal kids. And fuck, that couldn't be good.

A small orb of light floated through the room coming through the wall up from below, to beside the crib, changing instantly into a regular size person. His blood-red hair was pulled up on his head into a mass of a curled updo, and clothes, while they looked like a pair of jeans and a T-shirt, had too much texture in their green lines to be anything more than magic.

Bryar glanced at me. His eyes glowed just as bright as the babies since he was a fairy. "I'm bringing the babies to Jamie's room," Bryar told me. "Jamie and Kelly are holed up over there."

"Seiran going too?" Because he really needed to. Whatever it was that was downstairs none of us needed to see. I suspected I already knew what it was and the wards were working the way they should.

Bryar frowned. "He said he would follow in a little bit."

This martyr bullshit needed to stop. "Is it who I think it is?"

"Yes," Bryar said.

I sighed, feeling sluggish, and not up for another battle. Stupid sun. I rubbed the bracelet on my wrist, forgetting I hadn't taken it off and suddenly a burst of warm energy slid through me. Well that was nice. Maybe I could get Sei to make me a whole shit-ton of these bead things.

I left the room in search of Seiran and Gabe. Because that tugging at me was the ghost of a broken tie, Gabe's severed bond. I felt it like a phantom limb, tugging and flailing, painful, raw, and not at all normal. No one said that broken bonds could be mended, or even used to trace an old tie, yet that's exactly how it felt. I could feel Gabe pacing, his agitation and irritation, raging like a caged beast, both from the severed bond, and from his link to Seiran. Another tangled web. I sighed. Someone needed to help me work out this siphon bullshit.

Seiran stood at the giant sliding door that led to the arboretum. In the actual arboretum, which wasn't more than a plot of dirt and a few tiny trees surrounded by glass and pretty architecture, paced Gabe. His skin was pink from the sun overhead, but he didn't seem to notice it at all. Waves of anger and irritation rolled off of him. He grumbled things that I couldn't make out. Seiran seemed frozen at the door. Unsure of what to do.

"The wards are working," I said. They pulsed on the edge of my senses. "How come he got into the arboretum?"

"I didn't extend the wards that far," Seiran said. "Just to the edges of the actual house. The arboretum is an add-on."

We would have to fix that soon then. I watched Gabe pace. He kept looking up, glaring at us, trying to approach the door but not getting close enough to touch it. His eyes were completely red. Not glowing with the monster, but dark, blood-filled orbs that reminded me of pictures of demons. Was he already a revenant? His arm hadn't healed at all. He kept the battered remains of it hugged tightly to his chest, the flesh appearing to be rotted and blackened, the earth eating away at it slowly.

"It's hurting him to not be close to me," Seiran replied. "I can feel it." He closed his eyes and shuddered. "He's so broken. Memories, thoughts, everything about him is a jumble of chaos. He's not healing at all."

Which worried me as much as the red eyes. "How long until he becomes a revenant, Ronnie? Could any of us bring him back from that?" I waved my hand at the giant dirt pile Gabe paced. "Have the earth take him back before it's too late."

"Maybe if I explain..." Seiran whispered. He put his hand to the glass and tears rolled down his cheeks. He reached for the door handle, and I grabbed his hand.

"No," I said firmly.

"He won't hurt me," Seiran said.

"He isn't Gabe right now."

"He is," Seiran insisted. "I feel him." Seiran put his hands to his face and sobbed into them. "He's so lost and alone."

"And how will you dying in his arms help that?"

"Seiran, come to me," Gabe said. His words barely audible, but I felt them like a punch to the gut. It wasn't a request, but a demand. Seiran trembled, hands fisted, pressed to the glass. I could feel the war inside him. The pull to obey and how he fought the compulsion. Vampire compulsion. That was one power that Gabe had always told me to use sparingly. Equivalent to mind rape, were the words that stuck in my head. That he would do this to Seiran made me want to rip him to shreds.

Seiran shut his eyes and his pain was so sharp in that moment I could almost feel it cut the both of us. "He promised to never do that. It's not supposed to really work now that I'm his Focus."

"You're not running to his arms," I pointed out, though I knew that was sheer willpower. I wasn't bound to Gabe anymore and had to fight the need to go to him. He hadn't even called me. Fuck.

Gabe stopped pacing a moment again, stared directly at us, then the demand came again, *"Come to me, Seiran."*

Seiran wiped at his eyes. "Let me just talk to him."

"What's to talk about, Ronnie? He knows what he needs to do."

"I don't know if he does," Seiran said. "He is so confused. Drowning in hunger, rage, and confusion. Maybe if I explain it again?"

"No," I said. "He doesn't get to keep hurting you. This is the whole abusive relationship nightmare everyone hears about, but tries to ignore."

"He wasn't always like this. He's not…"

"But he is now," I pointed out. "You can't keep living in the past, Seiran. Matthew is gone. Roman is gone. Your mother doesn't have any power over you anymore. Gabe needs to go to ground. You have a future to survive for. Children. A world of change to create in the Dominion. Don't let one man steal all of that from you. No matter how much you might love him. Love will not save either of you. You both have to make the choice to change. Him to go to ground and maybe heal this, and you to grow a pair of balls and fight back."

"Fuck you!" Seiran said.

"Truth hurts, Ronnie? How long will you play the victim? Yeah, the world fucking hates us. Sure, everyone is out to get us. But you know what? So what? We are stronger than that. You're Father fucking Earth! I'm some sort of weird super-rare siphon, apparently more powerful than the Tri-Mega. So tell me why it's okay to let people treat us like shit? Neither of us asked for this. Tell me that if Gabe were himself, and looking in on your relationship right now, like the *thing* pacing out there was someone else, that he wouldn't say you needed to end that?"

"Sam."

"Fuck you!" I screamed at Gabe through the glass as his strength rolled over me, trying to coax me out that door. His energy hit a metaphysical wall, Max's strength, and vanished like it had never been.

I took Seiran's face in my hands. "Don't let love break you. If he's in there, the way to get him back is to put him in the ground. If it worked for me, it can work for anyone. You said yourself I was an asshole when I went to ground and mellowed out when I rose."

"You're still an asshole," Seiran said.

"Love you too, Ronnie." I let go of him to stare out the door again at the pacing monster beyond. He'd been sane when he'd brought me over. Perhaps not completely in control like he'd made us think, but the thing that raged and growled out there was nothing like the man who'd mentored me in my first few months. That man had been quiet, reserved, and respectful. This was nothing but a beast barely held back from totally losing it to bloodlust.

Seiran sighed and pushed open the door but didn't step through it. Gabe did not advance. "Let me tell him one last time. Give him one last chance to make the right decision."

I sighed. Fucking martyrs. "Only if I come with. If he starts something, I will finish it. Do you understand that? That *thing* out there is on the verge of becoming what you saw from me yesterday."

"You came back."

"Because Max took control. I feel him even this second. I'm not sure how he did it, not after I apparently took down Galloway. Do you think he's strong enough to bond Gabe too? Gabe is like a billion years old."

"Tresler bonded Gabe."

"Gabe willingly did that because Tresler convinced him he needed to so he could protect you. And I'm not sure how strong that bond is, it could just be what's driving him mad."

Seiran frowned, "Do you think that was his plan from the beginning? Tresler, I mean?"

"The fuck if I know. The old vamps really seem to have a skewed version of the world. I hope I don't get so stupid as I age that common sense eludes me."

We shared a look that I took to mean that he feared the same thing happening with him. A vampire Focus lived as long as his master, and Seiran as Father Earth might actually have been more than just mortal anyway. Would we both go mad over time? "We'll keep each other honest, yeah?" I prompted.

"Or become total enemies fighting each other 'til the day we die in the ultimate destruction of the earth," Seiran remarked.

I snorted. "Sunny view, Ronnie, but possible."

He reached for my hand, which I gave him.

"If he goes revenant you put him in the ground, Ronnie. Understand? I can hold him off, but not forever. He's stronger than me, lived long enough to probably tear me up. So you can't hesitate. You get that? You need to live because you have super-babies upstairs who need you. Think of how pissed you were that your dad wasn't there 'cause he died before you were born. Don't do that to your own kids."

"Bastard," Seiran grumbled.

"Jerk," I threw back.

Seiran took one step out the door, then down the stairs onto the dirt-packed ground of the arboretum. I followed, giving rise to the connection between us and the power that he kept locked away. Flowers bloomed beneath our feet. Well, flowers for Seiran, cacti for me. I'd have to ask him about that sometime.

Gabe took a step in our direction. Seiran held up a hand to ward him off. "No."

"You belong to me," Gabe said. He sounded almost normal, but the raging red of his eyes said otherwise. "Why would you put a wall between us?"

"You need to go to ground, Gabe," Seiran said. "You need real rest."

"I need *you* to stop trying to make decisions for *me*."

"What decisions have I made for you?" Seiran demanded. "Everything I've done is for you."

"Right," Gabe snarled and went back to pacing. "Moving out and leaving was for me."

"Yes," Seiran said. "You know what you need to do, and obviously I'm holding you back. Removing myself from the situation was best for both of us."

"You're not safe. I can't protect you if you're not with me."

"You're not with me," Seiran pointed out. "You were at some club feeding on groupies and trying to mind rape teenage girls. How is any of that protecting me? How is you abandoning me when I'm caring for the twins, helping me? You were part of my mother's scheme to beget heirs. Now they are here and you don't get to say that you don't want to be part of it and still be in my life. That's not fair to me, or to them."

"They make me hungry," Gabe admitted quietly. "Their power, your power…it's too much. I crave it so much, it's better if I'm not home. If I feed off others. I'm not sure I could stop…"

That was news neither of us had expected. I wasn't tempted by the twins at all, despite their crazy power. In fact their super energy set my own power on edge, a warning of biting off more than I could chew was the idea I got from all of it.

"If you can't be with me why not go to ground? Heal?"

"You don't know that it will fix anything," Gabe said. "And you'll be alone."

"I'm *already* alone," Seiran said. "You've been gone for months." He tapped his forehead. "Even from here. And now you're open to me. Why? Just so I can see how mad you've become? It's such a mess in there that I don't know if I'm the one angry, anxious, or sad. Is it me or you? Am I going mad? I think you're driving me mad. You promised you'd love me forever. This isn't love, Gabe." He let out a long sigh. "I'm not sure you can feel love right now."

Gabe rushed forward and I tried to pull Seiran back, but he wouldn't budge. The green rose up through the earth into his body, crawling up his legs, Father Earth coming to roost, but Gabe only put his only good hand on Seiran's face, and kissed him soundly.

Seiran returned his kiss for a moment, then pulled away to reach up to pull Gabe's hand off his face. "You can't keep breaking my heart. It's not fair."

"You can't leave me," Gabe said, baring his fangs. "You belong to me."

"I belong to no one," Seiran said. "You taught me that. You taught me that love was respect, not ownership." Seiran turned his head to the side as though he just couldn't look at Gabe. "You told me once that a vampire's Focus was often the death of the vampire. Now I understand why. You're not Gabe. You are just his shade. Go to ground before I put you there."

Gabe growled, and before I could react, he was on Seiran. Not kissing him, but his teeth digging into Seiran's throat, arms wrapped around him like a vice.

"No!" I leapt at him, trying to pull him off Seiran. Gabe's grip was like granite. My strength was not enough. And wasn't that just the worst feeling again? I couldn't save anyone. Not myself, and certainly not my former mentor and my friend. Fuck Seiran Rou for insisting on becoming my friend.

Seiran shoved at him not just with strength but with power, throwing him several feet away. It was a blast of energy so strong it felt like fire on my skin. Gabe leapt forward, more animal than anything human I'd ever seen. I was too slow to react, I needed more practice fighting fucking vampires instead of witches, but I felt Seiran's tug on our bond. In that moment I was his Focus as he directed the energy. A giant root latched around Gabe, catching him in midair. Gabe struggled against it, ripping at it, but unable to really free himself.

Max nudged at me, his power asking for a claim over my body. I had no idea what he planned but just let him roll through me, settle over me like some sort of costume. Not an illusion, but a full-on presence. His power nearly sent me to my knees as the weight of it wrapped around me. Only his will kept me standing. This was Max, I thought. The part of him he kept restrained around everyone. The power he hid from the world to maintain the status quo. It wasn't even magic. Not really. More just force of will and a presence so large he could have brought any congregation of worshipers to their knees proclaiming he was God.

His power slammed into Seiran and Gabe. Gabe stumbled back a few feet, only held up by the root, blood covering his mouth and chin like he was some sort of monster. The root broke and Gabe fell on his ass, shaken, disoriented, but at least several feet away. Seiran sank to the ground, his hand pressed to his neck, earth rising upward in vines along his skin like it sought to heal his wounds.

"Enough, Gavril," Max said through my lips. "You've spent your life destroying that which you love, will you continue that cycle or finally break free of it?"

Gabe stared at me, blinking, confusion on his face.

Seiran looked my way. "Max?"

Did I look like Max? I could feel him laced over me like a skin of some sort, but hadn't thought anyone could see it.

"You failed me lifetimes ago, and now you will fail him?" Max asked.

Gabe took another step away from us. Something warred on his face changing his expression from anger to confusion to rage and back to a lost look that clearly said he was having trouble focusing on whatever he was seeing and thinking.

"Titus? I…" He looked back at Seiran, who sobbed into his knees, broken by being attacked by the one person he loved and trusted before anyone. I knew from experience it was hard won affection. A lifetime of the world fucking with us made us cynical bastards, the few who got through were either super loyal or would destroy us.

"This is your last chance," Seiran said. "Go willingly or I will put you in the ground."

The red haze in Gabe's eyes faded, and for the first time I

could remember since I'd woken from the grave the second time, his eyes were green. He dropped to his knees just feet from Seiran.

"Seiran...what did I? Oh, my God... What did I do?" He looked around the room, looking confused at where he was, lost.

His eyes met mine and through me, Max. "I didn't mean to..."

"But you did," I said, forcing my own words through the visage of Max. "You've done exactly what you promised you would never do. How has any of this helped Seiran who you claim to love so much?" I demanded, pissed, wanting to rip Gabe apart just for causing the pain I could feel rolling off my best friend. Fuck, Seiran was like the twin brother I'd never asked for. We were linked through magic and emotions. Stupid emotions. Stupid powerful emotions. They could either build us up or tear us apart.

"I do love him," Gabe whispered, his gaze falling back on Seiran. He dropped forward, hands to the earth, head down. "I didn't... I don't understand what happened..."

"You need rest," I repeated. "You once told me not to fear it."

Gabe looked at Seiran again. "I'm so sorry, my love. I never meant to hurt you." He stared at his remaining good hand for a moment, which was flecked with Seiran's blood. His damaged arm looking like little more than bone charred by fire. He touched his jaw and the smear of Seiran's blood came away bright red and fresh. Seiran still clutched his neck, though he was healing. He was curled in a ball over his knees, shaking his head and refusing to look up.

"Seiran," Gabe whispered, "I'm so sorry. I love you so much. I didn't mean... I would never hurt you..." But he had. A thousand times over. Gabe bowed his head. He swallowed hard, put his hands back to the earth, then stared at Seiran when he said, "To the earth I commit myself."

The ground began to bubble around him, a living thing, sucking him down. He didn't fight, or struggle, just sank into the ground like fast quicksand swallowing him whole. Seiran lifted his tear-filled gaze and it was a sad moment of their eyes meeting as Gabe vanished into the earth. The dirt settled, lying flat as though nothing had happened.

Seiran stared at the spot, his arms wrapped around himself, emotions blank, locked away in a vault erected out of bricks built with pain. Max retreated, though he knew I had a million questions for him.

The sun overhead made my skin ache, but it wasn't burning me for which I was grateful. I dropped to my knees beside Seiran and wrapped my arms around him. The wound at his neck still oozed blood, but it had slowed. I leaned over and licked it, willing it to close.

Seiran slapped the wound. "Gross, Sammie. You licked me."

"Okay, well next time you're bleeding out I'll just kick some dirt in it, yeah?"

"Bastard," he said without heat.

"Jerk." I used the bottom of my shirt to wipe his face free of blood spatter and tears. "You need some sleep. Maybe the big guy will be back in a few days."

"It's probably better that we have some space," Seiran said.

"If you say so, Ronnie," I allowed. The pain would fade in time. But Gabe had gone willingly to ground. Would it absolve him of everything he'd done in the past few months? Was there a need to, when we knew he hadn't been himself? It was likely something Seiran would be debating until Gabe resurfaced, but that was okay, he overanalyzed everything anyway. I was less conflicted. If Gabe came out calm and normal, the past could be left in the past. If he came out stupid and raging, we'd have to find a way to make his grave permanent. But I'd cross that bridge when we got there.

Seiran let me help him up and leaned on my shoulder. I'd always thought of us as about the same size, but in reality Seiran was smaller. Slightly shorter, a lot thinner, and much more delicate. Sometimes he was so strong that we all forgot just how breakable he was.

The shot that rang out ripped him from my arms and splattered me with his blood.

CHAPTER 24

I stood there for a stunned few seconds, trying to figure out just what happened. Blood poured from a huge wound in Seiran's skull. He hit the ground as though we'd launched into a slow-mo mode of a movie, my arms stretched out toward him. His eyes were open, staring blankly upward. I had only the barest moment to think that Seiran was dead before the ground began to tremble and the release of power rolled upward. Instinctively, I reached for it, trying to put a cap on the energy, quell it before it destroyed us all, but it was just too much and I hadn't had enough practice using power that wasn't really mine. I could only equate it to standing in the middle of a lava field, trying to hold back the flow, while the melted rock ate away at my very being.

I pressed my hands to Seiran willing the earth back into him like it was a bottle with a leak, trying to keep it filled. The power rushed through me. Needles of pain prickling over every inch of my skin. The ivy and tiny plants climbed through my flesh like they had Seiran's only moments before. The earth didn't recognize me. It rejected me, jumping from me back to Seiran and crawling across his skin, headed toward the head wound. Was there any way he could survive that? Would Father Earth be strong enough?

Red pooled across my vision as the other inside me crept out to play. It offered me strength even as the raging power of the earth battered at us. I tried reaching for my link to Max. Maybe he'd know what to do. Maybe he could save Seiran, or at least redirect the earth energy. But there was too much power. His energy seemed to drown in the intensity of the flow of earth, making our link almost invisible.

I briefly thought of Jamie who'd been upstairs, maybe the power would fall to him. Or even one of the twins, and wouldn't we all be screwed then? If I didn't have enough control to reign in the earth, how the hell could a baby?

I only had a second to glance back, to see Tresler standing in the door of the arboretum with a gun in his grasp, aimed at me. Another shot rang out. I waited for the hit, the pain, maybe death, though bullets alone were unlikely to kill me. Instead Luca collapsed on top of me, his blood spattering me in a bright wash of crimson.

A hawk flew at Tresler as I caught Luca and eased him down beside Seiran, the power of the earth Pillar burning my skin. Luca gasped for breath, the shot having taken him in the lower back. I reached for him, hearing the squawk of the hawk as it raked its huge talons over Tresler's face. The vampire waved his arms and tried to shake the bird off.

"Kill him," Luca gasped. "Devour him like you did Galloway. It's our only chance."

I registered his words, felt the world slow to a maddening moment of chaos. Seiran dead, yet healing, the earth struggling not to tear us apart as I barely held the reigns like a mere mortal trying to hold back the tide of the ocean. Luca bleeding out at my feet and Con risking everything to buy us time.

I jolted forward, leaping the distance no human ever

could have, to slam a fist into Tresler's gut, adding to it a blast of fiery air as I felt Con's powers awaken something familiar inside me. Tresler flew back into the wall of glass, the length of it splintering around him. His skin blistered with the heat from the blow. I'd hoped he would have dropped the gun, but no such luck. He lifted it even as he sank to his knees, aiming it in my direction.

"Take my bond, Mueller. Save your friends," Tresler offered. "I can control the earth if you just give me your bond."

Who was he kidding? Give another crazy control over me? Not a chance. Did he forget I was no longer that kid everyone got to abuse? I was no one's slave. I was a fucking vampire!

My movement became magic. I wasn't sure how it happened, just that one moment I was twenty feet away, the next I was in front of him, ripping the gun from his grasp and crushing his hand with little effort.

He gasped as though he hadn't seen me move either. The red in my vision gave me an edge of comfort as I glanced down at my hands, talons extending from my fingertips. Sharp enough, I thought. All those years of hunting beside Matthew, learning to survive by killing things bigger and badder than me. Now I was at the top of the food chain.

My *other* and I were finally aligned in one thing. Death of the Tri-Mega. Destruction of Tresler. These things appealed to us both. For him, the release of rules and restrictions, and for me, an end to the constant attacks on my friends and life by idiots who thought their power could dominate everything. Madness, isn't that what Seiran had said? Power drove people mad, and that's what he feared. But we could keep each other sane. Or at least have a lot of fun bickering until insanity took us both. If we survived. First, I had to destroy the monster who thought I was still a victim.

With a flick of my wrist I took off Tresler's head, nails slicing through him like razorblades. The first key to killing a vampire was decapitation. Ensuring he stayed dead was about destroying the body. I think it was more about disintegrating the magic that held the vampire together. Not so much physically, but metaphysically. Though that was more philosophy shit I wanted nothing to do with.

I could have done as Luca said, fed on the power. It pulsed in waves of broken energy. Stolen magic, not all that unlike Galloway. Through it I could see an endless web of ties cast into the distance in the thousands, other vampires. Galloway had not had such ties. Perhaps he had created or bonded so few vampires that he was truly alone in his power. Tresler had built up his web like a barrier around him. Hundreds, if not thousands, of threads woven together like a tapestry of slicing strands to keep anyone who got close away. He also wasn't dying, despite his head coming off. Instead it snarled and gaped at me while the body twitched convulsively, each movement bringing it closer to the head. The power seemed to stretch between the severed parts like it could somehow metaphysically bind it all back together.

Fuck.

That chaotic web of power wasn't something I wanted any part of. The strands of it darkened and dripped as though covered in blood. Was he pulling energy from the vampires he was bonded to? If I fed on him like I had Galloway would that make those vampires mine? Fuck, no. I didn't want that kind of responsibility. I hated people on a good day, tied to thousands? Yeah, I was pretty sure I'd go mad and kill them all.

I screamed and kicked the head into the opposite corner. It landed with a sick thud. Tresler's power stretched like taffy over the distance, his web of vampire ties trying to pull him back together. Damn it!

I called the earth, willing it to take the vampire, return it to the soil as nutrients, devour the power and spread it back across the universe. Seiran had described it a time or two. A well of particles that made up all the energy of the earth. Sometimes it glowed with the power, sometimes it was quiet. I shoved at whatever my power was, begging the earth to feed on Tresler if that was what it needed to take him back permanently.

The link of energy from the earth felt like worms crawling through the dirt and rising up. Only it wasn't worms, it was branches, vines, roots, and trees. They wrapped around Tresler's body and began to rend it to pieces. The head was pierced a second later, spearing it between the eyes and sprouting new growths that broke up the head, despite Tresler's stunned expression, into a thousand tiny grains of compost. The body decomposed that quickly, feeding the earth and releasing the last hold on Tresler's stolen power. All those tiny webs spanning into the distance shattered, as the power of the earth ripped them apart, flinging small daggers of energy outward. I felt them hit me like shrapnel from a bomb, cutting into my soul in places that really fucking hurt.

I remembered vaguely back to when Matthew had died in the fire. The barn burned, but he'd begun to move despite my taking his head. So I'd dragged him into the fire, thinking to myself that it all just needed to burn, and the entire place had blown. Not just with heat and flame, but an eruption of magic. How I'd survived, I still wasn't sure. I had simply woken up a few hours later outside in the cold, next to the smoldering heap that was the barn. I'd thought it was all the power that Matthew's null ability had been restraining that had caused the explosion, only now I think it was the opposite. It was a release of his power, the destruction of his soul, or whatever it was that made us vampires. Tresler's death seemed to be on the verge of causing the same thing on a much larger scale.

The ground shook so hard I thought it might split open any second. There was just too much. Too much power, too much wild magic, too many emotions. I looked back at Luca. Con was back in human form, curled around Luca and Seiran as though he could somehow protect them. I could see a bubble of air swirling around them. But if the ground fell apart beneath them it wouldn't matter, they'd all die.

I could hear Max very quietly in my head telling me to redirect the power. The extra energy Tresler's destruction released into the earth was too much, like a bomb directed underground that just needed to explode. Our tie burned. The power igniting the bond, traveling through me to him like wildfire. Max's skin burned and began to flake into little pieces of dirt from being open to me and then a wall came down and he was gone. His last bit of help controlling the power vanished.

An explosion smashed through the arboretum, throwing me into the wall of the house and shattering the glass into a rain of daggers. I felt them pierce my skin. A thousand cuts leeching energy from my flesh. I collapsed, crushed into the ground and motionless by the weight of the energy pouring out around us. I could see Con and Luca, both looking at me, sadness on their faces, like they knew we were all dead. And Seiran, whose open eyes should have been dark, glowed like the babies.

We were still linked, he and I. I could feel it, even if he was dead. Was he? His body had been lost last year. Death, we'd all thought, though Gabe had claimed to still feel their link. Since the earth hadn't come apart we wondered, while the Dominion had speculated if he'd really been accepted as Pillar. We'd all wondered if maybe Gabe had just gone mad with grief until Seiran appeared at the back door of the house a few days later. Alive. Whole. Something different. No longer human.

My heart leapt at the thought that maybe, just maybe... But that was stupid, wasn't it? People didn't just survive a gunshot to the head. Not normal people at least. Was there anything normal about Ronnie?

Shit. No wonder his blood tasted divine. Fucking Rou. Letting us all think he was vulnerable when he was practically a god. Not that I'd ever tell him that. Wouldn't want it to go to his head.

Something separated from his physical body. It wavered in the light, transparent, but somewhat human-shaped, moving toward me. I couldn't make out any features, just a wash of colors, green, brown, orange, and blue. Like the swirling of a storm over an island in the sea.

Seiran? I thought instead of vocalizing as I couldn't even move to breathe. My cheek was pressed into the dirt, my blood leaking into the ground, pooling around me. At least Con and Luca had been protected from the glass by whatever shield Con had created out of wind. *Get back in your fucking body and stop this!* I screamed at him through our mental bond having no idea if he could actually hear me.

Plants surrounded us. Shooting out of the ground in a rain of dirt around stalks and roots a hundred sizes larger than their normal versions. The ceiling of the arboretum began to splinter and crash down around me. I prayed Con and Luca were safe, but feared this was only the epicenter of what was likely to be the end of the world.

The hand in front of my face began to dissolve, even as I fisted it into the earth like it could help, crumbling to little grains of sand, as it slowly disintegrated under the weight of the earth's power. I didn't feel it. Couldn't feel anything really. Nothing but fear for Con and Luca. Maybe the babies who hadn't yet had a chance to live. I was so mad for a moment as something dark covered my vision, and I tried to blink. My vision didn't clear. I sucked in a breath, feeling the glass in my lungs, the power crushing my bones, body dissolving to mix with the earth and feed the growing plants. I let go of the struggle, releasing it all and sinking into something dark and luminous all at the same time.

~

A fire flickered, flame bursting to life, warmth spreading through my soul. Was this Hell? I deserved Hell, right? I'd killed lots of vampires. Hurt people. Stolen enough to enjoy my sorry life. The short time with Seiran wasn't enough to absolve me of those ills. It seemed momentarily justified that I'd burn when I died. I always hated being cold anyway. Though it made me more than a little pissed off that I had such a short time with Con and Luca. Just a few days to be happy. But life wasn't fair. Isn't that what they always said in church? Maybe if I'd thought to repent?

Who was I kidding? I wasn't sorry for anything I'd done. The past was done and over. No point lingering on it now. Or was that the purpose of Hell? An endless monologue of our sins? Wow, that would be Hell. Like watching the stupidest TV show you'd ever seen on repeat for eternity. Painful until it just drove you mad.

Shouldn't it burn more? I expected burning, searing pain. Yet, it was just warm. Floating in a pool, maybe, or through the breeze on a warm day. It was a struggle of consciousness. Was I awake? Asleep? Dead?

But my eyes opened and the world below was still growing. Apparently, I'd tossed my body aside again to become a bird. Only my wings weren't black, they glowed orange, red, and yellow. Like a fire.

I flew above the madness. Seiran had vanished, likely

absorbed into the earth as his clothes were left behind. Jamie knelt on the steps, hands to the earth, probably trying to control some of the earth's power. Con tried to hold the vines back with his wind, but they squeezed at the bubble he'd created around himself and Luca. His bare back and the tree of birds reminded me of the comment Con had made: *"We're all connected through the earth, so that's why it's the tree. Birds land in the tree, rest, and nest in a tree. Earth and water make the tree grow. Fire burns it down to make way for new growth. It's a balance."*

Life was a balance. All the elements were part of that life; earth, water, air, and fire. Without any of them the whole balance shifted, and entire species died. Life was a delicate thing. It was why all witches were elemental since all witches were part of the earth and the chain of life and death.

What were we missing from that teeter-totter? Fire?

I glanced at my blazing wings and thought, *maybe we weren't*, though where it had come from was unclear to me. Was Max a fire element? I think I would have sensed it in him. His power came across as non-magic. Something more physical than metaphysical. Luca maybe? Same issue.

Either way something needed to be done to stop this insanity and put the genie back in the bottle. But how did one cut back the earth? I swept down toward the bubble wrapped in squeezing ivy. I squawked at it, sounding like some sort of eagle, warning it to let go, only fire spewed from my mouth with the sound.

Shit!

The vines lit like they were soaked in gasoline. They burned away quickly, leaving a bewildered Con staring at me from inside his weakening bubble. Luca lay unmoving beside him, barely breathing, but alive. Tiny vines had begun to curl around his limbs like they were planning to drag him under. I glared at those nasty little vines trying to steal him from me and they burst into flames, falling away from him somehow without singeing him.

Okay, so I was fire. I could work with that. I flapped my wings, turned and headed for the largest growth, which had burst forth from where I'd kicked Tresler's head. Gross. I briefly entertained visions of a live Ent-like tree with Tresler's mad gaze coming at me. But it was just a tree, gnarled, blackened with corrupt power. I shot fire at it, pretending I was a mini dragon instead of just some orange bird. It took a few passes to get it to ignite, but the flames began to crackle and the branches moved, mimicking the Cthulhu of old, tentacles raging toward the sky. I lit all of them up, too.

Watched Jamie drag a weary Con into the house, which appeared untouched by the rage of magic, earth, and freed vampire power. Jamie reappeared a moment later to scoop up Luca. I kept raining fire down on it until it all burned, crackled and stopped writhing like a thing of nightmares. The fire began to devour what was left of the arboretum, melting metal, bursting the last of the glass, and sizzling through the lower drywall layer. The plant matter fell to the dirt as nutrients, ready to fuel the soil into new growth. I hoped the fire wouldn't overtake the house. Wouldn't that just suck. Sam Mueller absolving himself by saving the world, only to burn everything down by accident. Yeah, that was the story of my life.

We needed fucking water. Good thing there was a water witch nearby. I could feel him, close. Not anywhere near the door, but it didn't matter. He'd used my power to amplify and focus his own before, so the seed still sat in my gut. I pulled on the metaphysical link, demanding water, even if it was a burst in the ground beneath where I flew. I thought *cleansing*, which is what we needed, not unlike Seiran's California house, or the river beside the old ranger tower where

I'd been forced to carve into my own flesh for evil spells. It all needed to be cleansed to rebalance. Earth, air, fire, and water.

Kelly appeared in the doorway, the look on his face ashen, but he glanced upward when Jamie pointed toward me. Con put a hand on Kelly's shoulder. They shared a look and a few words I couldn't make out, then the sky darkened overhead as clouds amassed in the sky. A crack of thunder rumbled loud enough to shake the house. I fumbled in my flight, banging into a blazing branch and trying to right myself. Then the rain began. Not a gentle spring shower, but a full-on downpour so thick I couldn't see them anymore. The fire sizzled out, water pooling like a lake in what was left of the arboretum. The beat of the downpour battered at me with the weight of an anvil.

The bright fire of my wings vanished and they felt suddenly heavy. I flapped them trying to stay in the air, only the drenching of my wings became lead weights and I dropped like a stone. I hit the water with a thud, struggled for breath and direction as the water bubbled and swirled, cleansing, but also fighting with the earth. A moment later someone swept me up in firm arms and lifted me free.

Without the fire I looked like a raven again, black wings, talons, and beak, what little I could see of it in the reflection on the glass in the door.

The rain began to ease, and slowly trickled to a stop, while Jamie waded back through the now waist-high water with me held against his chest. He climbed the stairs up into the house and carried me through the doorway. Con was wrapped in a sheet. Kelly held out two towels, one for Jamie and one for me. Jamie carefully placed me in the outstretched towel before taking his own. Kelly rubbed at my wings, and I was grateful when the towel began to leech away some of the water.

After a few minutes I flapped my wings again and the orange reappeared. Kelly took a step back, holding me away from his body, as fire reignited in my wings, though didn't touch the towel. "Whoa!"

"Holy crap," Con said.

"Call him," Luca said. "Make him change back." Luca was alive. He lay on the kitchen floor, a professional-looking bandage on his abdomen. It was probably a good thing the muscleman nurse was on hand.

"Change," Con said. "Sam, change back."

Yeah? How did I do that? How had I done it before? I'd thought I'd been dreaming the first time it happened. Hadn't realized it had been real, but then I had only thought about it and it had happened.

I breathed in a deep breath and just let the idea of being me again fill my head. The change washed over me like a flame burning through a piece of cotton candy. I hit the floor because my limbs didn't want to work, and Con was there a moment later to share his sheet with me. He pulled me into his arms, me unable to help.

"Holy fuck," I groaned, feeling as limp as a baby. "What the hell was that?"

"Um..." Kelly said staring at Jamie who appeared thoughtful.

"Restoring balance," Con said. "Can't you feel it? It sings in my power, not a vibration, exactly. More like a soft hum?"

"Yeah," agreed Kelly, "I feel it too. Everything is quiet. Calm. It was like the release at the California house, only more contained. I think Seiran contained it to just inside the arboretum because nothing beyond has been touched."

Jamie stepped up to the door, peering out into the broken remains of the arboretum and the yard beyond.

"He's not dead," I said.

"No," Jamie agreed. "I feel him."

I think we all did. Flowers began to bloom throughout the barren ground. The last of the giant plants created by wild magic dissolved and became a small grove of trees.

Con dragged me to Luca's side. I reached out for Luca with a hand that felt like it weighed a ton. He took it, squeezed it and let me lay my head on his chest. His breathing was steady and solid. Eyes clear, though tired. I guess a dhampir was pretty hard to kill with a bullet too.

I stared out into the arboretum for a minute and saw the shadow of Seiran there, crouched over where Gabe had gone to ground. Only I knew it wasn't really a vision of this world but something beyond what I'd seen before. Seiran never spoke of the place beyond the veil he'd gone when he'd ascended to Father Earth. Bryar mentioned it a time or two as an actual place and Jamie had speculated once that it was a parallel dimension of power. I suspected it was all tied together.

"Hey, Ronnie," I called to him with my mind, feeling like maybe he could hear me, *"get your ass back here. Those babies need you and I think the big guy is going to start crying soon."*

"Bastard," I heard faintly. Was it in my head or for real?

"Jerk," I said out loud. I closed my eyes, resting for just a moment, and then jerked awake a second later. When I opened my eyes again the spot where I'd seen Seiran kneeling had become a grove of red roses, thick with thorns and lush buds. Father Earth knelt at the edge, both fists clutched around stalks of painfully sharp spikes and dripping blood. I feared for a moment that it would wake Gabe too early. He'd need more time to rest. But then I realized the truth. Gabe wasn't there anymore. In fact, all vampires who went to ground were eventually reabsorbed by the earth. When they rose it was because their souls, or whatever it was that animated them, had regained enough strength to be rewarded a new body from the circle of power.

Life and death. Two sides of the same coin. Both a formidable and intertwining circle with that of the elements. There was no balance without life and death. Seiran had pulled Gabe back once when his body wasn't yet absorbed into the earth to regenerate. It was why I hadn't risen faster or responded to their bloodshed over my grave. I rose when I'd been ready. Gabe would have to do the same.

Seiran let go of the roses and got to his feet. The wounds on his hands healed almost instantly. He turned toward us and as he came up the stairs the green visage of Father Earth faded and he was back to himself again. Jamie gave him a sheet to cover himself, though I suspected he could probably do like Bryar did and create some sort of ethereal clothing made from strategically placed leaves if he thought about it.

"Fire, eh?" Seiran said to me. "Been holding out on us?"

"I have no idea what you're talking about," I said. "Too many hits to the head from giant plants maybe?"

"You or me?" He wanted to know.

"Both?" I squinted at him. "I'm not sure where the fire came from."

"That was you," Kelly said. "I totally felt it. Opposition to my water."

"And my wind," Con added.

Seiran nodded. "It makes sense. All witches are elemental. We've all been wondering what yours was. I think you just hadn't manifested it yet, or maybe you did and didn't realize it." He thought for a minute. "Like that barn...when Matthew died...it should never have exploded. Burned sure, but not exploded."

"That was magic," I insisted. "The destruction of Matthew's power."

"I think that was the release of your power. You'd been living under his null influence. Null's dampen power, they don't increase it, not even in death. Your siphon powers enhanced his while your own were just beginning to emerge. That's why no one tests until college. It can take that long for a witch's power to manifest. And when Matthew died, the void-effect of his power over yours vanished." Seiran looked thoughtful. "It explains the blast of heat we always get when you touch me in my Father Earth form."

"And maybe the cacti," Con pointed out. "'Cause hot earth and all…"

"Sam is so hot," Luca said sleepily.

Seiran snorted. "And the vampire baby is loopy."

"I gave him some pain meds," Jamie said.

"Not a baby," Luca said. "I'm older than all of you."

Seiran waved his hand like he was trying to clarify his thoughts. "Sam is the youngest of us. So it makes sense. Just because my powers showed up early doesn't mean everyone's does."

"Didn't start having to change until I was almost eighteen," Kelly said.

"Mine really evolved in the past two years," said Con. "Sam is barely nineteen."

"Right 'cause the rest of you are all geezers," I remarked. Early twenties was not old.

"No, but none of us had a null suppressing our first years of power."

"Seiran was with Matthew when he was a kid," I reminded them.

"My powers hadn't manifested yet," Seiran said.

"Okay, so I'm a fire elemental as well as a siphon? Is that a thing?"

"Apparently. I'll have to talk to the Dominion. See if we can get you a one-on-one fire witch to help train you." He looked back at the fire ravaged structure. Not much remained of the arboretum. "Just so you don't burn the house down."

"I didn't mean to burn the place down. I was trying to save the world."

"Now who has the white knight syndrome?" Con asked.

I glared at him. "Whose side are you on?"

He kissed me. "Whatever side keeps us breathing."

I sighed into his lips while I listened to Luca's steady heartbeat. Okay. I could be on board with that.

CHAPTER 25

The broken vampire bonds were a mess. My fault, I guess. Since I'd refused to take them from Tresler. Some vampires died, destroyed by the police, too broken to take themselves to ground to heal. Others were bonded *en masse* to the few strong vampires, who had not bonded to Tresler, that were left. This included Mike and Max.

Which was how I ended up standing in a brand-new tailored suit in Max's office with twelve other vampires, all of which I'd never met. Apparently Max was now doing the bonding thing. He'd cited some bullshit about his government contracts when I'd made a comment about it.

He seemed unaffected by the incident. Whatever wound he had received from our bond, was long gone only a few days later. He'd given Luca a week to rest, and me along with him, though he set goals to be completed before I'd arrive in his office, like getting the suit. Fucking suit felt like a million ants crawling on my skin. And how did people breathe in this shit?

All the vampires were dressed up, like little dolls, all watching Max with devoted eyes. It annoyed me. If he was looking for a zombie ass-kisser from me, he'd picked the wrong vampire to save.

The edge of Max's lips curved up in a tiny smile and I felt his gaze on me. I met it with defiance, daring him to challenge me. Could he hear my thoughts? Maybe, and so what? Fuck him. I didn't have a daddy kink. It was Seiran who'd begged him to save me.

"Everyone has their assigned mentor," Max said as he walked around the desk to stand before the group. We had already gone through a long list of expectations, guidelines, and issued equipment. I'd never had such a stuffy job before. "I expect great things of all of you. Treat your mentors well or my use for you will find an abrupt end."

Well wasn't that friendly.

Luca got up out of the chair beside the desk. He looked good in the light gray Armani suit that hugged his frame. He'd lost a little bit of weight while healing, but I knew the wound to be nothing more than a slightly raised pink scar. Not the first bullet, he told me, but I really hoped it was the last. Seiran promised to feed him up and had been cooking up a storm. At least it kept his mind occupied.

Luca crossed the room to my side as the crowd began to disperse to their assigned areas. I was apparently going to be Luca's assistant, which might have sounded fun for about two seconds before I realized it was a lot of phone calls and scheduling in order to free up his time for phone calls and scheduling for Max. Add to that a regular fight schedule, two shifts a week at the bar, and required Dominion training on the weekends, and my days were about to get really long.

"Did you get your reading done?" Luca asked as he waved goodbye to his father and directed me into the elevator.

I sighed. "Con read to me while I played video games. Does that count?"

"Do you remember any of it?"

I thought for a few minutes. "Maybe."

"We'll keep working on it."

"I'd like to work you out of that suit," I told him honestly after the last group got out of the elevator and we were finally headed down to the parking garage.

Luca threw me a sexy grin. "That can be arranged." He'd kept himself clean-shaven, which while making him look several years younger, just did crazy things to my dick every time I saw him.

"Con won't be home until after three," I reminded him. Con was working until close at the bar tonight, which meant two a.m. and then cleanup. Since it was just after eleven p.m., that left us some time before our third could join us.

"I'm sure he won't mind us starting without him. He'll join us when he gets home."

I still hesitated to spend time alone with Luca. It was odd, because of the two, he was more indestructible than Con. The whole getting shot and healing in less than a week thing proved that. However, I wasn't tempted to throw Con up against a wall and fuck him through it. Con and I together were more slow exploration until we were both about to pop. Romance some might call it, though I hated the term. What I felt for Luca wasn't so much romance, but full on lust. I really liked him. Like panicked at the thought of him going anywhere, *liked* him. Con told me it was love, but the whole love thing still had me confused. Philosophy bullshit in my opinion. Luca was mine just as much as Con was mine, and that was all that mattered. I wanted both of them badly in very different ways. It didn't mean I didn't enjoy slow kisses and exploration with Luca, or rough grips and a bit of teeth with Con, but more a mix of the two. What I wanted from Luca came more from the vampire side. A sense of ownership I didn't feel I had a right to. It was very visceral and related a little to the fact that I was feeding from him regularly.

Territorial, Luca reminded me when I got bitchy about Max's other vamps looking at him like he was dessert. He experienced the same thing. My caveman attitude over him had taken several blood exchanges to develop. And while it was no longer specifically related to the feeding, it bothered me a little that it was related to blood at all.

Luca's strength made my masochistic and sadistic sides come out. I liked to manhandle him, liked when his grip bruised me, or if occasionally my claws came out to mark his beautiful skin. We hadn't done more than hand jobs or blow jobs between the three of us. That was my fault. More old baggage I tried to pretend didn't exist.

"Isn't there work stuff we should do?" I tried to get my mind off the idea of having Luca naked and all to myself.

"Nah, my stuff is done from noon to midnight. It's easier when I have calls to make. Most of the businesses are normal human businesses run during daylight hours. A handful are overseas which is why I'm working so late most times. I'll go over the computer and handbook stuff tomorrow."

Each of us had been given a laptop, a fancy phone, a black diamond credit card—to be used for business expenses only—and a handbook of rules and guidelines expected from employees who represented the company. In our case, not so much the company, but my bonded sire, Maxwell Hart.

I was also being handed a bunch of contracts, in Chinese, to review. That was going to suck. Because not only did I hate reading, but my reading of Chinese was pretty rusty. I hoped it came back like riding a bike.

"We should stop in and check on Seiran." He'd been pretty quiet all week. Back to work, with his mother, Kelly, Jamie, Bryar, and even me on rotation to watch the twins. When Luca and I had headed to the meeting earlier he'd been spread out in the second floor family room, which we hadn't noticed before, twins playing on a blanket on the floor, and papers of some new mystery from his job as an investigator for the Dominion, spread out around him. He didn't seem happy, but also not completely broken. I just worried about him.

"Do you not want to be alone with me?" Luca asked.

"Not at all. I have visions of throwing you against the wall, but worry about the property damage and a pissed off witch."

Luca laughed. "So much snark. I mean it, though."

"Mean what?" I played dumb.

"Do you not want to be alone with me?"

"I just said I did."

"You can throw me against a wall anytime. I'll pay for any property damage."

I just grunted. Stupid insecurity.

"Do you need to fight?"

I didn't, and wasn't that sad? 'Cause fighting with Luca was hot, sexy, and a super turn-on, but I was as calm as I'd ever been. "No."

"So what's wrong?"

"I'll blow you when we get home," I offered. I was getting better at that.

"I want you to fuck me."

Just the idea of that made me hard, and terrified all at once.

"Do you not want to fuck me?"

"I just want it to be good for you," I admitted.

He laughed. "Um, yeah, that's why I'm requesting it, 'cause your cock and my butthole need to become fast…hard…friends."

Fucking Luca. I felt like my face was on fire and the stupid suit was far too tight and revealing all at once.

"Maybe we should wait for Con and he can…"

"Sam?" Luca demanded. "What is wrong?"

"Nothing. I've just never done that before." There was a pause. Silence that stretched a few seconds longer than comfortable and I immediately felt like an idiot. "Never mind," I said.

"You've never fucked someone before?" Luca asked.

"I've had sex before."

"But you've never topped," Luca clarified.

"No," I said, mad at him and myself now.

"Would you rather Con be your first? He's okay with bottoming, though he prefers blow jobs over anything else."

"No."

"But you don't want to top me?"

I did. I fucking fantasized about it a thousand times a day. "I just want you to enjoy it."

"I plan to," Luca said. He glanced my way as we finally pulled into the driveway of the big house. All the lights were off other than the front motion sensor. Everyone was probably asleep, although Jamie's car was missing from the big circular driveway so he might have been working. Luca parked the car but made no move to get out. He stared at me and I couldn't look at him until he reached across the giant beast of his Hummer to touch my face. "Hey," he said. "Why does this freak you out?"

"It doesn't freak me out," I defended.

"Right, 'cause you're a badass motherfucker who has no trouble throwing me over a table and fucking me until we both see stars."

"God!" I cried, pants tightening until it damn near hurt to be wearing any clothes. "You're such a fucking tease."

"Not teasing. I'm legit. Wanting you to fuck me."

I sighed and looked at him, really looked. He was concerned, and so beautiful. Men like him didn't normally want guys like me. Not for more than just a warm hole. Fuck. "Stupid emotions."

"Yeah, they're a real bitch, right?" Luca smiled. He had a little boy's smile full of delight and mischief that I just loved. "But you trust me, yeah?"

"I do."

"It's you, you don't trust."

And wasn't that the truth. "I'm good at breaking things. Fucking things up."

"If you expect a particular result often you get it. Sometimes you have to shift your perception to really find change."

"You mean believe it will be great and it will be great? Thanks, Mary Poppins," I said.

"Well, yeah. I know it will be great because you and I have a fuckton of chemistry. Every time you enter a room, I feel your pull. I look your way and think, God, I can't wait to have that. And he's *mine*."

"I feel the same way. About both you and Con." I sighed thinking about all the things I'd fantasized doing with both of them. Luca's many teasing comments put more visuals in my head that might never have been there before. Like the idea of him spit-roasted between Con and me. Porn did not mirror real life, but that didn't mean we couldn't play.

"So let's work on that." He got out of the car and headed toward the house. I followed, though at a slower pace, thinking hard. Wasn't this what I'd promised to leave behind? All this self-doubt and fear of really living?

The house was quiet and dark. I followed Luca upstairs to our room, passing Seiran's closed door and the twins before finding ours. Furniture had been added, window treatments, a slight color change, a reorganized closet, and the three of us looked like we'd been living together forever. It was weird to have the world align in just a week, but we fit. And that was all that really mattered.

Luca closed the door behind me and shoved me up against the door, his lips capturing mine in a fierce kiss. He tugged off my tie and pushed the jacket off my shoulders. "I'm not afraid of you," he said.

But I was afraid of me. Worried about the monster I'd once become and some of the fierce need that burned in my gut with an intensity I'd never experienced before.

He sighed when I didn't touch him and pulled away to begin stripping out of his clothes. It was always sensual with Luca. Just the way he moved. So even when he rolled his shoulders to ease off his own jacket and began to unbutton his shirt one button at a time, it was an erotic dance. I watched him, already hard and aching. His little smile devious and sexy all at once. Fucking Luca.

He swayed his hips a little and flicked open the button of his pants. I couldn't help but watch every move. He shoved off the pants to reveal the tiniest little jock strap ever, which framed the most perfect ass ever. The realization of him wearing that under that tailored suit did crazy things to me. Him sitting in that office chair, looking so prim and perfect, with those naughty little undies beneath…

He turned to wiggle that fine ass suggestively. Luca waxed everything. I knew this for a fact as he had an appointment two days ago in which he'd grumbled about getting his asshole waxed. I didn't know why as I thought hairy men were just fine. But the perfection of those globes was something to behold. Like some sort of Adonis or sculpture of male perfection. Luca wasn't a giant man covered in muscles and monstrous pecs, but he was the sleek elegance of a well put together man. I loved the smooth slide of his skin against mine, and the sun kissed tone of his flesh, though I knew he spent little time outside.

He pulled off the strap, letting it slide suggestively down his leg before he dropped it on the pile of his clothing. His cock was hard and as always he was confident in his skin, letting himself stand on display for me. I drank in the sight of him, sleek muscles, honeyed flesh and need. I hoped to someday have that confidence.

I sighed as he dropped his discarded pile of clothes in a chair and went to the night stand. He retrieved a bottle of lube and squirted some into his hand before climbing up onto the bed and kneeling, then leaning forward, offering a tantalizing view of that amazing ass in the air, spread wide.

For a moment I was at a loss as to what he was going to do, but he reached back, fingers slick with lube, and began teasing himself. I bit my lip to stifle a groan as the first finger disappeared inside his clenching hole. It was a slow process, one that locked me into place, watching, fantasizing that it was me playing with him, pulling little sounds of pleasure from his throat.

The first finger vanished inside him, his hole clenching around it, but he didn't really move. Then he pulled it out and added another, sliding them in and out, turning them slowly and then pressing them deep. I heard him gasp, and his hips moved. He reached for a pillow and put it under his chest, head to the side, hugging the pillow with his free arm.

His ass in the air, legs spread wide, cock hard and dripping a fine line down his chest and onto the bedspread, made a stunning view. Those fingers fucking his ass made some need in me clench hard. I wanted it to be me. I knew he wouldn't care if I crossed the room and fucked him. It was what he wanted. Fuck, it was what we both wanted. Yet I still stood there frozen.

He added a third finger, then a fourth, his pace quickening, and the little sounds that fell from his lips made me tremble. I stripped out of my clothes in a hurry, willing to at least rub off while I watched him play. That was something, right?

When I was finally naked, I crossed the room to stand beside the bed and stare at that amazing ass as Luca fucked himself with his fingers. His hips moved in a rhythm with his thrusts, but he made no attempt to touch his own cock.

"Touch me," Luca begged.

I worried at my bottom lip with my teeth, but reached out to stroke his bare ass cheek. I could feel the muscles of his ass clenching under his rhythm. Watched his fingers turn and twist, playfully for a bit then thrust hard for a few seconds before turning to playfulness. I climbed up onto the bed beside him and leaned forward to kiss the cheek I'd been petting.

His moan was sweet. "Yes," he said.

The view from this angle was much nicer, that fine hole gaping with need each time he pulled his fingers out. I traced my fingers down his crease, gathering a bit of extra lube and circling his hole as he thrust his fingers back in deep again.

He reached for my hand. He wrapped his lube-coated fingers around two of mine and jacked them as though they were my cock. Fucking Luca. He was going to make me come just from watching him. But he stopped and instead guided those two lube-coated fingers to his hole and eased them inside.

They were incased in soft, clenching heat. I didn't move for a moment, just reveling in the texture and warmth, the rippling strength of the muscles around them. I turned my hand, sliding my fingers around the space, exploring the spongy walls. Luca shivered and let out a little half-groan, half-sigh.

"Is this okay?" I asked him. I slid my fingers partially out and then back in again, the sensation odd, but not unpleasant.

"Yes, oh fuck, yes."

I slid them out again, circled his rim, watching his muscles tremble with sensitivity, and added a third finger. This was a bit more of a stretch, his channel clenching at them as I pressed in and rolled them around, feeling inside him and watching his body for reactions. He pressed back into my fingers forcing my touch down a little, and I felt a little nub of tissue, maybe that bundle of nerves every gay man knew was supposed to be our hot spot. Was that his prostate?

I rubbed at it for a few seconds and he growled, his cock twitched and a second later spurted down his chest, and all over the blanket. He let out a long sigh. I pulled my fingers out.

"No, don't stop," Luca begged.

"You just came without anyone touching your cock," I remarked, thinking hard, and studying his body which was still tense and shivered with need. It had never happened to me. Even the many hours of porn Matthew had made me watch had never featured such a phenomenon.

"Yes, and I can come probably another half dozen times tonight. Part of being a dhampir. Super-charged libido." He rubbed his spend into his chest and it looked dirty and so fucking sexy all at once. I was still rock hard of course, but a thousand ideas ran through my head of things I wanted to do and see.

I rubbed his crease again, tickling his rim. I was close enough to smell a slight orange scent. How was that possible? "Why do I smell orange?"

"Flavored lube," Luca said. "It's one of my faves."

Why would lube need to be flavored? I leaned forward and tentatively licked a tiny drop that rested on one of his ass cheeks. It wasn't disgusting, just a mild flavor of sweet orange candy.

"Fuck, do that again," Luca begged. He was growing hard again.

"Kiss your ass?" I laughed at the thought.

"Yes," Luca said. "Please. Touch me."

I pressed my fingers back inside him, he let out a long sweet hiss of pleasure, and then I kissed his crease. It took a few seconds of internal pep talking but I licked a line down his crease, tasting orange and a musky, but not unpleasant flavor of him. Huh. Not bad. His hips shook with need.

Maybe I could do this. We didn't have to fuck, I thought briefly, though I wanted to. However, I could make him come until he was too exhausted for anything else. And that was appealing in its own way, watching him come undone because of the little things I did to him.

I tasted his rim, again just the bite of orange candy and him. And the way my tongue made his hips shake spurred me on. I fucked him with my fingers, adding a fourth and pressing in deep, nudging his prostate as I licked around them.

The little sounds falling from his lips made my cock drip and ache, but I didn't touch it. No, I wanted to see him come apart. Watch him drown in pleasure under my touch. He gripped the comforter and moved his hips back into my thrusts and lips, grinding himself into me when he could. It was too hard to maintain a solid pace, so I took hold of his hips with both hands to steady him, which meant I didn't have enough hands to fuck him.

I frowned at his gaping hole which opened and squeezed like it was begging to be filled, while I held his hips in place. He tried to move, but I held him firm, hard enough to bruise, though he didn't protest, instead he growled and groaned saying over and over again, "Please."

That delicate hole begging for attention, I thought. So I teased at the rim again, flicking the tip of my tongue over him, fighting his strength as his body tried to press back for more. When I pushed my tongue into him for the first time, I worried that this wasn't a thing, that he'd pull away, but his little "please, please, please," turned into "yes, yes, yes."

His cock dripped again, hard and dark, begging for touch. I was tempted to lie down and take him down my throat. He'd enjoy that, had every time I'd done it so far, but it wasn't what he wanted right now. And I wasn't done playing with him.

I licked at him then, inside and out, flicking into him, then around the rim and back inside. His breath came out in pants like he was running a marathon. Legs trembling to hold him up, but that was okay because I had him. Where his strength ended, mine continued. I traced my tongue across the side of his crease up to one round cheek where I carefully set my teeth and applied a little bit of pressure, just the slightest bite, no breaking of the skin, but Luca came again, his cry muffled in the pillow as he'd turned his head to fill his mouth with it.

Holy fuck he was so hot when he came undone. His body swaying like a dancer, come trailing over his perfect skin, face flushed and the indent of my teeth slightly marring his skin. I squeezed my cock so as not to come. Not yet. Fuck. I wanted to see him fall apart at least one more time before I came.

His entire body shook. "Fuck."

"You okay?" I asked.

"You talk too much."

"Okay?"

"Fuck me. Please."

I stared at his still clenching hole, wondering what it felt like. The way he'd moved around my fingers and my tongue had been amazing. But I was much longer than my fingers.

He shoved the bottle of lube my way. "Please."

And I wanted it. Wondered at how he would feel around me, muscles squeezing me, pulling me in. Would it hurt him? Did it matter? He didn't seem to care, should I?

I opened the bottle and squirted some onto my hand, enjoying the smooth scent of it, not overly strong or sweet, and it felt smooth going on too. Luca's gaze was locked on my cock as I stroked myself, coating it in lube.

Was I really going to do this?

"Please," Luca begged.

I put the bottle aside and got to my knees, adjusted his hips for a better angle. Not so high, but still open, I pressed the head of my cock to his hole, expecting resistance, maybe his pain. I don't know exactly.

The tip popped inside, and Luca's little chants of please once again turned to "yes, yes, yes." I wasn't sure if I should keep moving forward. I knew from experience that the first entry was always more than a little bit of a burn. But Luca reached back and gripped my hip, guiding me forward.

I slid into his heat, breathless, devoured, and soon trembling myself. There was no resistance, just his body clenching and pulling me deeper. I waited for him to tell me stop, but it wasn't until my sack rested against his taint and the back of his balls, and my cock was fully encased that I stopped. I leaned over him, breathing hard, trying to work out all the sensations and emotions rolling through me. His body still shivered around mine, causing his channel to contract and squeeze me until I was aching to move, cock begging for the friction.

"Fuck," I groaned.

"Yes," Luca said. "Please fuck me." He pressed his hips back against mine, grinding up together. "So fucking good. Sam…please."

I put my hands to his hips again, steadying myself as much as positioning him, then pulled back slowly, leaving the tip inside and sliding back in. This wasn't about speed right that second, though I knew it would be too much to hold back soon. It was about the feeling of him around me. The sensation of bare skin swallowed by delicate heat. Both of us aching with need.

I rolled my hips in an easy rhythm, closing my eyes to bathe in the sounds of Luca's moans and the grip of his channel around me. Every few seconds I would shove in deep, grind my hips into him, pressing hard into his recesses, then slide out for another slow dance. It was good in a way I'd never imagined sex to be. I flirted on the edge of release for a while, almost ready to come when I'd pull back and let the cool air calm my need, before pressing in to spear him again.

We danced for a while. I'd honestly never had sex last that long, but I found that rhythm of taking him to the edge, watching his eyes flutter as he almost came, then pulling back, and biting his shoulder, or his arm, giving him just enough pain to stave off the climax. He was covered in bite marks and sweat. He moved with my rhythm now, pressing back when I thrust deep, begging for release.

I even pulled him back into my lap, moved us to the head of the bed so I could put my back to the wall and hold his weight while he bobbed on my cock. His legs spread, resting over my thighs, leaving him wide open, bare to the room, cock jutting up toward his stomach. With this angle I could drive myself deeper, and bask in the heat of his body and the feeling of his heartbeat throbbing around my cock.

He tried to quicken the pace a dozen times. Only I put a stop to it with my strength. Luca was strong, more than human strong, but I was a vampire. He groaned as I pulled his back to my chest, and turned his head so our lips could meet. We battled for a time. Lips and teeth, tongue and mouth, chasing, nipping, tasting. Bodies sliding together. I could have fucked him hard, made us both come, but preferred the sweet dance of it.

The door opened and I froze, worried for a moment that it was Seiran, but it was Con who entered, pausing at seeing the two us entwined, then stepping into the room and closing the door. He looked tired, but leaned against the door and gave us an appreciative look. Luca wiggled his hips, trying to get me to move again. I shoved up into him and did that little rock again that had him gasping and begging for release.

"Give me five minutes," Con said.

"Better hurry," I told him, licking Luca's shoulder. Con began stripping and disappeared into the bathroom, leaving the door open where I could hear him turn on the shower. I pressed my hips into Luca's, not letting him move and putting a halt to the friction that was driving me to the edge. His body still squeezed and danced around my cock.

"Make me come again," Luca said.

"Once Con gets out here," I promised.

Luca whined. "I recover fast. Can come and come again."

I bit down on his earlobe then licked it. "That's the plan."

He growled and tried to move again, but I held him in place, letting just our breathing be the only movement. He trembled around me, begging until Con came out of the shower, naked, clean, and rubbing at his hair with a towel.

"He won't let me come," Luca protested to Con.

Con chuckled a husky laugh. "Is that so? How tragic. We'll have to see what we can do about that." He climbed onto the bed all sinew and ink, leaned over Luca and kissed me. We ate at each other's mouths for a few seconds before he turned and kissed Luca's cheek, and then reached down to slowly rub Luca's cock. He ran his hand down the length of Luca, tracing over his balls and below to where Luca and I were joined. He ran his fingers around the base of me, sliding along Luca's rim.

Luca grabbed Con and held on hard. "Fuck!"

"He's got a dirty mouth," I told Con.

"He's got a dirty everything," Con said. He ran his other hand over Luca's come stained chest. "Apparently already had a few orgasms tonight. Yet still complaining about not having another." Con's finger pressed against Luca's rim and I felt the added pressure, the tightening of Luca's body around mine as Con slid a single digit in beside my cock. Luca flailed, cursing, begging and writhing in our arms, body pinned between us.

"Oh fucking God," Luca said.

"He likes that," Con told me.

Hell, I liked that.

Con stroked his cock, finding the lube and adding some to ease his slide. His dick was thicker than Luca's or mine. Heavily veined and cut like most witches were, the head was very defined. I loved the feel of him in my mouth, the way he tasted and stretched my jaw. I also loved watching Luca's nose buried in Con's pubes, cock down the back of his throat.

I bent Luca forward, over Con's lap, adjusting Luca's hips like he was little more than a doll. "Suck him," I told Luca.

Con smiled and directed his cock into Luca's waiting mouth. Luca swallowed the head of Con's dick, taking that thick length down easily. He tried to pull back but Con shoved him down further, pressing his dick to the back of Luca's throat and rolling his hips. Luca made a little gurgling, wet, half-choke before Con let him go to pull back and thrust forward, repeating the action. Drool dripped from Luca's mouth. He held on to Con's hips, steadying himself, his hips wiggling in time to Con's thrusts.

I got to my knees again, moved Luca's hips a little and

began to slide in again, slow at first, contrary to Con's fevered pace. Watching Luca struggle to find his release as he danced on the edge. But watching them together was always too much for me. I could watch them for hours and come without participating. So my thrusts intensified, deeper, harder, faster, until I had to fight to keep my eyes open and watch them instead of just losing myself in the pleasure. I didn't want to come yet, not until they did, no matter how much Luca's little noises and tight body squeezed at my very soul.

The slap, slap sounds of flesh rose in a musical with the wet slurp of Luca on Con's cock. I rammed into him hard, not worrying about my strength in that moment as Luca didn't protest. In fact his little noises said he wanted more.

Con leaned forward to capture my lips, one hand still firmly guiding Luca's head, the other trailing over Luca's flesh until he found where we joined again, adding not one but two fingers. Luca screamed around Con's cock, his body spasming around me, gripping me like a vice, breaking up the pace of my thrusts and pulling at me so hard I came undone, spurting into him.

Con bit my lip, holding it there between his teeth as he came, shooting himself down Luca's throat and making me bleed. He licked at the wound, all of us breathing heavy, his cock slipping from Luca's lips, and Luca rested his head on Con's thigh. I thrust a few more times into Luca's warm body, enjoying how tight he became around me, before easing free and watching his hole gape in wanting.

"Fuck," Luca grumbled.

"Hmm," Con said into my lips. "That was nice to come home to."

"Better than dumbass drunks, right?" I teased.

"So much better," he agreed. He stroked Luca's ass, even putting his fingers back into Luca's still clenching hole.

Luca trembled and cried out. "Oh yeah, sensitive boy pussy."

I traced the rim with my fingers, slipping two in beside Con's. "He clenches so nice."

"Stretches well," Con remarked. "Bet we can both fuck him at once." He smiled down at Luca. "How many times have you boasted about being double-teamed?" Con added two more fingers, forcing Luca to stretch around us. "Bet I could put my fist in there, make you sing."

"Yes," Luca moaned. "Please."

I pulled my fingers out and put my hands on Luca's hips to turn him, giving Con better access by putting Luca on his back, ass facing Con. Of course, he was getting hard again. "He is like the energizer bunny," I remarked.

Con laughed. "Right? And so dirty." Con rubbed Luca's spend into Luca's skin. Some of mine leaked from his gaping hole and I spread that over him too. It was odd how comfortable I felt in that moment. Luca sprawled out between Con and me, all three of us in union of one thing, Luca's pleasure. My pleasure was great. Watching Con was good too, but unraveling the cool and calm exterior Luca showed at work? That was well worth basking in.

My stomach grumbled, reminding me I needed a snack. I leaned over Luca licking down his come covered chest as Con coated his hand in lube. I traced my tongue over Luca's hip and down to his thigh where the sweet smell of his blood was strong and throbbing along with his heart and his quickly filling cock. I nipped at the vein a few times playfully, feeling Luca nuzzle my cock, though it would take me longer and more blood to be ready to come again any time soon.

I watched as Con worked into Luca, adding fingers, which were long and thin, delicate looking despite the ink across the knuckles. He started with three, then four, twisting and pressing part of his hand in, tucking the thumb close and rounding the fingers until he got to the knuckles. Those he worked at Luca's ridge for a few minutes while I licked at sucked at Luca's thigh.

As Con pressed in, working past the knuckle and finally the palm, I bit into the vein in Luca's thigh. His blood filled my mouth, while I added thoughts of intensity to go with the pressure of Con's entire fist disappearing inside Luca's body.

Luca screamed again, body bucking in pleasure, while Con rolled his fist and I fed from Luca's lifeforce. This was both the beauty and the horror of being a vampire. It was all about the blood. Feeding it, feeling it race in pleasure, and tasting the release beneath the copper bite. And that was okay. Watching Luca's pleasure, sharing it with Con to create our own? That was worth living for.

EPILOGUE

Seiran Rou (From the short Samhain)

The house flickered with eerie lights as I pulled my minivan into the driveway. I wondered if the effects were intentional since it was Samhain. It was just after six and almost completely dark. Every other house I'd driven by had already lit their pumpkins to shine into the night and ward off spirits. But most of the world celebrated Halloween, and the day was all about candy for them.

I glanced back to the two carriers strapped into the second-row seats. My babies both mumbled unintelligible things and moved their little fingers. At almost five months, Mizuki and Sakura were quickly outgrowing their baby stage. Mizu was sitting up and rolling over often, on the verge of crawling, and Kura was fighting hard to not fall behind her big brother. I could put the two together on a play mat for hours and they'd entertain each other. It was often how I worked, only interrupted on occasion by infectious baby laughter, which had the rare power to make me smile.

They kept me going. Without the twins I wasn't sure how I'd wake up each day. I was learning to be stronger thanks to therapy that often added my friends and family to help work things out in a group rather than just leaving it all in my head. My kids deserved better than what I'd had growing up, and I was trying to provide that for them.

I put the car in park and stared at the house. It'd been a while since I'd actually gone inside. Hanna and Ally had bought the mansion late last year with my mother, and my older brother, Jamie's help. It had been a fixer-upper, now it was grander than the Rou Mansion. It was in the heart of downtown St. Paul just off Grand Avenue. The street lined with amazing houses and architecture that inspired awe. The yards were small, but they'd had it fenced for security. It was smaller than the house my mother had built for me, but not by much. It was also a little too close to the neighbors for my liking.

The main door of the house opened. Hanna stepped onto the porch. She wore a black dress that swept her ankles in flowing dark spider webs of lace and had a pointy witch hat on her head. "I guess they are waiting for us, babies. Let's go celebrate the harvest."

I got out of the van, walked around the side, and then stripped off my coat and threw it on the passenger seat before opening the door to free my babies. Mizu's eyes were wide.

"What, you don't like it?" I asked him as I twirled in my catsuit. It was molded brown leather custom ordered from a cosplay website. With a few minor modifications, including a dark green leather kilt to hide anything the suit showed off since there would be kids around, the outfit was perfect for the mini-masquerade that Hanna was hosting. "Daddy's a tree. Can't you tell?"

I lifted my arms to display the branches and multi-colored leaves I'd woven through the fabric. Those leaves were real like the ones in my hair. My hair was green, a bit of my Father Earth power let out to play. The flowers and leaves real there as well, though I'd had Bryar help make it look nice. I'd styled it up so it would be out of the way and not a tempting handle for small grabby hands. Both babies had watched me play with the leaves with fascination on their faces. The fact that I'd made them from the brightest fall colors possible probably helped as all the books I read about babies stated that their eyesight would still be developing.

Mizu squinted his eyes, and then sneezed. Sakura giggled.

"Oh goodness, we better make sure you're bundled up." I crawled inside the van to unlock the baby seats and stepped into a pile of leaves. "How did those get in here?" Had I left the door open? The leaves crunched beneath my feet as I kicked them out the door. "Earth just follows us everywhere, doesn't it babies?"

The twins were dressed as pumpkins. Matching orange jackets, quilted and padded like pumpkins, though the jack-o-lanterns on the front were different, thick gloves and a brown stem hat that covered their ears, made up the outfit. Once they were both unstrapped, and put in the stroller, I double checked their zippers and ties. Everything was in place. Time to go inside, couldn't avoid the crowd forever. I pushed them toward the door and where Hanna waited. She had known to give me time. They were all walking on eggshells around me, and it was annoying but I was still grateful for the space.

"Look at our beautiful babies! Oh Ally, come look!"

Hanna squealed as she came around the car to help with the carriers.

Ally, her spouse, stepped out of the house looking like Marilyn Monroe, blond hair teased up, and frilly white dress. She barely spared me a glance, though since she treated the twins well, I ignored it.

Two seconds later she too was squealing over the twins and talking baby talk. Mizuki and Sakura could reduce anyone to single syllable and high-pitched tones in half a heartbeat. "Their costumes are great! Perfect."

I'd been working on the costumes for weeks. Hanna had asked me a million times if I just wanted her to buy them something cute and simple, like a lion or those weird penguin suits. But I'd been adamant. My babies were going to celebrate Samhain the right way. Costumes were handmade, candy simple, the night began with lighting candles and ended with blowing them out.

Jamie, my older brother, stepped out of the house and he was dressed like a giant teddy bear, pawed mitts and all. Kelly, his lover and my best friend, came down the steps behind him dressed as a hockey player, though instead of ice skates he had roller blades.

"So this is what you were working on," Kelly said. He kissed each of the twin's foreheads. "Making them perfect little pumpkins."

"Press their tummies gently, right where the nose is," I told him and pointed to the jack-o-lantern grin.

Kelly pressed Mizuki and a pale glowing light poured through the little pumpkin.

Hanna squealed again and turned Sakura's suit on.

"Had one of the IT people at work help me with that part," I told them all. "But it's LED so it's safe and won't burn out."

"That is amazing, Sei." Jamie whipped out his phone and began taking pictures.

"Oh I have to get mine too!" Hanna rushed back into the house. Ally took Kura out of her seat, and I got Mizu. Hanna came back out and called, "Everyone pose with the twins." I let her snap a few pictures.

Mizu yawned, and Kura snapped her lips wanting her nook. I had them in the pocket of my kilt, but was hoping to keep the kids awake a little longer by holding on to them.

"The twins are already sleepy," I said, though they'd had a nap today. Hanna had talked about taking them trick or treating. I had protested briefly, worried more about their safety, but as long as we did the normal Samhain stuff, I didn't care if their momma wanted to walk them around and gather candy they couldn't eat anyway.

"Dinner should be ready," Hanna said as she led us inside.

"Seiran," my mom called as we walked in the door. She was positively glowing with happiness as she crossed the room and kissed me lightly on the cheek before bending to kiss each baby. Mizu opened sleepy eyes and reached for her. She took him from me with an ease of movement only a mom could have. Kura made sleepy noises, but looked pretty comfortable in Ally's arms. "I hope you're hungry. The soup should be ready."

I followed her toward the dining room. The harvest theme ran throughout the house. My mother always hired professional decorators to make it memorable, but this year's design was simpler, less commercial Halloween and more true Samhain. Maybe that was Hanna's influence. The double glass doors from the dining room were open to let in the brisk air of the evening. Two tiny pumpkins and one larger one sat on the end of the table. My mom went to the door and shut it, closing out some of the cold and immediately the warmth of the fireplace eased some of the shivering in my bones.

"The big pumpkin is yours. The little ones are for each of the babies. I thought you might want to light them before dinner," my mom motioned to the chair on that end of the room. I took Mizu from her as I made my way across the room. His eyes were all over the bright orange blobs on the table. The past few weeks, each time we'd gone to the grocery store I'd pointed them out to him and Kura. I'd even taken them to a tiny patch that a co-worker owned so they could touch the leaves and take in the bright colors of the fall.

The large pumpkin was carved with an intricate tree spanning almost the full length of one side and was duplicated on the opposite side. My name was written in the base of the tree in large letters. The two smaller gourds were similar, only instead of a large tree, they were little seedlings, sprouting out of the ground, each of the twins' names carved into the tiny stalk.

Baby fingers on my cheeks brought me back into the now as I realized tears were falling from my eyes. Mizu's little fingers reached for my hair on one side, and touched my face on the other.

"Sorry, baby. Daddy's okay. Just tired." I glanced around the room and realized that other than immediate family, no one else had entered the dining room with us. When Hanna had said it was a small party, I figured she would have invited some friends from work.

Everyone took their seats, and waited for me it seemed, to light the candles and get on with it. "Sorry, everyone."

"No worries, Sei. Do you want me to take Mizu while you light the pumpkins?" Hanna appeared at my side, and held out her arms. I let her take him. Jamie handed me a lighter stick. I flicked it on, opening my pumpkin first, and reached inside to light the little white wick.

The candle inside roared to life, casting the flickering shadow of a tree on the wall. When the two smaller pumpkins began to glow too, I felt more lighthearted. It would all work out. Sure being alone sucked, but I was really only as alone as I wanted to be. Everyone in the room was more than willing to come when called, whether it be for baby patrol or just a last-minute movie night. I stared around the room at my family and really loved them for being there. Even though there was an empty chair beside me, I didn't feel as though he were far away. Maybe since this was the night of thin veils he was here somehow.

That was just wrong. He wasn't dead. He wasn't really there anymore, I reminded myself. Even if I couldn't feel him in my head most of the time. The earth told me he still had some sort of existence, but couldn't clarify it for me. The earth was a simple thing despite all its complexity. The earth had reabsorbed Gabe's mortal form, though it told me the pulse of his energy had not been broken. Which I took to mean someday he'd return.

I thought briefly of Galloway who'd gone to ground for five hundred years, leaving his Focus to fall into madness. Would that be my fate? I wasn't sure I'd last five hundred years alone. Especially not if I outlived the family that surrounded me right that moment. What would I have left without them if Gabe was still gone? My heart still ached too deeply to even contemplate finding love again.

My eyes went blurry. Damn tears. I blinked them back, refusing to let them fall. Waiters began bringing out bowls of pumpkin soup and slices of the cornbread I'd been craving all day. I could focus on food and family. It was the twins first Samhain. I had already taken dozens of pictures and done a little walk around our house with them, a small tea candle lit to cleanse the space and make way for prosperity. Sakura and Mizuki seemed to like the flickering of the candle, or it could have been the fairies that trailed along with us as we walked.

Hanna and I set up the twins in their highchairs. I was used to my food being cold by the time the kids had eaten, but the waiters didn't even bring our bowls until the twins had finished their pumpkin soup and were gnawing on pieces of bread. Both were my recipes, and I could feel the warmth of having them served for the holiday spread through me.

Jamie cleared his throat as I was pushing my bowl aside. When I looked up all eyes were on him and Kelly.

"Kelly and I have talked about this for a while." Jamie looked at Kelly who nodded. "And we wanted to announce this tonight, not to take away from the holiday, but as a symbol of upcoming growth."

I blinked at them. Were they saying what I thought they were saying?

"We've decided to have a baby."

The room sat in dead silence. Jamie smiled at me. "You've shown us how much we really want our own, Sei. We want our babies to grow up with yours, so Kelly and I are in the process of choosing a surrogate."

"Will she be a witch?" My mother asked.

"Only if she gives up all rights to us," Kelly replied. "The baby will be ours. In fact my older sister has volunteered to donate a few of her eggs, so the baby will be part me, part Jamie. We just need someone to carry our baby to term."

"A water-earth mix?" Had that ever been done, I wondered? Would the baby inherit water since that was the stronger element? Baby. There would be more babies. I burst into tears.

Jamie was at my side rubbing my back in an instant. "I

didn't want to upset you. We were going to wait. But we really want our baby to be close in age to Mizuki and Sakura. We just don't know how long..." Gabe would be gone. I knew what he was trying to say. No one wanted to wait on the unknown.

I let myself fall into his arms and just cry it out. I was happy for them. Really, I was. My babies would get to play with their babies, and they'd all get to grow up in one big happy family. Only Gabe was supposed to be there too.

The sting of his absence ached more than the memory of his decline. Jamie often reminded me not to dwell on the last few months before he'd gone to ground. Sam had said that Gabe wasn't Gabe. And that was the truth as far as I could tell. Time eased a bit of the pain, but holidays would always be hard.

A bustle of activity came from the front of the house, and I heard Sam's voice echo through the hallway. "Leave it to the witches to make things cliché."

"Bastard," I grumbled.

Sam entered the dining room followed by Constantine and Luca, looking like the street thug he pretended to be in tight jeans and leather. "Heard that, Ronnie," He said. He set a stack of gifts on the counter. "Harvest stuff from us and Max. Seeds for the garden and toys for the twins. Gift cards for expensive shit for everyone else, 'cause you know Max is an old rich white dude."

Luca snorted.

"We chose the gift cards," Constantine said. "So they are to places you all like."

"Thank you," I told them sincerely.

Mizu was nestled in my mother's arms, and Ally was cleaning up Kura with a damp rag. Sam reached for Mizu who immediately cooed and wiggled himself into Sam's grip. Sam took my boy and bounced him a little before settling him back to rest. The small smile on Sam's face belied his tough exterior. He adored those kids and they adored him. He could spend hours lying on the floor, with them curled around him babbling incoherently, and he wasn't at all bothered by their spit-up or dirty diapers. Part of the baby-gig, he told me often. But being with the guys had mellowed him a little.

"We're walking with Hanna for the trick or treating," Luca said. He was dressed in leather too, like a street fighter from an old video game. Con was much the same, though he'd put on a suit of fake muscles over his lean tattooed frame. "Think of us as security."

I breathed hard, the anxiety of the reminder that I would be letting them out of my sight almost sending me into a panic attack. I missed the way Gabe had been able to soothe the attacks, but had spent enough time practicing my breathing to ease them myself now. The kids were safe. Even if the vampire and a room full of witches wasn't enough, I knew my mother had guards watching the house and that they would follow Hanna and the kids at a distance just in case.

"We've got the babies, Sei," Hanna told me. "If you need to go for a little while, it'll be fine." Everyone was nodding in agreement. My whole world was unraveling, had been for months, but here they all were, united, wanting to help. It just made me want to cry again. I'd lived alone a long time. Denied needing anyone, and then put all my desire, hopes, and dreams on Gabe. It had been unfair I realized, to put so much pressure on him. I was working on that. Finding my feet again.

"How about I drive? You look a little shaky. Maybe talking to Gabe will help," Kelly offered.

I hesitated because it had been a long time since I'd spoken to Gabe. Was that what I needed? "But the twins…"

"Are fine. They have plenty of family to take care of them. I bet you have nooks in that fancy pocket on your kilt. You'll have to tell me where you got that, by the way, 'cause I want one." Kelly pointed to the kilt.

I dug out the nooks, and wanted to protest, after all it was Samhain. I wanted to be with my kids on their first Halloween, even if they couldn't really understand it, but my head was still swimming with the craziness of too much change at once. How did anyone become equipped to deal with this sort of thing on their own? Or were we born with the ability, only to lose it when we found someone to depend on?

"You'll take lots of pictures?" I asked Hanna.

"Of course. And we won't be out long. Just down the block and back."

I kissed my babies, holding each one for a few moments before breaking away to breathe. I headed for the door, thinking maybe it was okay to talk to Gabe tonight, avoiding him for months meant I'd earned it, right? It was okay if he didn't respond. Sometimes therapy was what I let go of rather than what I held on to.

Kelly's new car was much smaller than the minivan. I knew it was big enough to hold the kids, but I'd never been a passenger in it before myself. The car steered nice, and didn't smell like babies, which just made me sad.

It was a long drive back to our house, which was dark and silent, a mausoleum really. Technically we should have been going to the big vampire graveyard on the opposite side of the city. Gabe had an official tomb there in which we let the government think he'd gone to ground, even if the truth was more complicated than that.

Once at the house we headed inside and toward the back. Kelly gave me a tight smile. "I'll wait here. Take as long as you need."

The arboretum in the back of the house had been restored, fully expanded, and bloomed like an entire forest of magic plants. The fairies had taken over. Fruit trees decorated every few feet while flowers and ivy covered the walls and climbed up to cause nets of green. The flickering orbs of lights weren't bugs, even if sometimes they felt that way.

Near the entry, down the stairs and off to the left was a patch of roses. They still bloomed, months after first appearing. At first they'd been red like blood, but after a few days had turned black and had been black ever since. It worried me, though the earth felt no different.

Gabe wasn't technically there beneath the soil. Part of the truth that vampires hid from humanity is that truly going to ground meant being reabsorbed by the earth only to regenerate later. It was a power that would have terrified mankind. Godlike, and immortal. Only vampires weren't really immortal.

Sam spoke about breaking up the energy of a vampire. True death, he called it. I read books Max had provided, most of which was philosophy that I needed to ask questions to understand. I could have asked Max. He offered. But I avoided him. That last day still fresh in my mind. Max was Titus. Gabe's Titus. The man Gabe had died for all those years ago. The reason Gabe had become a vampire. Had Gabe known?

More questions I wanted to ask Max. Yet feared the truth. If Gabe hadn't known, but came back, would it be to me or to Max? We were polar opposites, Max and I. Him sophisticated, tall, dark, and muscular. Me, small, delicate, and broken.

"Hey, Gabe," I whispered to him opening the bond between us. As always I felt nothing, just that endless void that couldn't tell me whether he was still there at all or not. "I miss you."

ABSOLUTION

I drew in the dirt, tracing my name and his together in a heart. Then I added Mizuki and Sakura to the list. "Your babies need you. I need you. But I suppose you know that."

Gabe was a vampire with more than two millennium of life lived. He'd warned me when we first met that sometimes things happened. Sometimes the pressure and memories became too much. I'd known only vaguely about redouts, and what they were. I knew vampires could go to ground, sometimes for years, even centuries.

I suppose I never thought that Gabe, who had always been a rock of strength and stability, would have to take a time out. He'd been prepared, as he was for most things. Accountants and lawyers came to me for decisions, all while I juggled two brand new babies, a fairly stressful job, and the responsibilities that came with being the Pillar of earth. Max had taken control of a lot of the business things, managing the mad tangle I hadn't even really known existed before. More than just the bar, Gabe had a dozen businesses and over a hundred properties, a lot of which generated income, but I had no idea how to run. Max's company specialized in management. So I'd hired him to figure it all out. So far the accountants gave me glowing reports, and Sam insisted he was keeping an eye on things as well. Mike took over the bar, but more than that was beyond him as he now had six newer vampires to watch after as well. It was a lot for anyone and I was grateful for the help. Even if I still didn't trust Max.

"It was really crappy timing you know," I told him and sat down on my ass in the dirt, and folded my legs beneath me. "You could have waited for the twins to be a few years old. Or maybe even out of college. Or maybe after we were married? What a way to get out of that." I laughed tightly at the thought. We'd put it off originally, planning to do it after the twins were born, but then everything had gone to hell.

He'd been so far gone. Almost a revenant when finally

committing himself to the earth. I remembered the expression on his face that day, the pure blood lust that turned his eyes red, skin ashen, arm eaten away by my magic and refusing to heal. The last bit was a hint that the magic which held him together was unraveling. Gone had been the affection and sweet smile I loved so much. Gone was his patience and understanding. Instead he'd compelled me several times, trying to force his will over mine. Then ravaged my neck, cast away only by my Father Earth power.

In all our time together, he'd never shown me that side of himself. Sure I knew subconsciously it was there, all vampires had it, but Gabe always seemed so human to me. I think that's why it hurt more when he was suddenly staring at me without recognition, like I was food. He'd apologized in those last moments before sending himself into oblivion, told me he loved me. I hadn't even had the chance to say goodbye or tell him that I loved him.

"I wish I could at least hear you in my head. Feel your mind or something. Anything other than this endless silence." We sat together for a while, and I remembered how he'd always massage my hands. Sometimes he'd just hold me for hours and neither of us would need to speak. If it weren't so cold, I might have been able to imagine him holding me.

"Sam is doing good. Happy. The three of them work well together even if their teasing drives me nuts. Hart's been taking good care of him in your absence. That was one thing you didn't plan for." His abandonment of Sam, forcing Sam to go revenant was still something that hurt. But Gabe's tie to Sam had struggled since the moment Sam had reawakened as a vampire. Too much power in that little fire witch for a very tired vampire. "Hard to believe he's fire, right? No wonder his temper burns fast and hot. You should see his phoenix form. It's pretty. Not at all like the pictures, but he's getting better at mastering the form, turning the heat off and on.

Doesn't hurt him at all to change either, no matter what time of the month it is. I wonder if that's a vampire thing or because he's a siphon. There is nothing in any of Max's books about siphons changing shape. I'm still searching the archives at work."

I laid down and pressed my cheek to the dirt, wishing I could feel him there. The arboretum was always warm, soil moist and full of nutrients, work of the fairies and my strong bond to the earth. I closed my eyes and breathed in the scent of soil, flowers, pollen and earth. For a while I dreamed of changing to my lynx form and just letting the simplicity swallow me whole. Being human hurt and sometimes I just got so tired of hurting and being alone.

I'm sorry. The whisper was so faint I wasn't sure I heard it. *I love you.*

Was it him? Or just wishful thinking?

I lay there a while longer, curled up amongst the black roses, eyes closed while whirls of bright colors still zipped around me. Life constantly evolving, moving, living, and dying. Something brushed my cheek like the softest fluttering of lips. I opened my eyes, expecting one of the fairies, but there was nothing.

Tears blurred my vision again. I wiped them away with the back of my hand and got up, feeling a chill wind around me like the faintest of hugs.

I'm sorry. I love you.

I blinked into the distance of racing fairy orbs and greenery lit only by moonlight and stars. Was it an outline or wishful thinking?

"Gabe?" I felt a caress along my skin like so many memories of him touching my face. The link between us wide and open, down the distance there was a tiny spark, so small, barely the flicker of a candle. Was it him? Finally after months of silence would I at least hear him again?

I love you.

Or just wishful thinking. I rose to my feet and dusted off my pants. "I have to get back to the twins. You should see them. They're growing so fast. Walking soon I'm sure." I stared at the flowers a bit longer, the one at my feet was edged in white. Odd. I'd never seen a black rose with white tips.

"I'll try to come more regularly," I promised. I'd been avoiding the garden—too many memories—buried myself in work and my children, gave the fairies free reign over the yard and arboretum. It pulsed with life that gave me energy and connected me to the earth, even when I hadn't set foot inside until today.

I'm sorry. The voice was so faint I really couldn't tell if it was my brain trying to comfort me or something from that tiny spark that linked us together. I headed back into the house and found Kelly scarfing down bacon in the kitchen.

"Don't look at me like that, it's bacon. I'll take bacon any day over pumpkin soup. Even your pumpkin soup which is amazing. Tradition I get, but bacon..."

I laughed, feeling a bit lighter. Even if Gabe wasn't coming back yet I wasn't alone. "A baby, eh?" I bumped his shoulder as we headed back to the car. "You ready for that yet?"

"No, but I get where Jamie is coming from and I think there's enough of us to handle it."

"I'm happy for you guys," I finally told him when we were back on the road. "Excited for Mizu and Kura to have a new playmate." Worried about the pressure that would put on Kelly who was in college full-time, struggling through the magic studies program that I'd barely just survived.

Kelly reached over and grabbed my hand, squeezing it tightly. "I've had your babies as a trial run, you know. It won't be easy, but nothing worth having is. Sam, Con, and Luca help a lot. It's nice having everyone in one place and still having enough space to be alone if I want it. The training I had over the summer…the time with Jamie, that cemented a lot for me."

The two months without them had been hard. I'd been afraid they wouldn't return to Minnesota.

"My home is here with you all, even the bastard vampire who always has some sarcasm to throw at us. I know I have someone to call when I need help and fuck if Sam hasn't been helping keep my powers in check. He's a quick study when it comes to magic."

Training Sam to use and control his element helped his amplifying power as well. I suspected Max had a lot to do with his control as I often sensed the vampire when I knew he was obviously not around.

"He looks all classy dressed up for work in a suit. Like a civilized person or something," I said.

"Then comes home and every other word is fuck."

"Or pussy," I pointed out.

"He's a jerk," Kelly said.

"Yeah," I agreed. But so were we all.

"Sam was complaining about the twins glowing eyes again," Kelly said. "Do you think my baby will do that?"

"Bryar said all babies have glowing eyes." I really had no idea. Normal kids didn't do that. But my kids weren't normal.

"Maybe fairy babies."

"Or really powerful witch babies." Kids didn't normally develop their witch powers until mid-to-late teens. My kids were already sparks of earth energy.

"What are we going to do?"

"Raise them. Train them. It's all we can do."

"They're pretty powerful," Kelly pointed out.

"And I'm Father Earth." Sam reminded me all the time.

Not much different than the vampires, he said. Immortal. Only the earth could retake me whenever it wanted to. Vampires too, as they were creatures of the earth no matter what power they had. It was a matter of faith, judgment, and balance. When humanity tipped the balance, the earth responded. When Tresler tried to usurp the circle of life the earth tore him apart, with Sam's help of course. The earth was life and death. It was also full of judgment.

Was I doing the right things? The earth would let me know if I wasn't. With or without Gabe I was going to be the best damn father I could be. Papa bear and mama bear all in one. After all, the future never had brighter prospects than my beautiful twins.

"Let's get back to the twins. I hope they're still awake. I'd like to dance with them under the moonlight." I thought about the waves of energy and tugging I felt of renewal as the veils thinned. Did they already feel it? Would they understand it at all? I'd have Bryar keep a close eye on them. He could travel through the veils without effort, tracking them if necessary.

"Dance sounds great," Kelly agreed, and we headed toward the family, my heart lighter and filled with hope.

Fin

ABOUT THE AUTHOR

Lissa Kasey is more than just romance. She specializes in in-depth characters, detailed world building, and twisting plots to keep you clinging to the page. All stories have a side of romance, emotionally messed up protagonists and feature LGBTQA spectrum characters facing real world problems no matter how fictional the story.

BOOK LIST

Also, if you like Lissa Kasey's writing, check out her other works:

Inheritance Series:
Inheritance (Dominion 1)
Reclamation (Dominion 2)
Conviction (Dominion 3)
Ascendance (Dominion 4)
Absolution (Dominion 5)

∽

Hidden Gem Series:
Hidden Gem (Hidden Gem 1)
Cardinal Sins (Hidden Gem 2)
Candy Land (Hidden Gem 3)

∽

Haven Investigations Series:
Model Citizen (Haven Investigations 1)
Model Bodyguard (Haven Investigations 2)
Model Investigator (Haven Investigations 3)
Model Exposure (Haven Investigations 4)

∽

Evolution Series:

Evolution
Evolution: Genesis

∼

Kitsune Chronicles:
Witchblood

∼

Survivors Find Love:
Painting With Fire
An Arresting Ride
Range of Emotion

∼

Under the pen name Sam Kadence

Vocal Growth Series:
On the Right Track (Vocal Growth 1)
Unicorns and Rainbow Poop (Vocal Growth 2)

Made in the USA
Lexington, KY
13 August 2019